THE FLOOFS
BRAVE THE WILD

To Mom and Dad.
Thank you for all your love and support.
— P.O.

Text and illustrations © 2025 Penelope O'Neill.

First Published in 2025 by Frances Lincoln Children's Books,
an imprint of The Quarto Group.
100 Cummings Center, Suite 265D, Beverly, MA 01915, USA.
T (978) 282-9590 F (978) 283-2742 www.Quarto.com
EEA Representation, WTS Tax d.o.o., Žanova ulica 3, 4000 Kranj, Slovenia.
www.wts-tax.si

The right of Penelope O'Neill to be identified as the author and illustrator of this work has been asserted by them in accordance with the Copyright, Designs and Patents Act, 1988 (United Kingdom).

All rights reserved.

No part of this publication may be reproduced, stored in a retrieval system, or transmitted, in any form, or by any means, electrical, mechanical, photocopying, recording or otherwise without the prior written permission of the publisher or a license permitting restricted copying.

ISBN 978-0-7112-9839-2

The illustrations were created digitally

Designer: Myrto Dimitrakoulia
Editor: Lotte Dobson
Production Controller: Dawn Cameron
Art Director: Karissa Santos
Publisher: Peter Marley

Manufactured in Bosnia and Herzegovina GP062025

9 8 7 6 5 4 3 2 1

Penelope O'Neill

THE FLOOFS
BRAVE THE WILD

Frances Lincoln
Children's Books

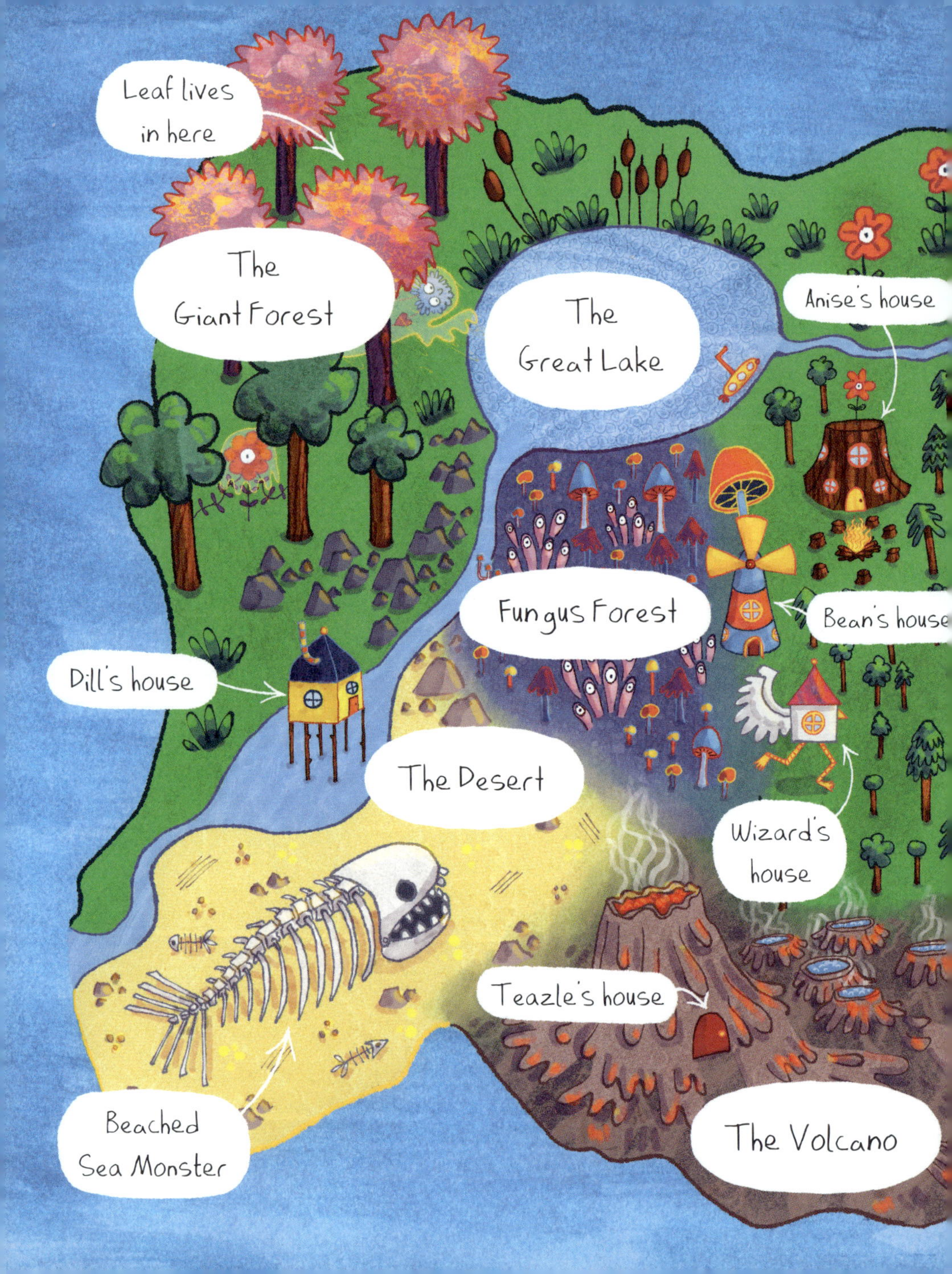
Leaf lives in here
The Giant Forest
The Great Lake
Anise's house
Fungus Forest
Bean's house
Dill's house
The Desert
Wizard's house
Teazle's house
Beached Sea Monster
The Volcano

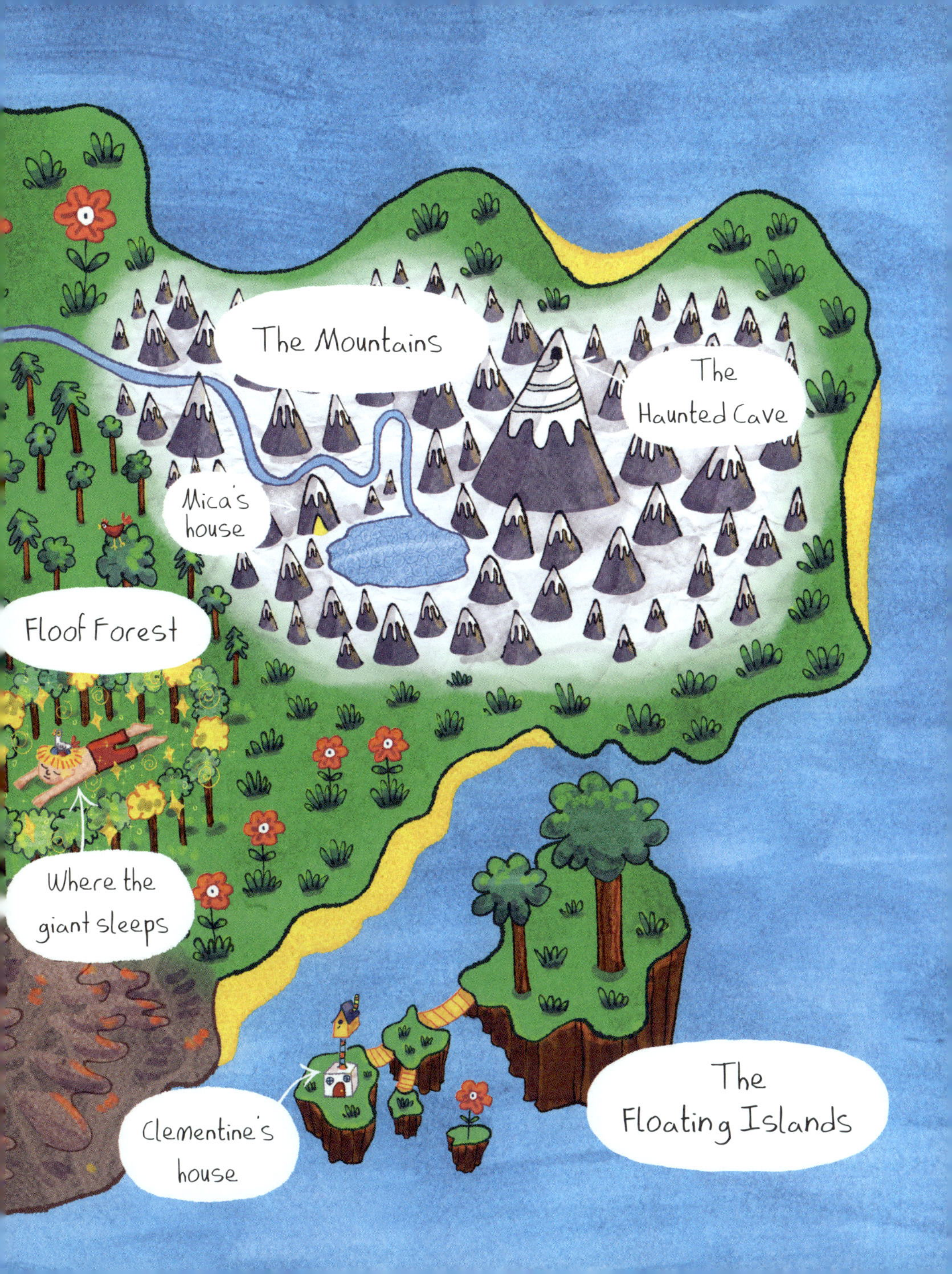
The Mountains
The Haunted Cave
Mica's house
Floof Forest
Where the giant sleeps
Clementine's house
The Floating Islands

Meet the Floofs!

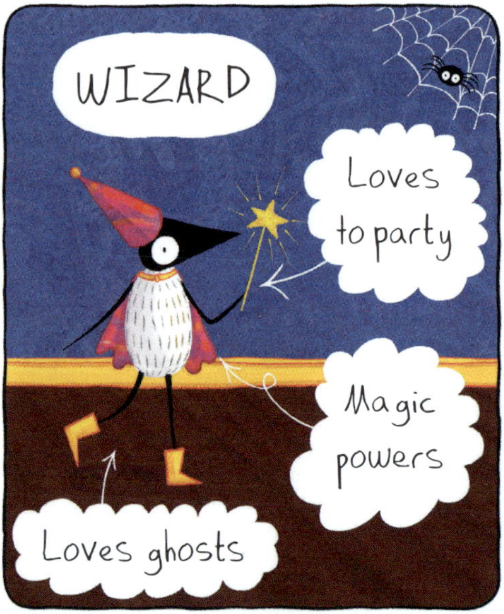
WIZARD
Loves to party
Magic powers
Loves ghosts

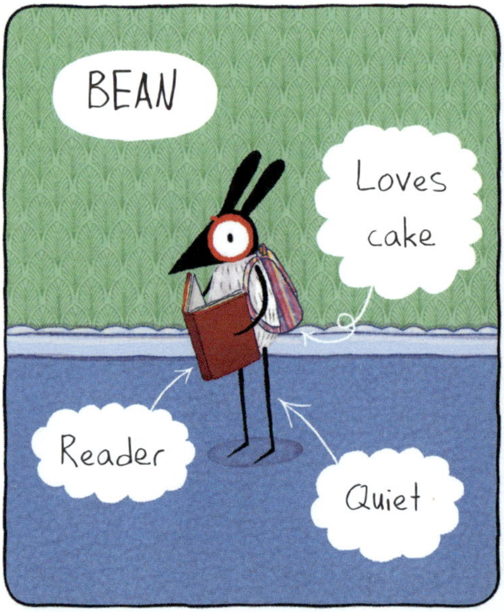
BEAN
Loves cake
Reader
Quiet

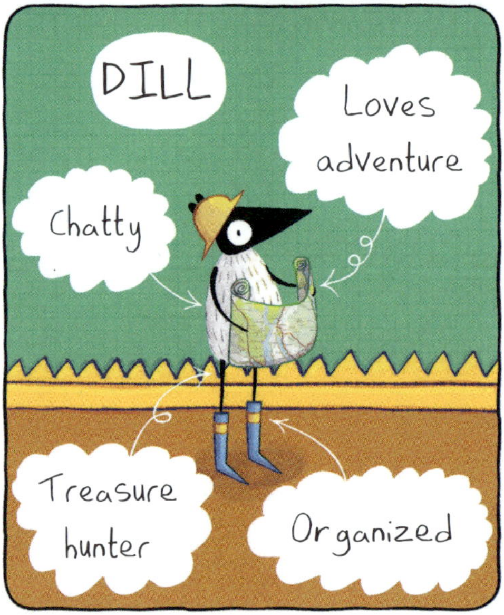
DILL
Loves adventure
Chatty
Treasure hunter
Organized

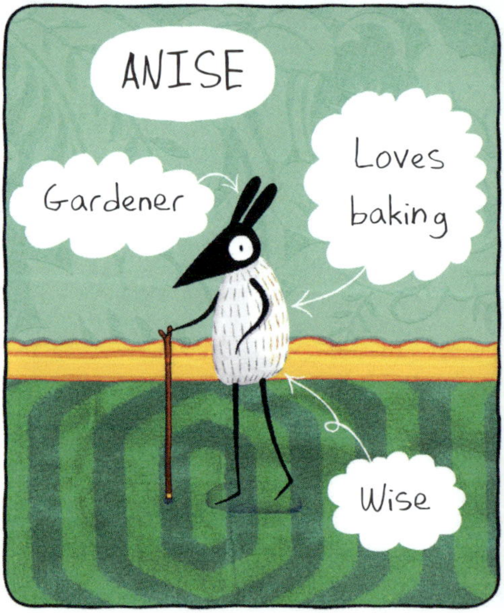
ANISE
Loves baking
Gardener
Wise

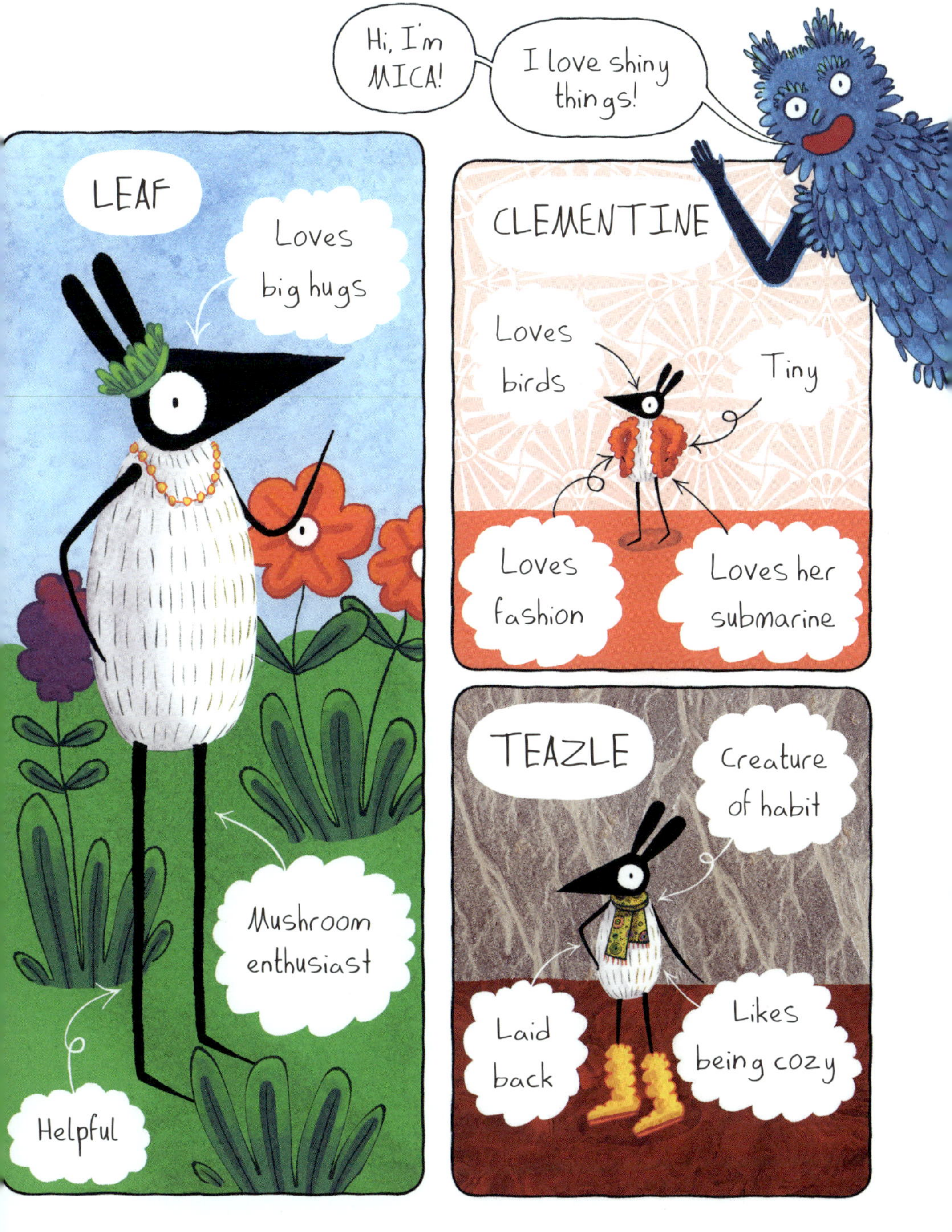
Hi, I'm MICA!
I love shiny things!
LEAF
Loves big hugs
Mushroom enthusiast
Helpful
CLEMENTINE
Loves birds
Tiny
Loves fashion
Loves her submarine
TEAZLE
Creature of habit
Laid back
Likes being cozy

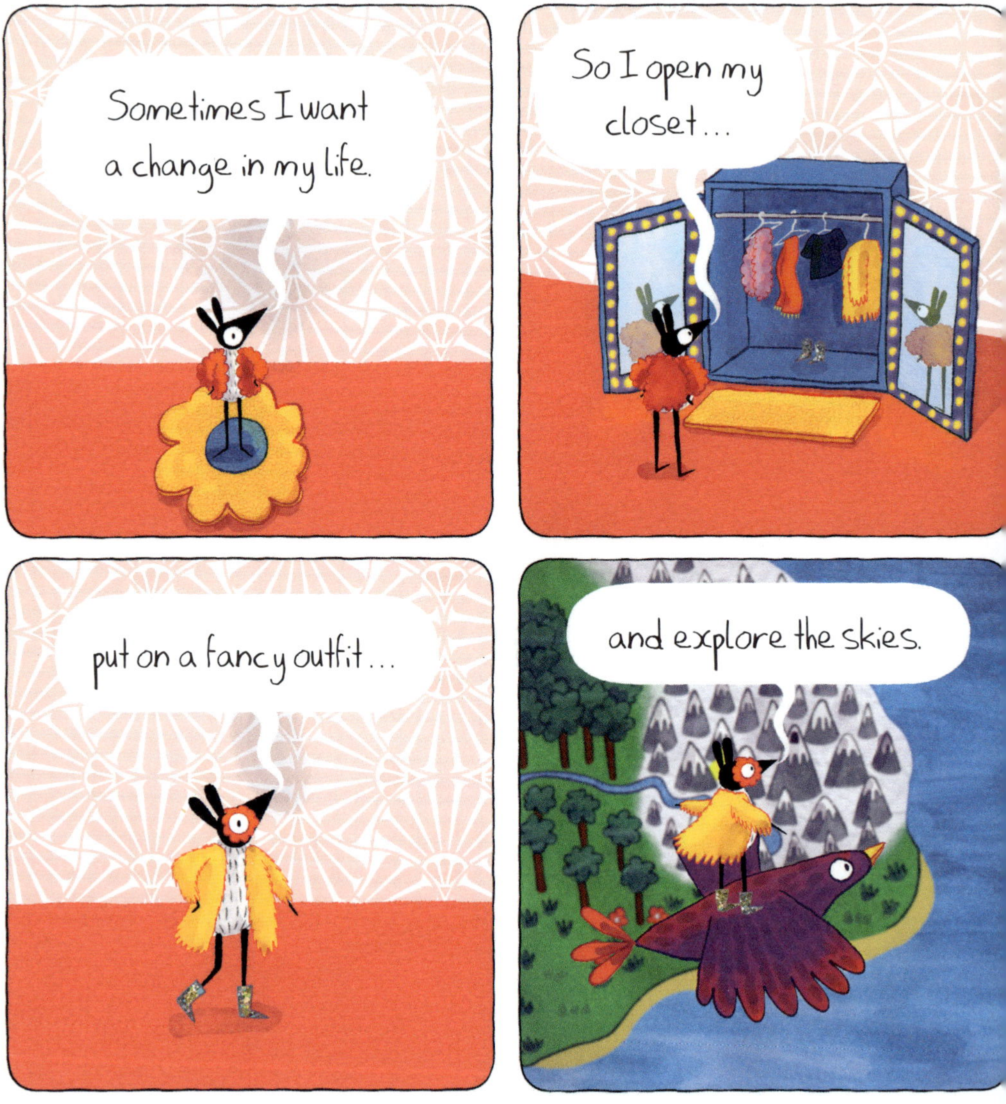
Sometimes I want a change in my life.
So I open my closet...
put on a fancy outfit...
and explore the skies.

FLOOF
AND THE AVALANCHE

One morning, Teazle is sitting in his volcano home deciding what to do with his day.

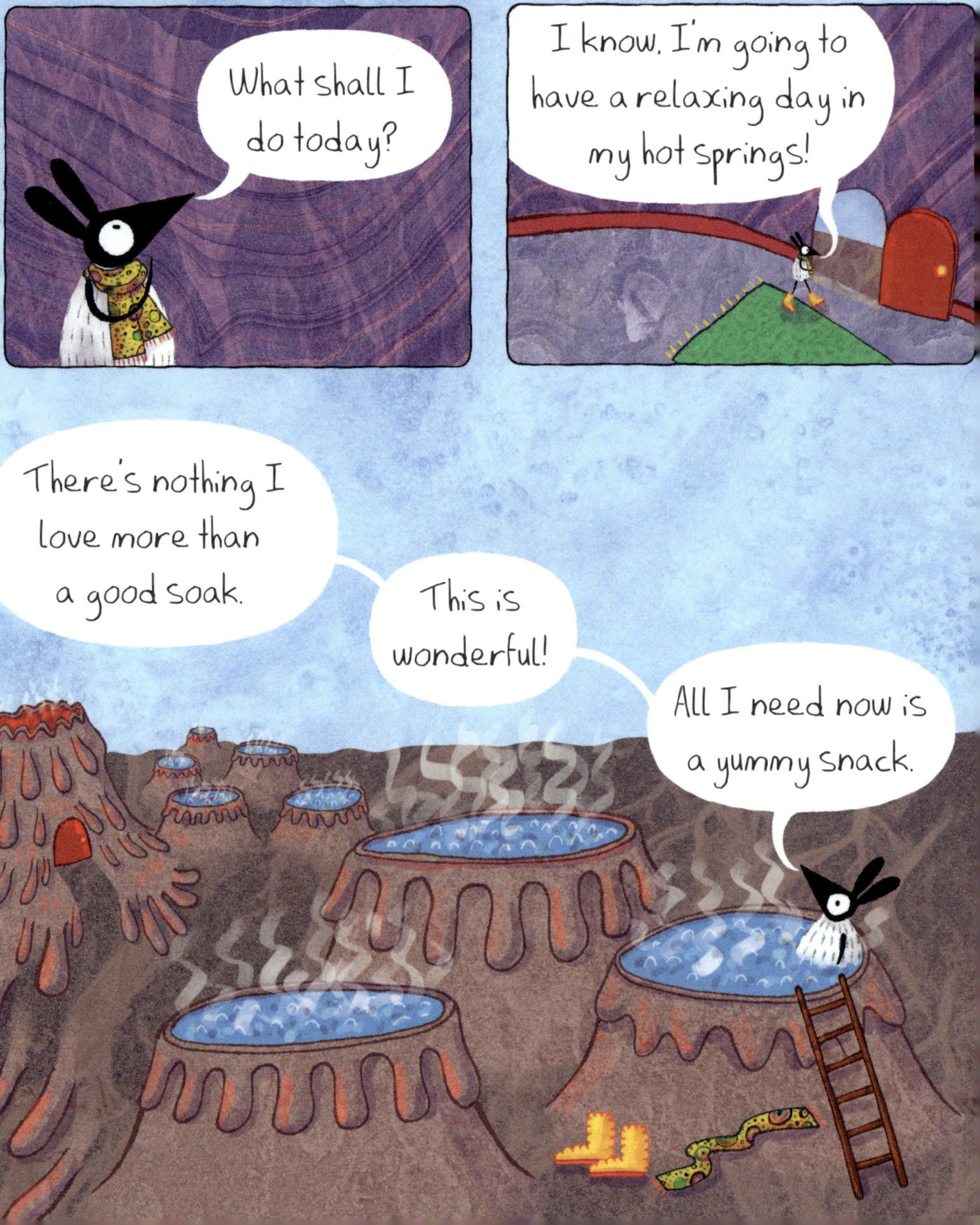
What shall I do today?
I know, I'm going to have a relaxing day in my hot springs!
There's nothing I love more than a good soak.
This is wonderful!
All I need now is a yummy snack.

Most of Teazle's days go like this. A nice morning bath, a few hours choosing an outfit for the day, then maybe a little walk if the weather is warm. Teazle liked his routine. But today feels a little different. Suddenly Dill arrives with an idea.

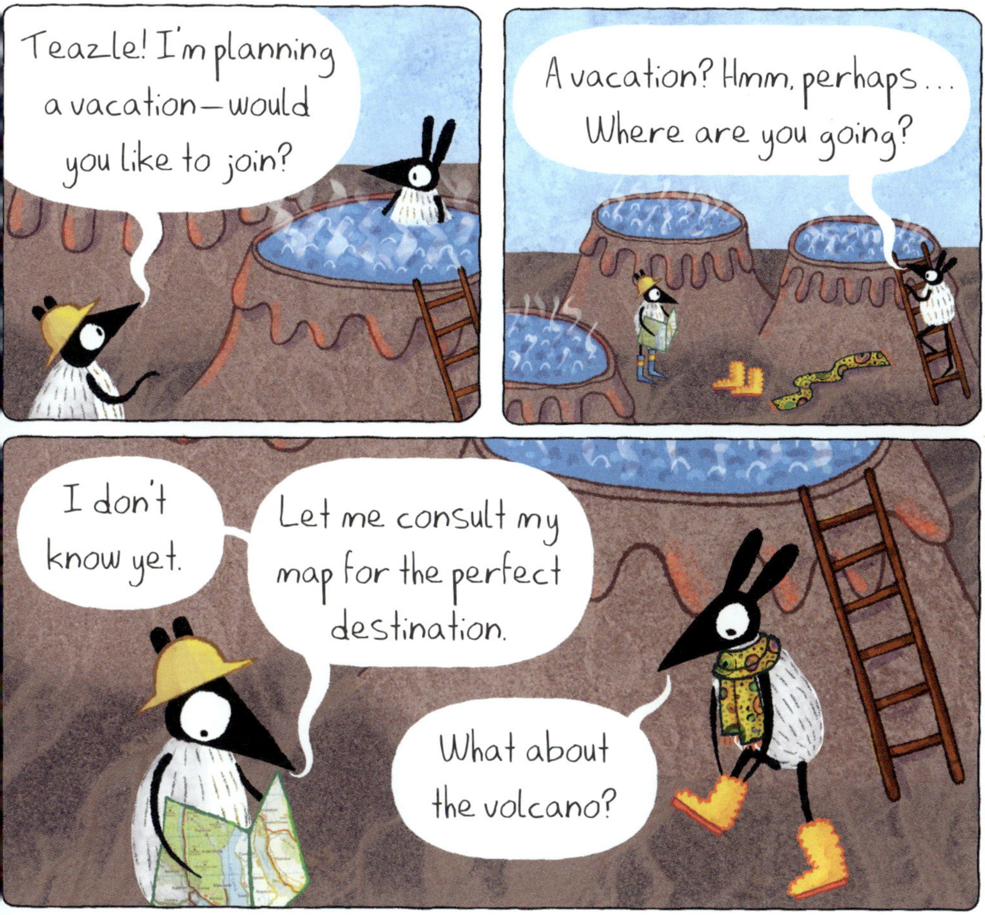
Teazle! I'm planning a vacation—would you like to join?
A vacation? Hmm, perhaps . . . Where are you going?
I don't know yet.
Let me consult my map for the perfect destination.
What about the volcano?

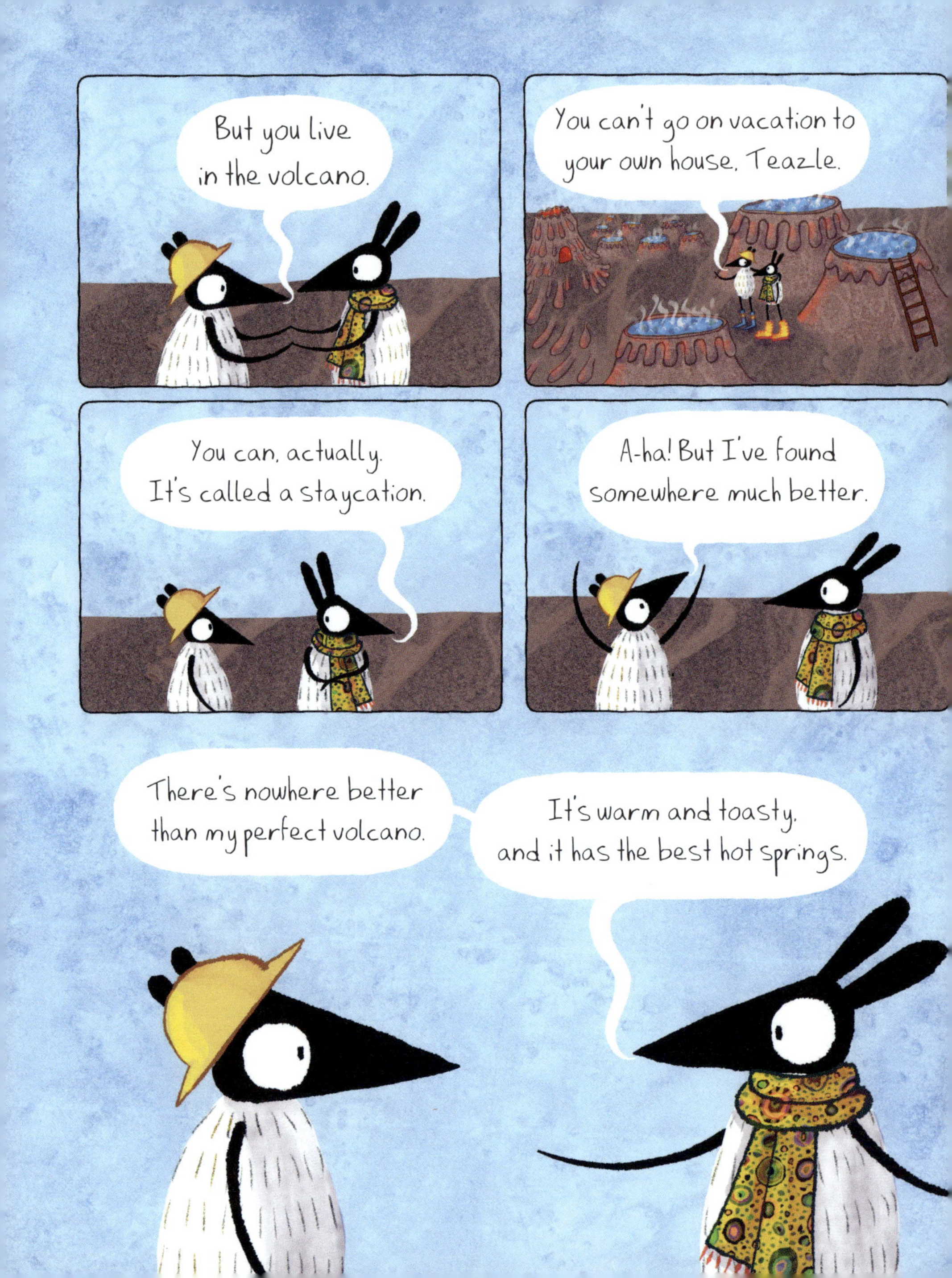
But you live in the volcano.
You can't go on vacation to your own house, Teazle.
You can, actually. It's called a staycation.
A-ha! But I've found somewhere much better.
There's nowhere better than my perfect volcano.
It's warm and toasty, and it has the best hot springs.

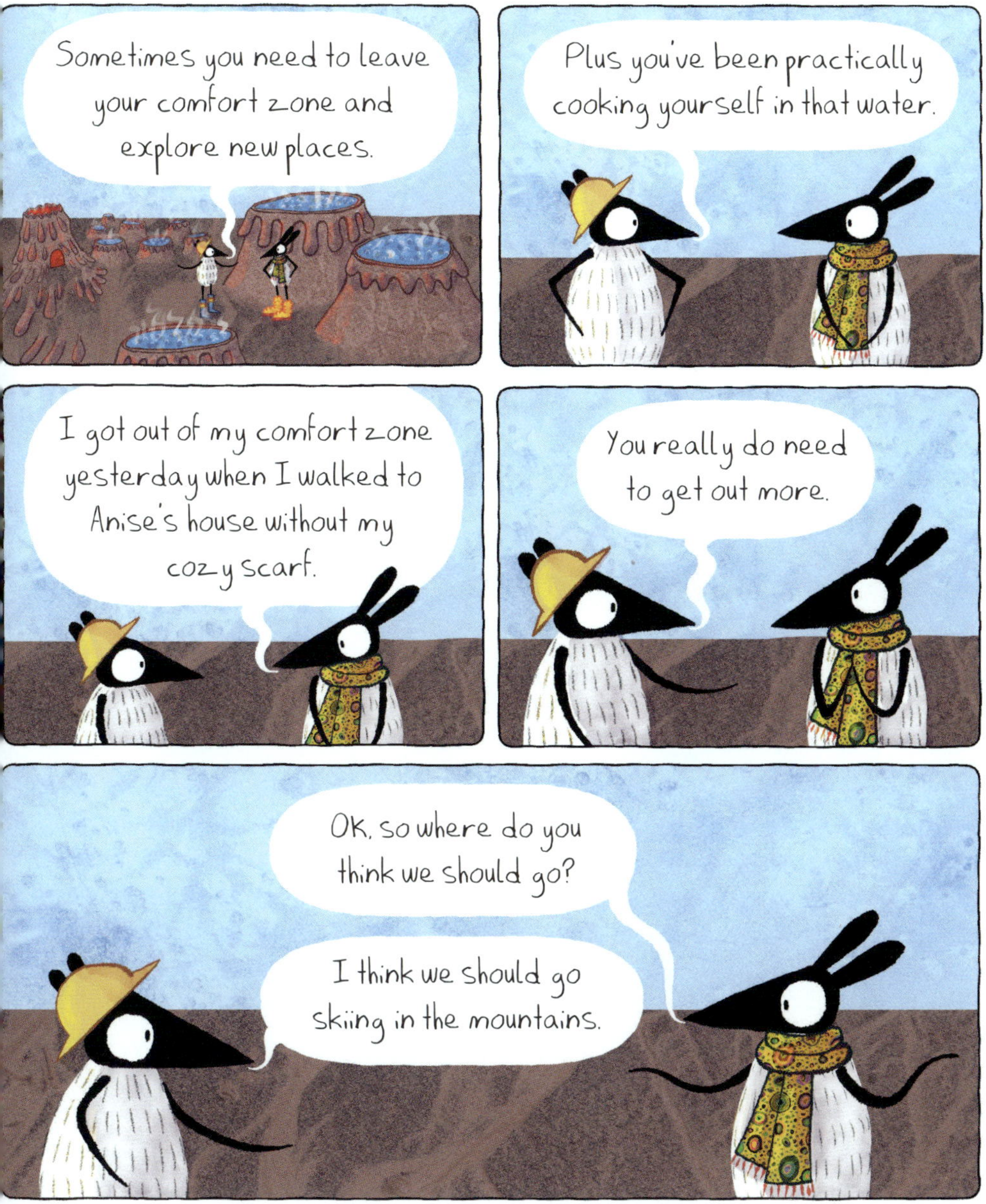
Sometimes you need to leave your comfort zone and explore new places.
Plus you've been practically cooking yourself in that water.
I got out of my comfort zone yesterday when I walked to Anise's house without my cozy scarf.
You really do need to get out more.
OK, so where do you think we should go?
I think we should go skiing in the mountains.

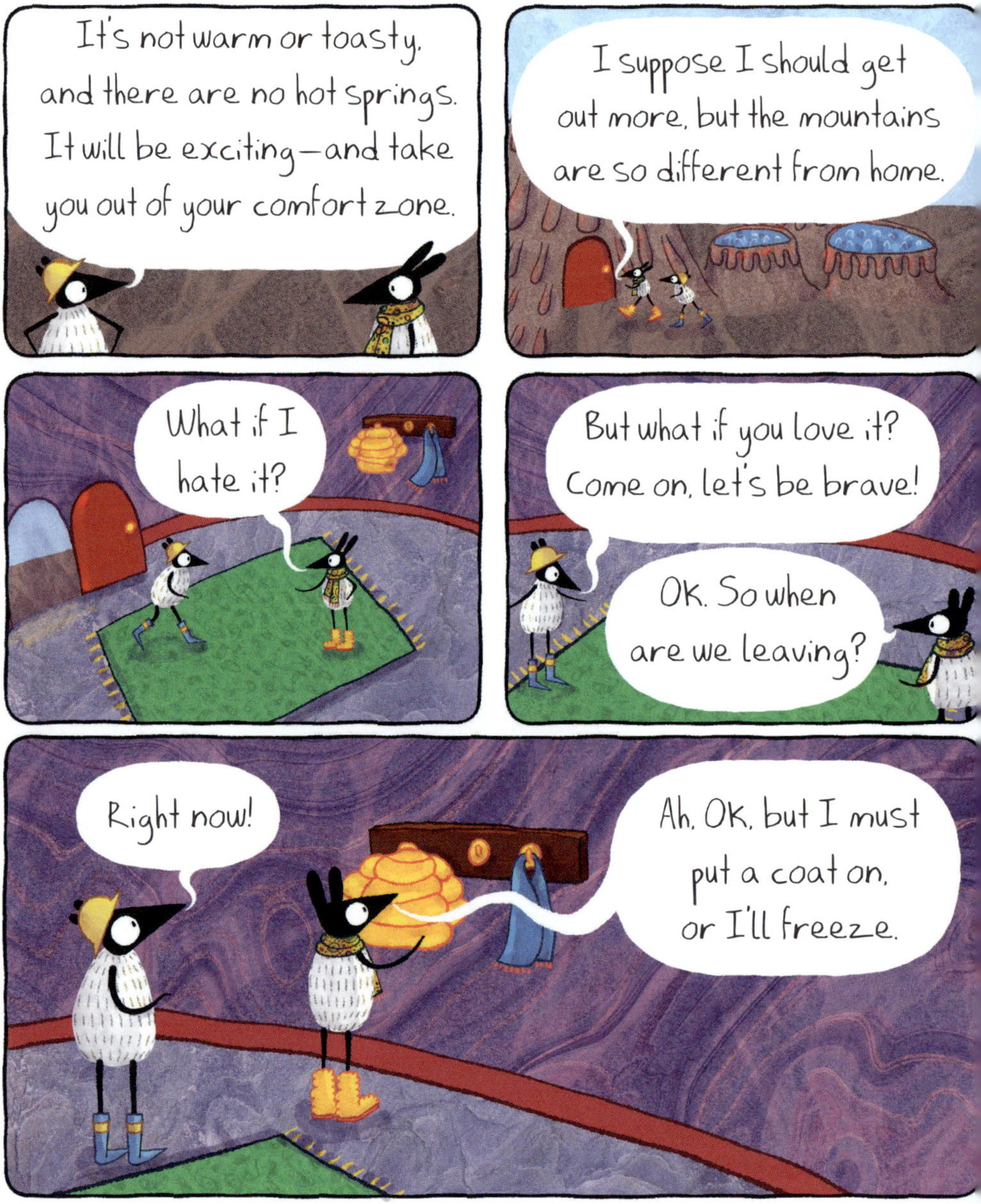
It's not warm or toasty, and there are no hot springs. It will be exciting—and take you out of your comfort zone.
I suppose I should get out more, but the mountains are so different from home.
What if I hate it?
But what if you love it? Come on, let's be brave!
OK. So when are we leaving?
Right now!
Ah, OK, but I must put a coat on, or I'll freeze.

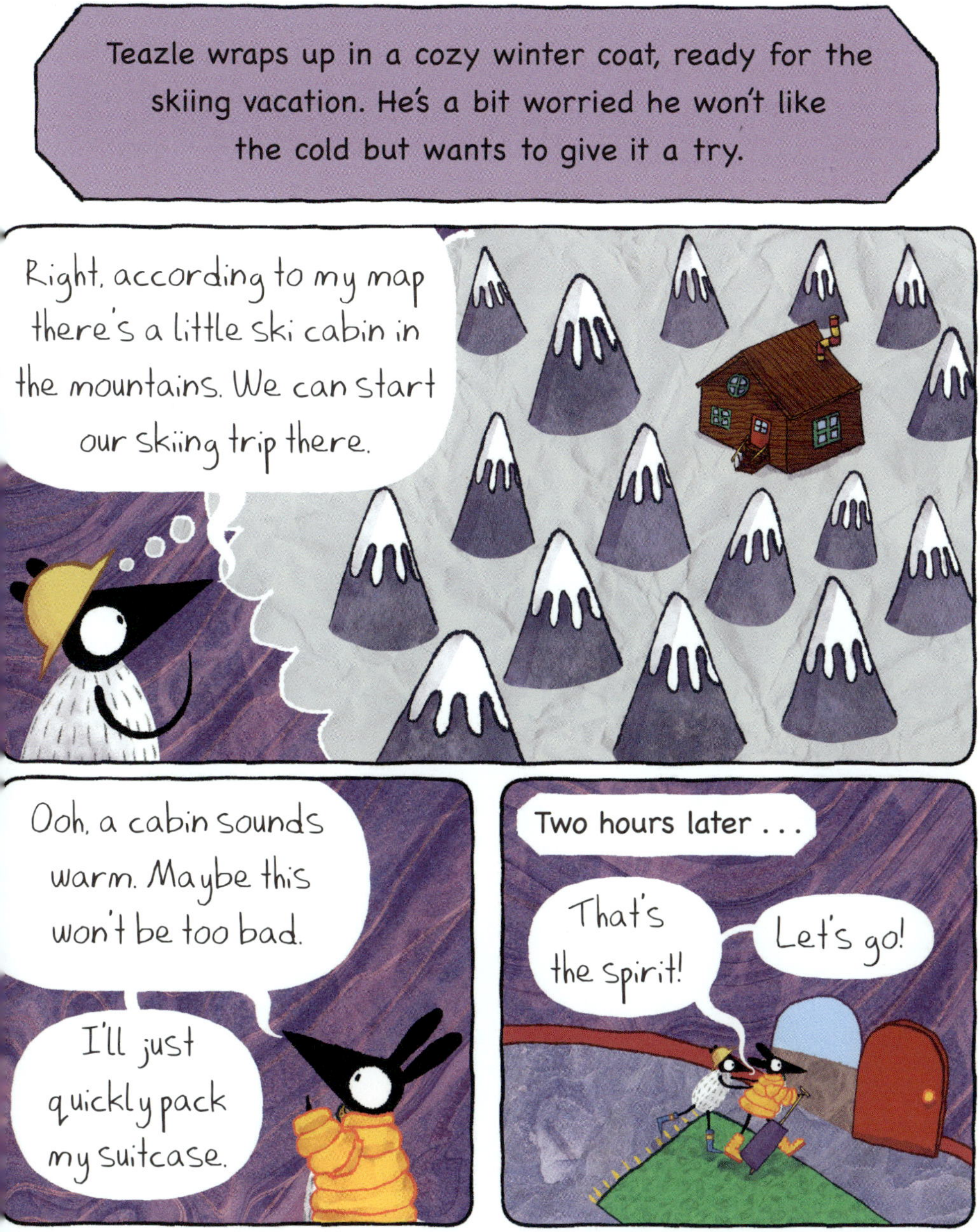
Teazle wraps up in a cozy winter coat, ready for the skiing vacation. He's a bit worried he won't like the cold but wants to give it a try.
Right, according to my map there's a little ski cabin in the mountains. We can start our skiing trip there.
Ooh, a cabin sounds warm. Maybe this won't be too bad.
I'll just quickly pack my suitcase.
Two hours later . . .
That's the spirit!
Let's go!

Teazle and Dill march off toward the mountains. Along the way, they run into Bean and Wizard.

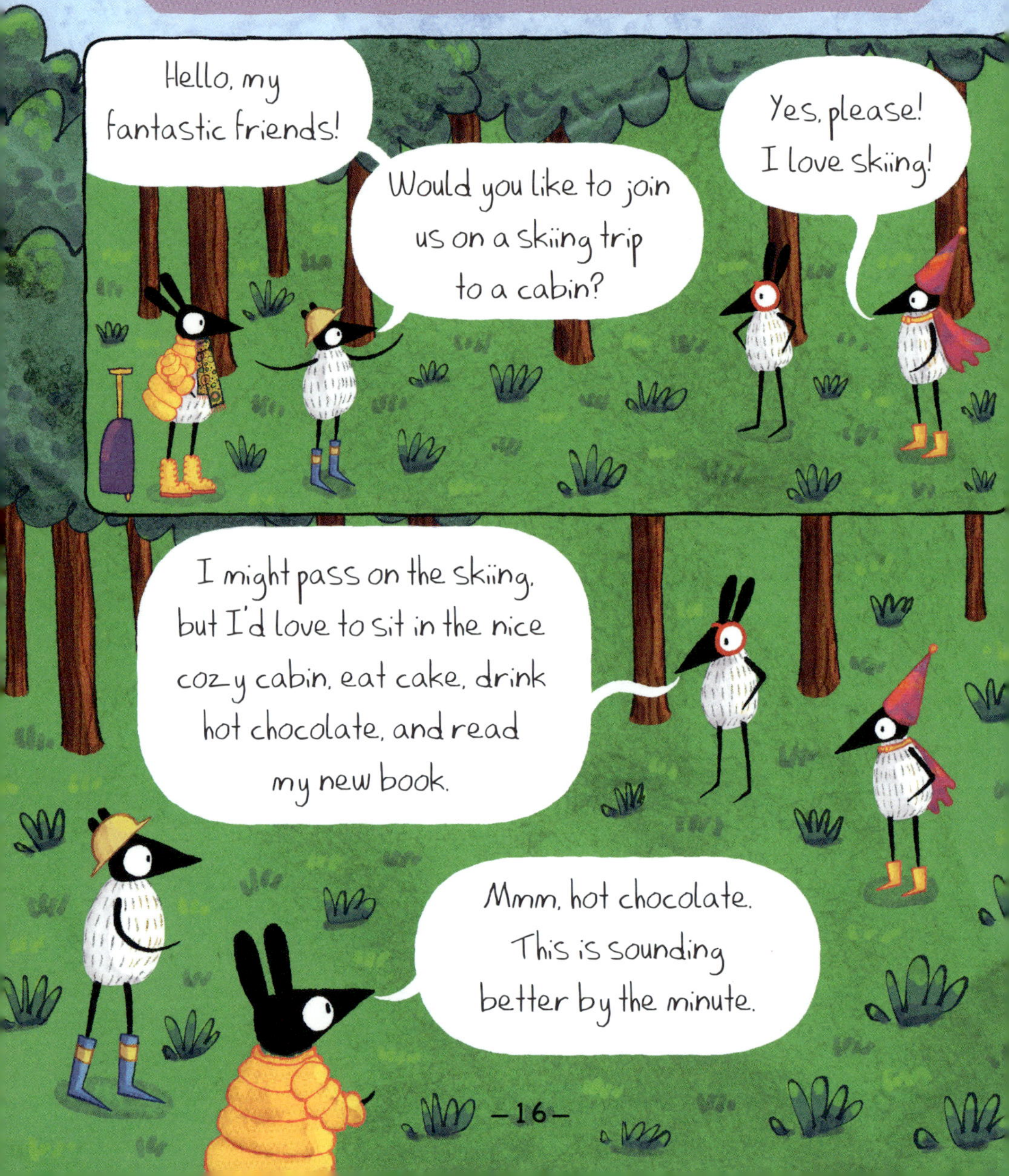
Hello, my fantastic friends!
Would you like to join us on a skiing trip to a cabin?
Yes, please! I love skiing!
I might pass on the skiing, but I'd love to sit in the nice cozy cabin, eat cake, drink hot chocolate, and read my new book.
Mmm, hot chocolate. This is sounding better by the minute.

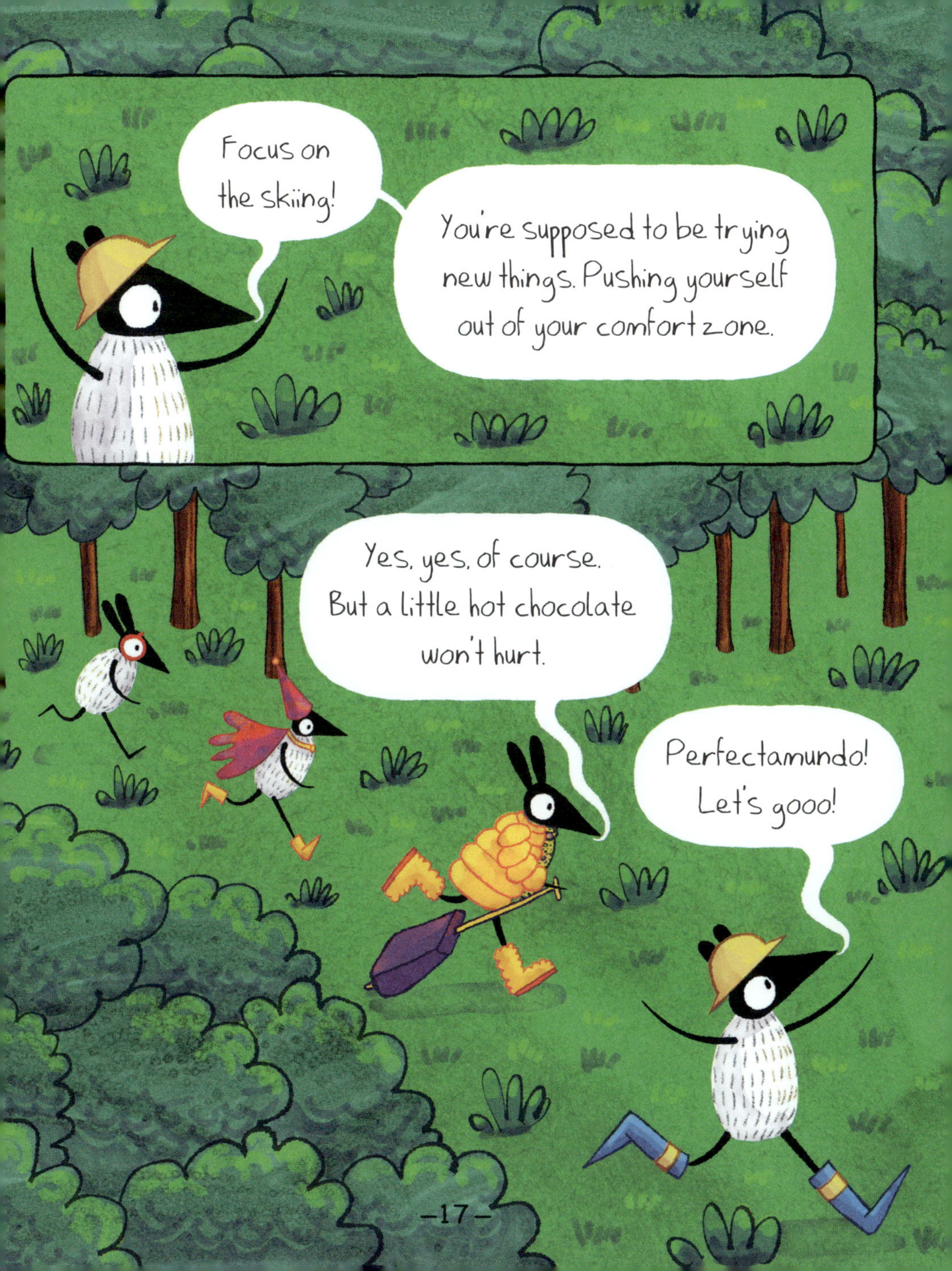
Focus on the skiing!
You're supposed to be trying new things. Pushing yourself out of your comfort zone.
Yes, yes, of course. But a little hot chocolate won't hurt.
Perfectamundo! Let's gooo!

The Floofs approach the mountain cabin. From a distance they can see the lights are on. Someone has beaten them to it.

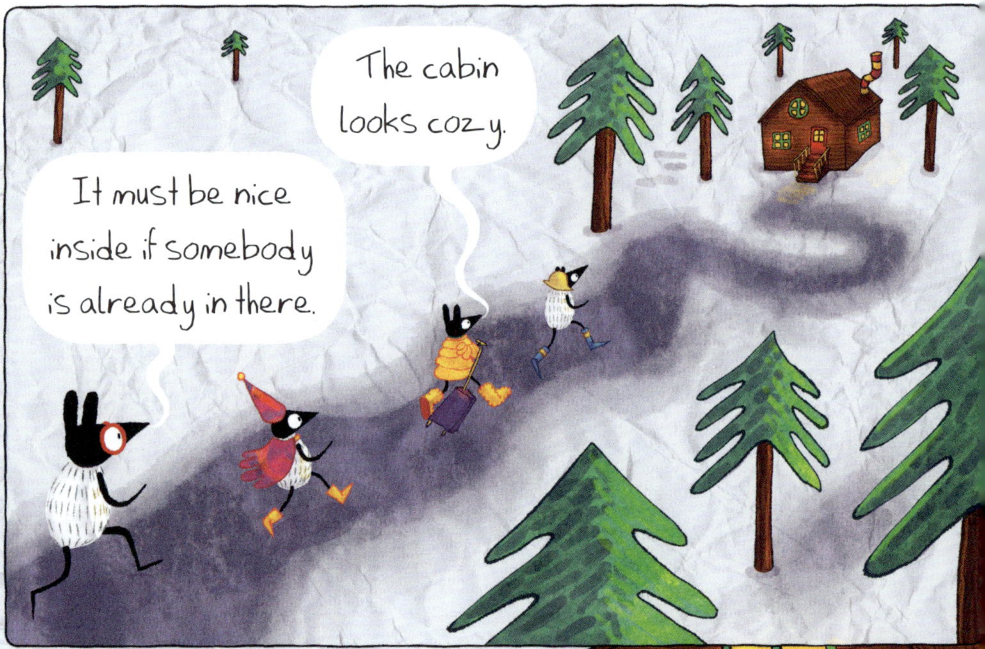

It must be nice inside if somebody is already in there.
The cabin looks cozy.

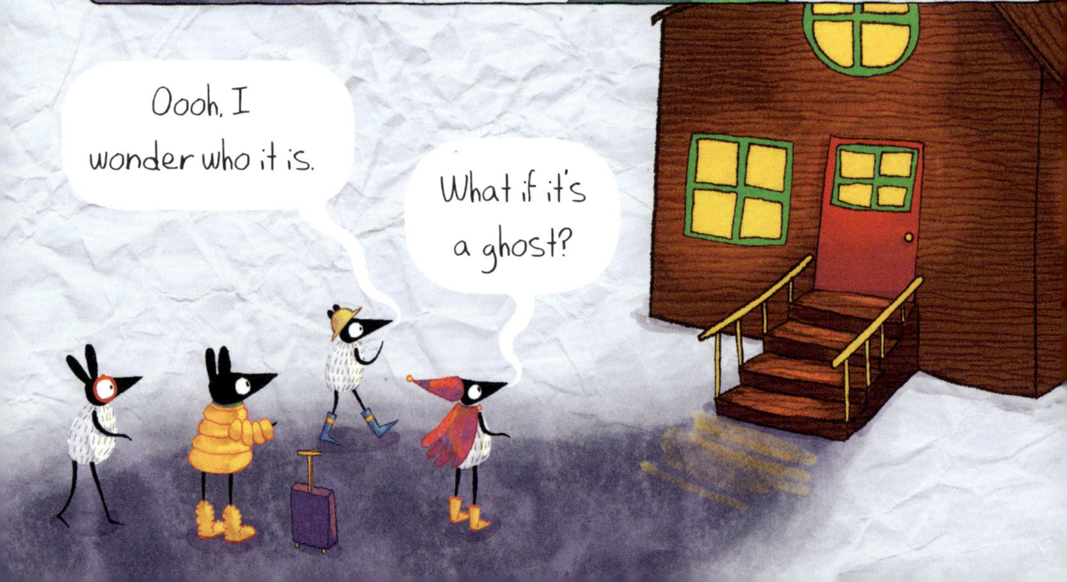

Oooh, I wonder who it is.
What if it's a ghost?

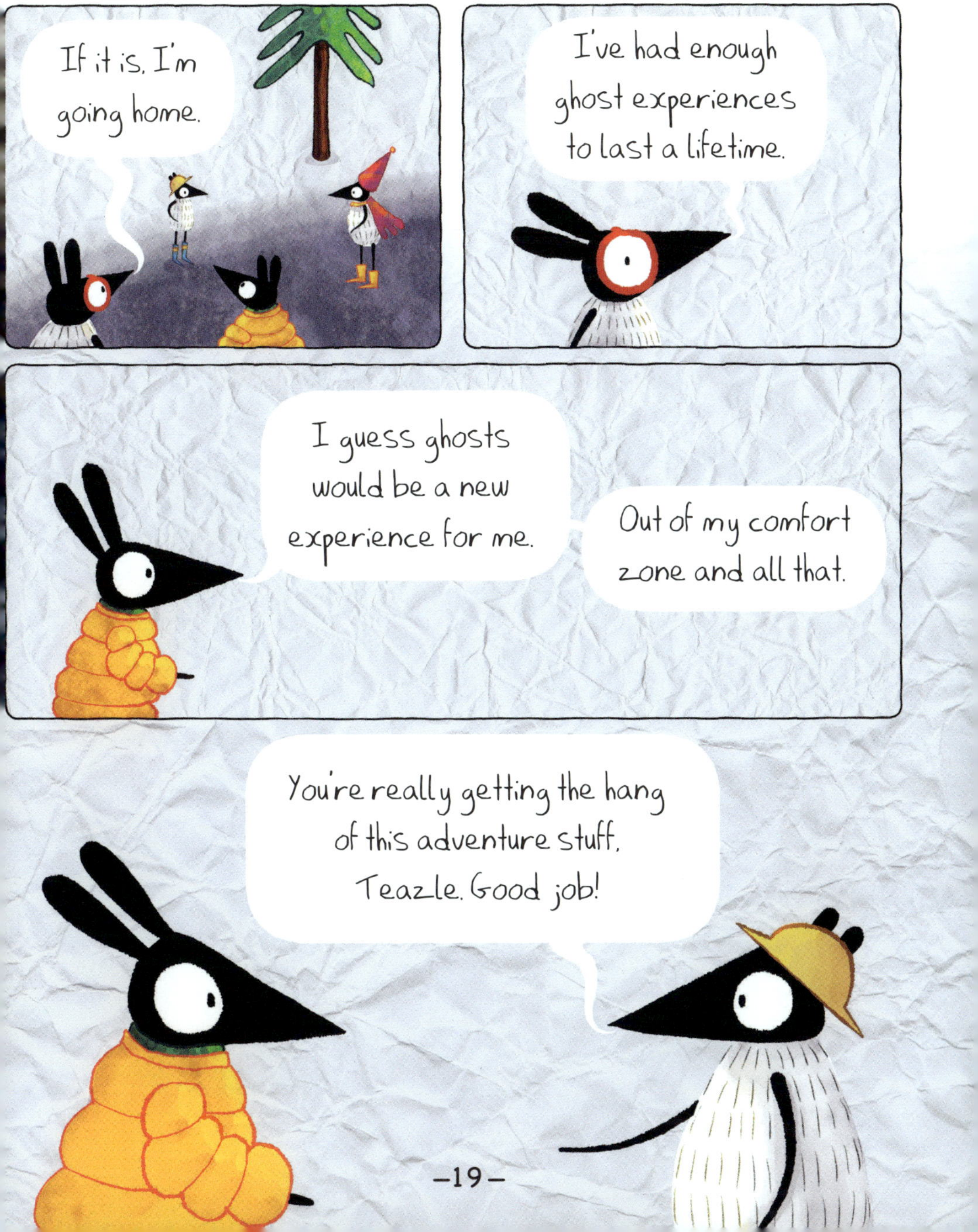
If it is, I'm going home.
I've had enough ghost experiences to last a lifetime.
I guess ghosts would be a new experience for me.
Out of my comfort zone and all that.
You're really getting the hang of this adventure stuff, Teazle. Good job!

The Floofs arrive at the cabin. Dill swings open the door. Inside is a cozy-looking Clementine. She's sitting on a large sofa in front of the fire, with the most perfect-looking hot chocolate.

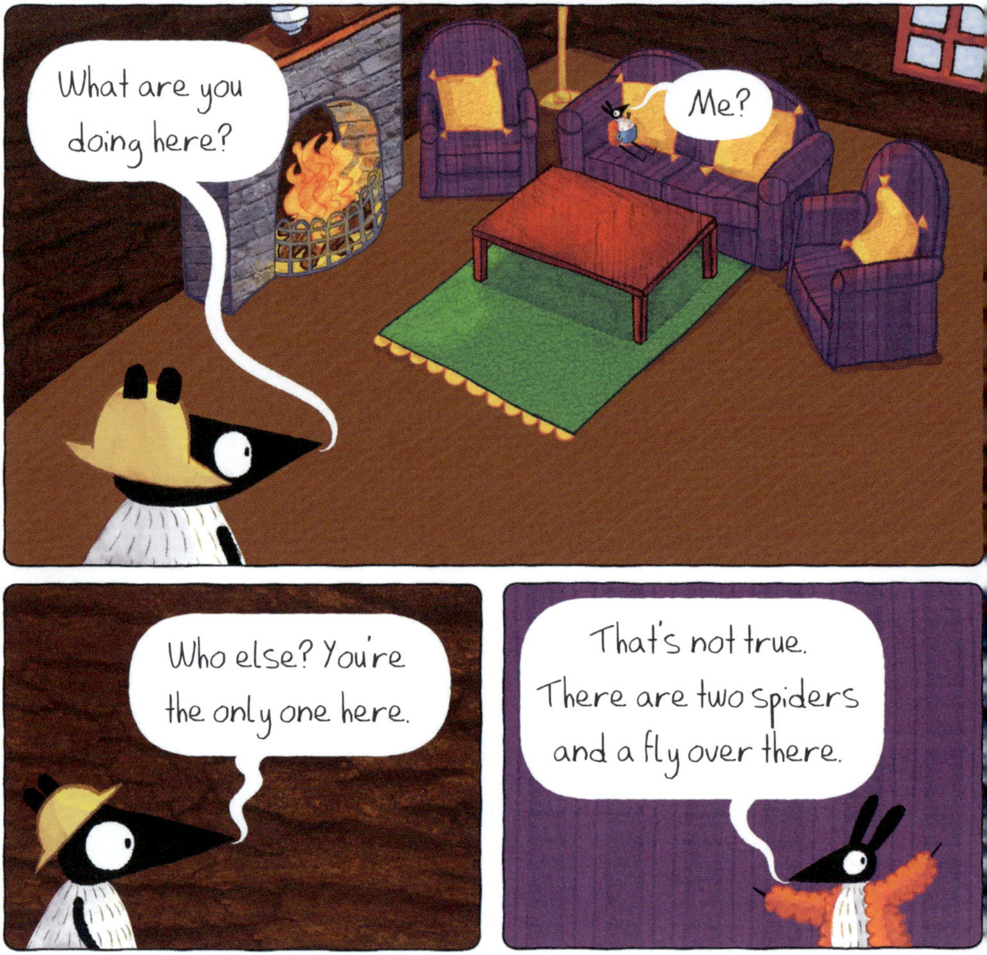
What are you doing here?
Me?
Who else? You're the only one here.
That's not true. There are two spiders and a fly over there.

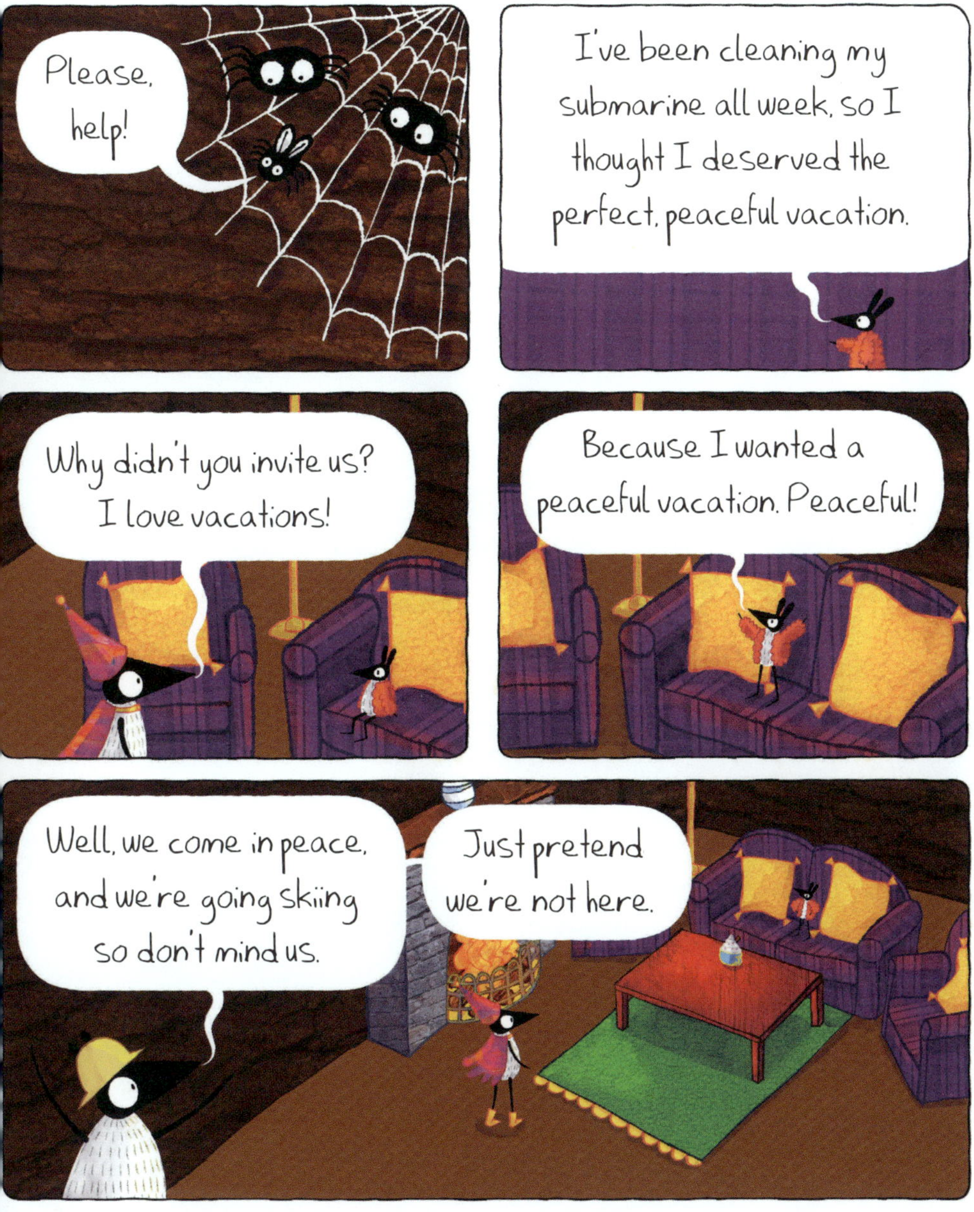
Please, help!
I've been cleaning my submarine all week, so I thought I deserved the perfect, peaceful vacation.
Why didn't you invite us? I love vacations!
Because I wanted a peaceful vacation. Peaceful!
Well, we come in peace, and we're going skiing so don't mind us.
Just pretend we're not here.

Bean joins Clem by the fire and makes herself a hot chocolate. Meanwhile, Dill, Teazle, and Wizard rummage in the closet looking for some skis.

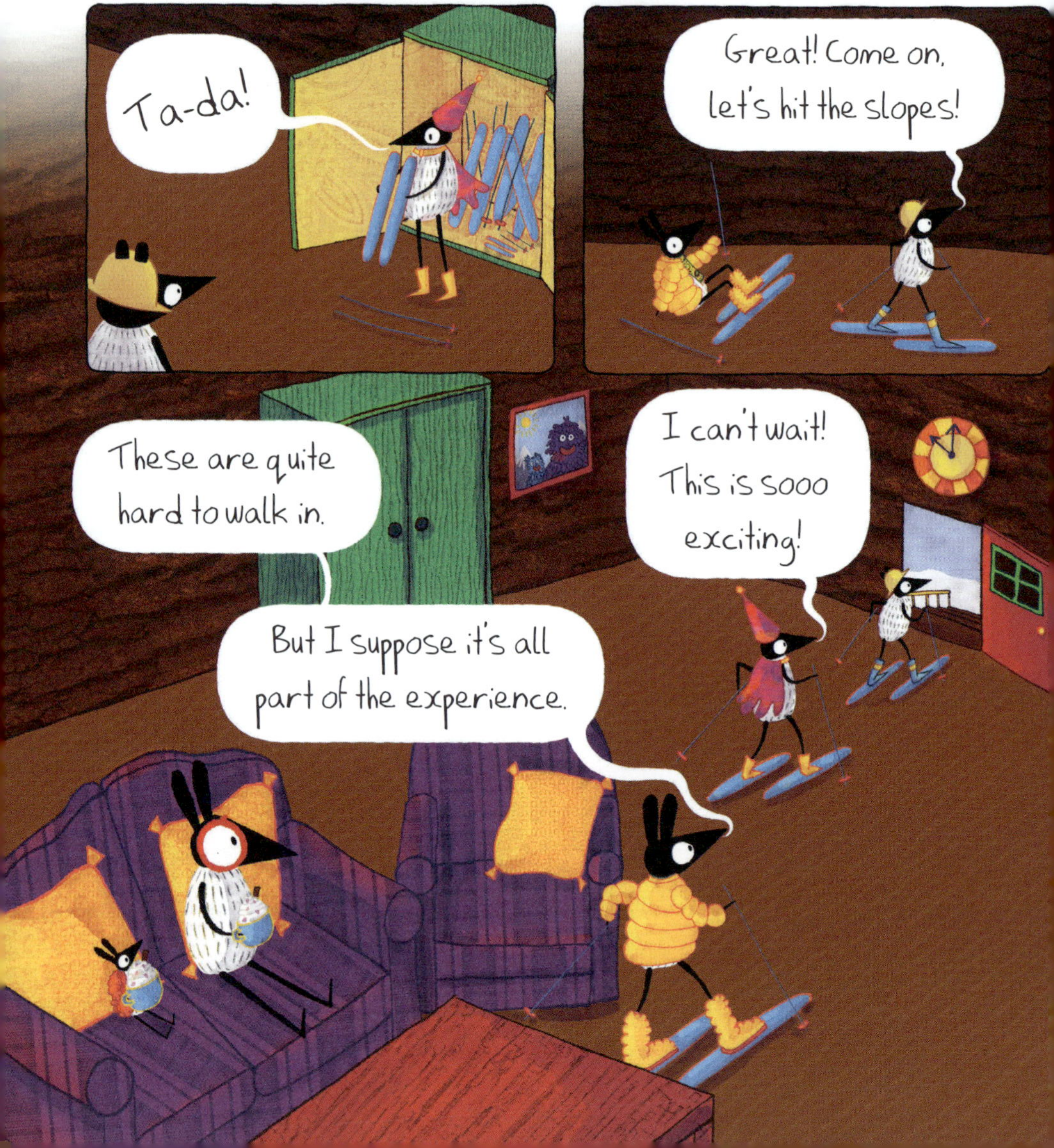
Ta-da!
Great! Come on, let's hit the slopes!
These are quite hard to walk in.
But I suppose it's all part of the experience.
I can't wait! This is sooo exciting!

Dill, Teazle, and Wizard trudge up the mountain toward the beginning of the ski slopes. The sky is beautifully clear: perfect weather for skiing.

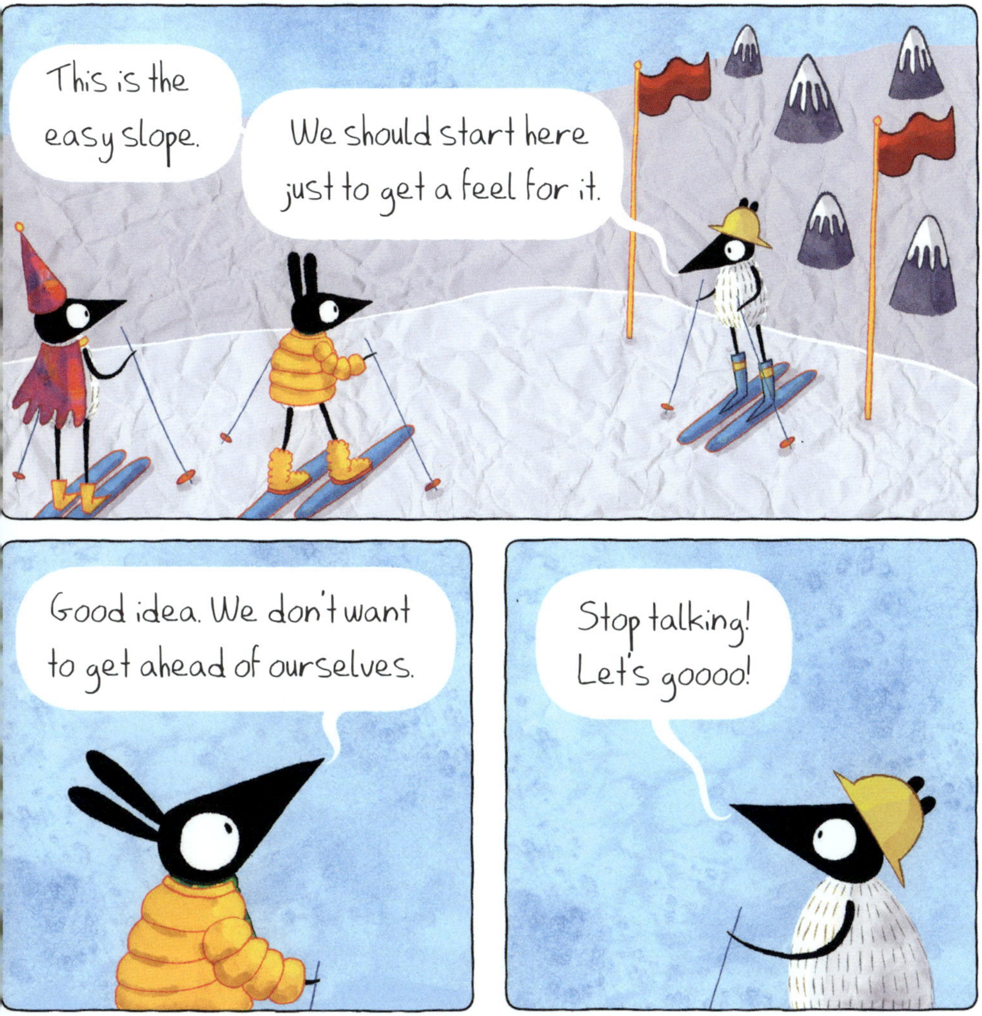
This is the easy slope.
We should start here just to get a feel for it.
Good idea. We don't want to get ahead of ourselves.
Stop talking! Let's goooo!

The three Floofs slide down the mountain, weaving in and out of the flags, the wind whistling in their ears.

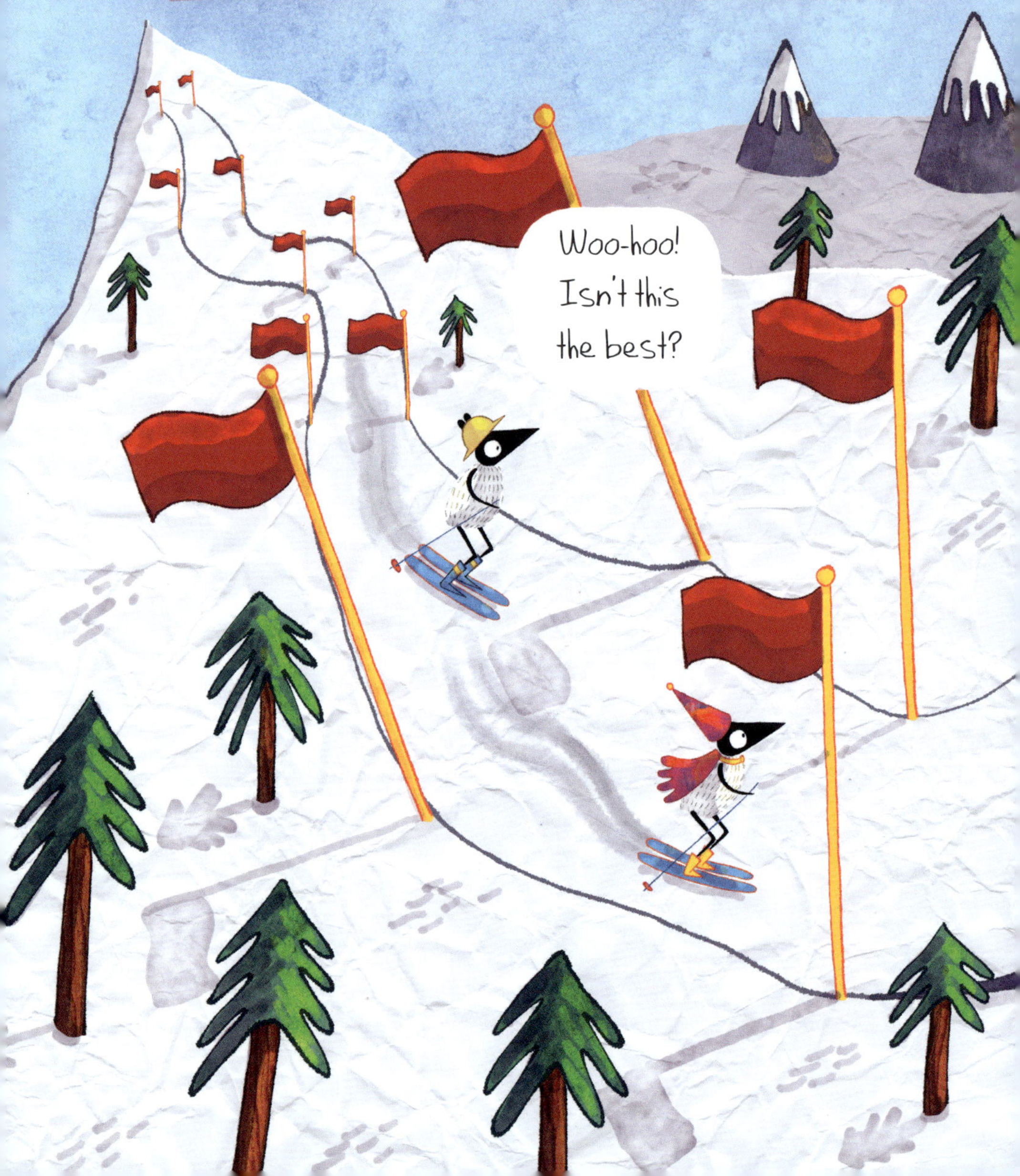
Woo-hoo! Isn't this the best?

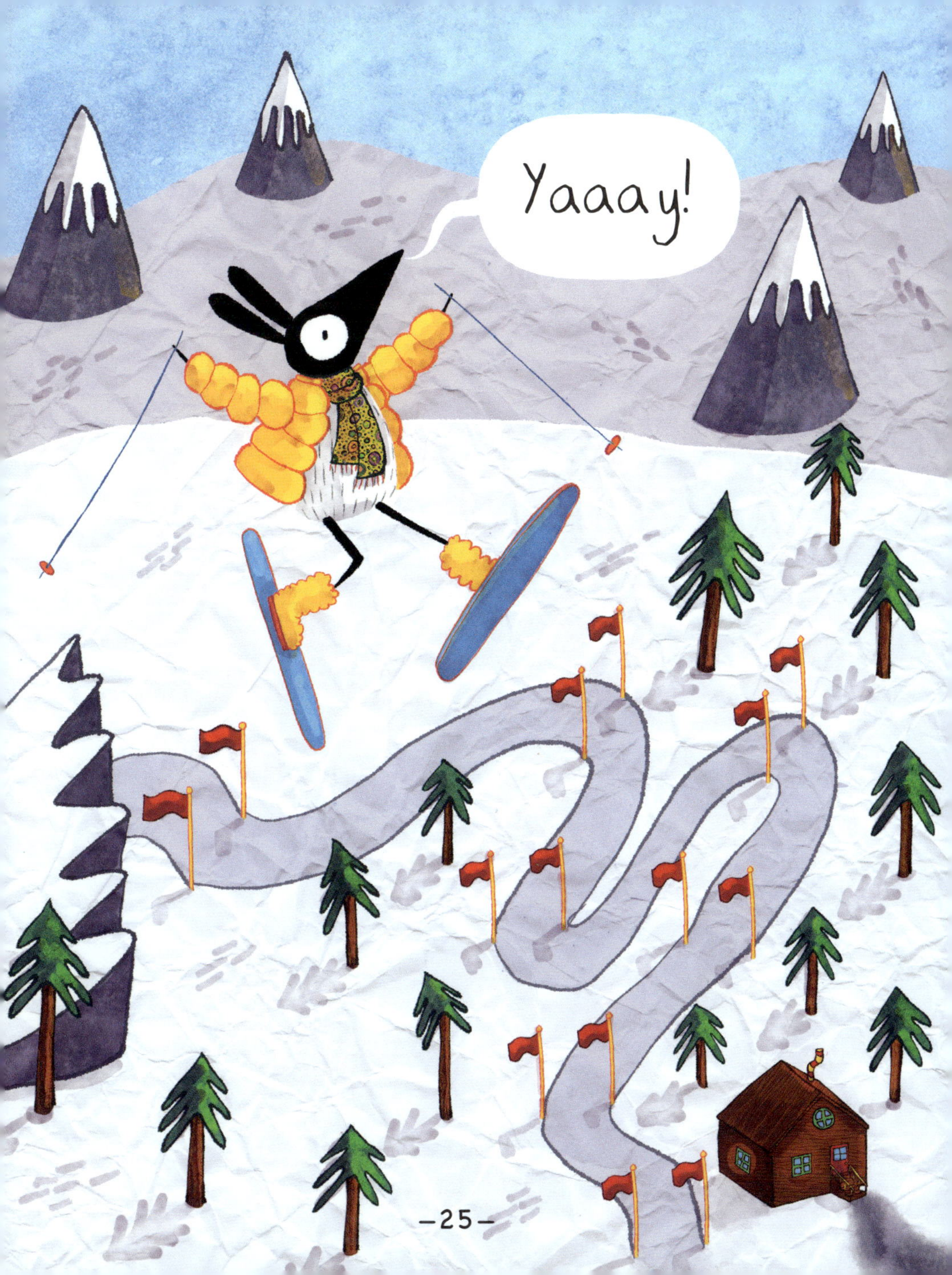
Yaaay!

The Floofs finish the slope, landing near the cabin.

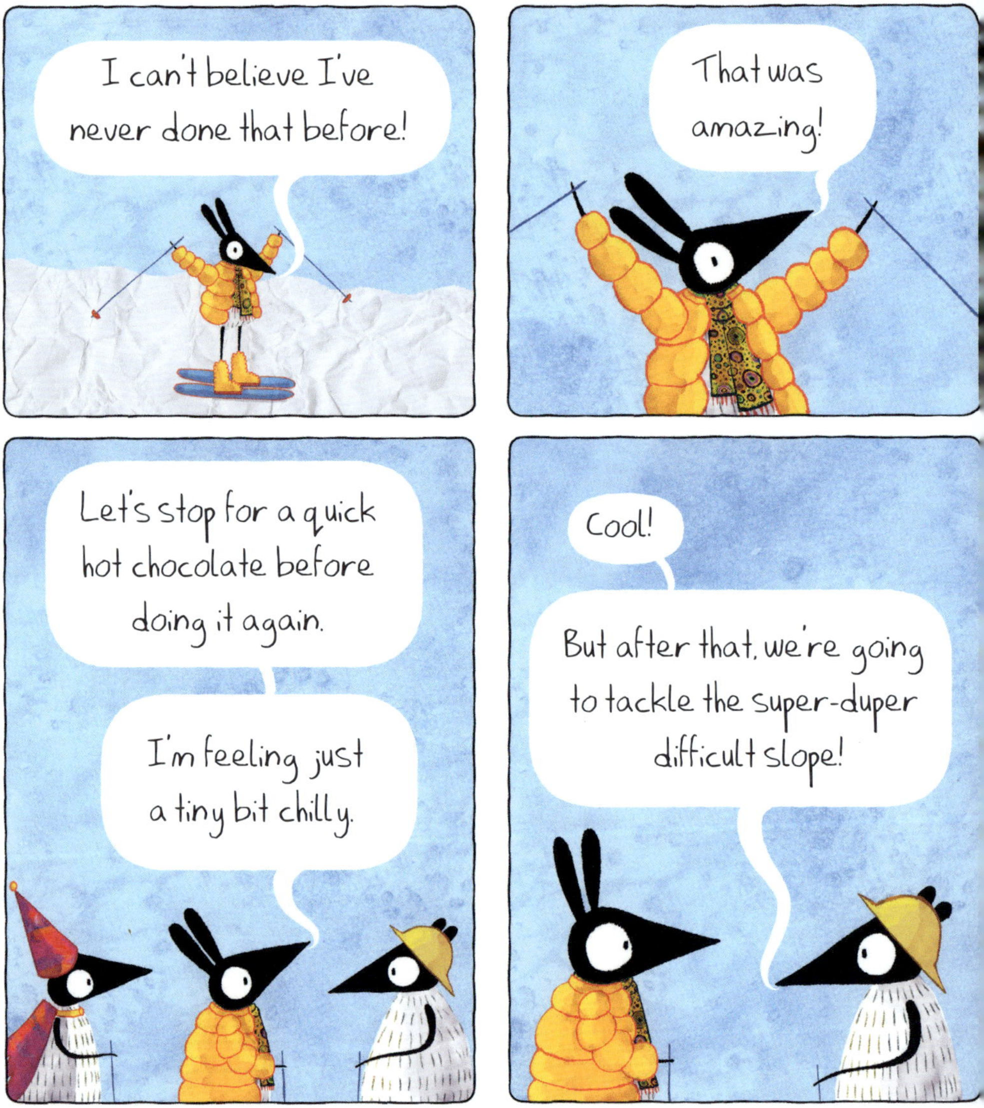
I can't believe I've never done that before!
That was amazing!
Let's stop for a quick hot chocolate before doing it again.
I'm feeling just a tiny bit chilly.
Cool!
But after that, we're going to tackle the super-duper difficult slope!

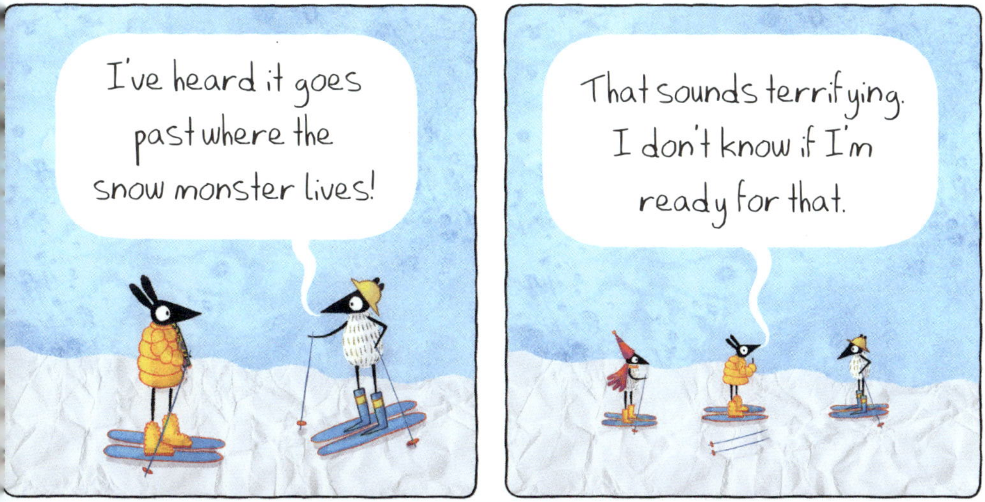
I've heard it goes past where the snow monster lives!
That sounds terrifying. I don't know if I'm ready for that.

Dill, Teazle, and Wizard go back into the cabin for a hot drink to warm up. By now, both Bean and Clementine are on their third hot chocolate.

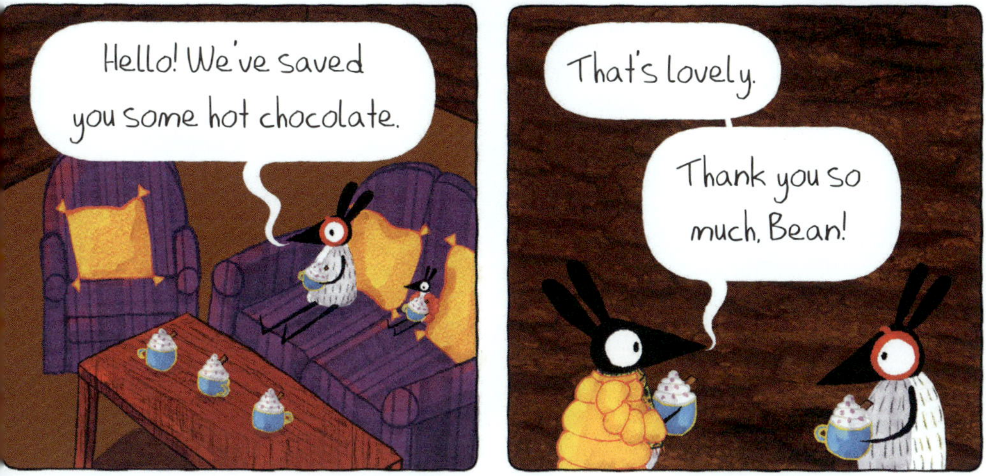
Hello! We've saved you some hot chocolate.
That's lovely.
Thank you so much, Bean!

The Floofs drink their hot chocolate, and Bean and Clementine listen to the others talk about their skiing experience. Suddenly, Bean points to the window.

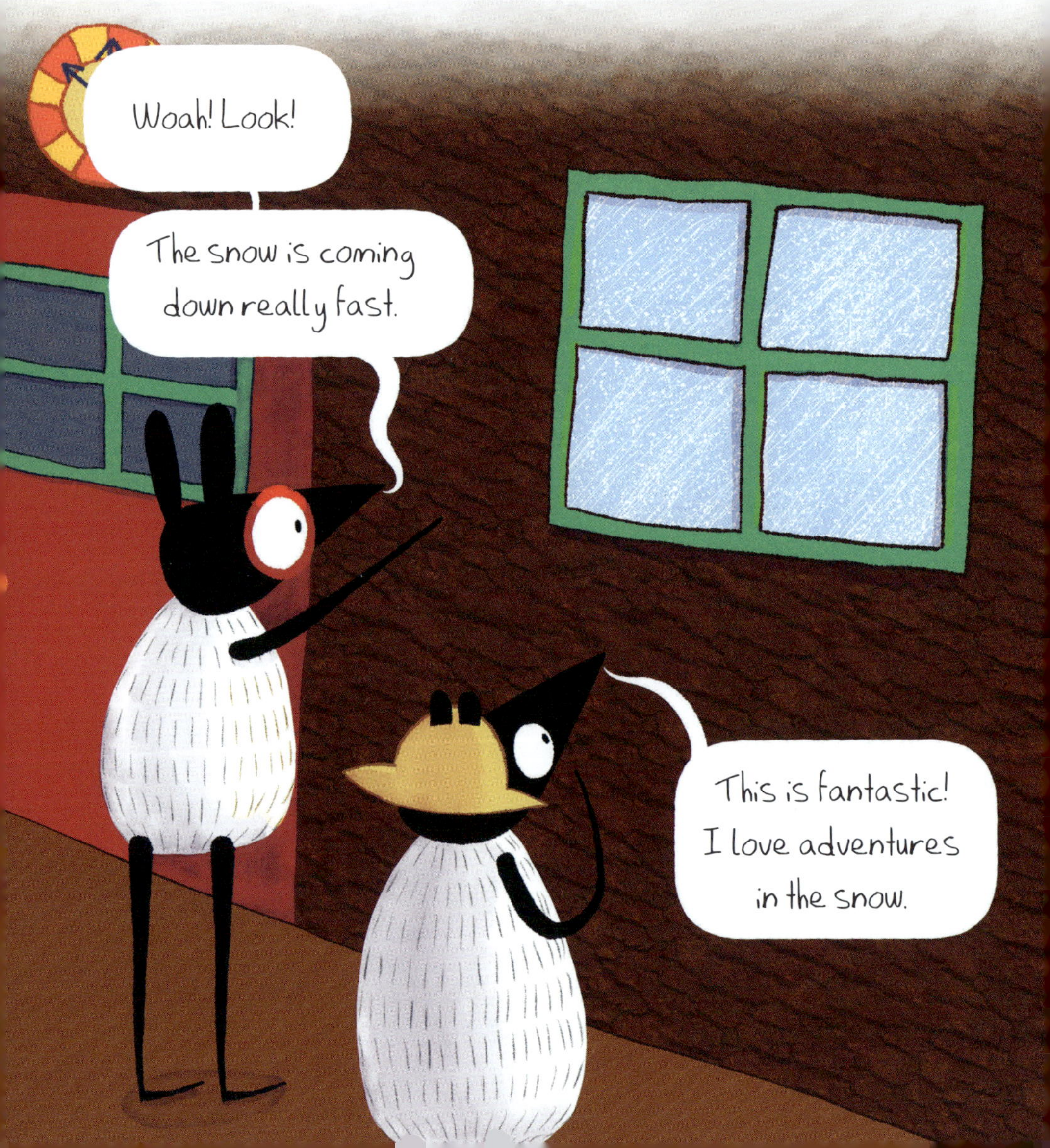
Woah! Look!
The snow is coming down really fast.
This is fantastic! I love adventures in the snow.

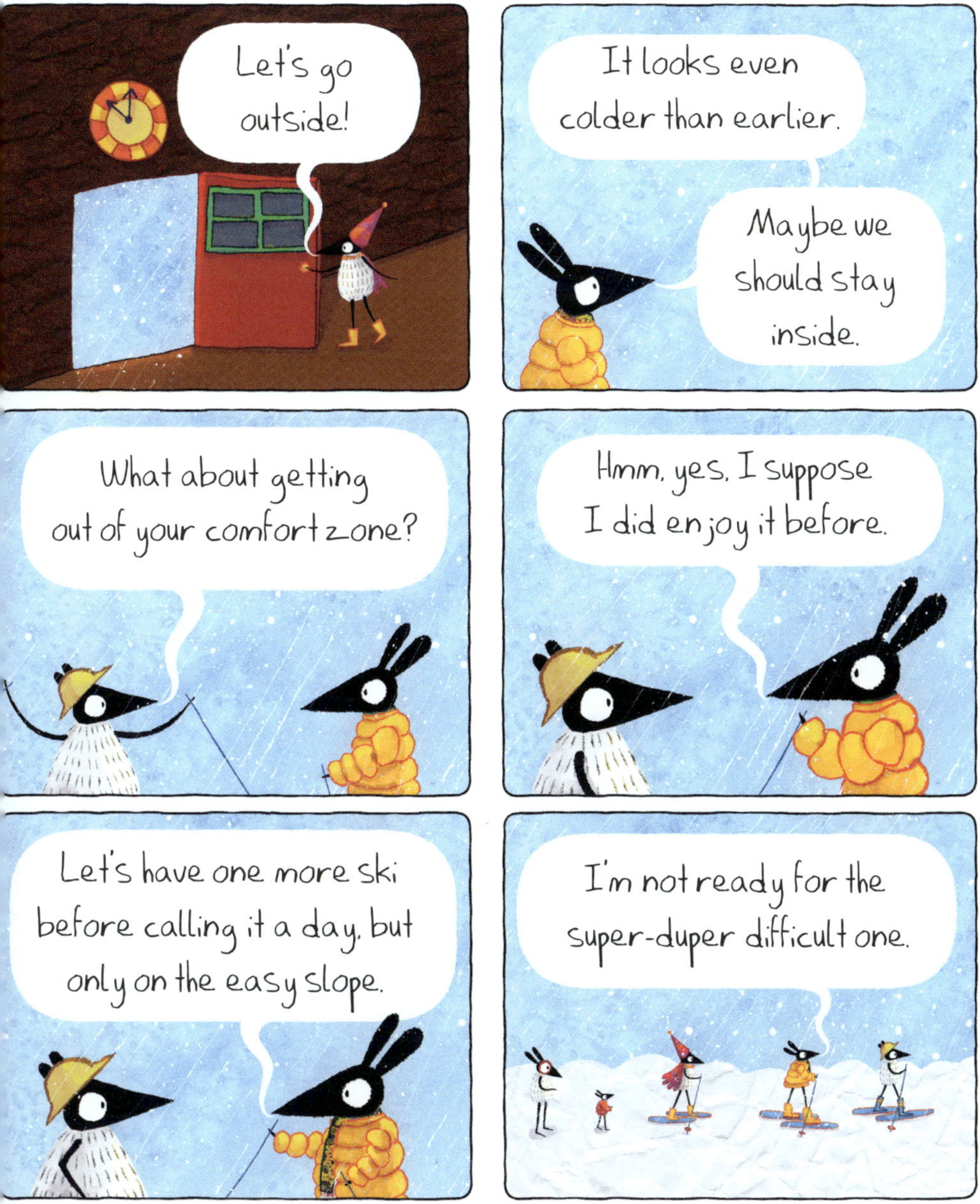
Let's go outside!
It looks even colder than earlier.
Maybe we should stay inside.
What about getting out of your comfort zone?
Hmm, yes, I suppose I did enjoy it before.
Let's have one more ski before calling it a day, but only on the easy slope.
I'm not ready for the super-duper difficult one.

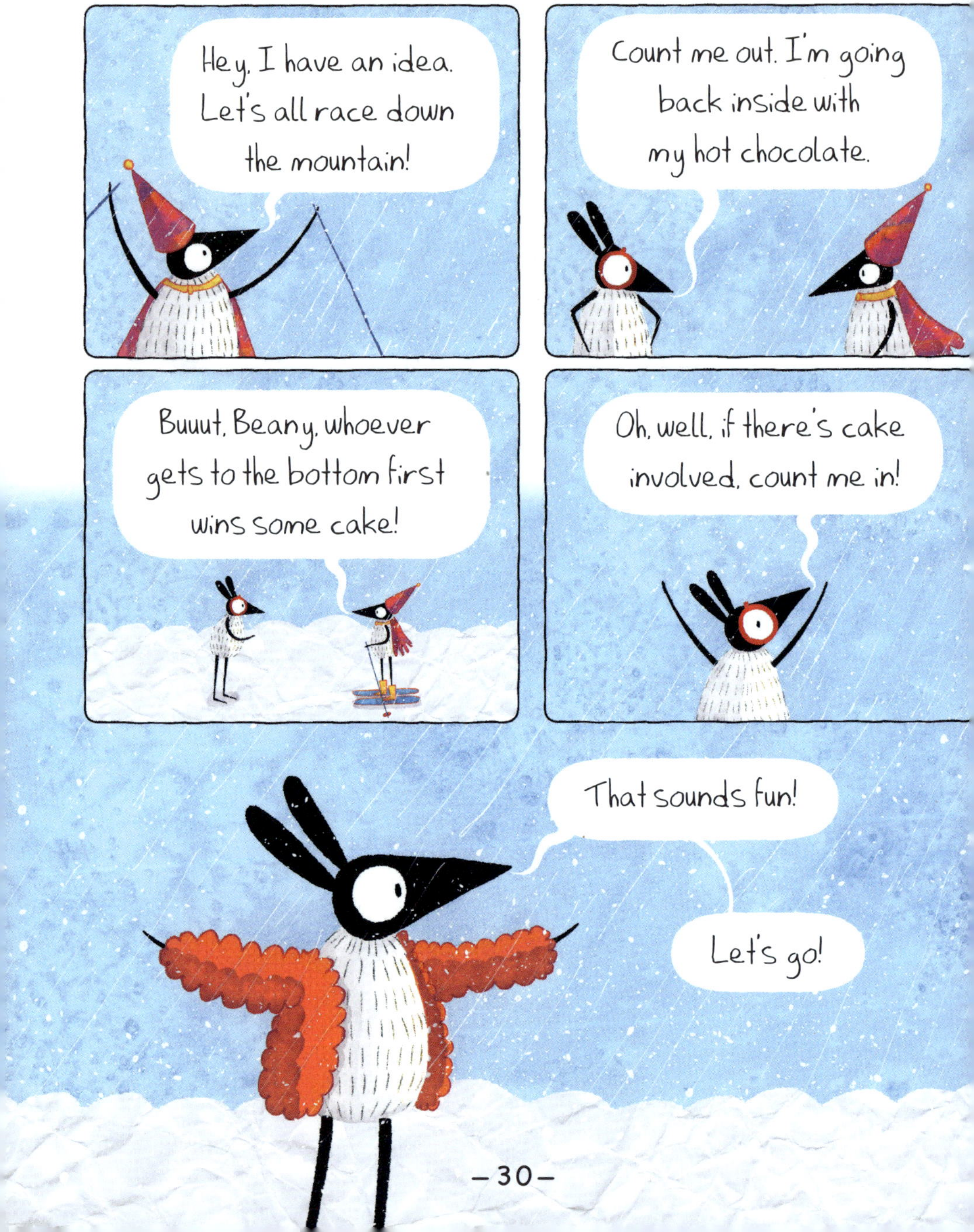
Hey, I have an idea. Let's all race down the mountain!
Count me out. I'm going back inside with my hot chocolate.
Buuut, Beany, whoever gets to the bottom first wins some cake!
Oh, well, if there's cake involved, count me in!
That sounds fun!
Let's go!

The Floofs go back up to the top of the easy ski slope to prepare for their race.

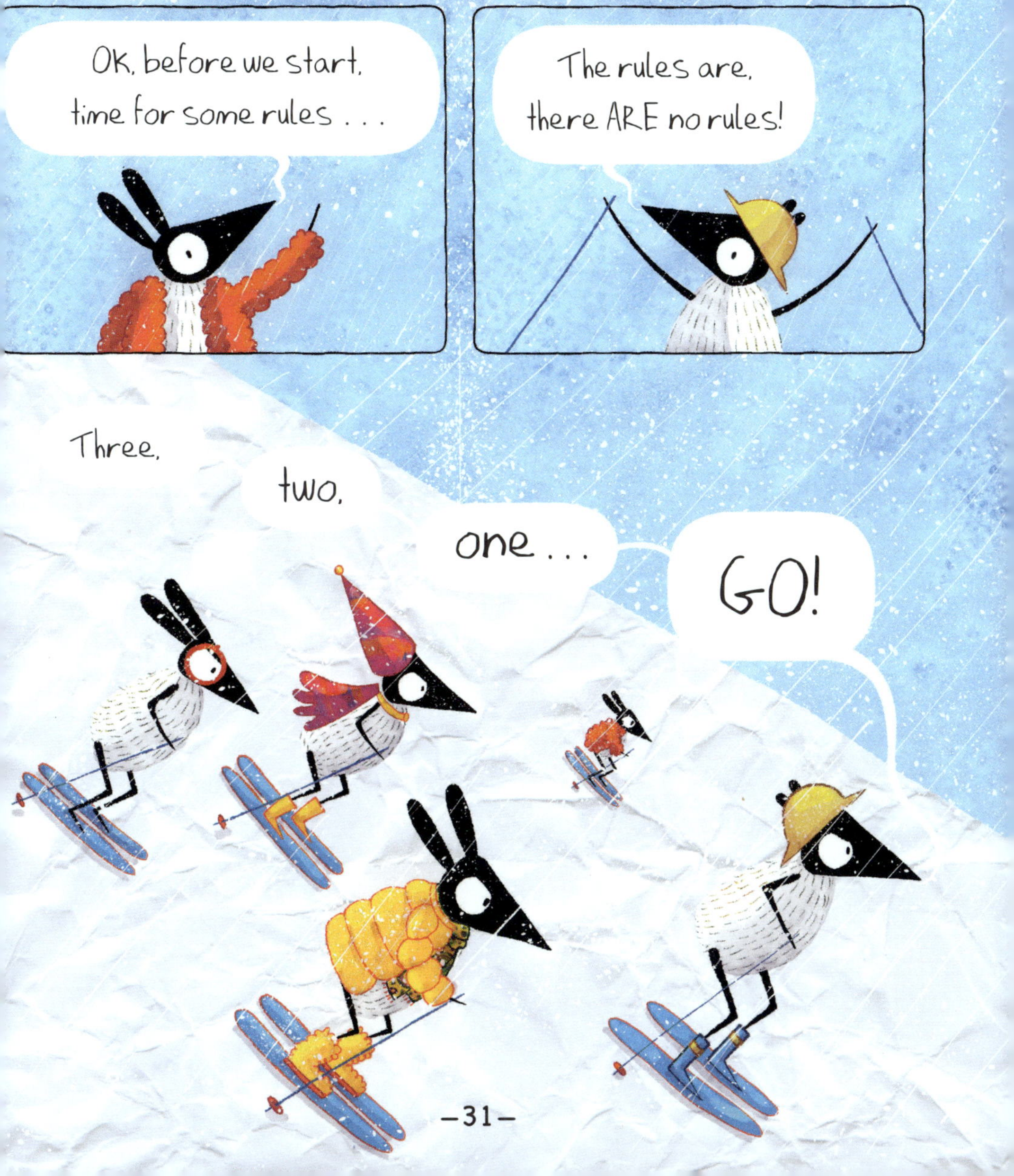
OK, before we start, time for some rules . . .
The rules are, there ARE no rules!
Three,
two,
one . . .
GO!

The Floofs shoot off down the mountain, with Bean leading the way, determined to win the cake prize. But the snow is getting heavier, and they can no longer see where they are going.

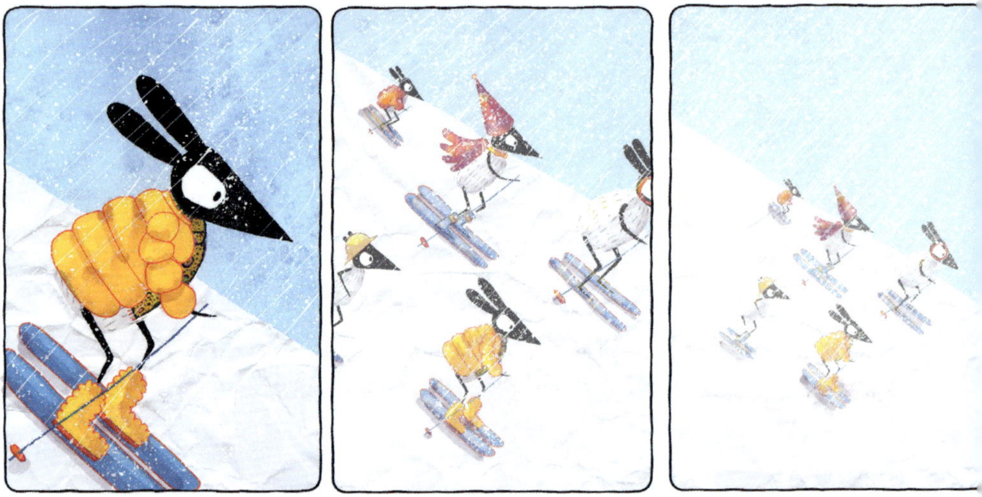

Suddenly, Dill and Teazle crash into a huge heap of snow while the others race ahead.

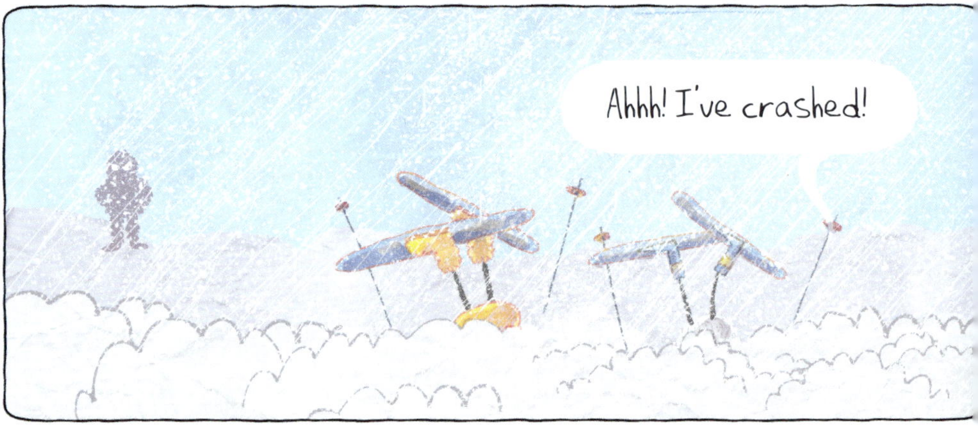
Ahhh! I've crashed!

Teazle pulls Dill out of the snow, but neither have noticed that a large, snowy figure has appeared behind them.

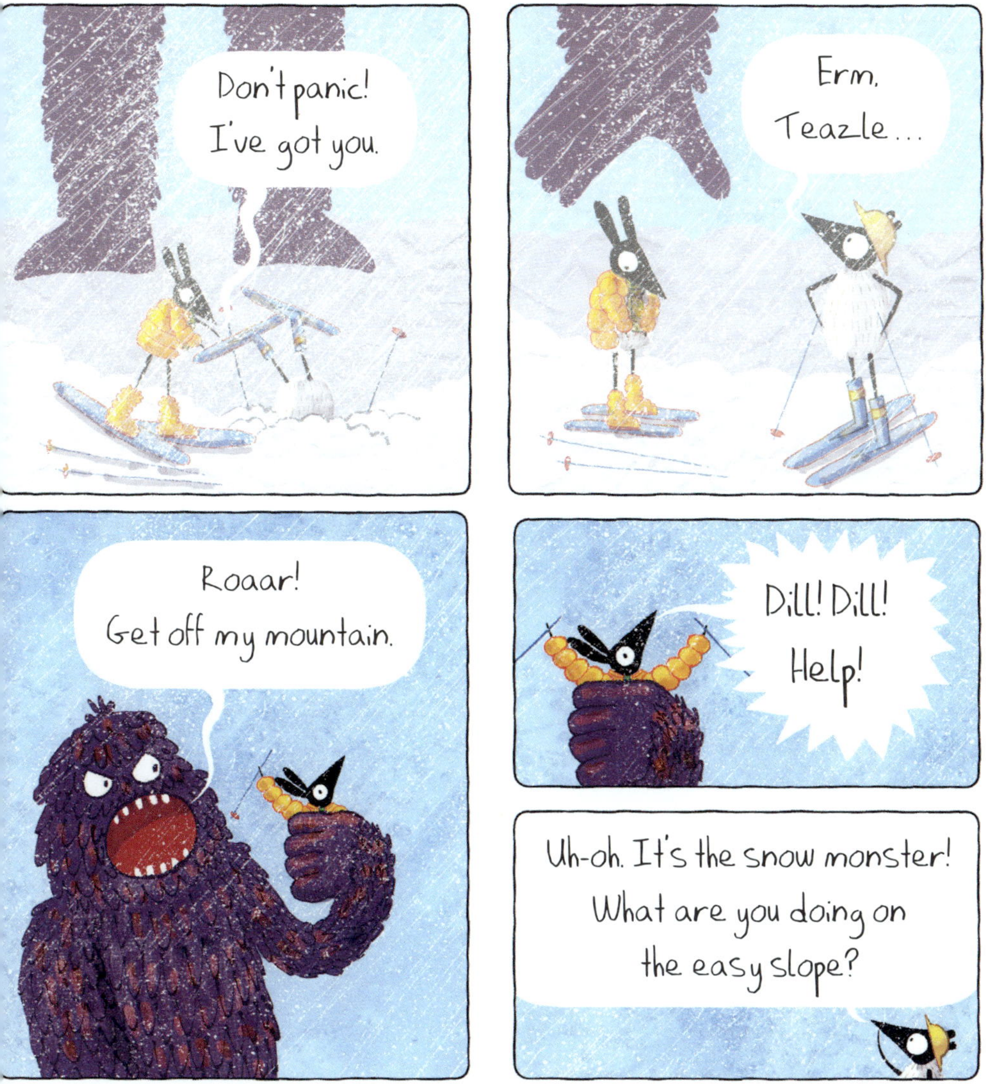

Don't panic! I've got you.
Erm, Teazle...
Roaar! Get off my mountain.
Dill! Dill! Help!
Uh-oh. It's the snow monster! What are you doing on the easy slope?

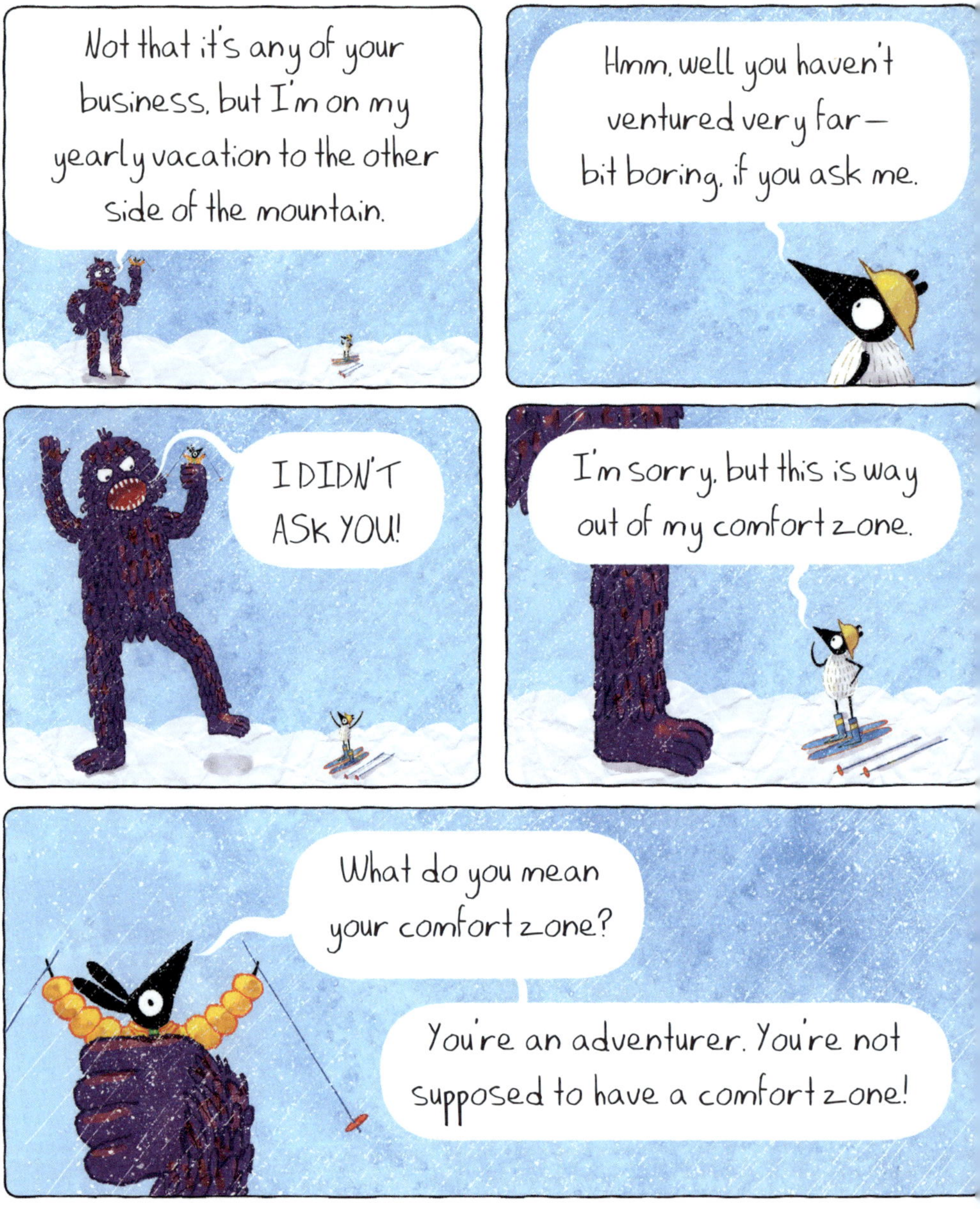
Not that it's any of your business, but I'm on my yearly vacation to the other side of the mountain.
Hmm, well you haven't ventured very far— bit boring, if you ask me.
I DIDN'T ASK YOU!
I'm sorry, but this is way out of my comfort zone.
What do you mean your comfort zone?
You're an adventurer. You're not supposed to have a comfort zone!

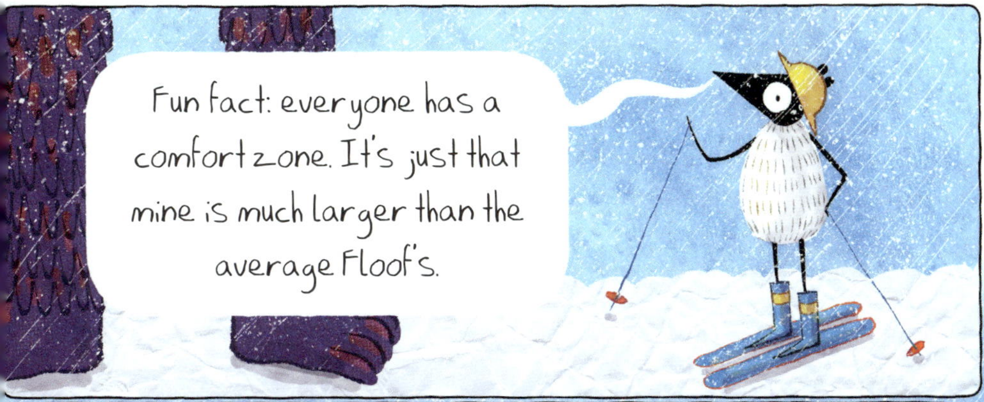
Fun fact: everyone has a comfort zone. It's just that mine is much larger than the average Floof's.

The snow monster doesn't care about any of this and decides the easiest way to get them off the mountain is to throw Teazle to the ground and scare them with his biggest stomping.

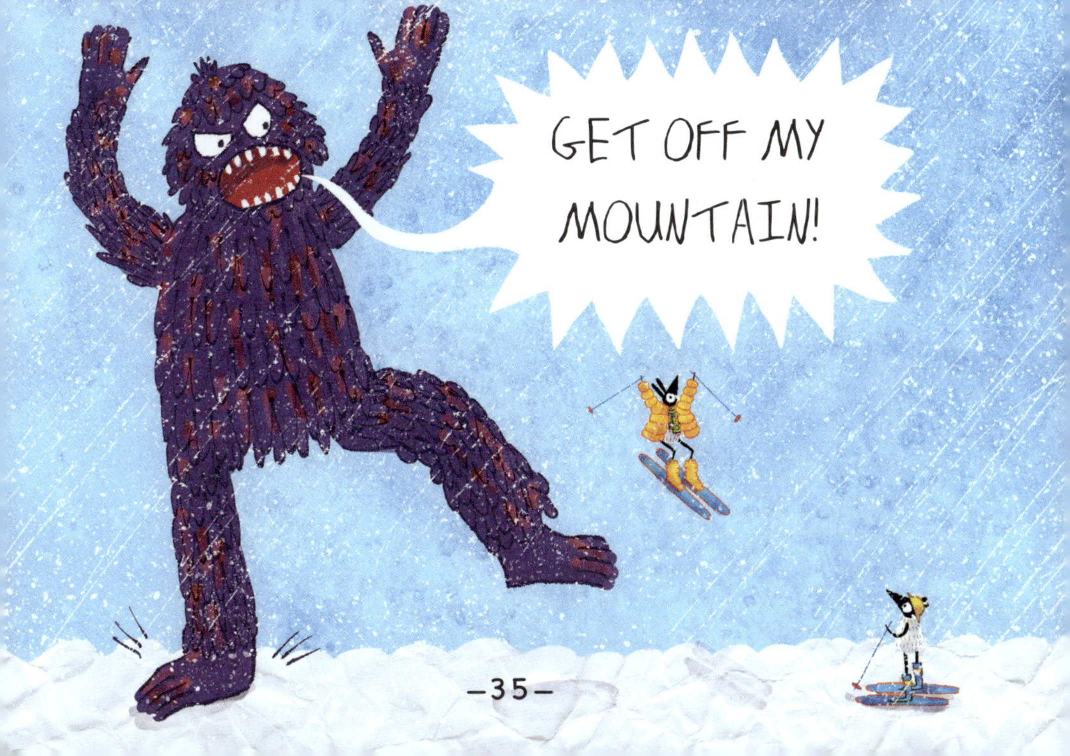
GET OFF MY MOUNTAIN!

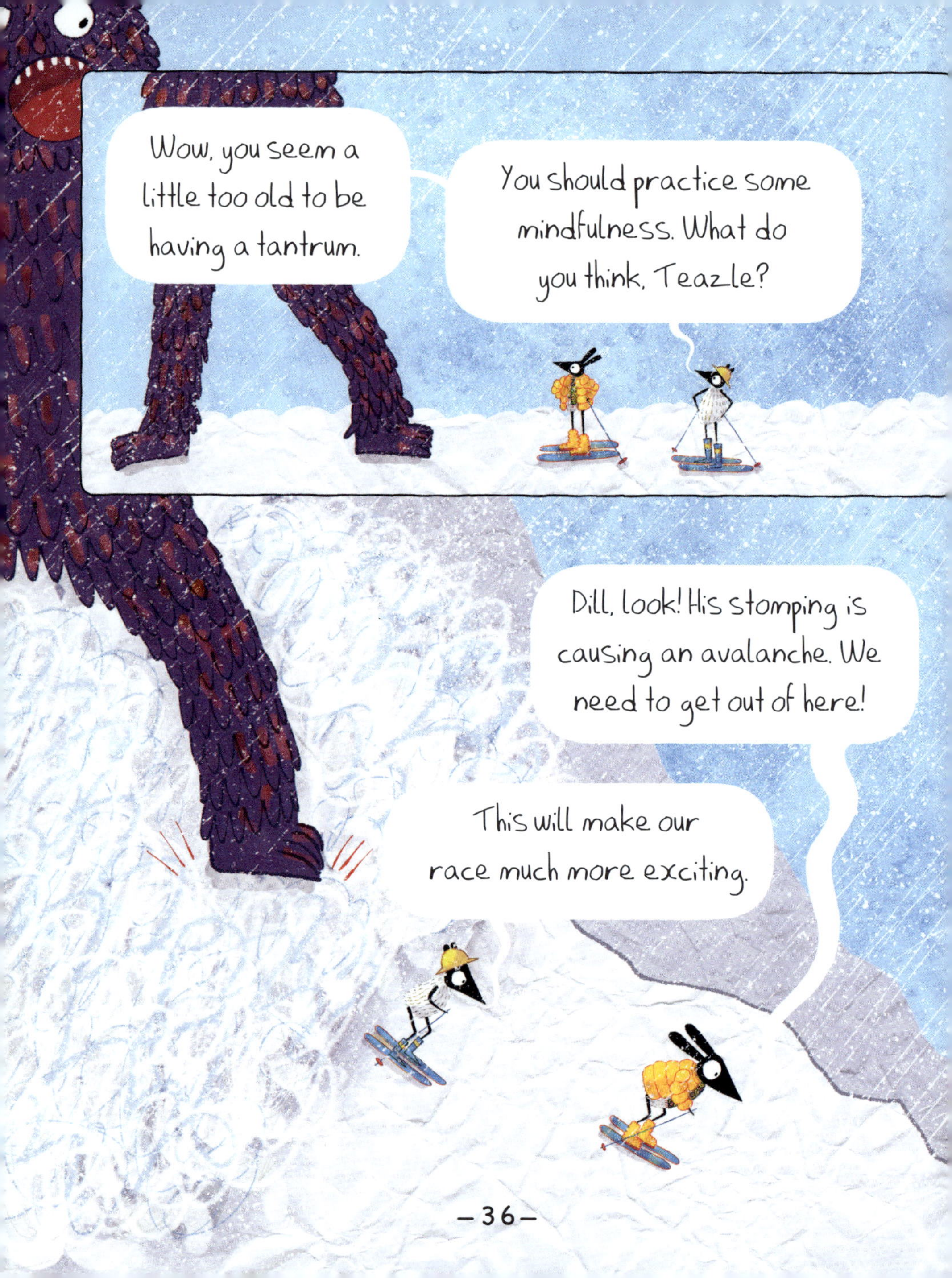
Wow, you seem a little too old to be having a tantrum.
You should practice some mindfulness. What do you think, Teazle?
Dill, look! His stomping is causing an avalanche. We need to get out of here!
This will make our race much more exciting.

Dill and Teazle speed off down the mountain, trying to outrun the avalanche that is about to engulf them. Suddenly, they get to a fork in the snow: the only way to escape is to take a turn to the super-duper difficult slope. Teazle knew he would have to be brave.

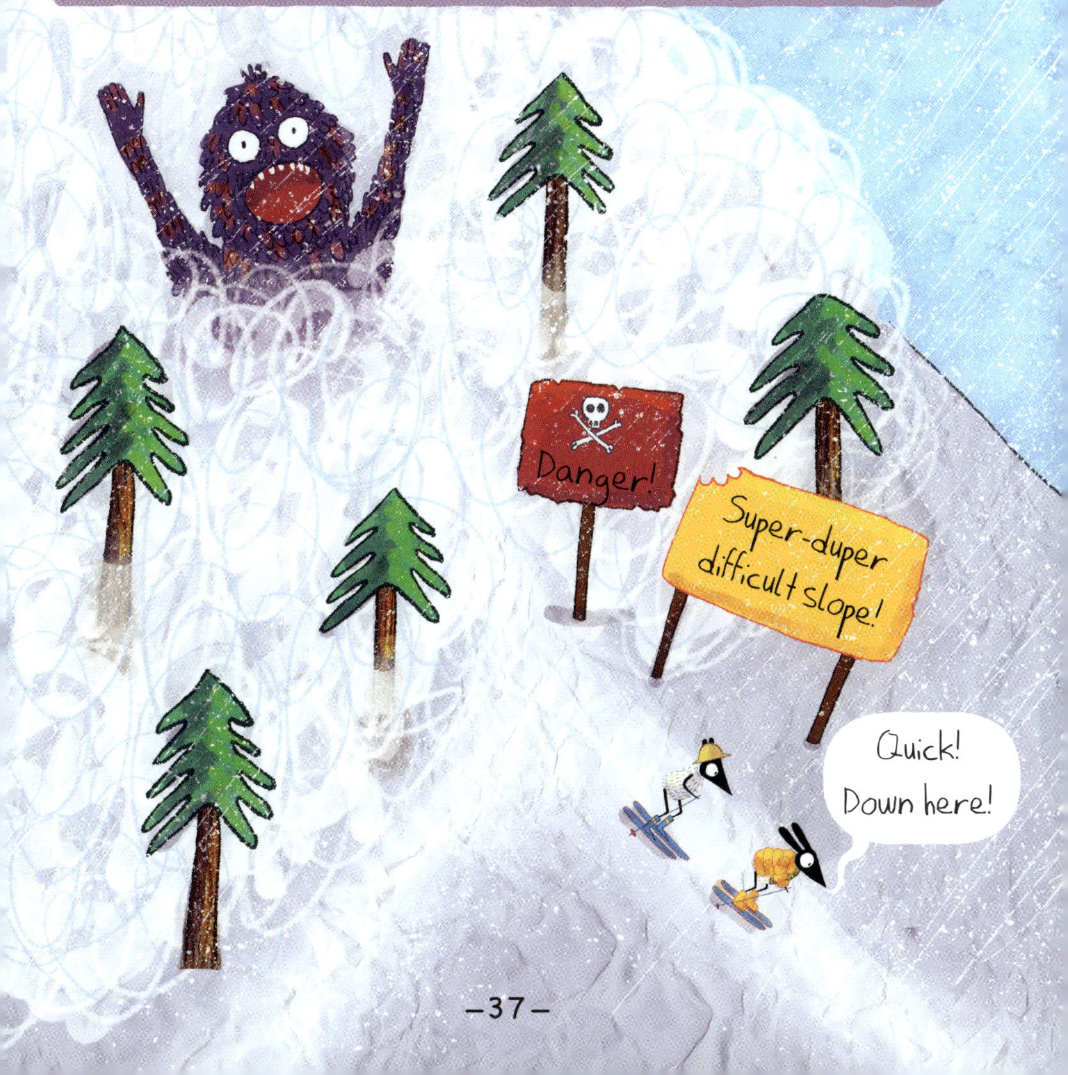
Danger!
Super-duper difficult slope!
Quick! Down here!

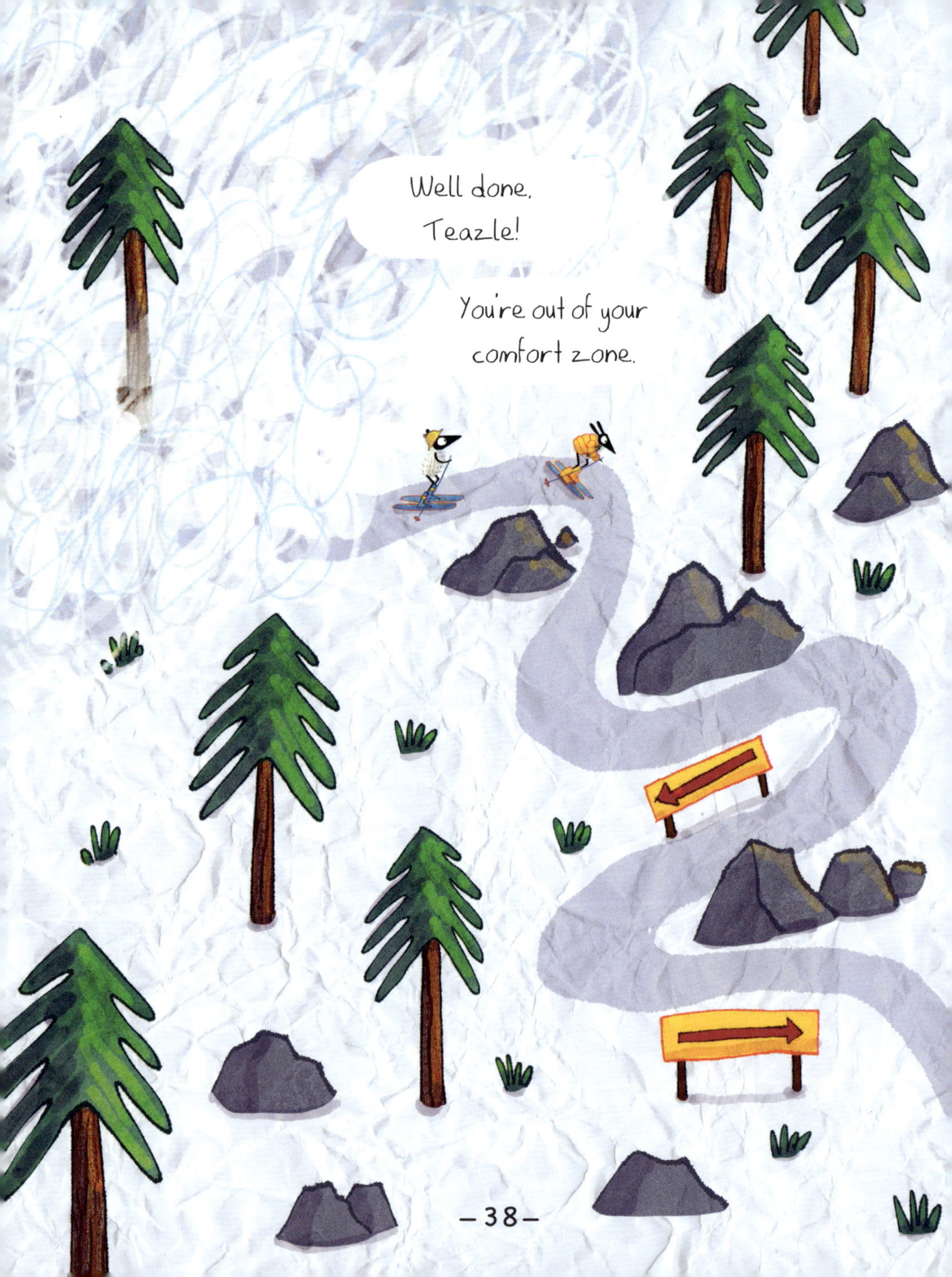
Well done, Teazle!
You're out of your comfort zone.

Dill and Teazle slip and slide down the super-duper difficult slope, dodging all the trees and rocks and outrunning the avalanche.

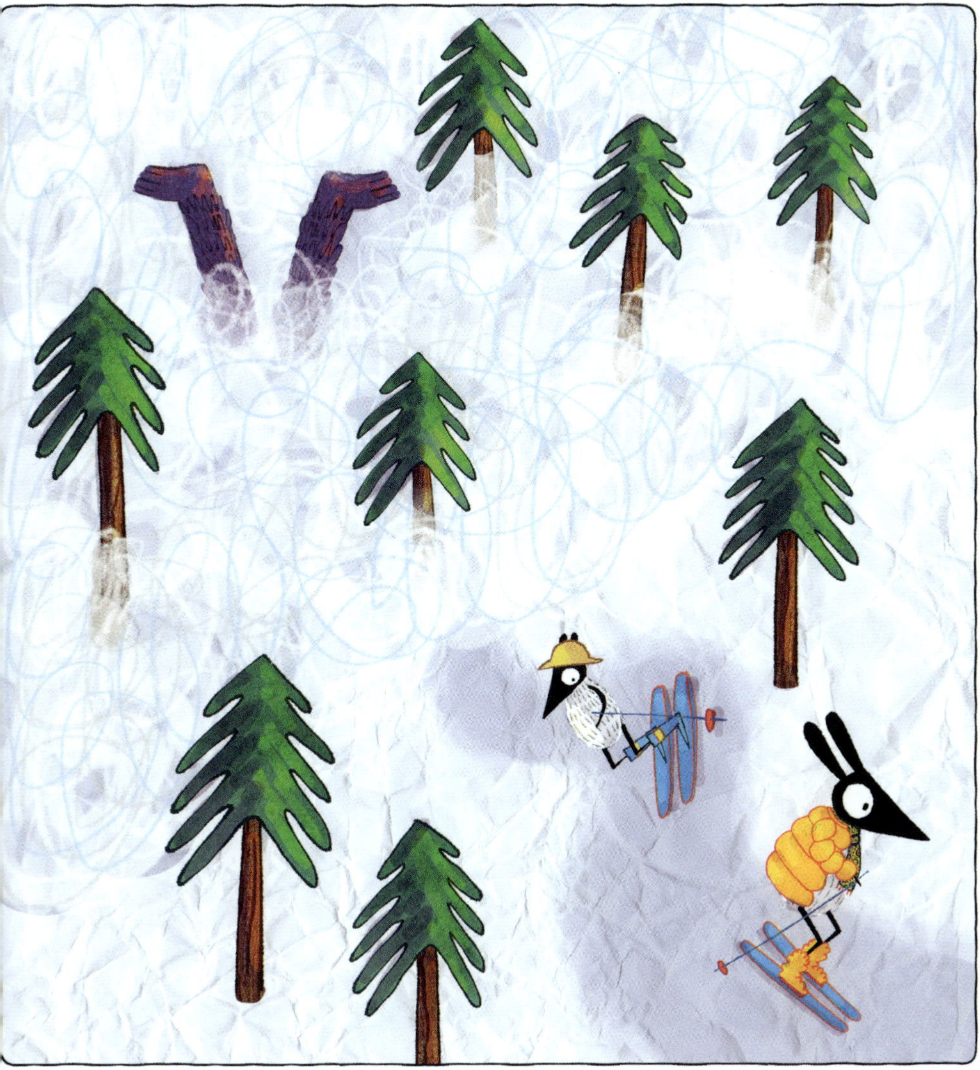

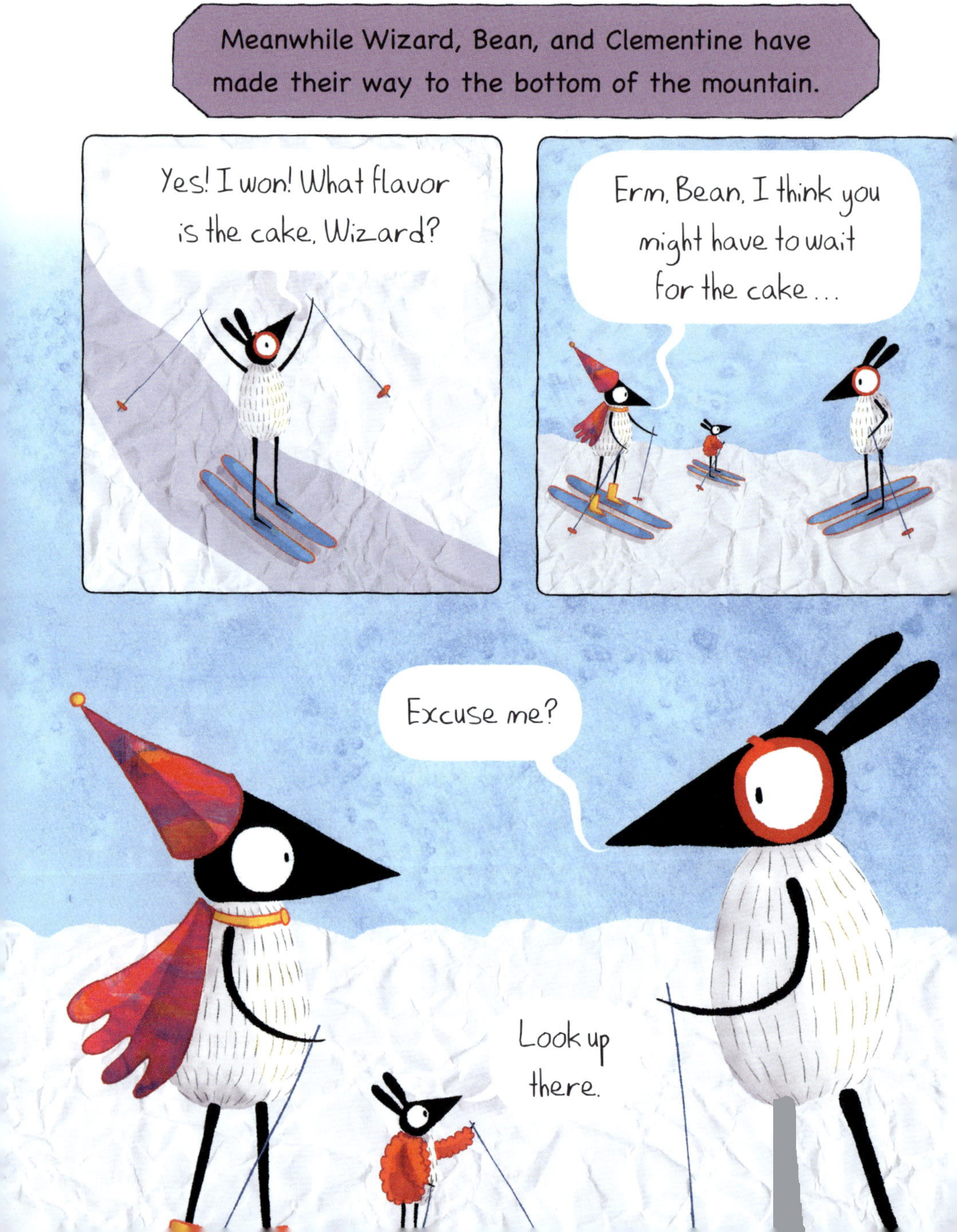
Meanwhile Wizard, Bean, and Clementine have made their way to the bottom of the mountain.
Yes! I won! What flavor is the cake, Wizard?
Erm, Bean, I think you might have to wait for the cake...
Excuse me?
Look up there.

The three Floofs look up to see snow streaming down the mountain, and Teazle and Dill rushing toward them.

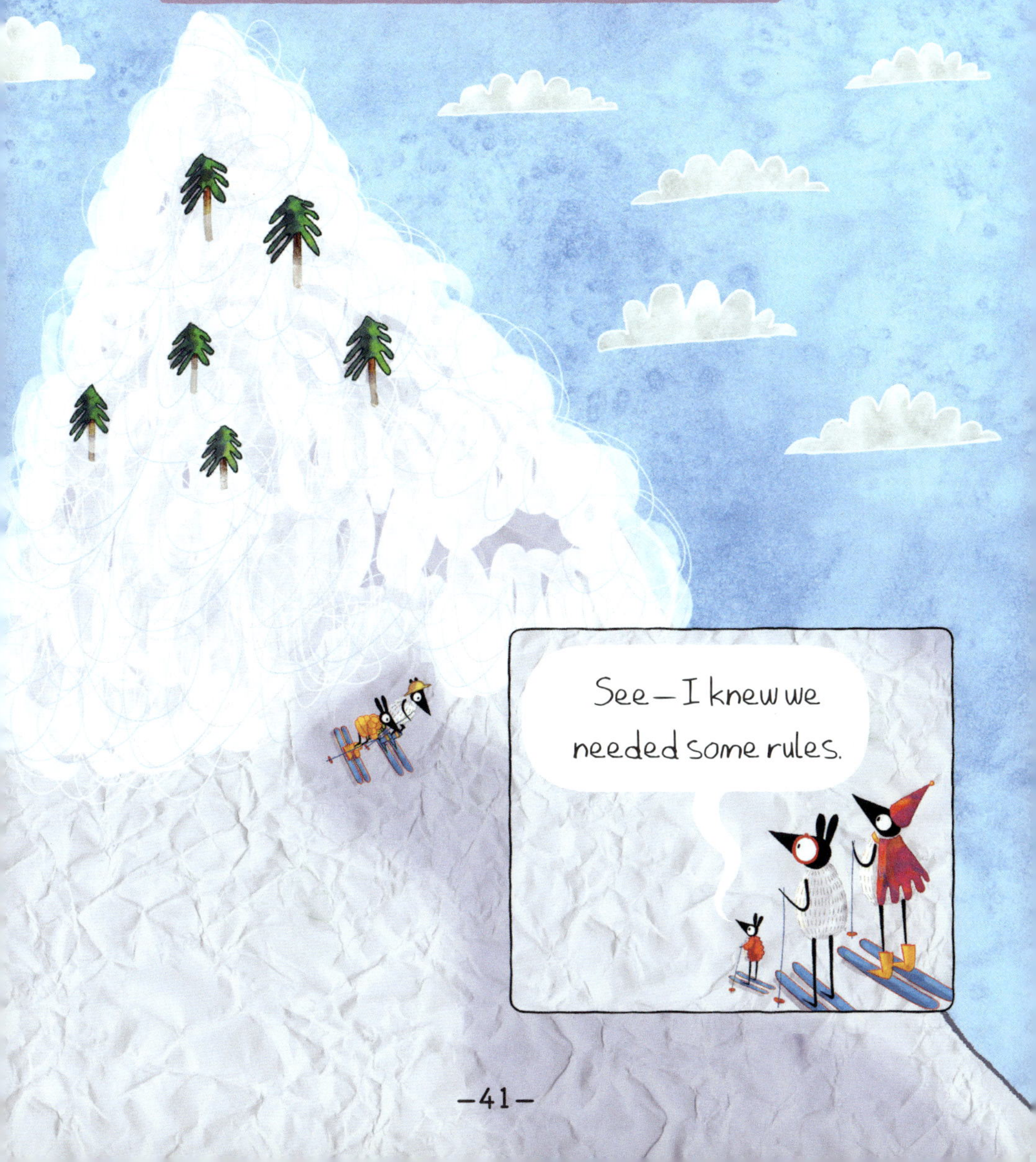
See—I knew we needed some rules.

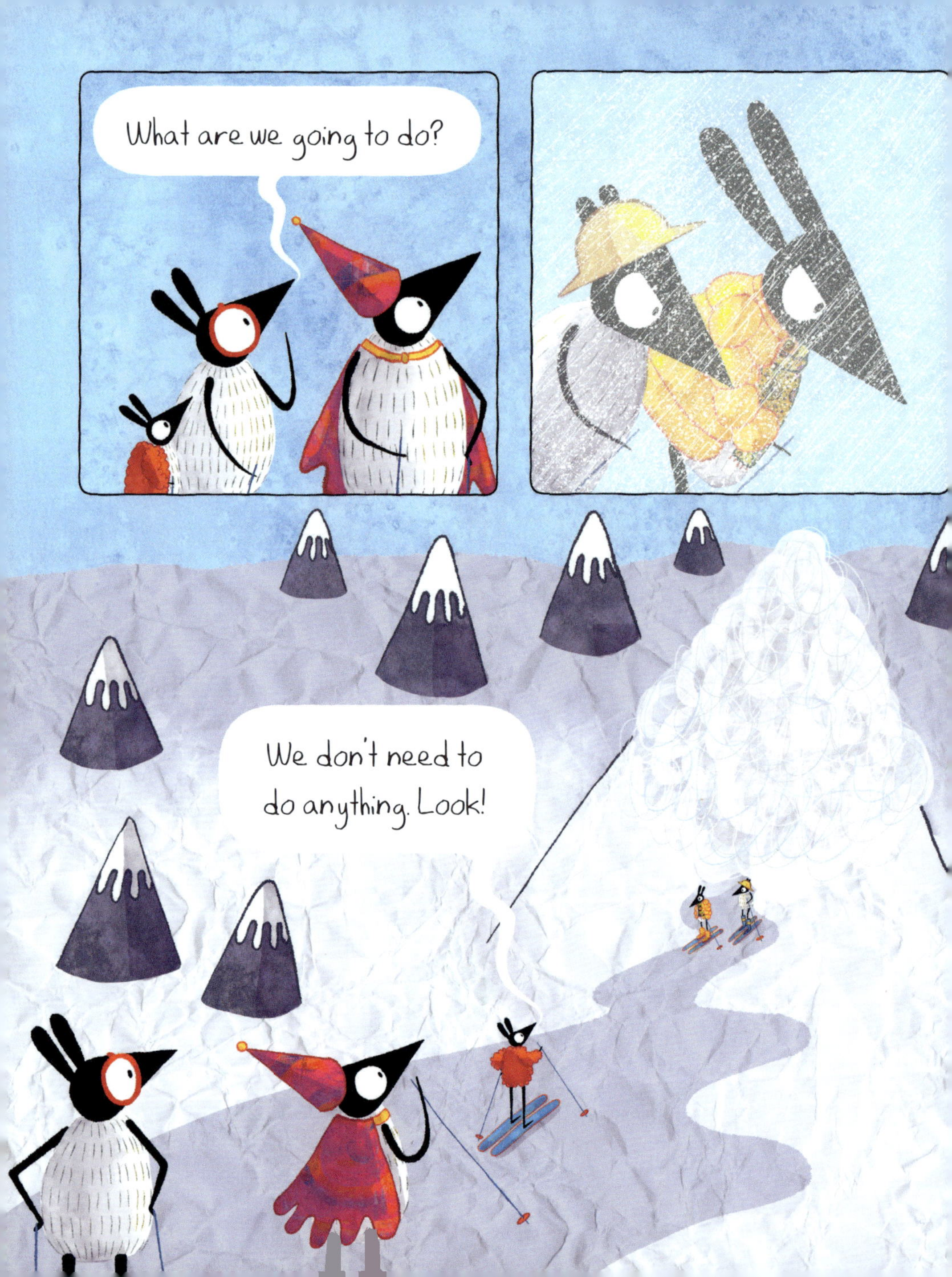
What are we going to do?
We don't need to do anything. Look!

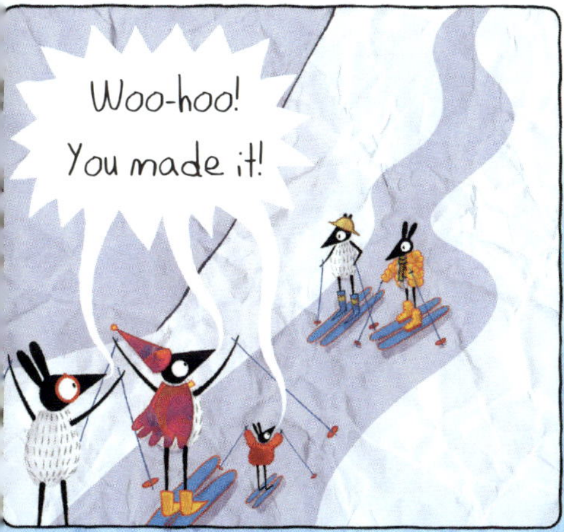
Woo-hoo! You made it!

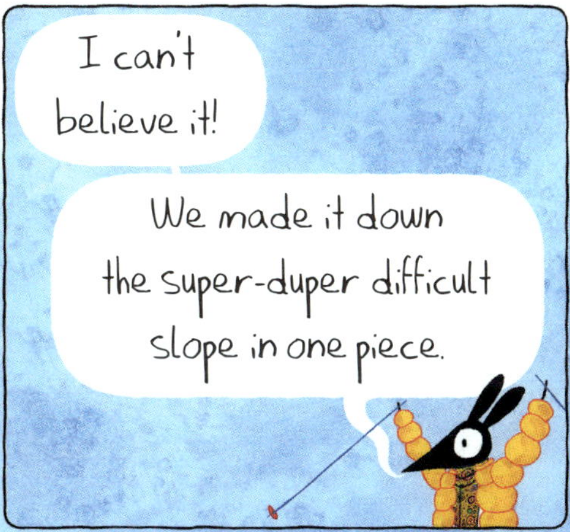
I can't believe it!
We made it down the super-duper difficult slope in one piece.

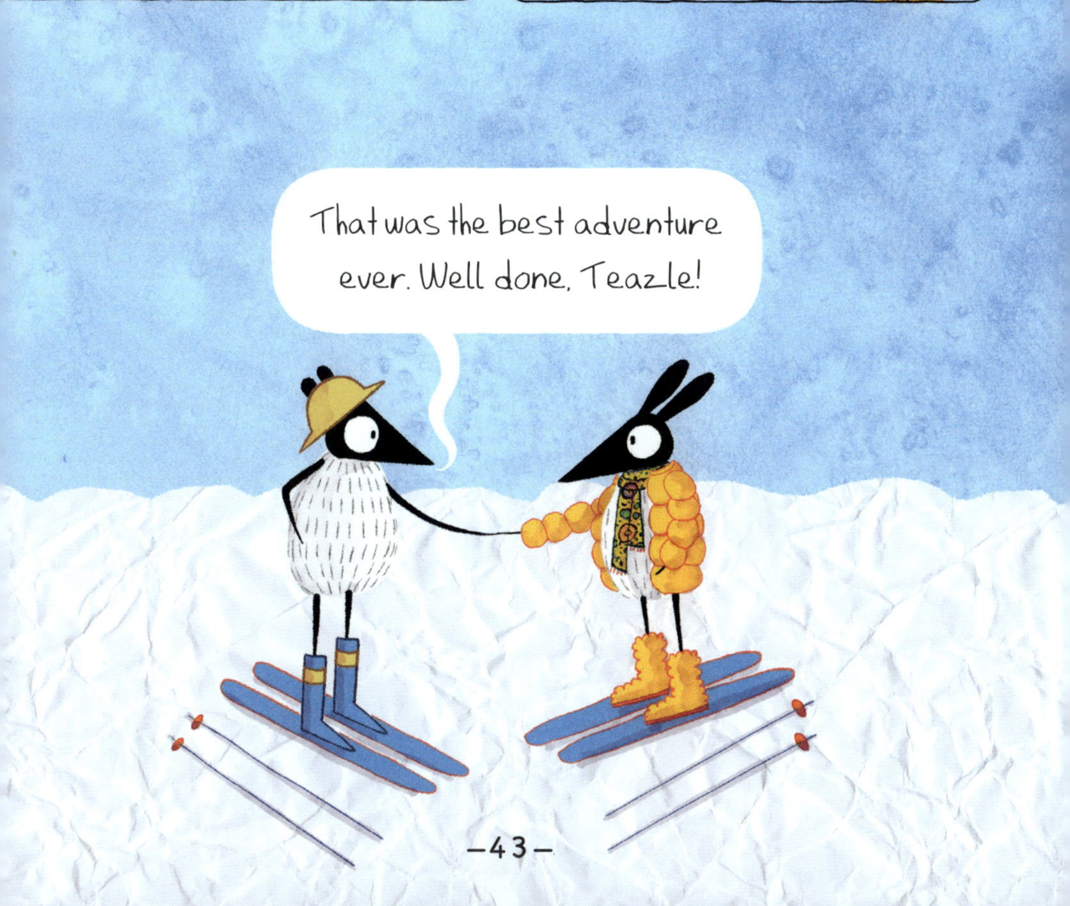
That was the best adventure ever. Well done, Teazle!

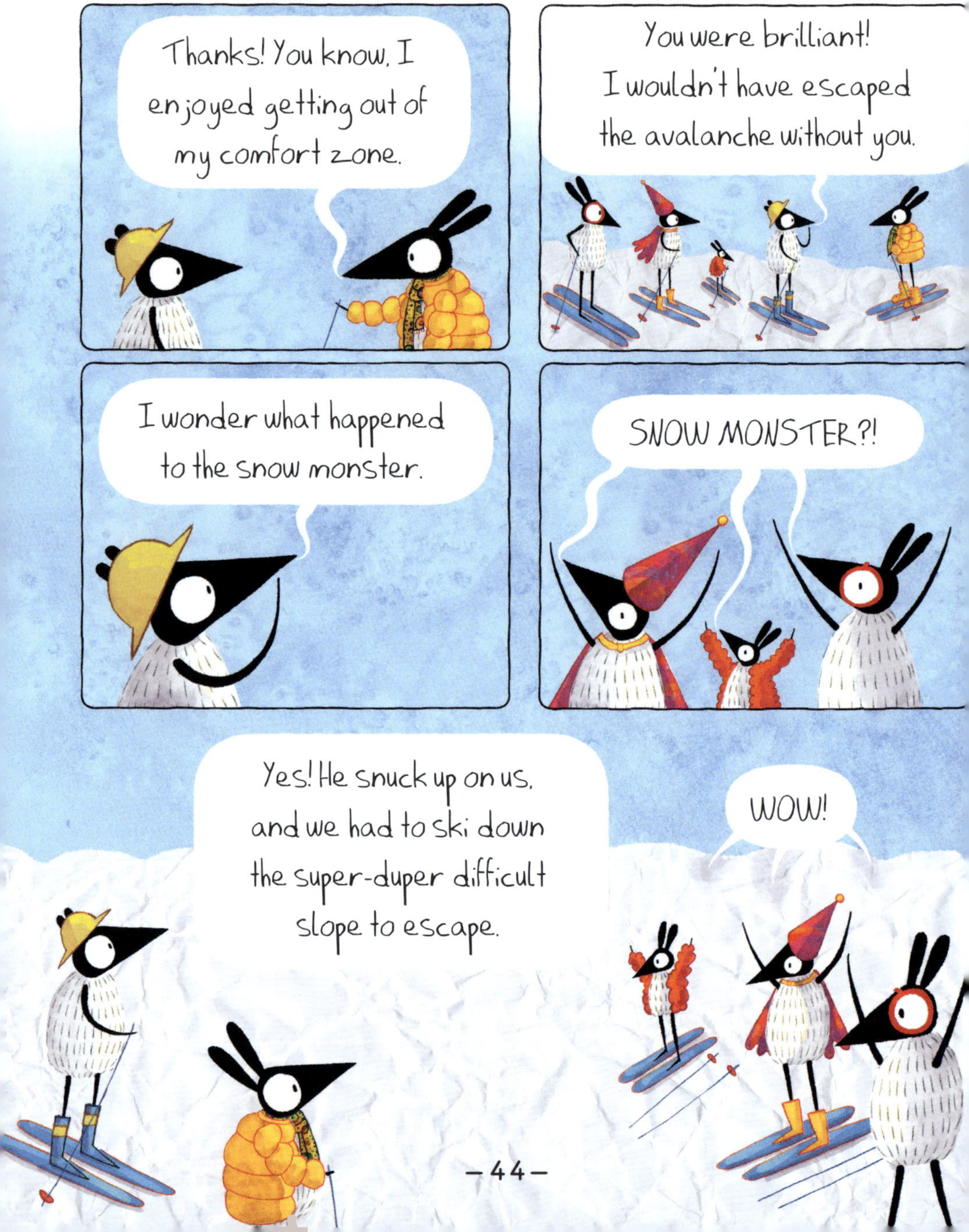
Thanks! You know, I enjoyed getting out of my comfort zone.
You were brilliant! I wouldn't have escaped the avalanche without you.
I wonder what happened to the snow monster.
SNOW MONSTER?!
Yes! He snuck up on us, and we had to ski down the super-duper difficult slope to escape.
WOW!

The Floofs look up and notice the snow monster climbing back up the side of the mountain.

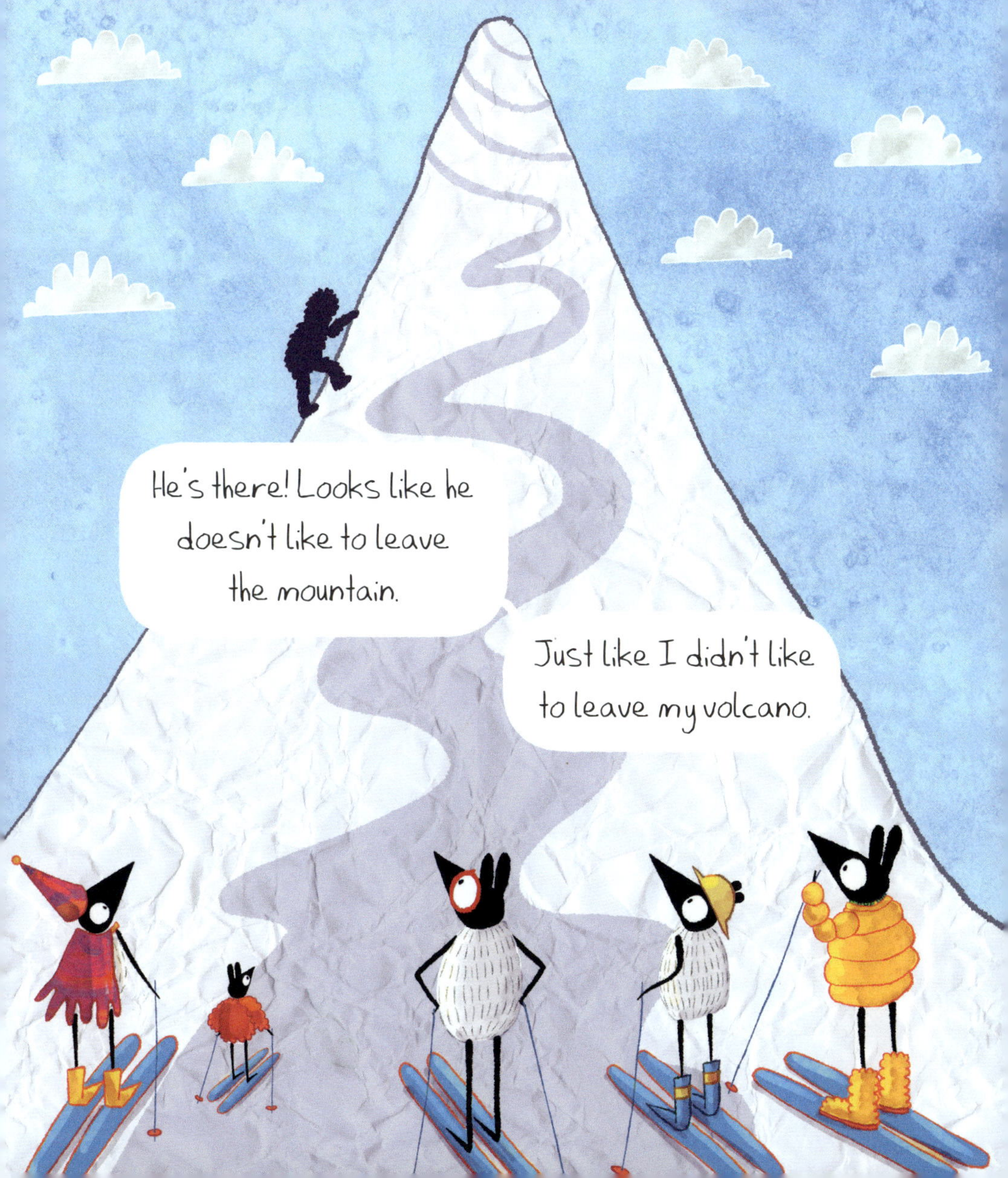
He's there! Looks like he doesn't like to leave the mountain.
Just like I didn't like to leave my volcano.

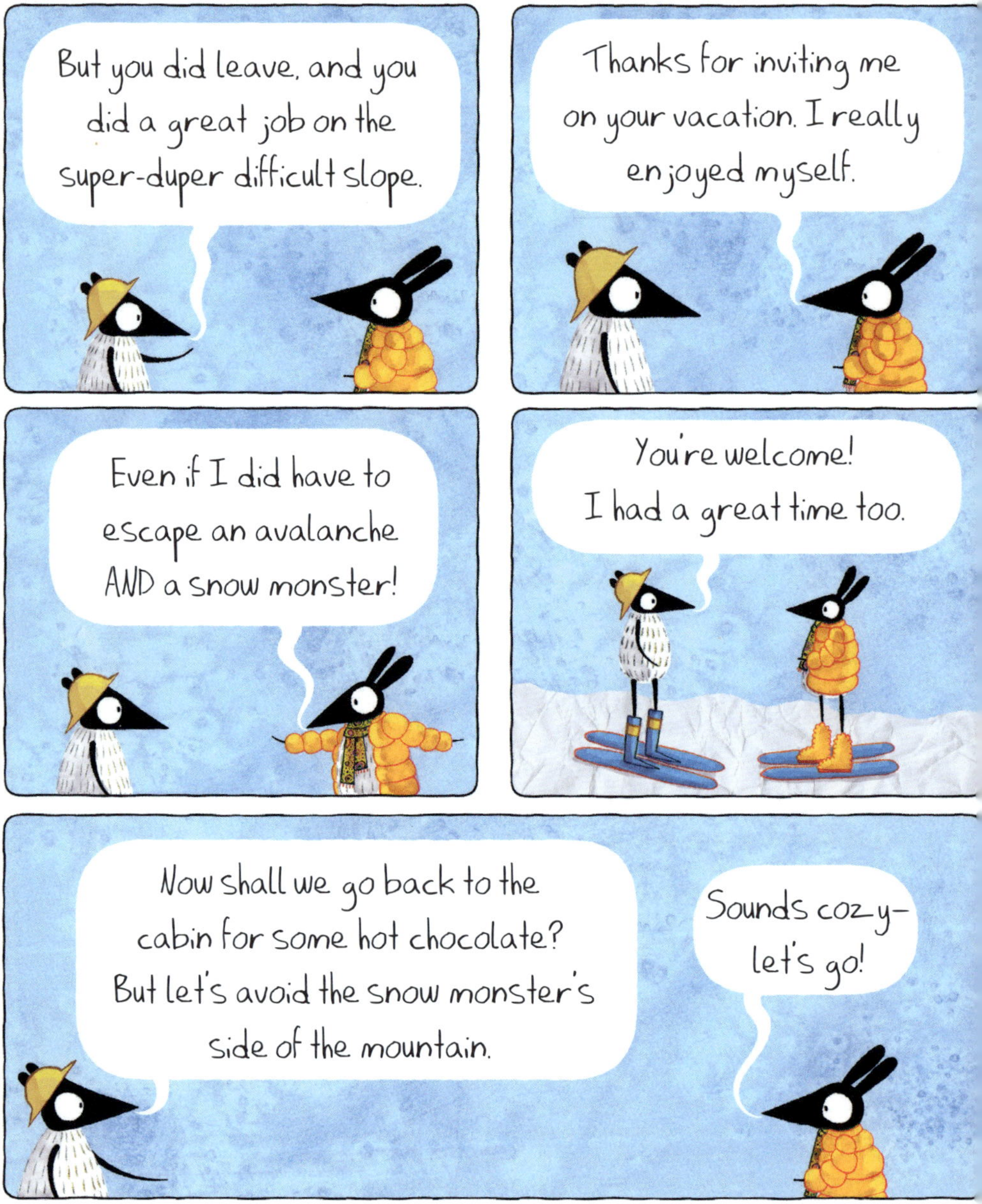
But you did leave, and you did a great job on the super-duper difficult slope.
Thanks for inviting me on your vacation. I really enjoyed myself.
Even if I did have to escape an avalanche AND a snow monster!
You're welcome! I had a great time too.
Now shall we go back to the cabin for some hot chocolate? But let's avoid the snow monster's side of the mountain.
Sounds cozy— let's go!

So in the end, Teazle was very brave and tried something new. He learned that although he loves his volcano home, he also enjoys getting out of his comfort zone once in a while, especially if his friends are by his side.

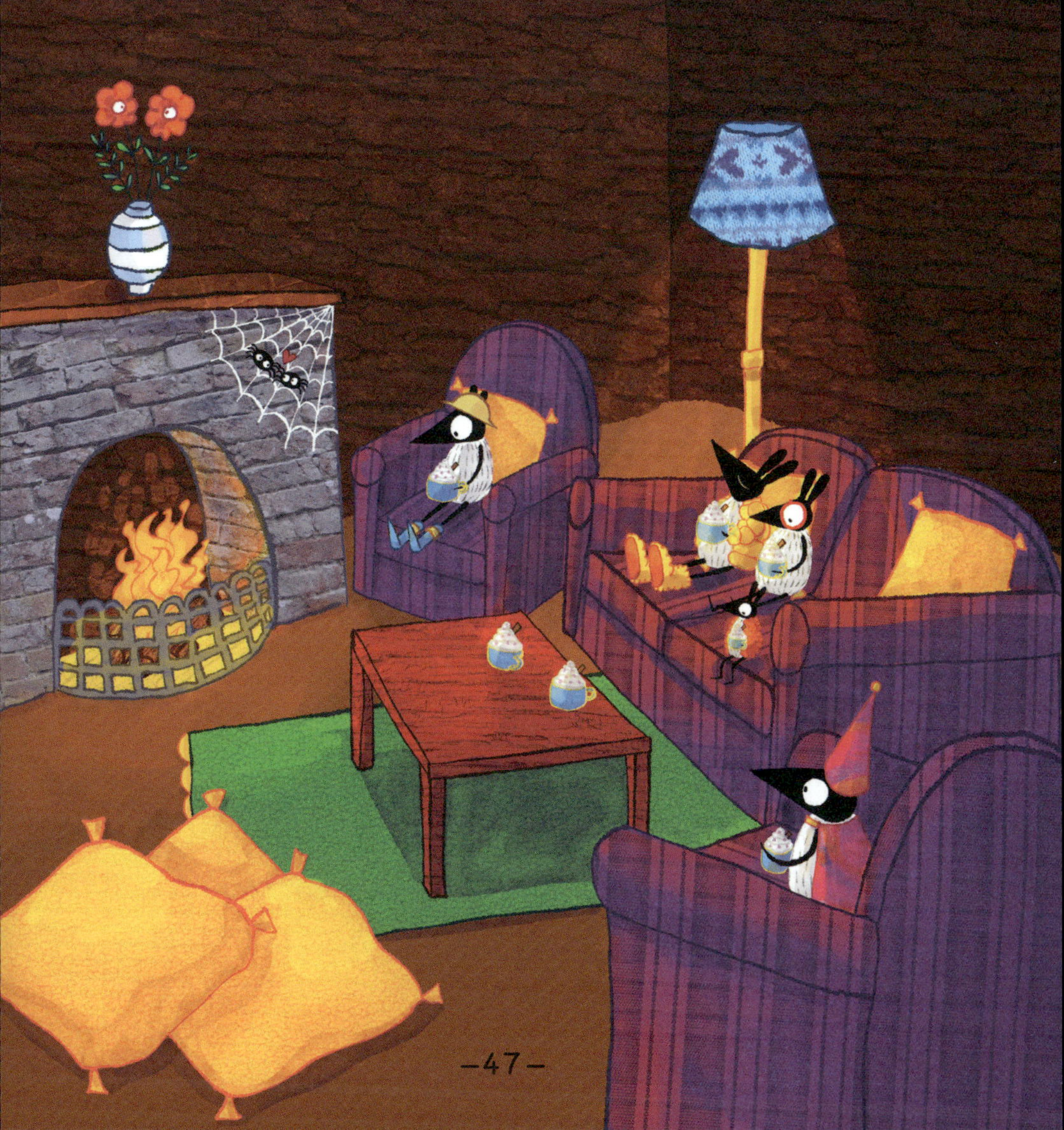

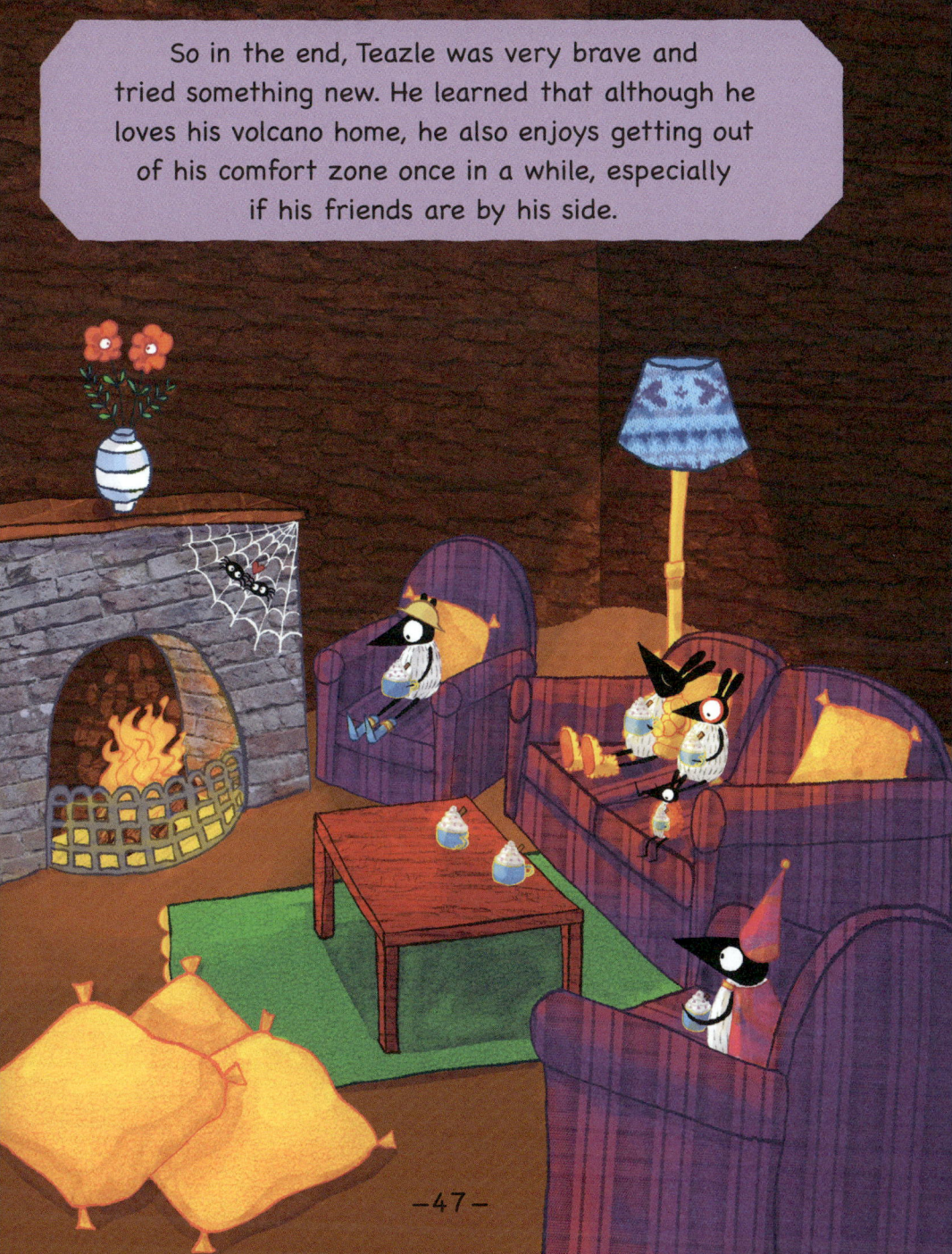

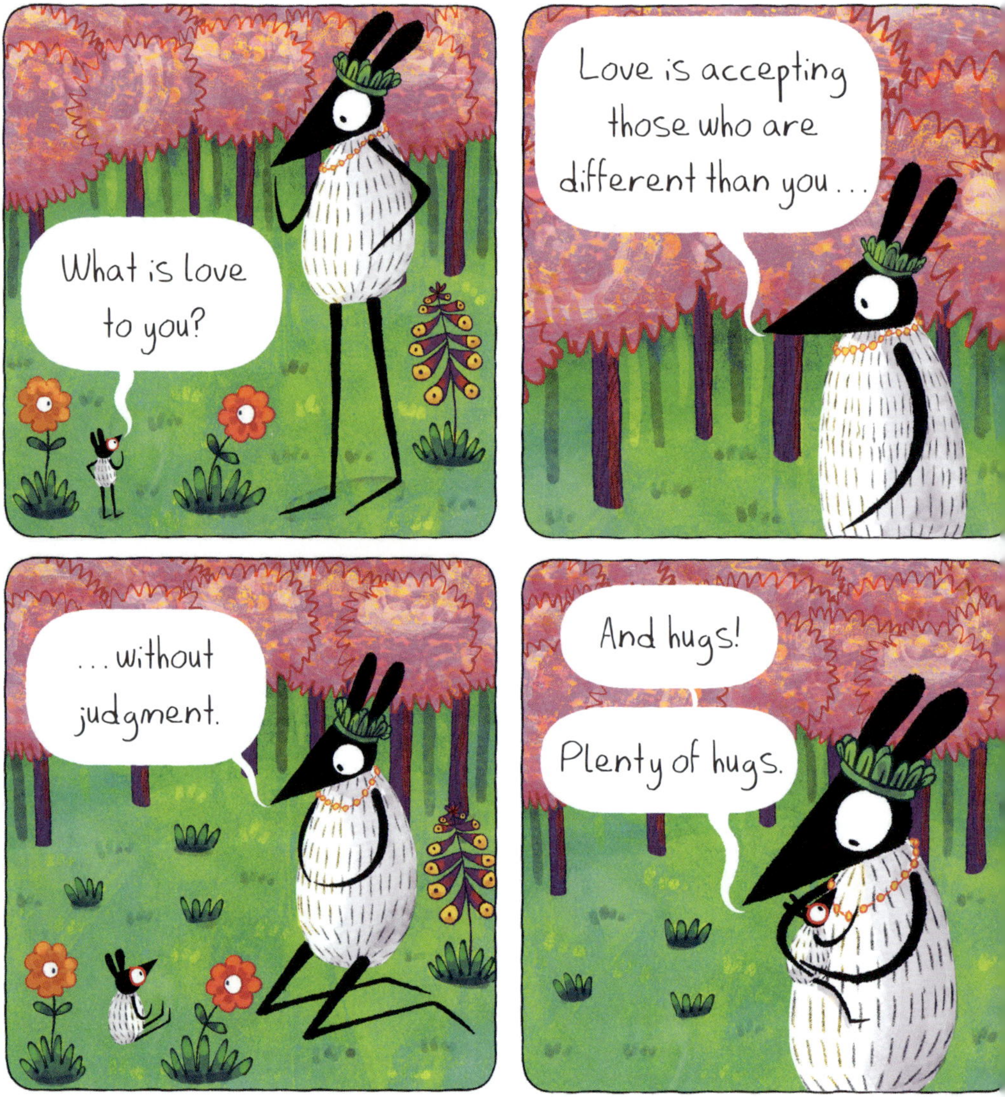
What is love to you?
Love is accepting those who are different than you . . .
. . . without judgment.
And hugs!
Plenty of hugs.

A DIFFERENT KIND OF FLOOF

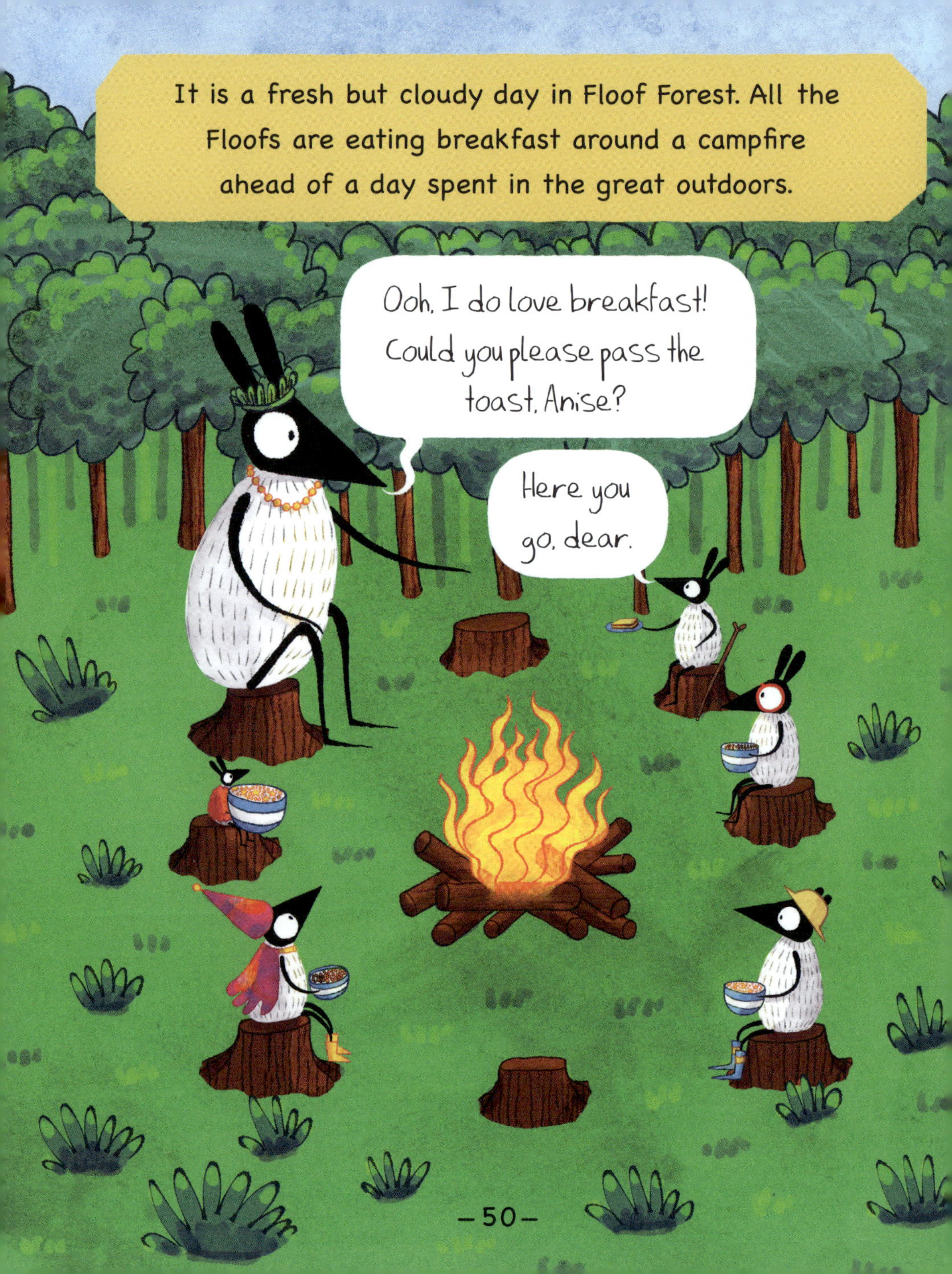
It is a fresh but cloudy day in Floof Forest. All the Floofs are eating breakfast around a campfire ahead of a day spent in the great outdoors.
Ooh, I do love breakfast! Could you please pass the toast, Anise?
Here you go, dear.

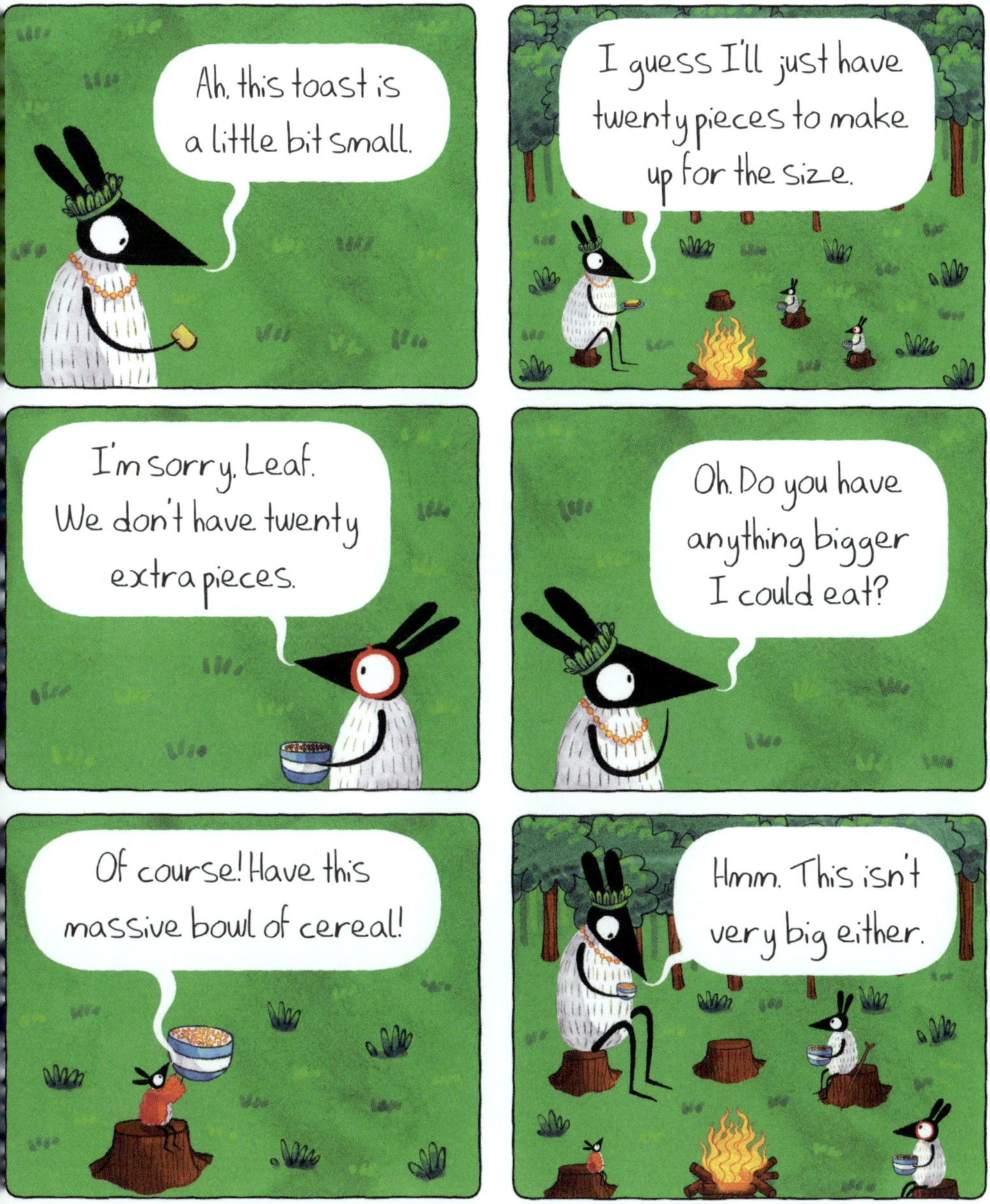
Ah, this toast is a little bit small.
I guess I'll just have twenty pieces to make up for the size.
I'm sorry, Leaf. We don't have twenty extra pieces.
Oh. Do you have anything bigger I could eat?
Of course! Have this massive bowl of cereal!
Hmm. This isn't very big either.

All of the Floofs had forgotten Leaf is much bigger than them. The breakfast they had prepared is too small, and Leaf feels a little bit left out.

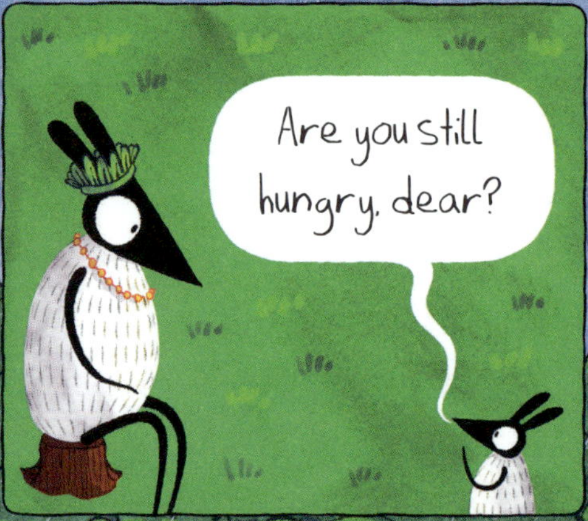
Are you still hungry, dear?

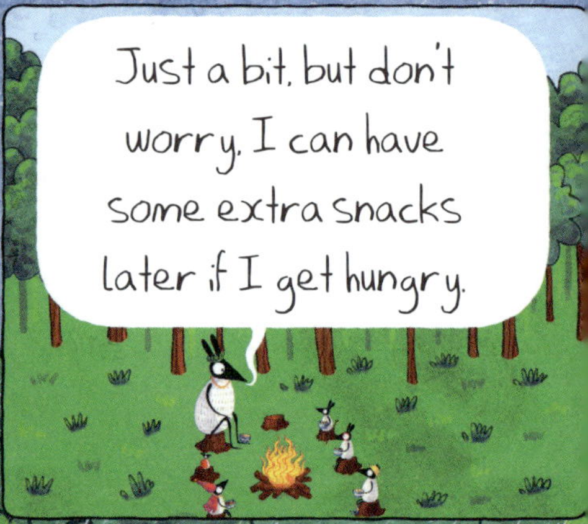
Just a bit, but don't worry, I can have some extra snacks later if I get hungry.

Leaf is left with his tummy still rumbling, but he ignores it as he doesn't want to make a fuss. Then the rain begins to pour. The Floofs are not prepared for the wet weather.

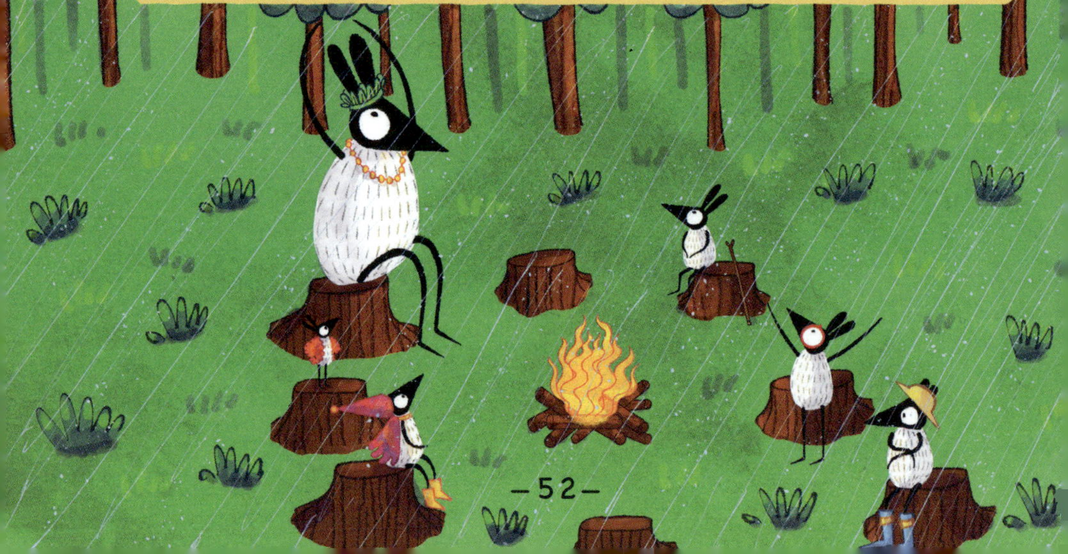

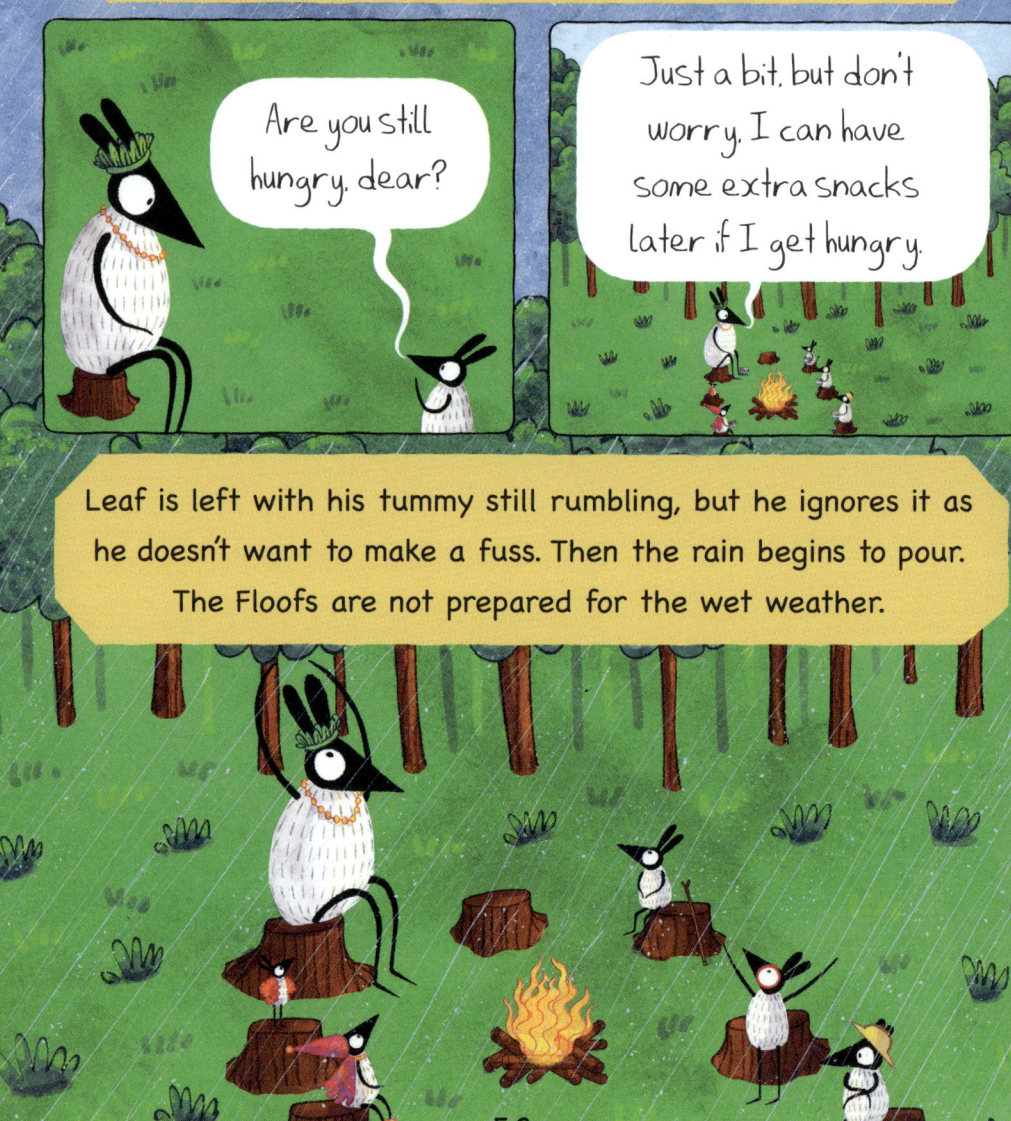

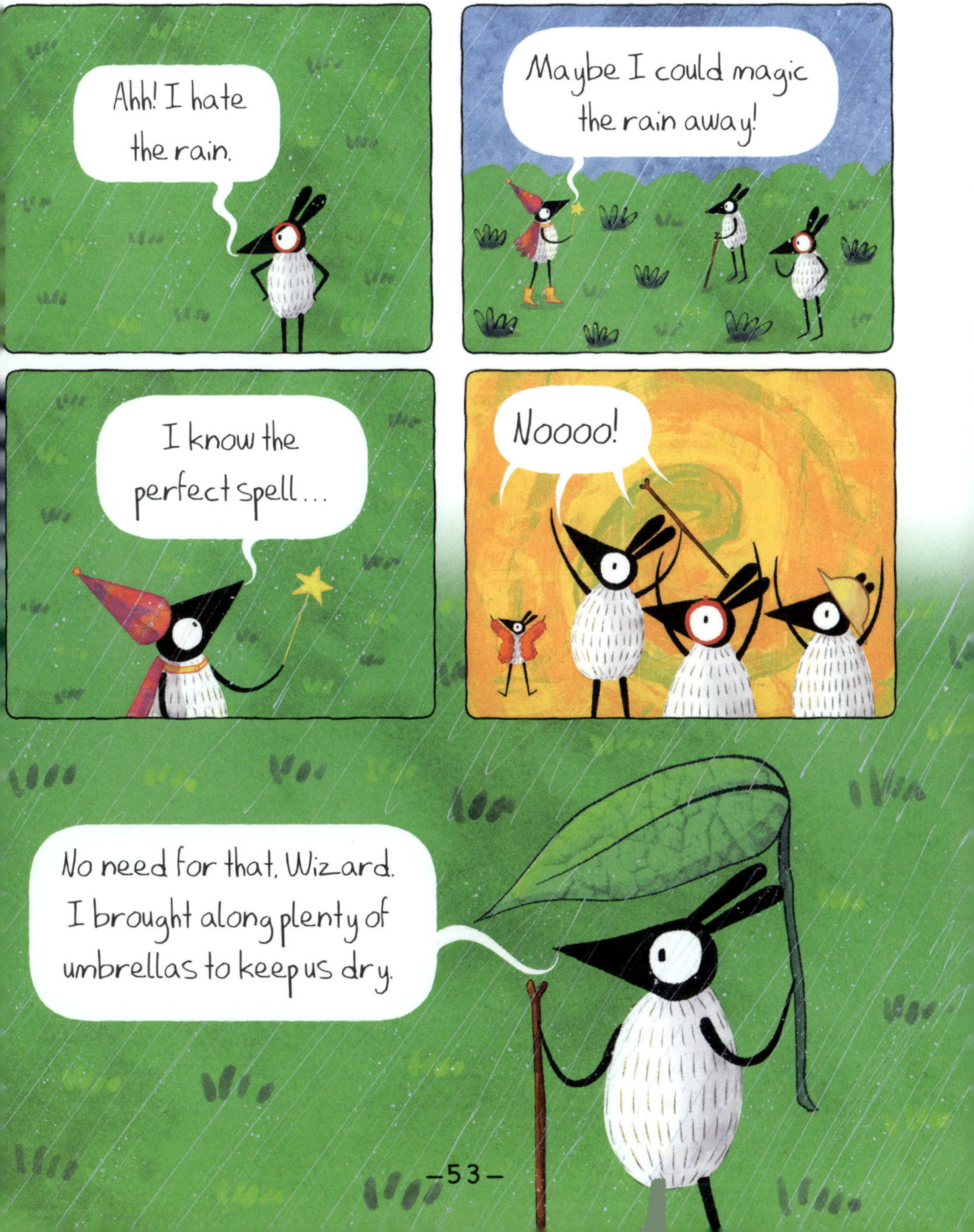
Ahh! I hate the rain.
Maybe I could magic the rain away!
I know the perfect spell...
Noooo!
No need for that, Wizard. I brought along plenty of umbrellas to keep us dry.

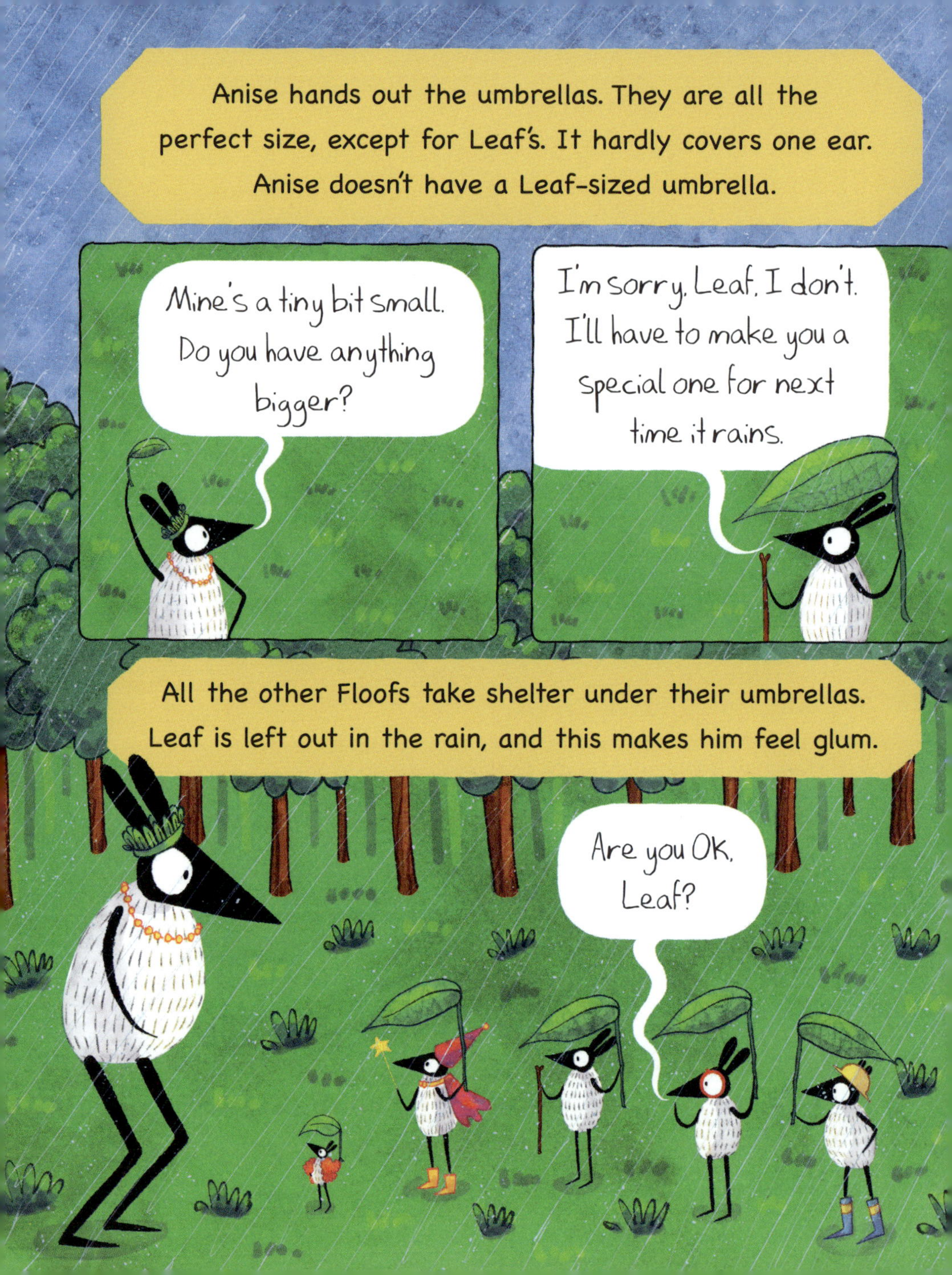

Anise hands out the umbrellas. They are all the perfect size, except for Leaf's. It hardly covers one ear. Anise doesn't have a Leaf-sized umbrella.
Mine's a tiny bit small. Do you have anything bigger?
I'm sorry, Leaf. I don't. I'll have to make you a special one for next time it rains.
All the other Floofs take shelter under their umbrellas. Leaf is left out in the rain, and this makes him feel glum.
Are you OK, Leaf?

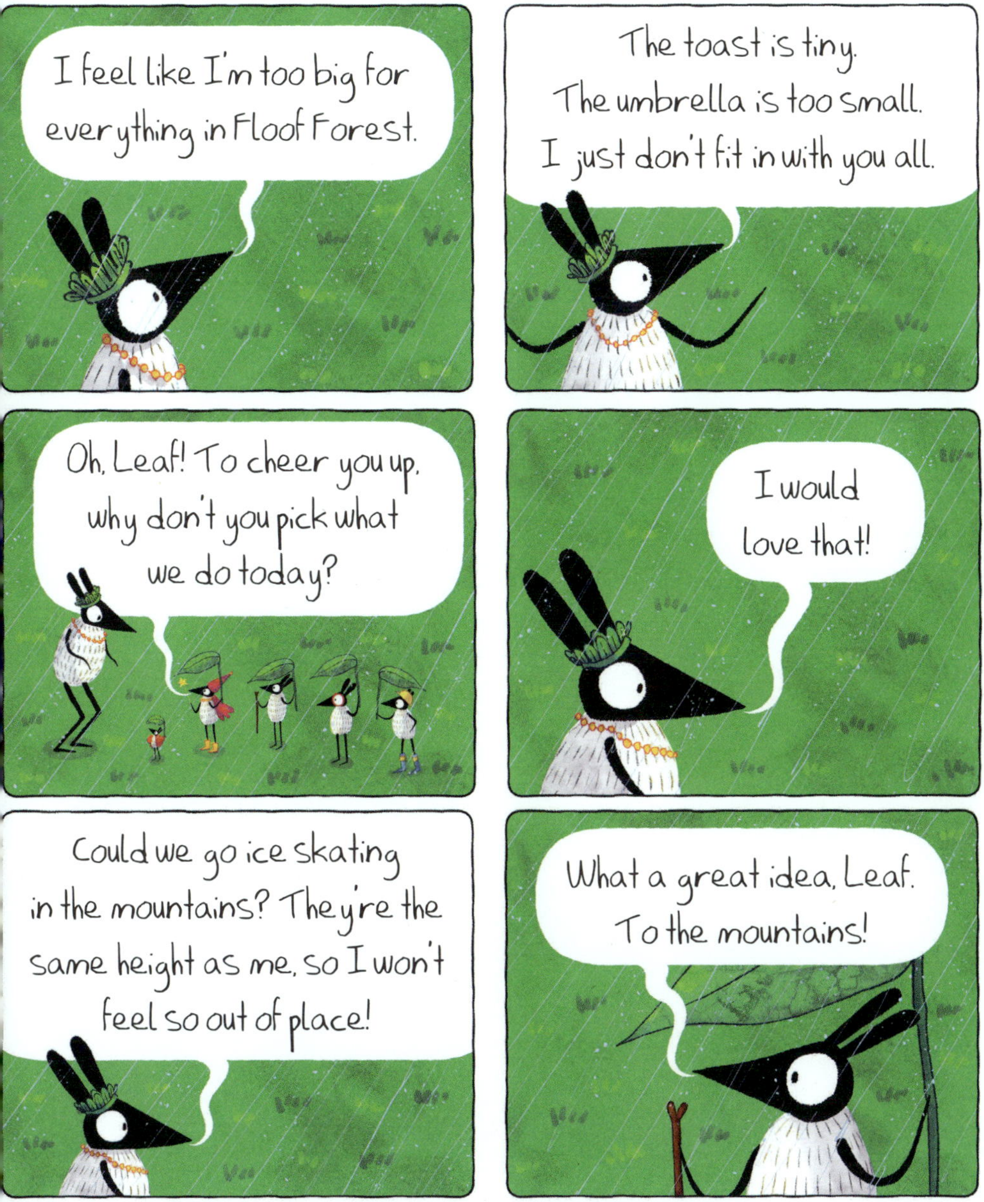
I feel like I'm too big for everything in Floof Forest.
The toast is tiny.
The umbrella is too small.
I just don't fit in with you all.
Oh, Leaf! To cheer you up, why don't you pick what we do today?
I would love that!
Could we go ice skating in the mountains? They're the same height as me, so I won't feel so out of place!
What a great idea, Leaf. To the mountains!

The Floofs walk toward the mountains.
As they get closer, it begins to snow gently.
Then they see a frozen lake ahead.

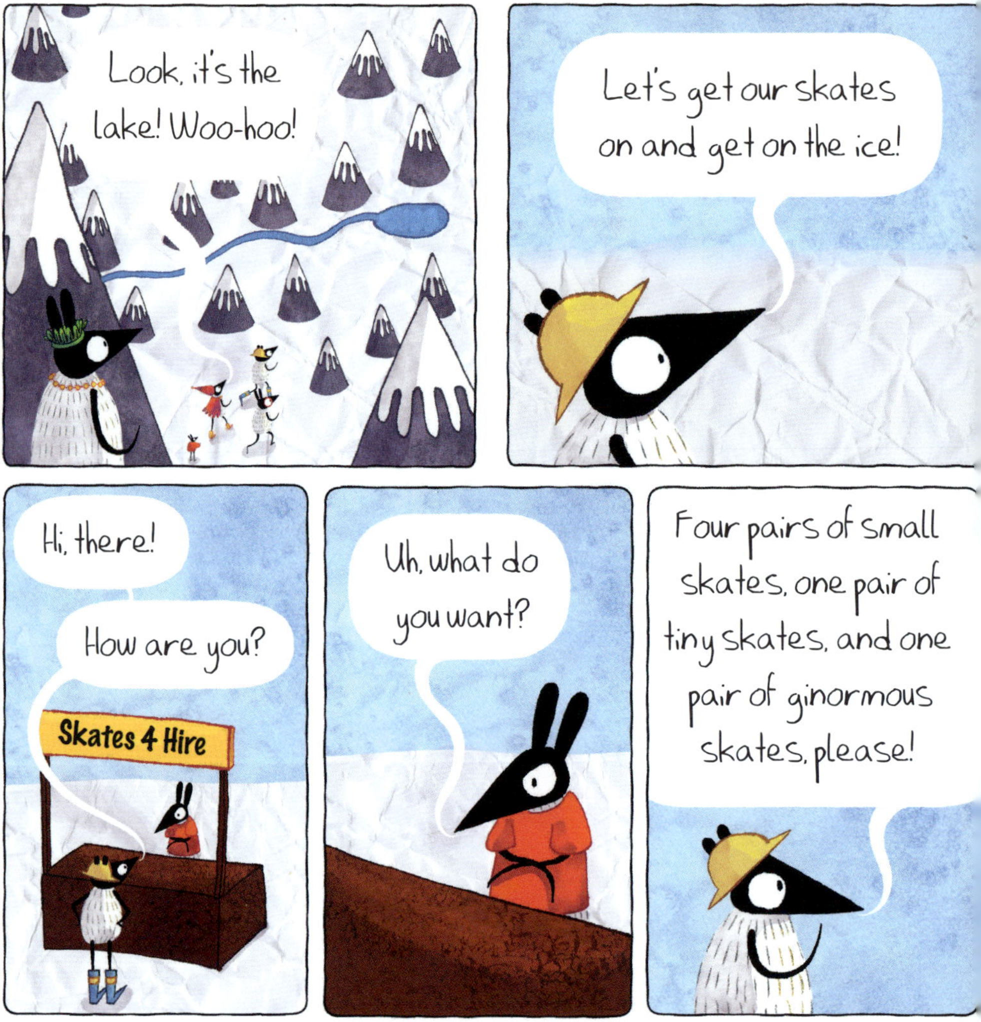

Look, it's the lake! Woo-hoo!
Let's get our skates on and get on the ice!
Hi, there!
How are you?
Skates 4 Hire
Uh, what do you want?
Four pairs of small skates, one pair of tiny skates, and one pair of ginormous skates, please!

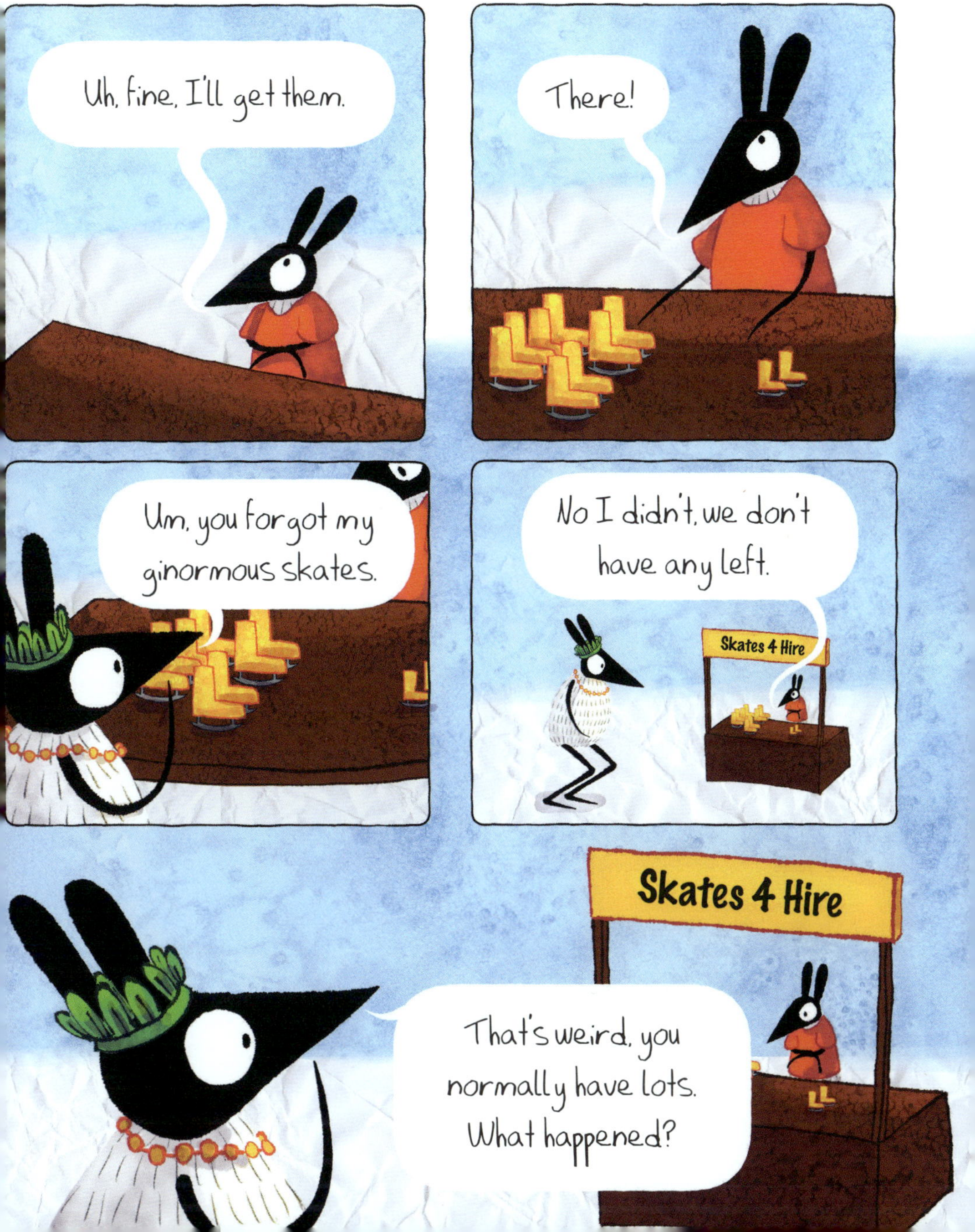

Uh, fine. I'll get them.
There!
Um, you forgot my ginormous skates.
No I didn't, we don't have any left.
Skates 4 Hire
Skates 4 Hire
That's weird, you normally have lots. What happened?

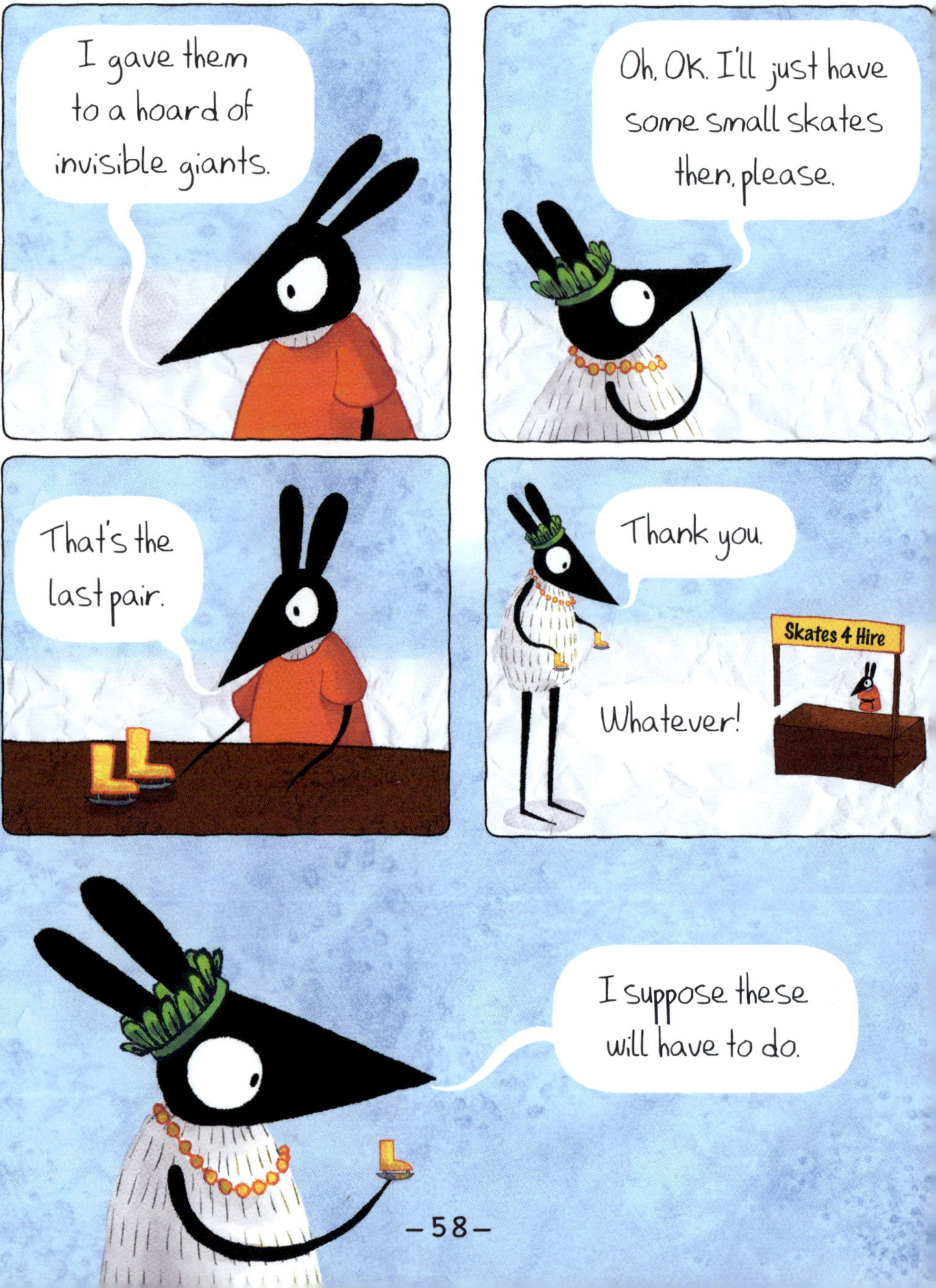
I gave them to a hoard of invisible giants.
Oh, OK. I'll just have some small skates then, please.
That's the last pair.
Thank you.
Skates 4 Hire
Whatever!
I suppose these will have to do.

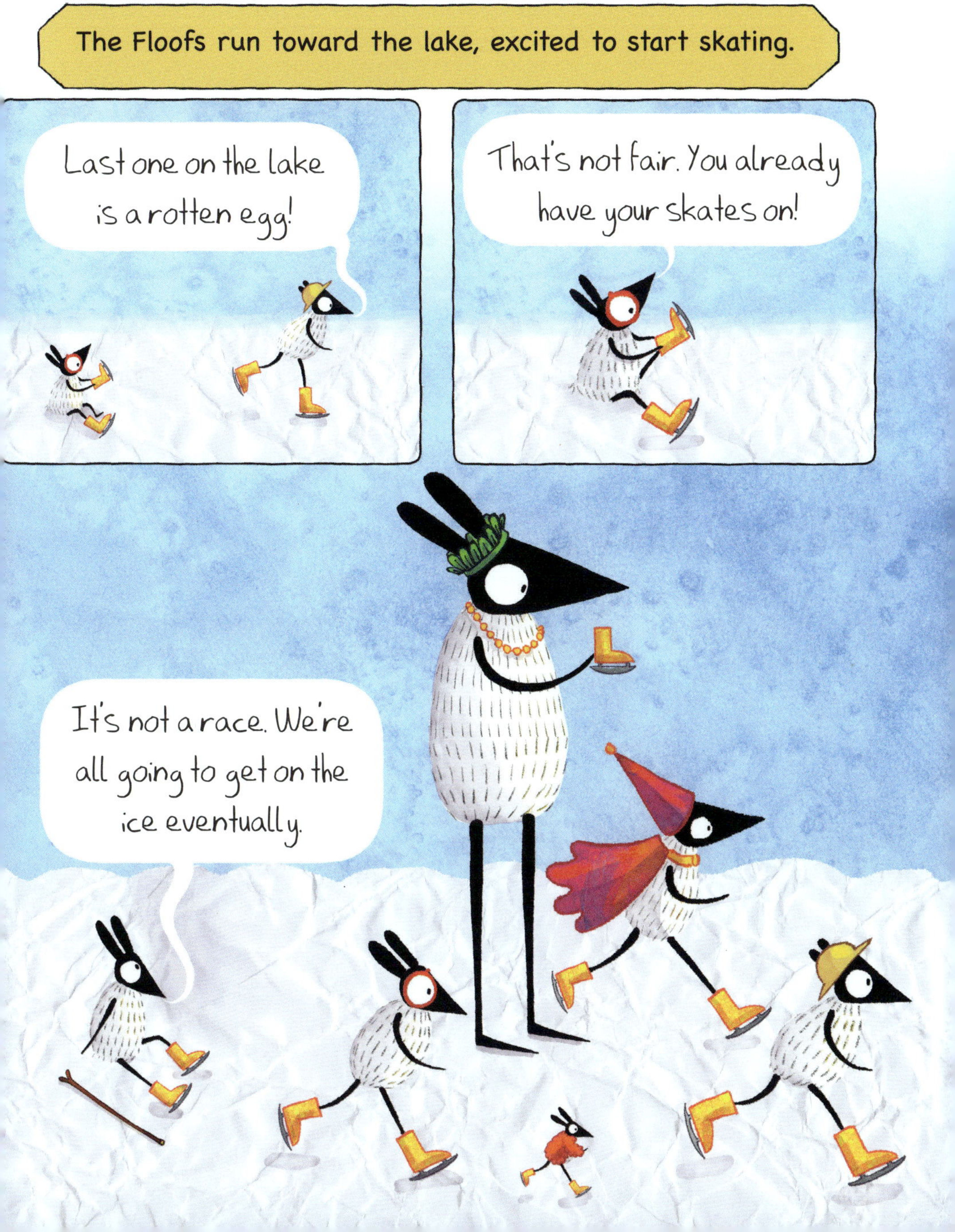
The Floofs run toward the lake, excited to start skating.
Last one on the lake is a rotten egg!
That's not fair. You already have your skates on!
It's not a race. We're all going to get on the ice eventually.

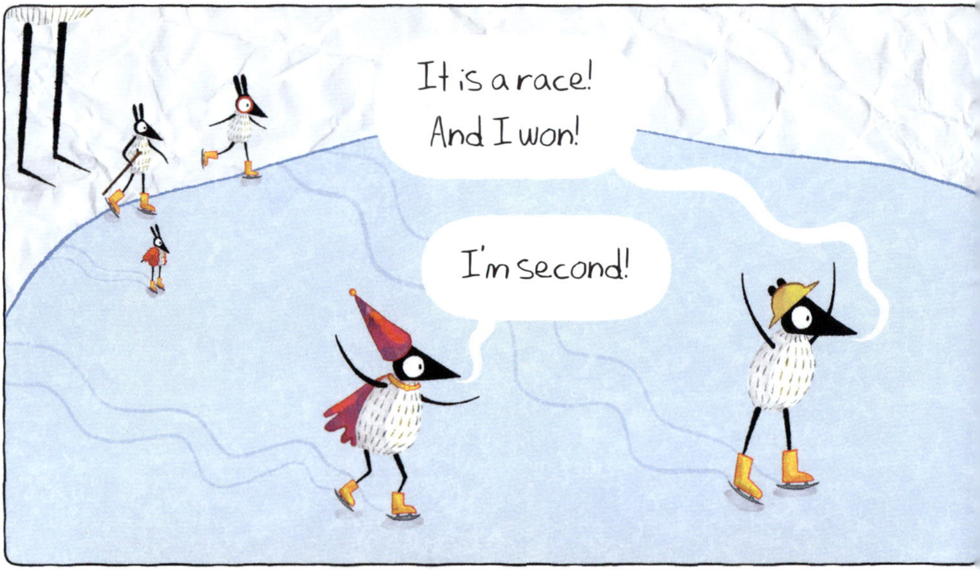
It is a race! And I won!
I'm second!

While Dill and Wizard celebrate, Mica skates over from the other side of the lake.

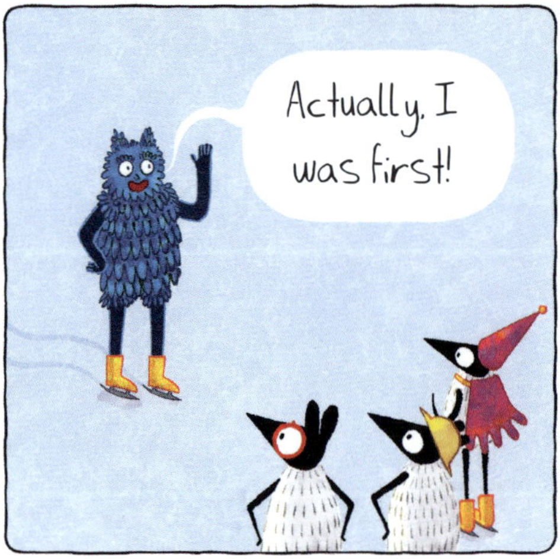
Actually, I was first!

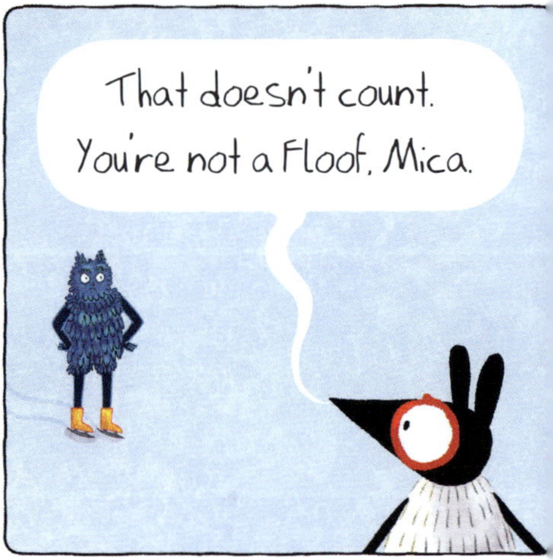
That doesn't count. You're not a Floof, Mica.

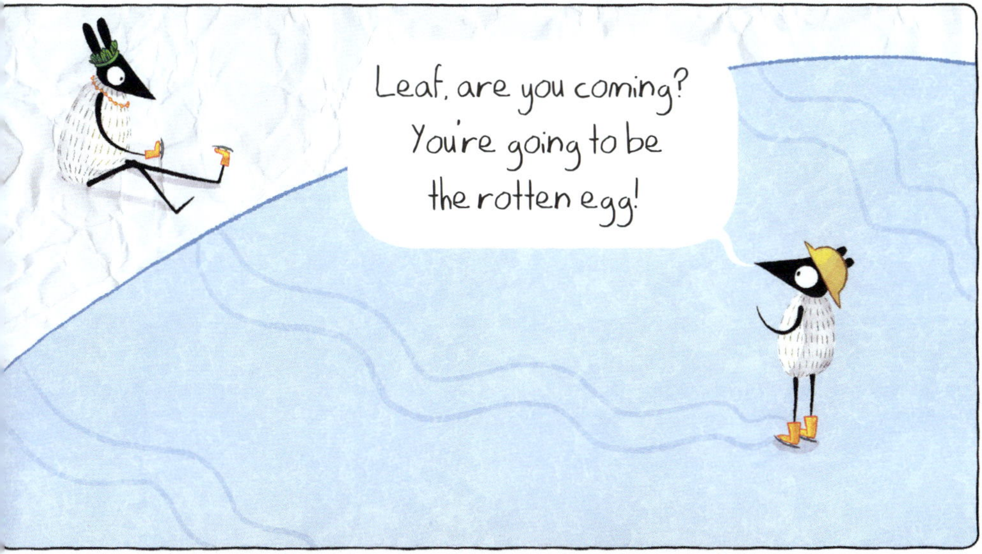
Leaf, are you coming? You're going to be the rotten egg!

Leaf is struggling to put the skates on. They are too small for his feet.

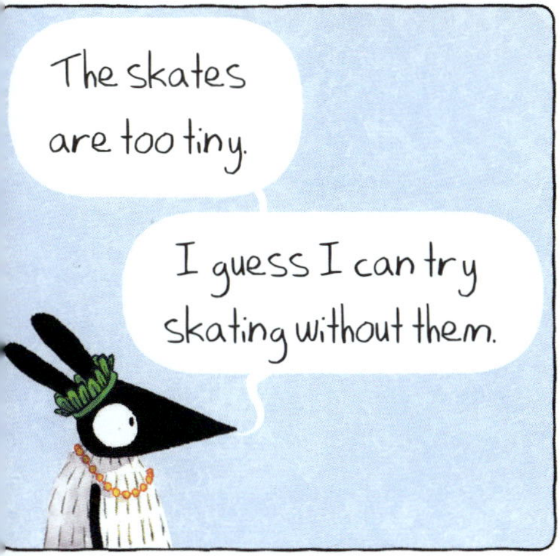
The skates are too tiny.
I guess I can try skating without them.

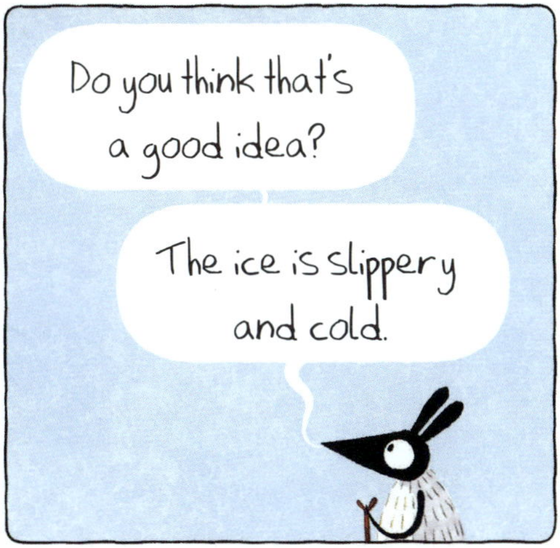
Do you think that's a good idea?
The ice is slippery and cold.

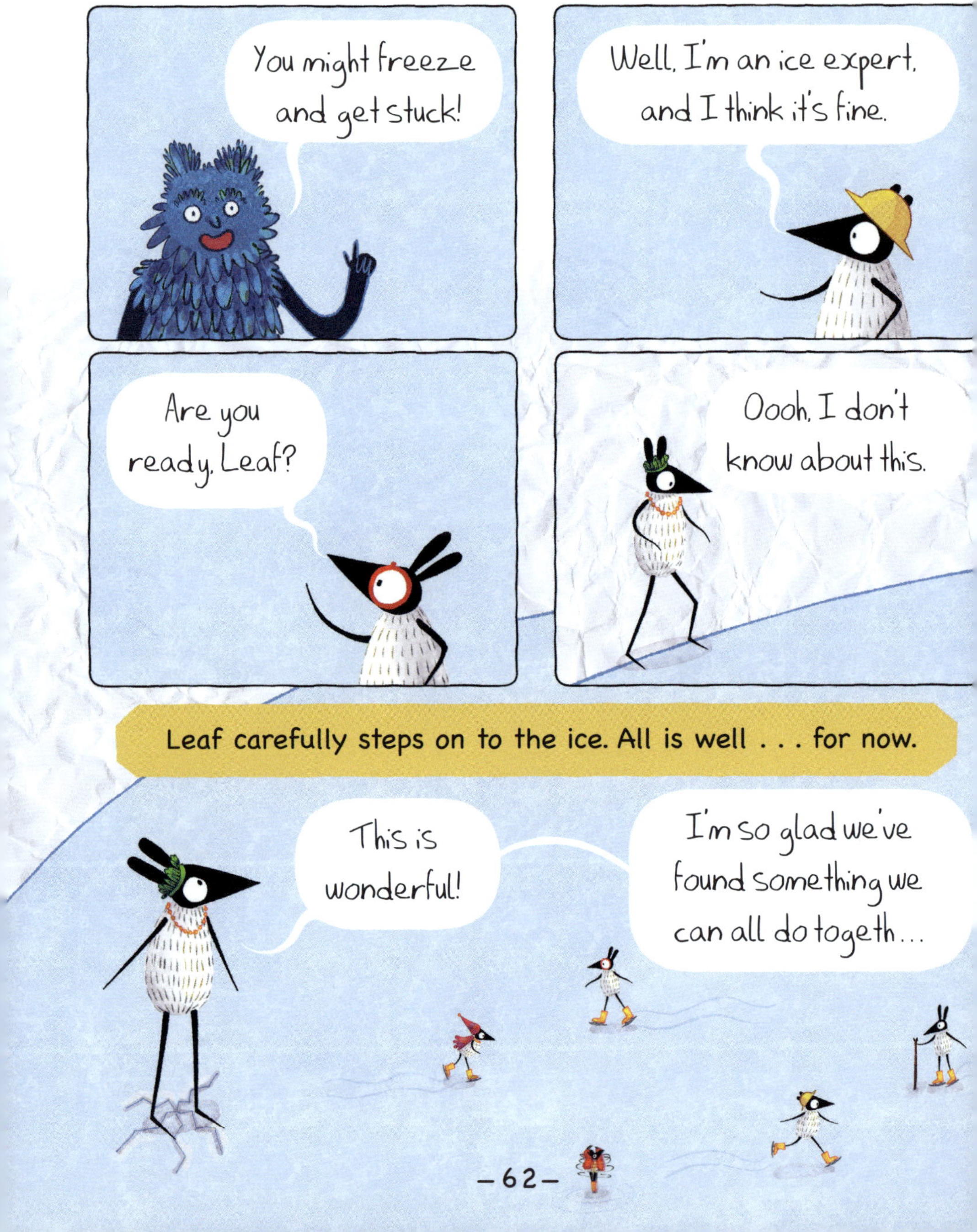
You might freeze and get stuck!
Well, I'm an ice expert, and I think it's fine.
Are you ready, Leaf?
Oooh, I don't know about this.
Leaf carefully steps on to the ice. All is well . . . for now.
This is wonderful!
I'm so glad we've found something we can all do togeth . . .

Suddenly, Leaf slips on the ice and falls with a bump. There's a humongous cracking sound, and he falls through the surface of the ice and into the freezing water below.

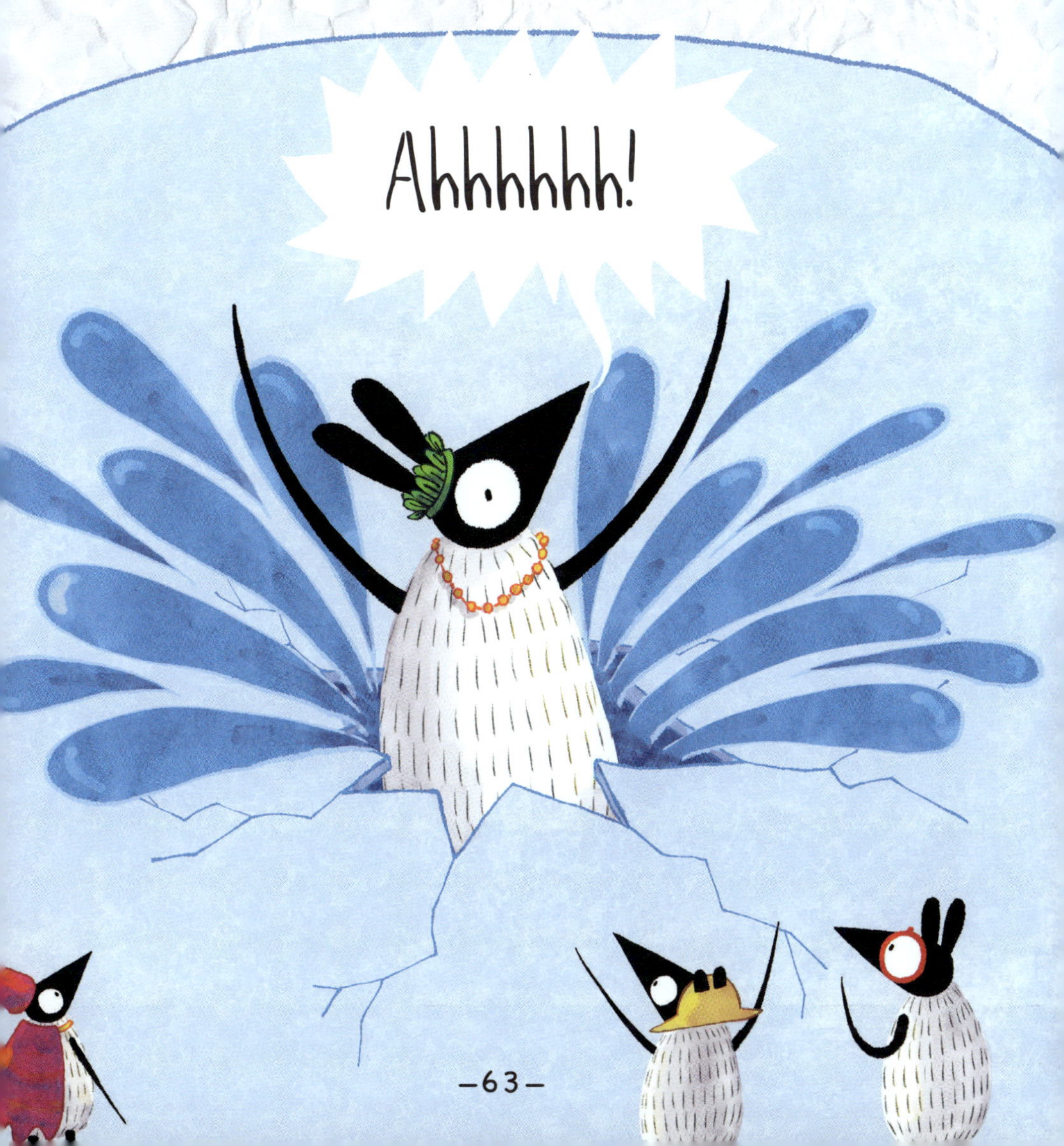
Ahhhhhh!

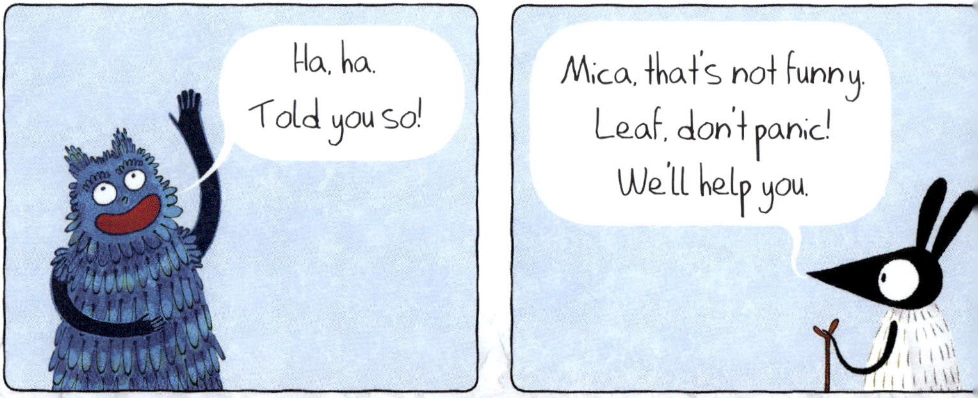
Ha, ha. Told you so!
Mica, that's not funny. Leaf, don't panic! We'll help you.

The water is so cold that Leaf turns to ice. But Dill has a plan to rescue him. Everyone comes together to pull Leaf out of the water and on dry land.

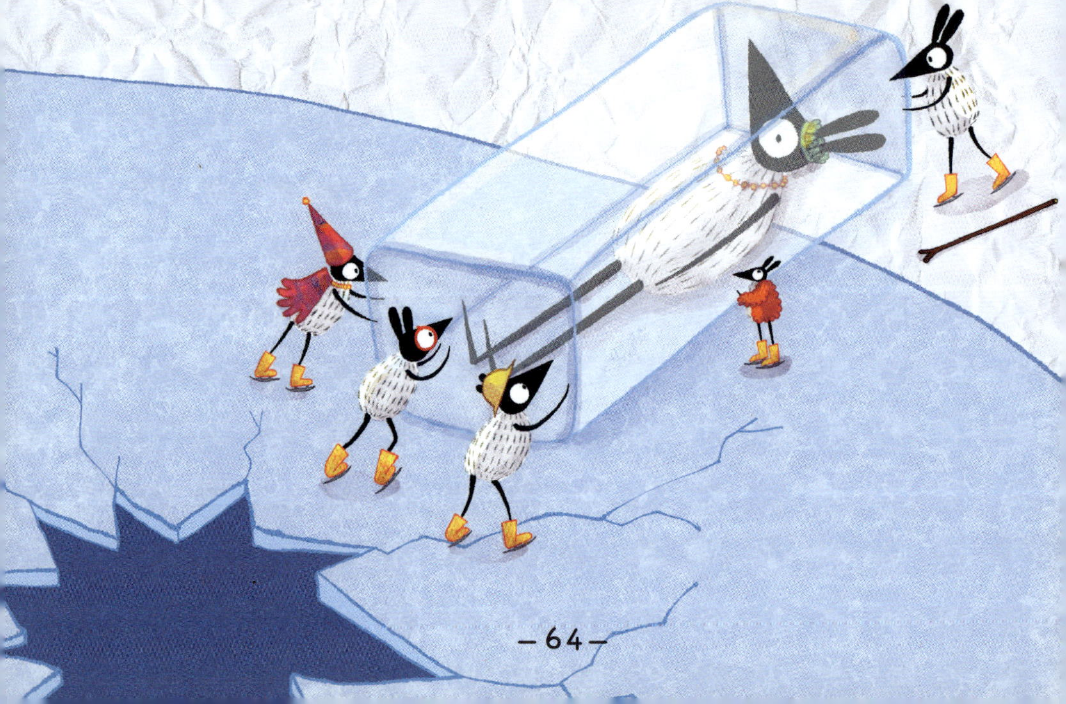

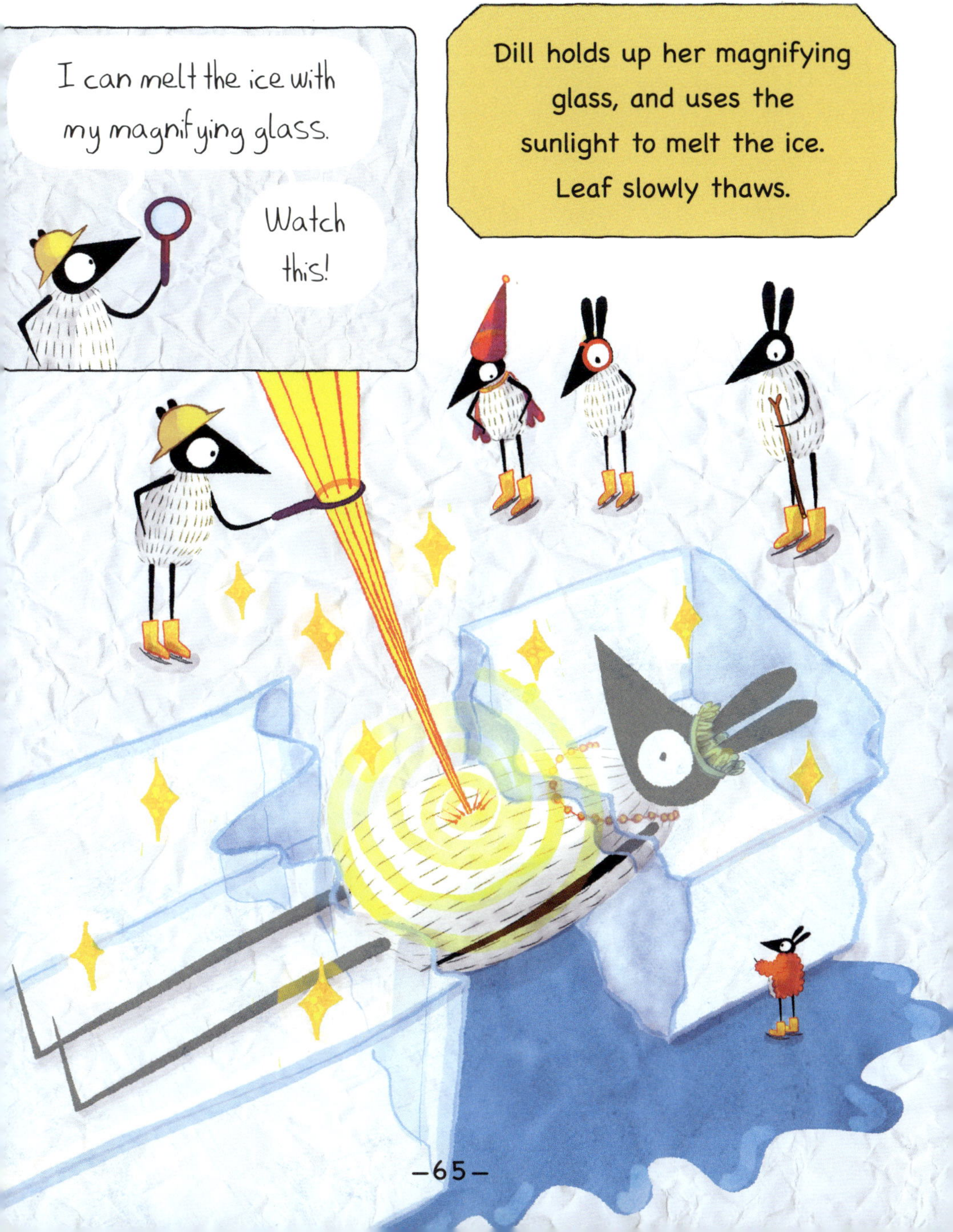
I can melt the ice with my magnifying glass.
Watch this!
Dill holds up her magnifying glass, and uses the sunlight to melt the ice. Leaf slowly thaws.

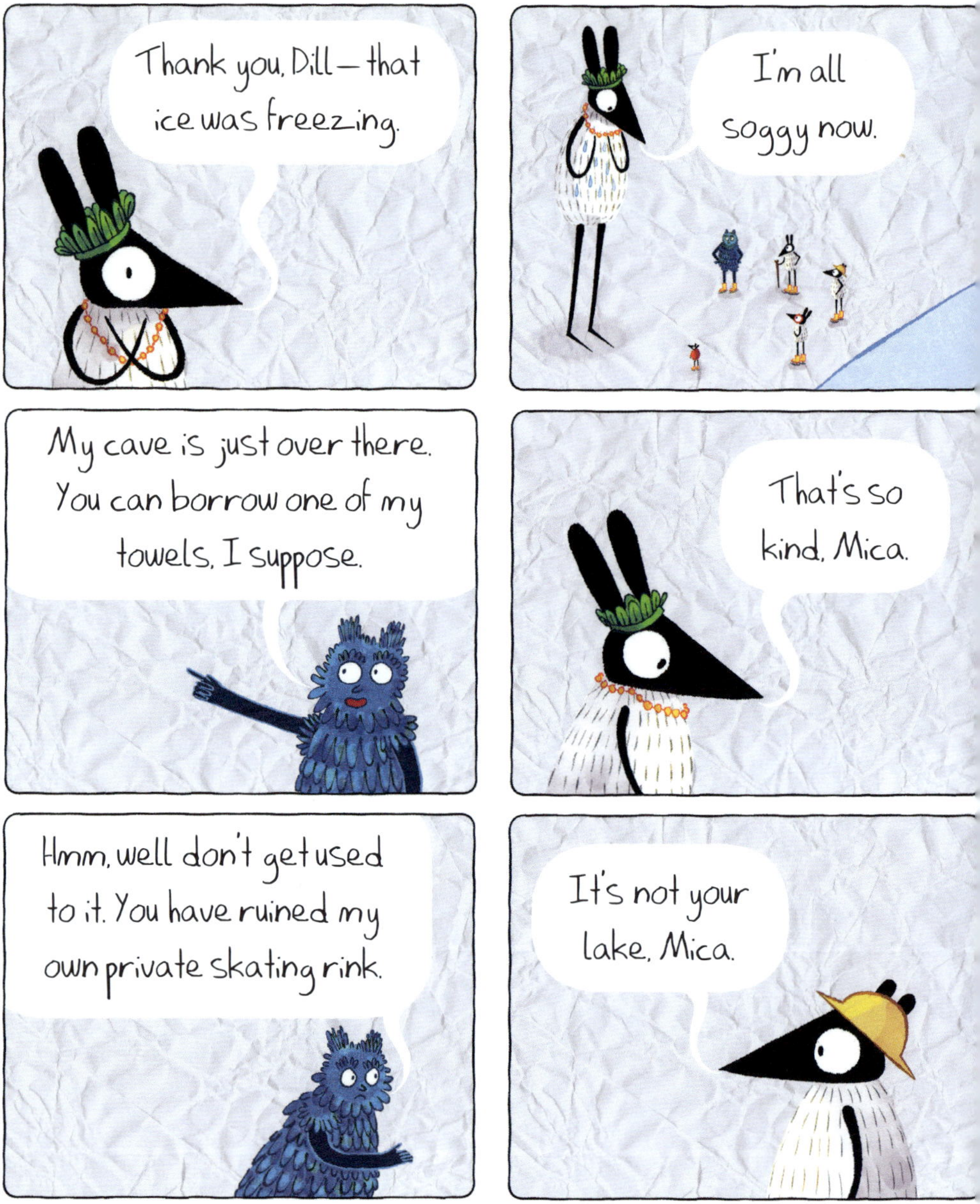
Thank you, Dill — that ice was freezing.
I'm all soggy now.
My cave is just over there. You can borrow one of my towels, I suppose.
That's so kind, Mica.
Hmm, well don't get used to it. You have ruined my own private skating rink.
It's not your lake, Mica.

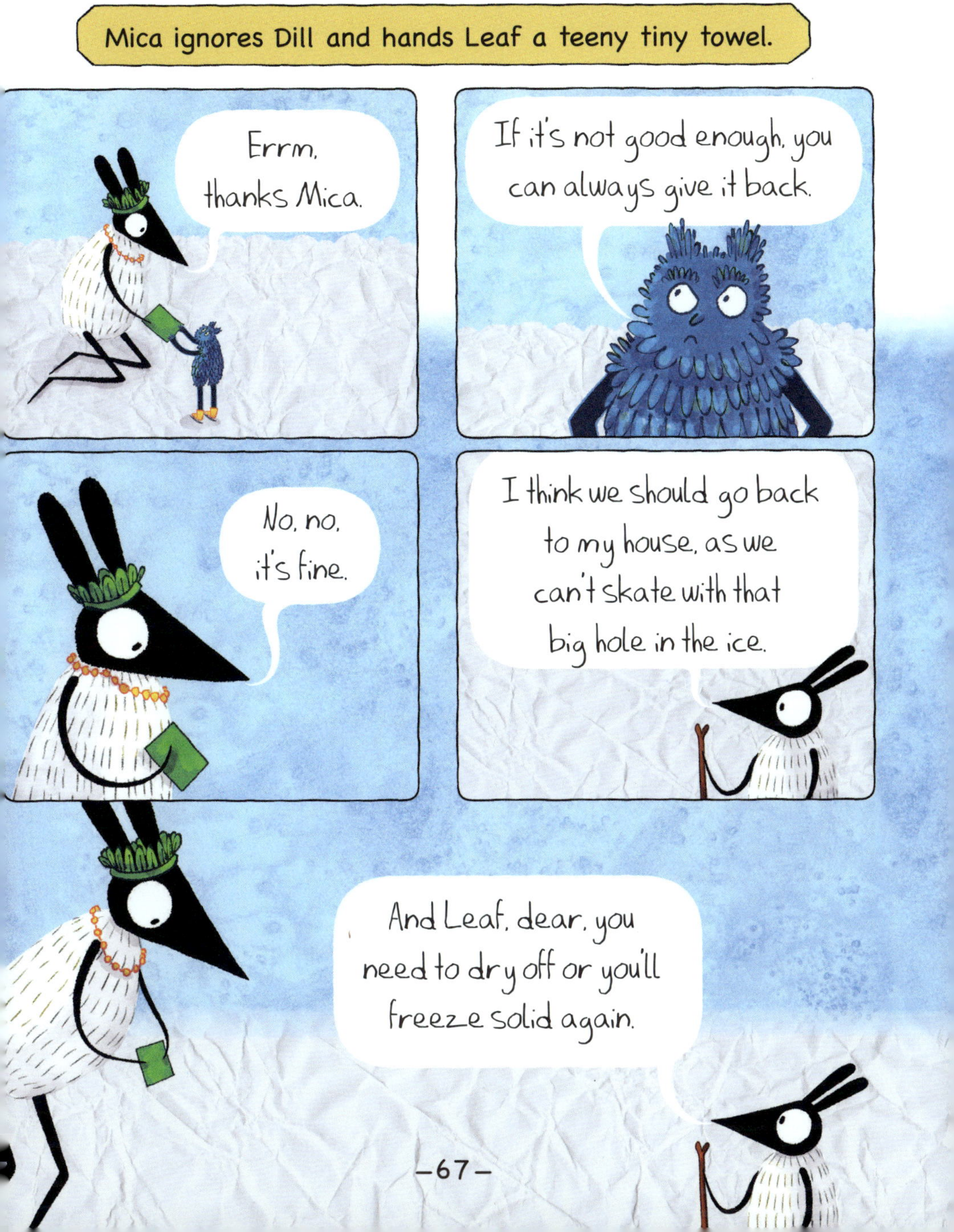
Mica ignores Dill and hands Leaf a teeny tiny towel.
Errm, thanks Mica.
If it's not good enough, you can always give it back.
No, no, it's fine.
I think we should go back to my house, as we can't skate with that big hole in the ice.
And Leaf, dear, you need to dry off or you'll freeze solid again.

Leaf is disappointed that the day has been ruined all because he didn't quite fit in. When the Floofs arrive back in the forest, Leaf is looking sad.

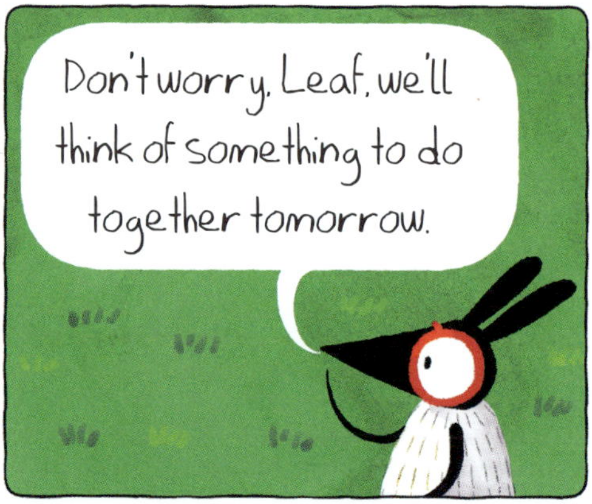
Don't worry, Leaf, we'll think of something to do together tomorrow.

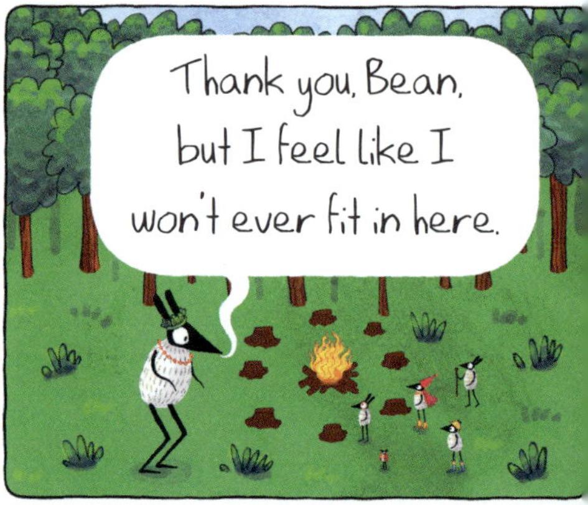
Thank you, Bean, but I feel like I won't ever fit in here.

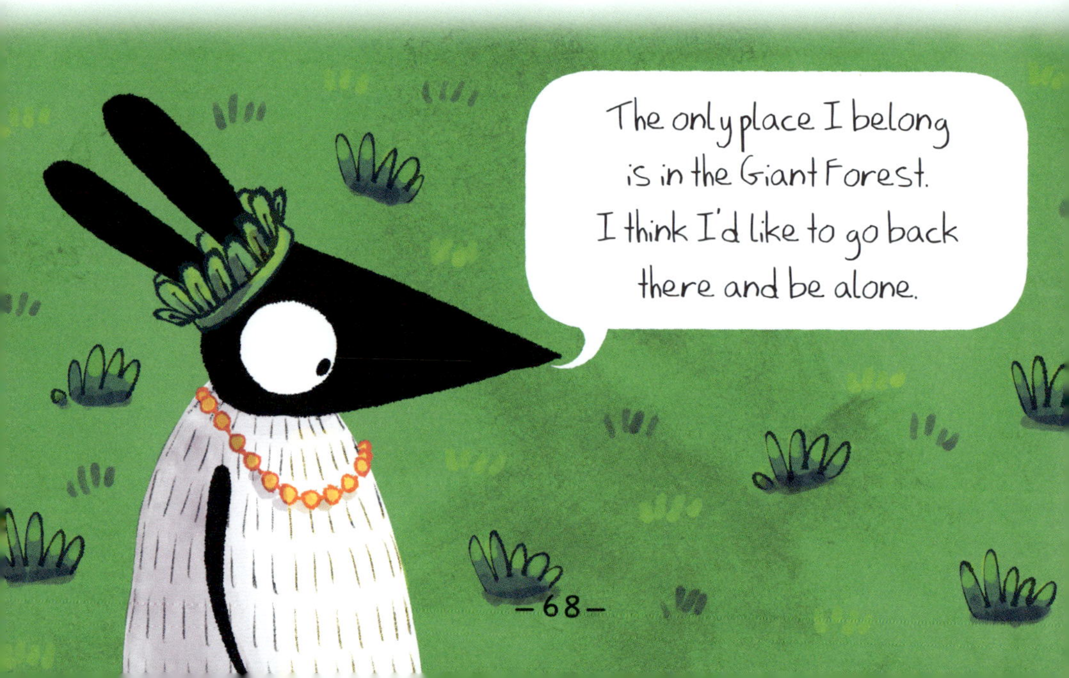
The only place I belong is in the Giant Forest. I think I'd like to go back there and be alone.

So Leaf gets up and walks back to his home in the Giant Forest—the only place he feels he fits in.

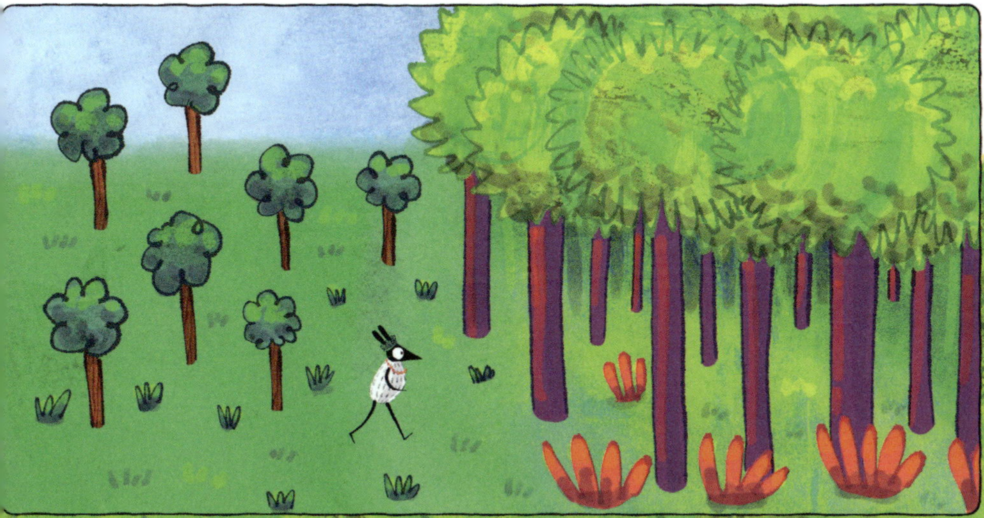

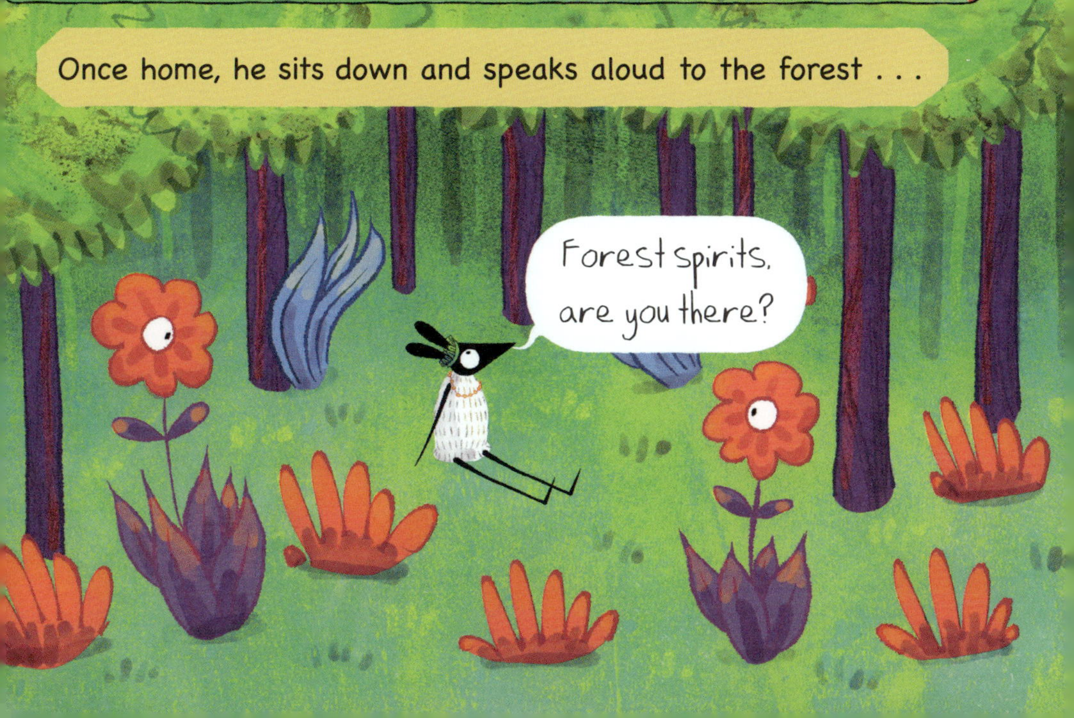
Once home, he sits down and speaks aloud to the forest . . .
Forest spirits, are you there?

Suddenly the forest comes to life. The flowers wake from their slumber, the trees ruffle in the breeze, and the spirits of the forest appear in front of Leaf.

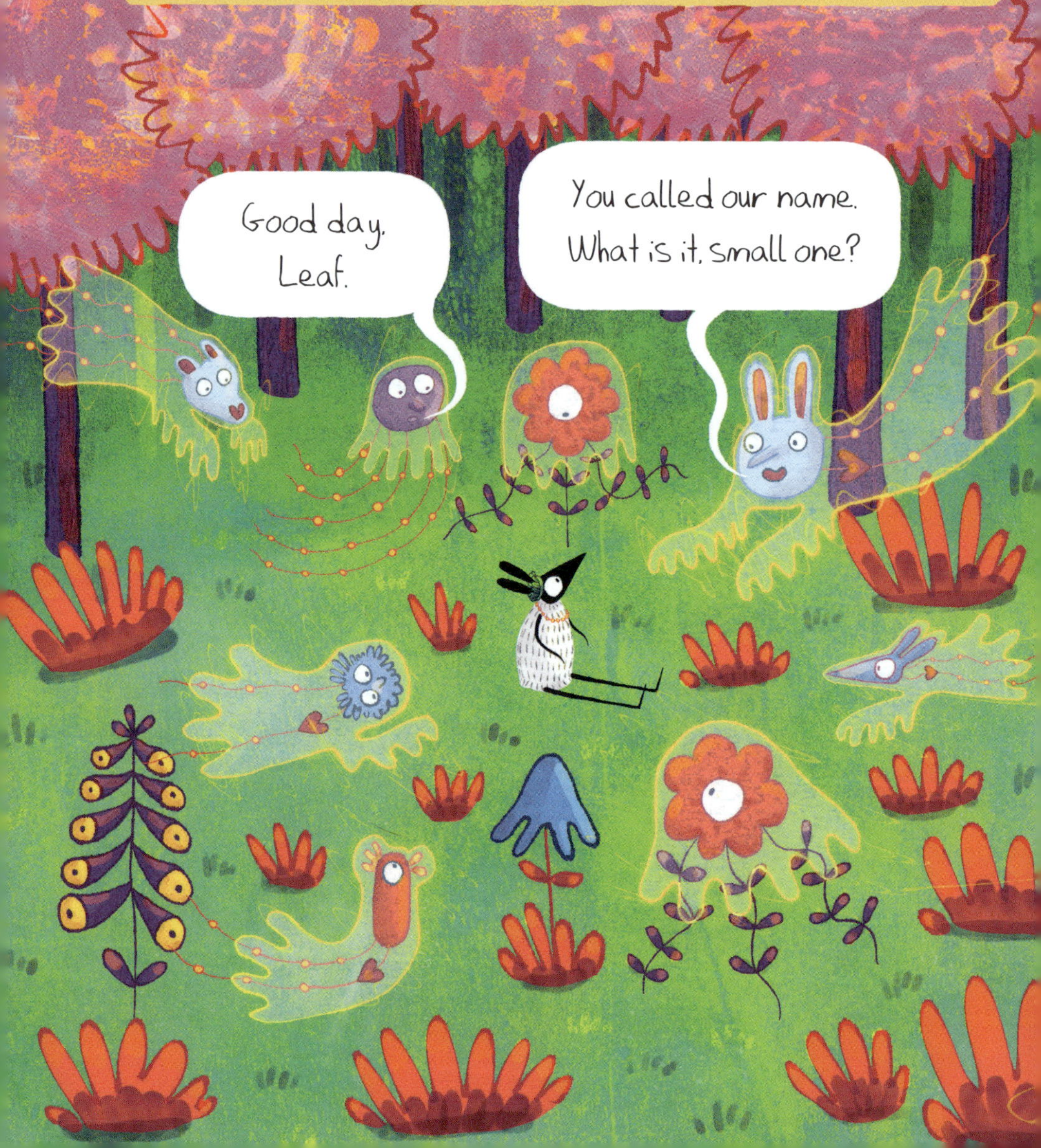
Good day, Leaf.
You called our name. What is it, small one?

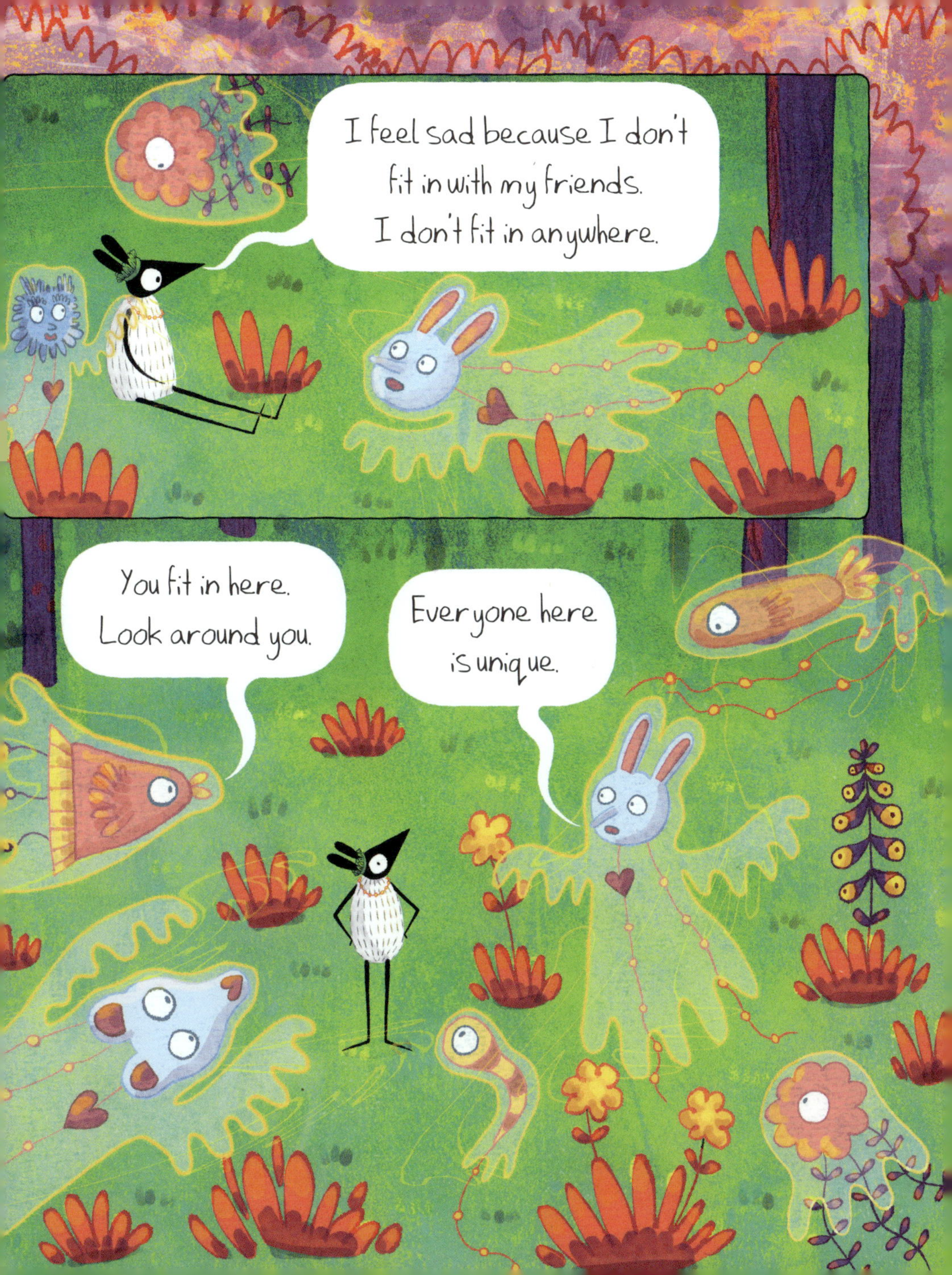
I feel sad because I don't fit in with my friends. I don't fit in anywhere.
You fit in here. Look around you.
Everyone here is unique.

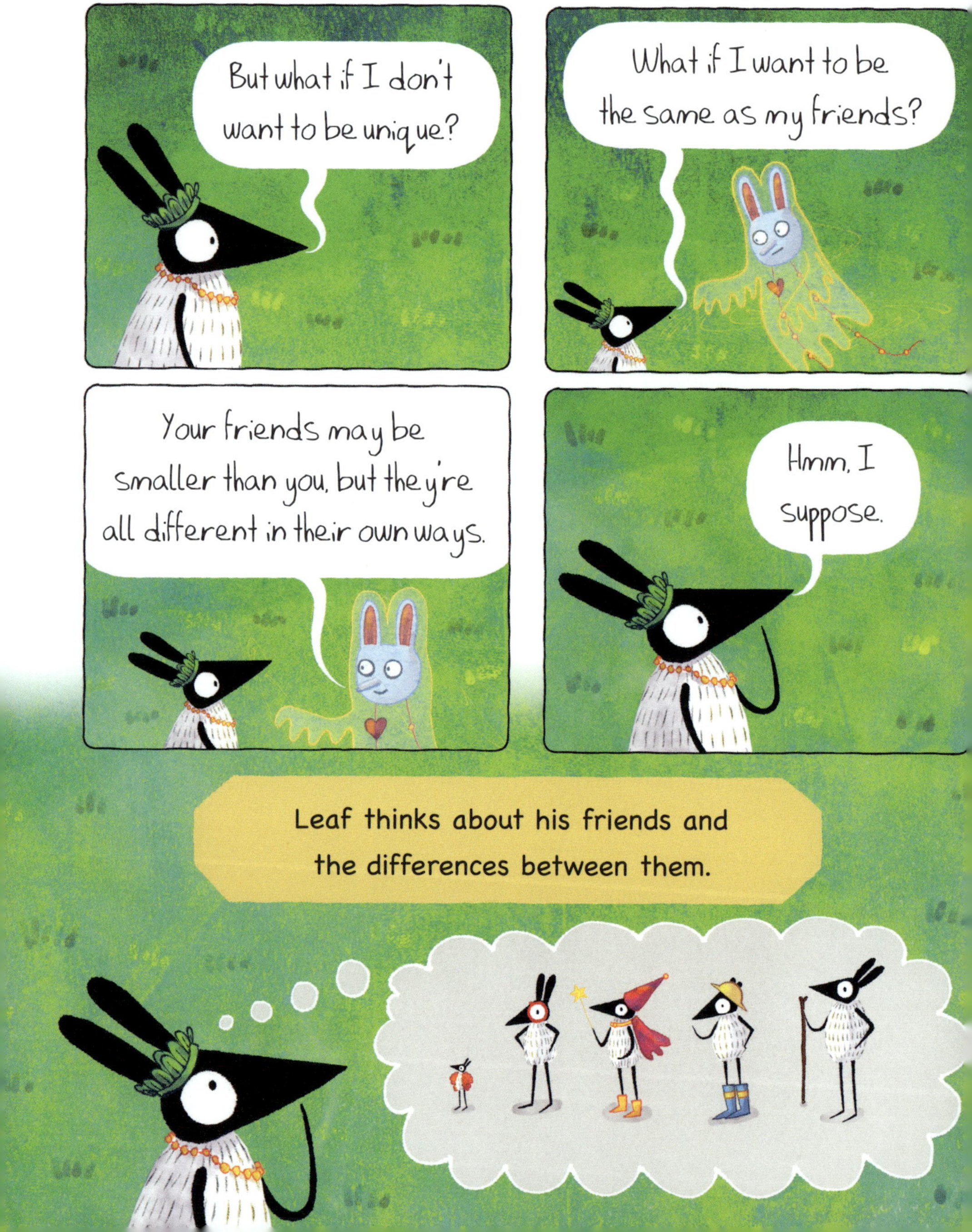
But what if I don't want to be unique?
What if I want to be the same as my friends?
Your friends may be smaller than you, but they're all different in their own ways.
Hmm. I suppose.
Leaf thinks about his friends and the differences between them.

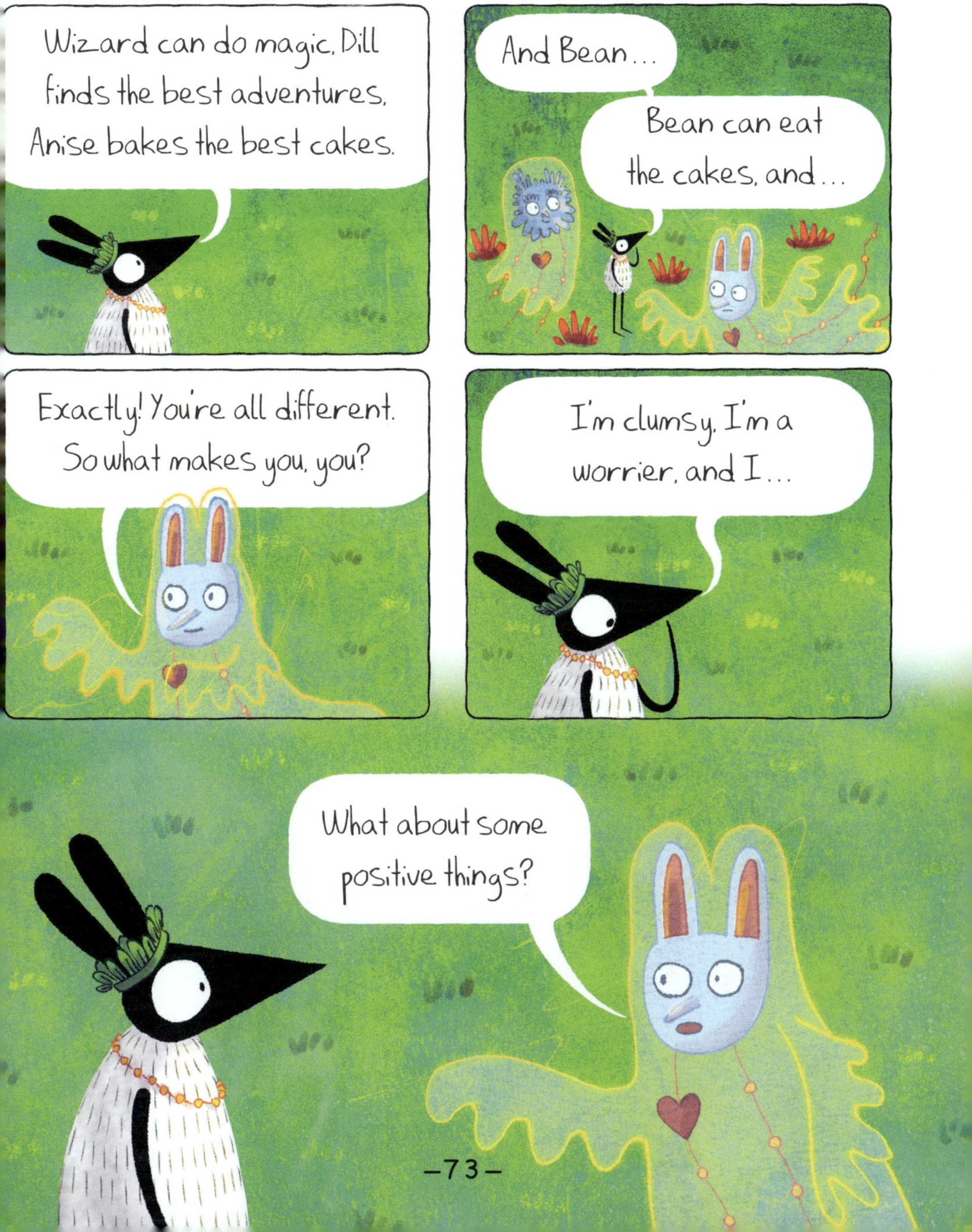
Wizard can do magic. Dill finds the best adventures. Anise bakes the best cakes.
And Bean...
Bean can eat the cakes, and...
Exactly! You're all different. So what makes you, you?
I'm clumsy. I'm a worrier, and I...
What about some positive things?

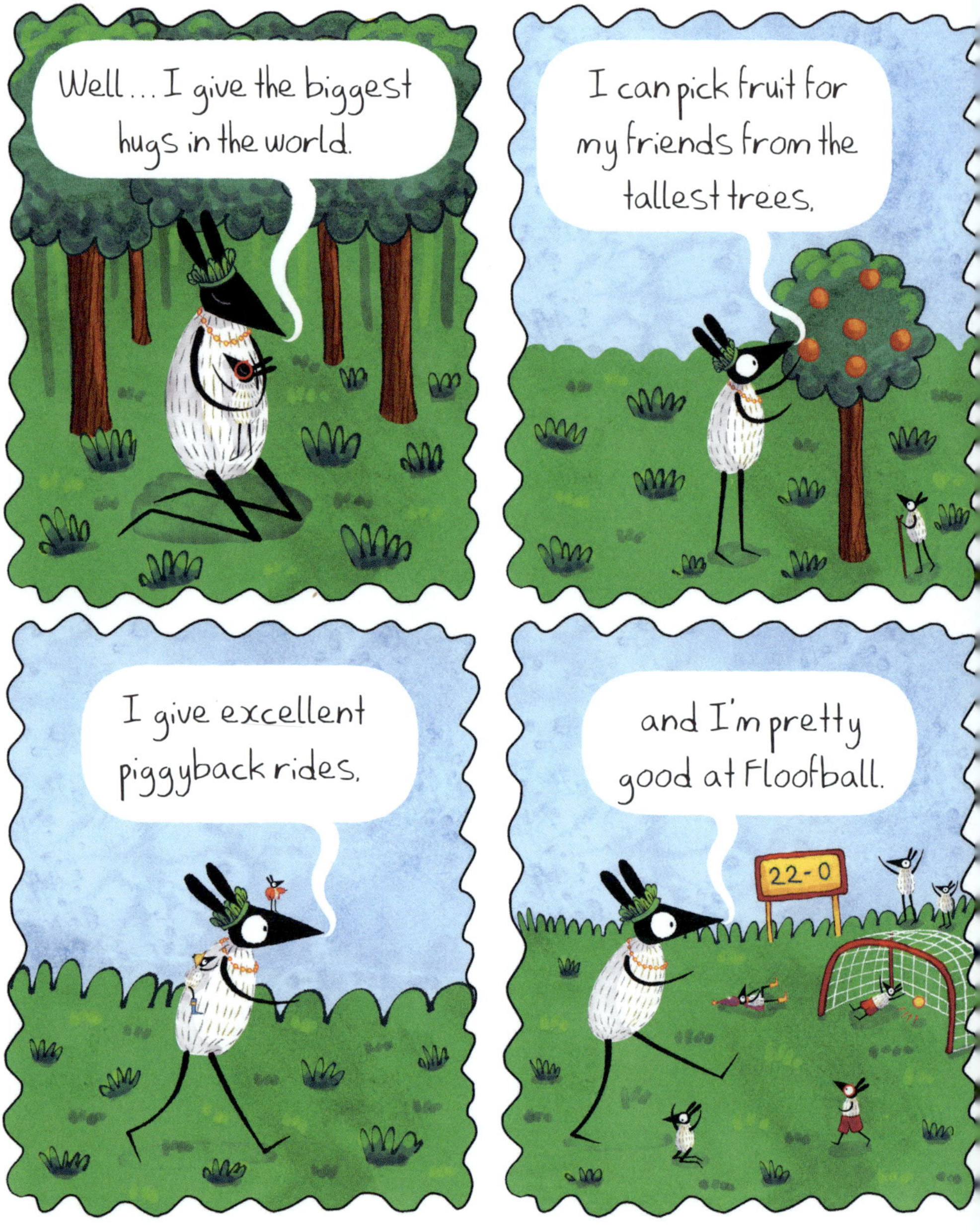
Well... I give the biggest hugs in the world.
I can pick fruit for my friends from the tallest trees.
22-0
I give excellent piggyback rides.
and I'm pretty good at Floofball.

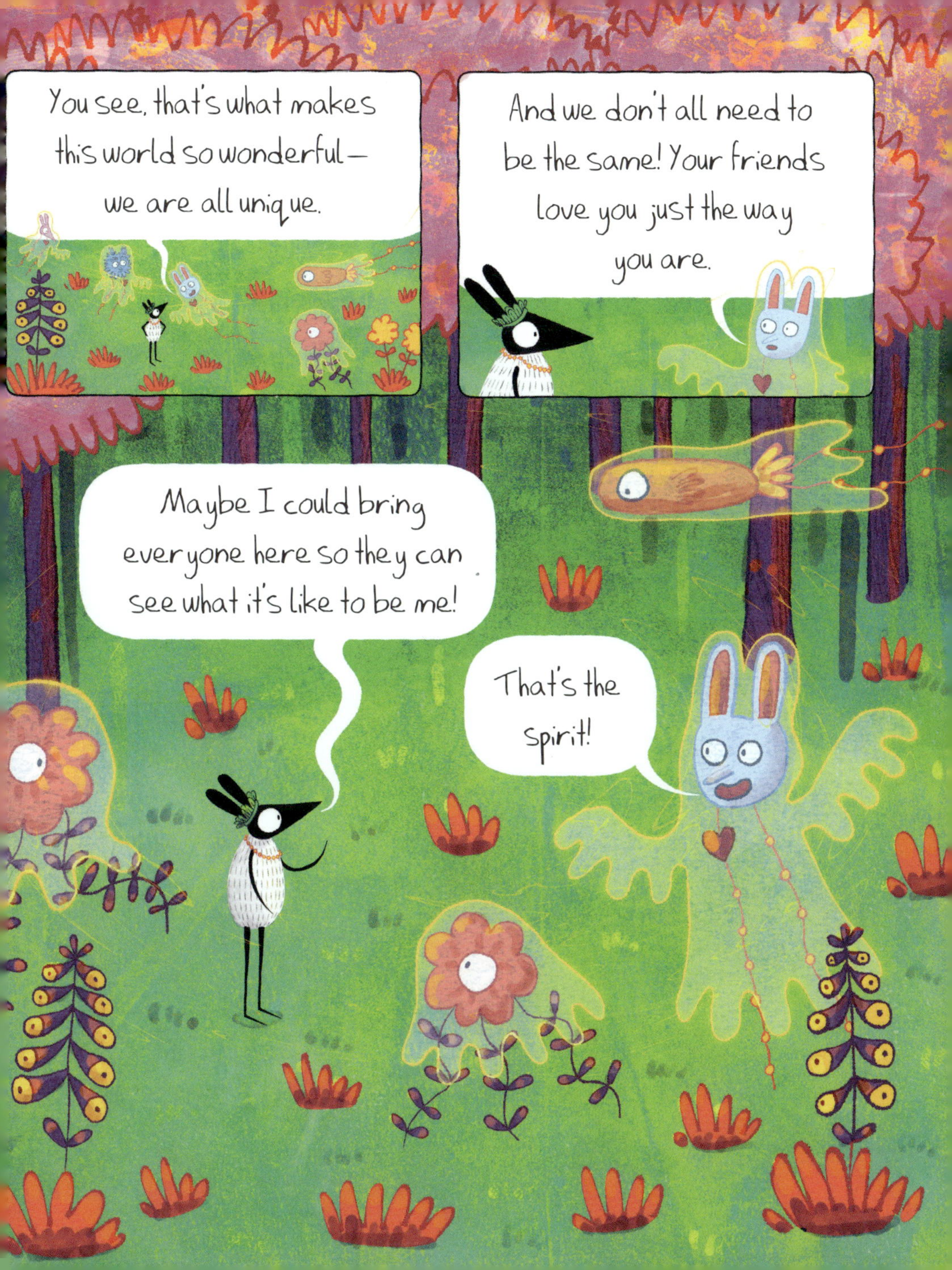
You see, that's what makes this world so wonderful— we are all unique.
And we don't all need to be the same! Your friends love you just the way you are.
Maybe I could bring everyone here so they can see what it's like to be me!
That's the spirit!

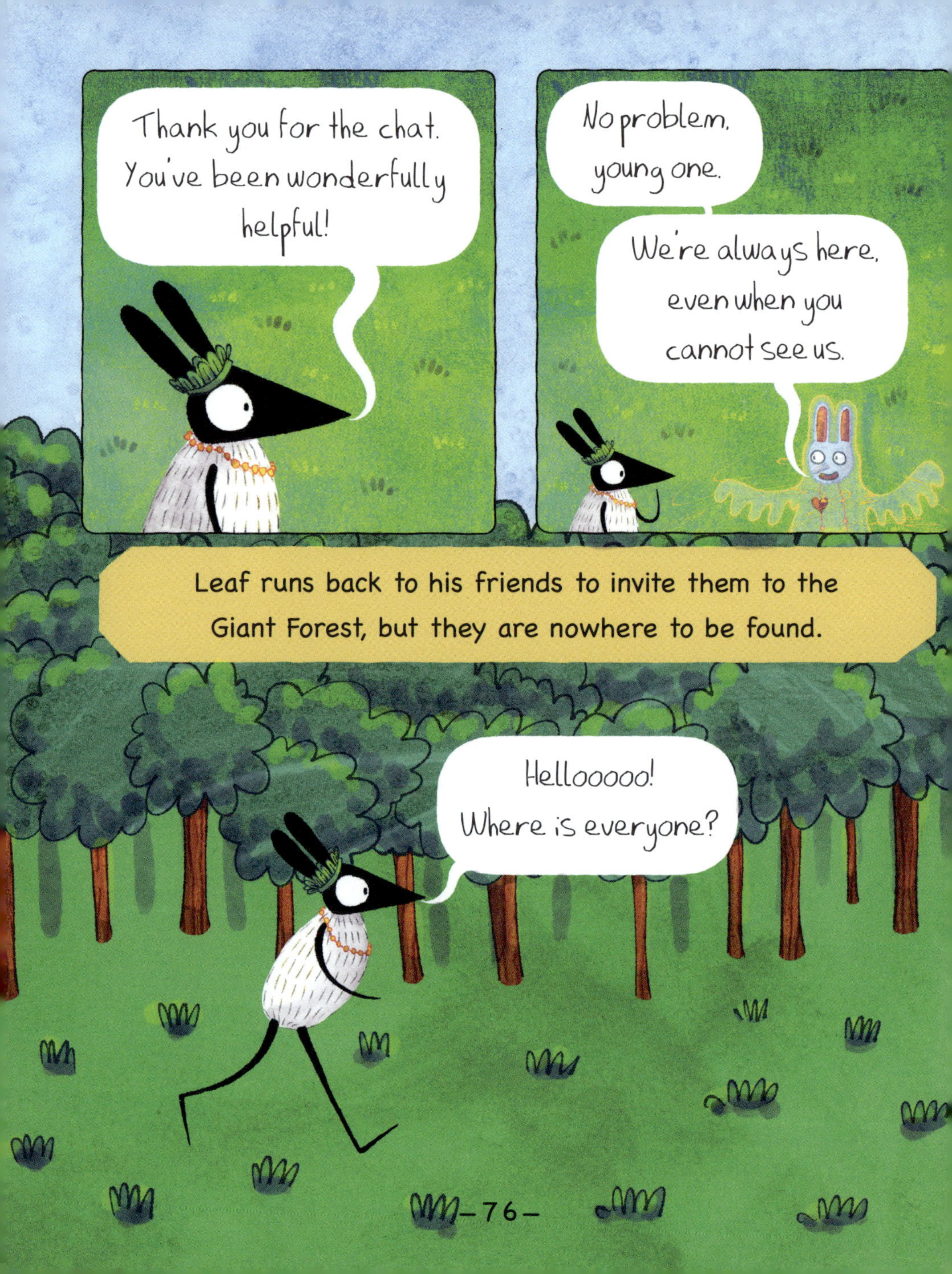
Thank you for the chat. You've been wonderfully helpful!
No problem, young one.
We're always here, even when you cannot see us.
Leaf runs back to his friends to invite them to the Giant Forest, but they are nowhere to be found.
Hellooooo! Where is everyone?

Leaf sits down by the fire and wonders where all his friends went. Just as he is about to get up and go home . . .

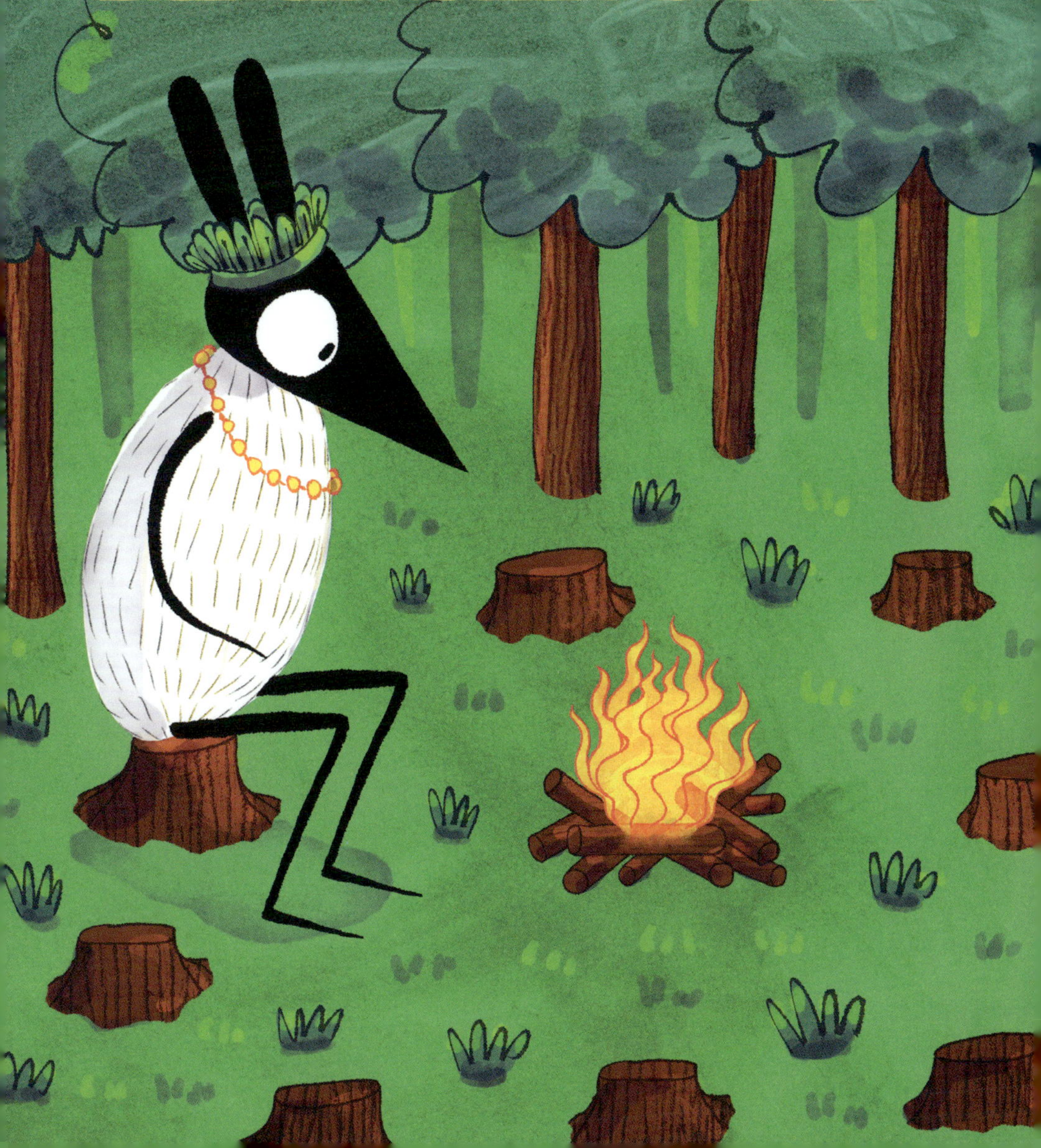

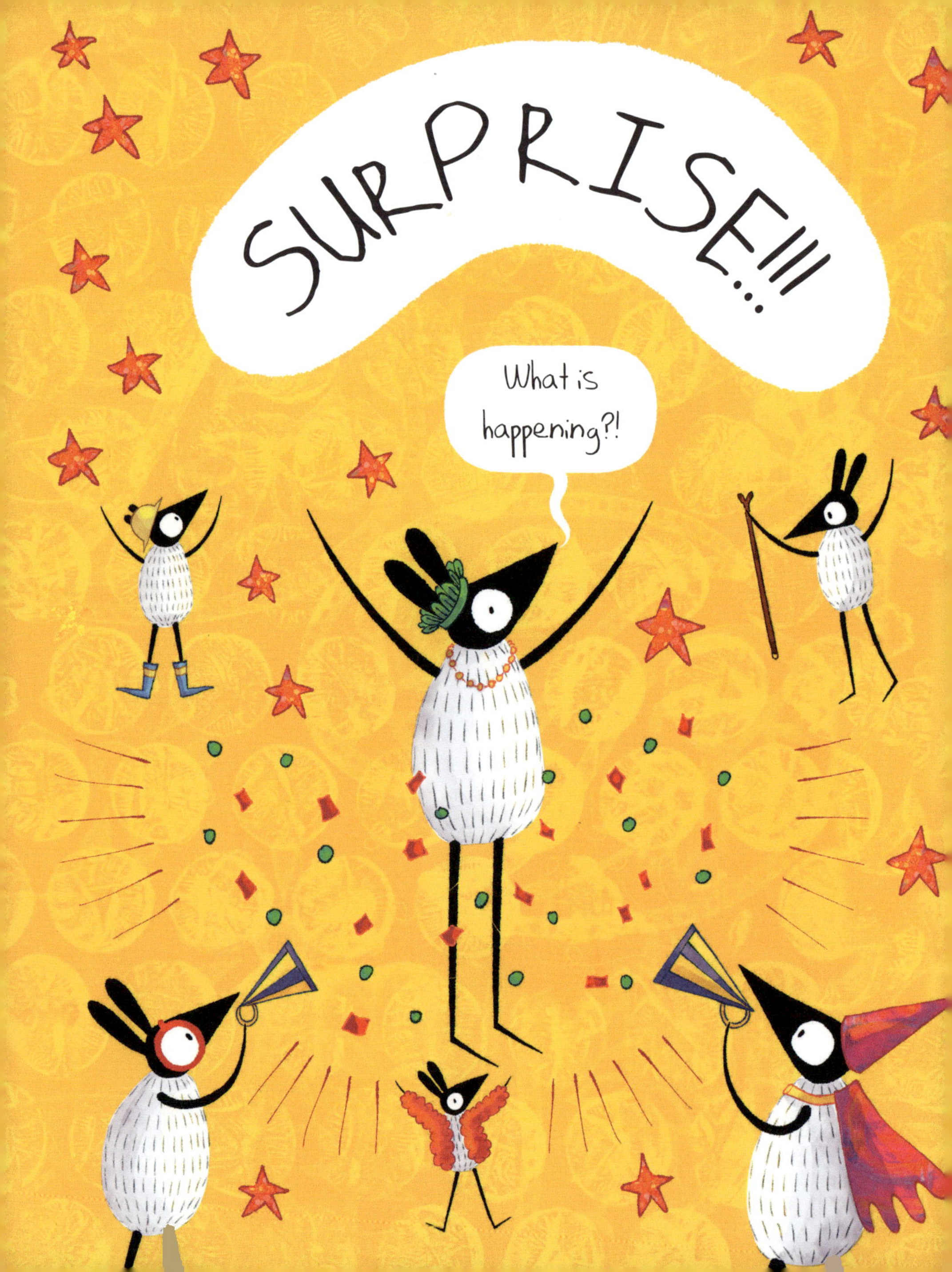
SURPRISE!!!...
What is happening?!

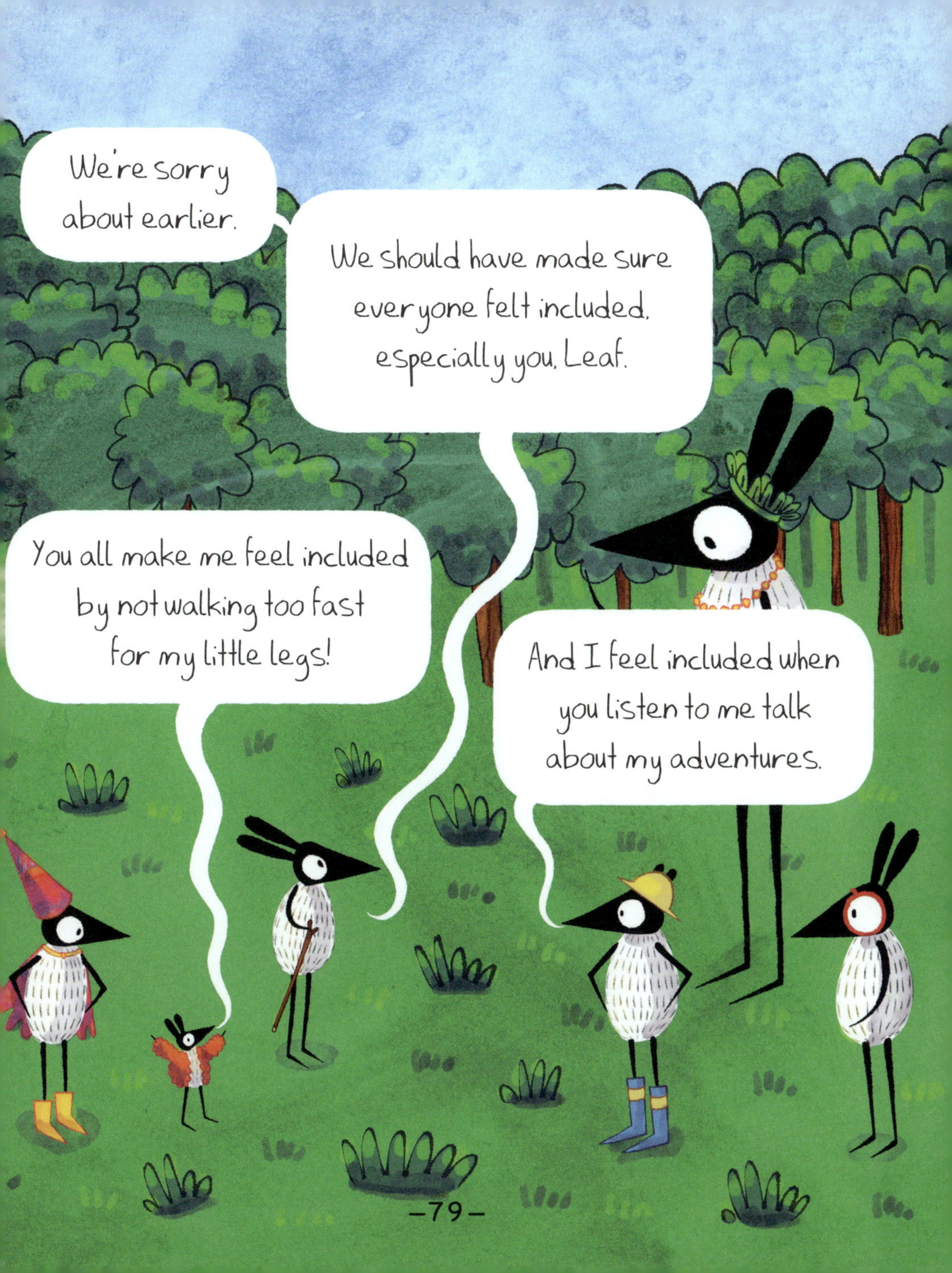
We're sorry about earlier.
We should have made sure everyone felt included, especially you, Leaf.
You all make me feel included by not walking too fast for my little legs!
And I feel included when you listen to me talk about my adventures.

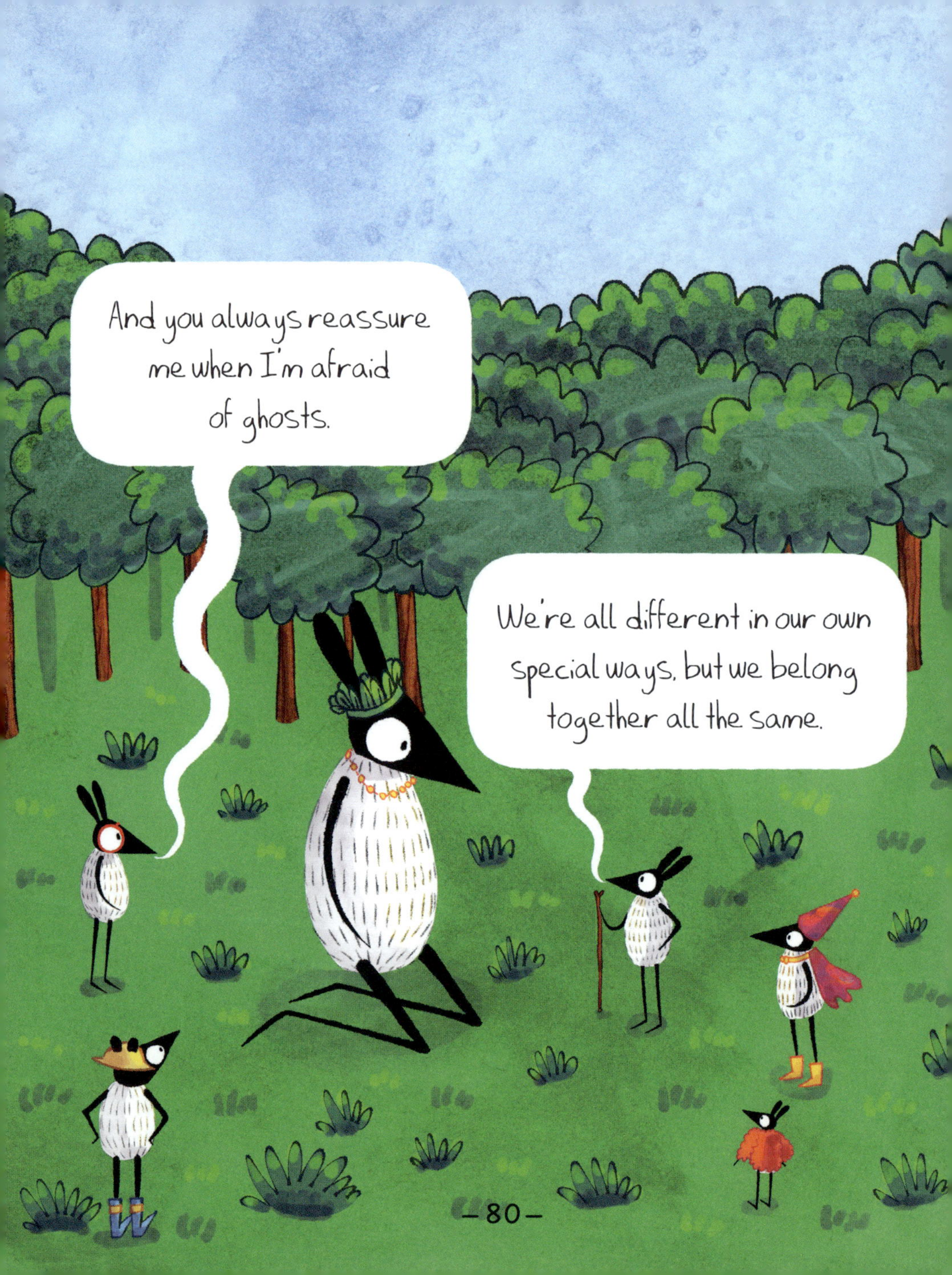
And you always reassure me when I'm afraid of ghosts.
We're all different in our own special ways, but we belong together all the same.

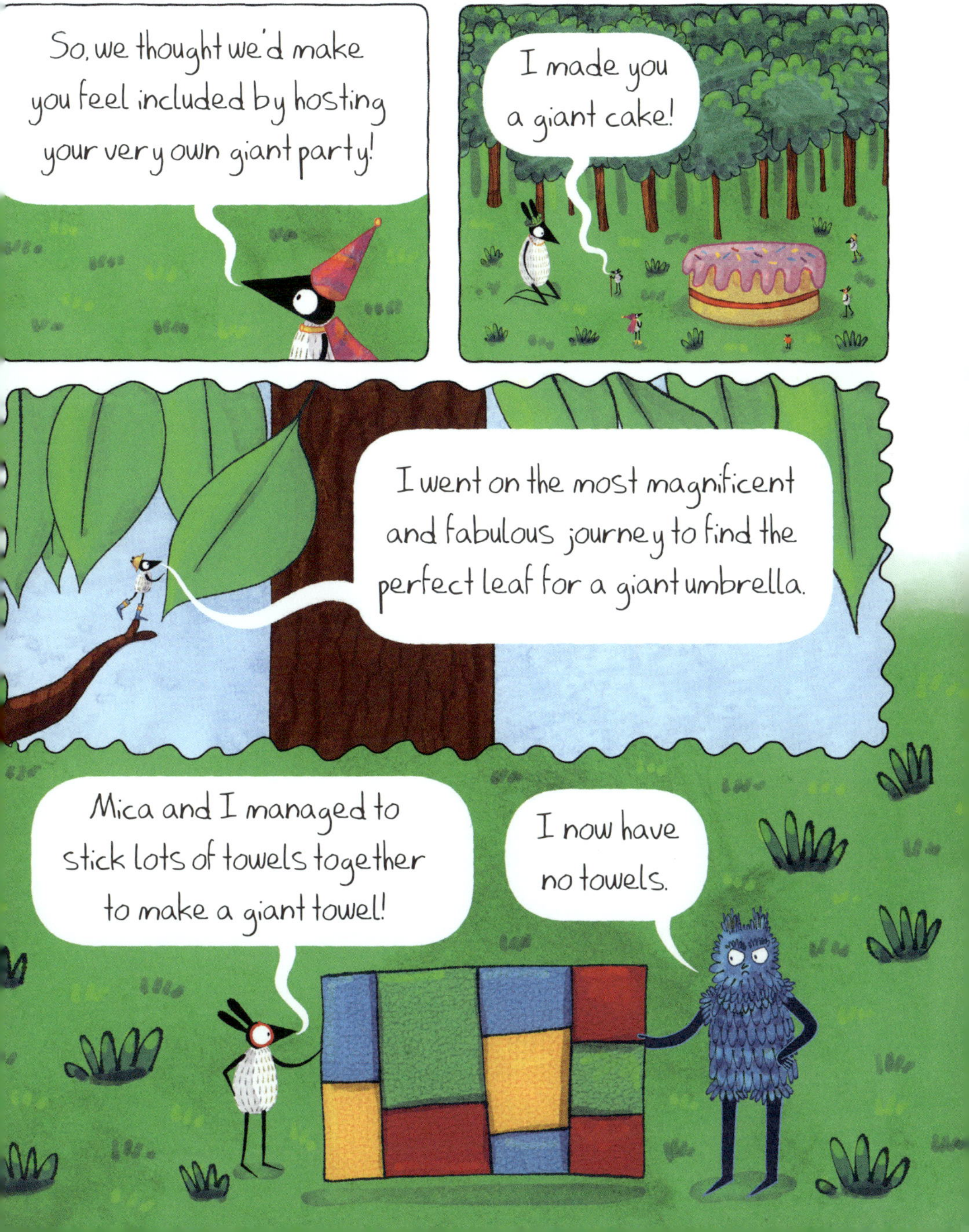
So, we thought we'd make you feel included by hosting your very own giant party!
I made you a giant cake!
I went on the most magnificent and fabulous journey to find the perfect leaf for a giant umbrella.
Mica and I managed to stick lots of towels together to make a giant towel!
I now have no towels.

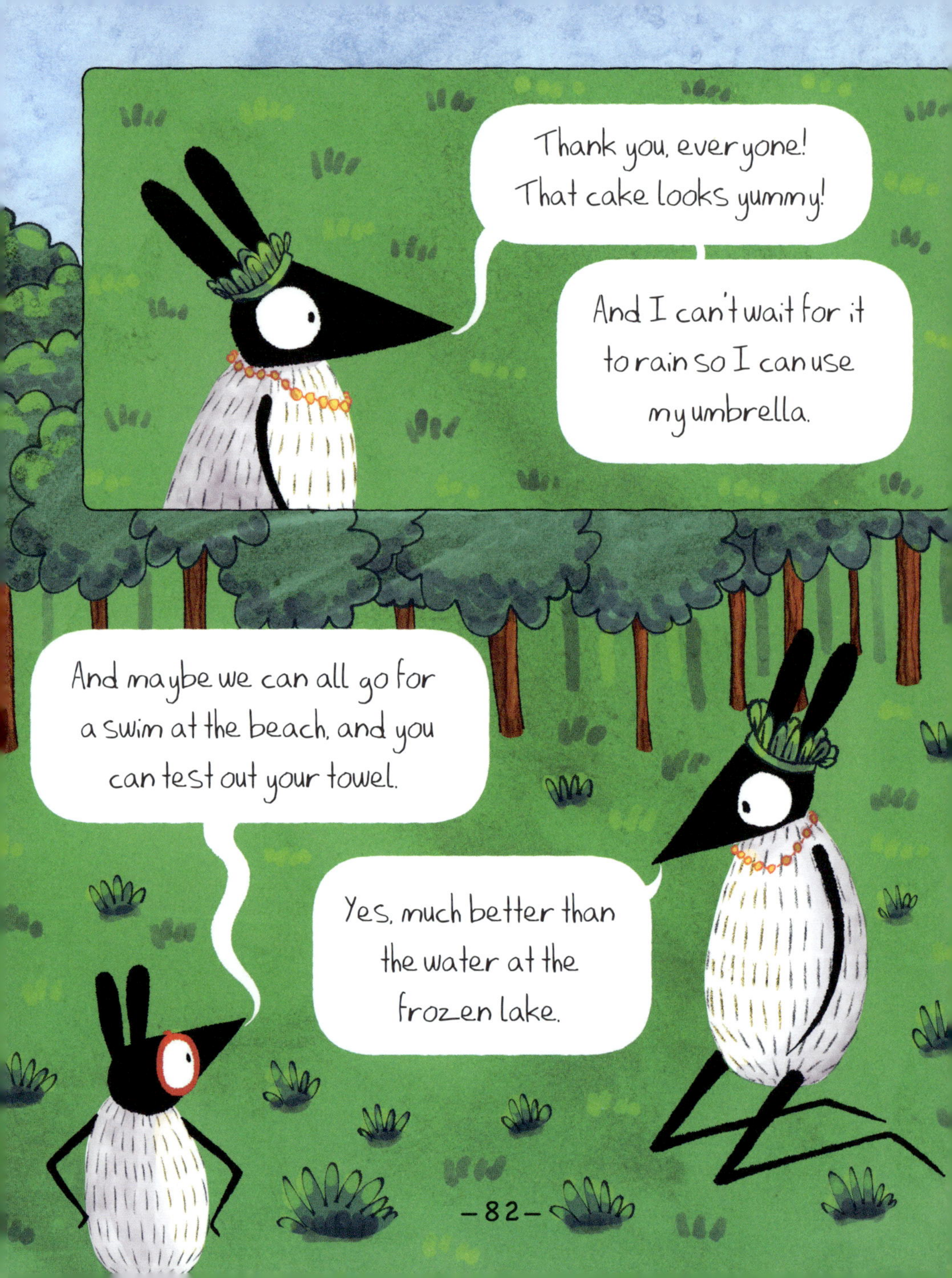
Thank you, everyone! That cake looks yummy!
And I can't wait for it to rain so I can use my umbrella.
And maybe we can all go for a swim at the beach, and you can test out your towel.
Yes, much better than the water at the frozen lake.

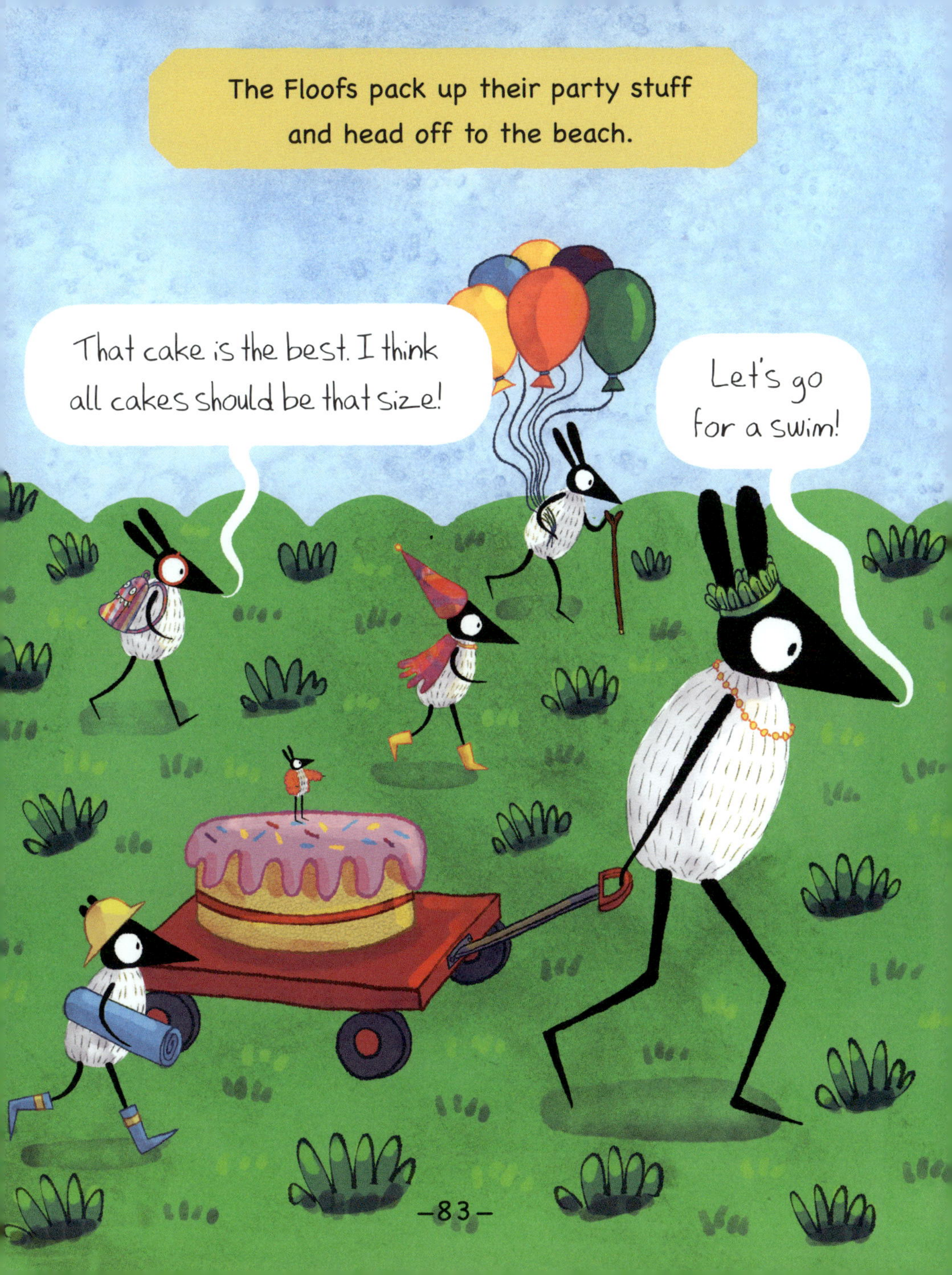
The Floofs pack up their party stuff and head off to the beach.
That cake is the best. I think all cakes should be that size!
Let's go for a swim!

The sun is blazing, so the Floofs can't wait to go for a swim in the ocean.

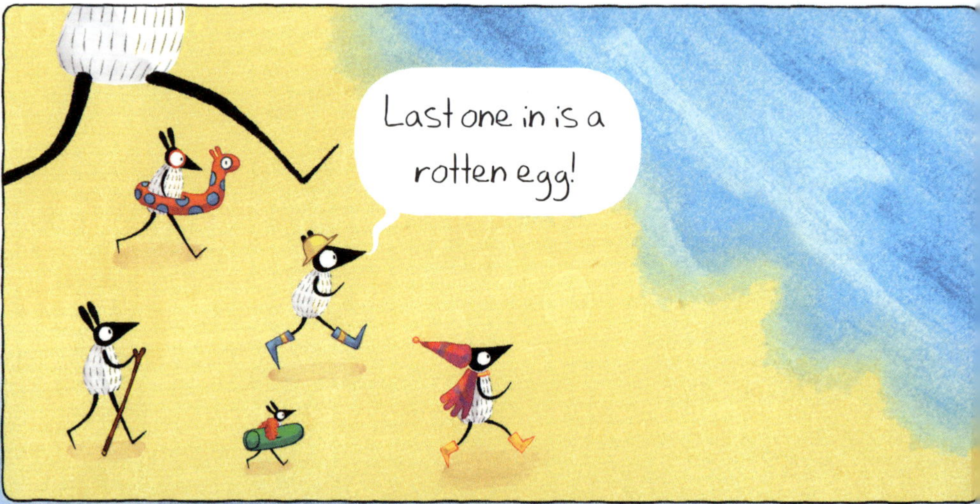
Last one in is a rotten egg!

All the Floofs run to the sea, and Anise is the rotten egg.

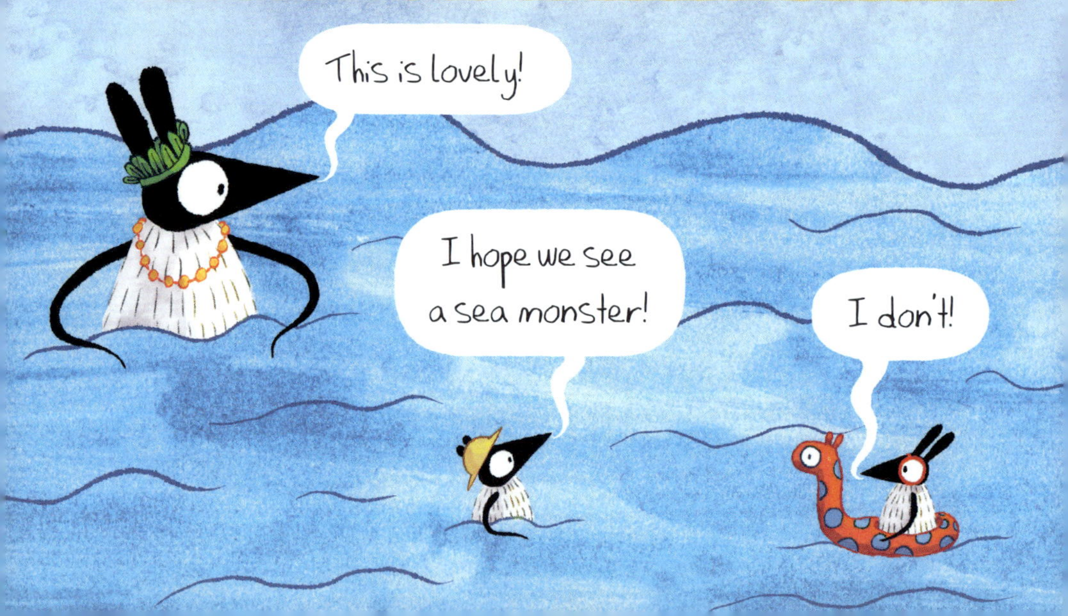
This is lovely!
I hope we see a sea monster!
I don't!

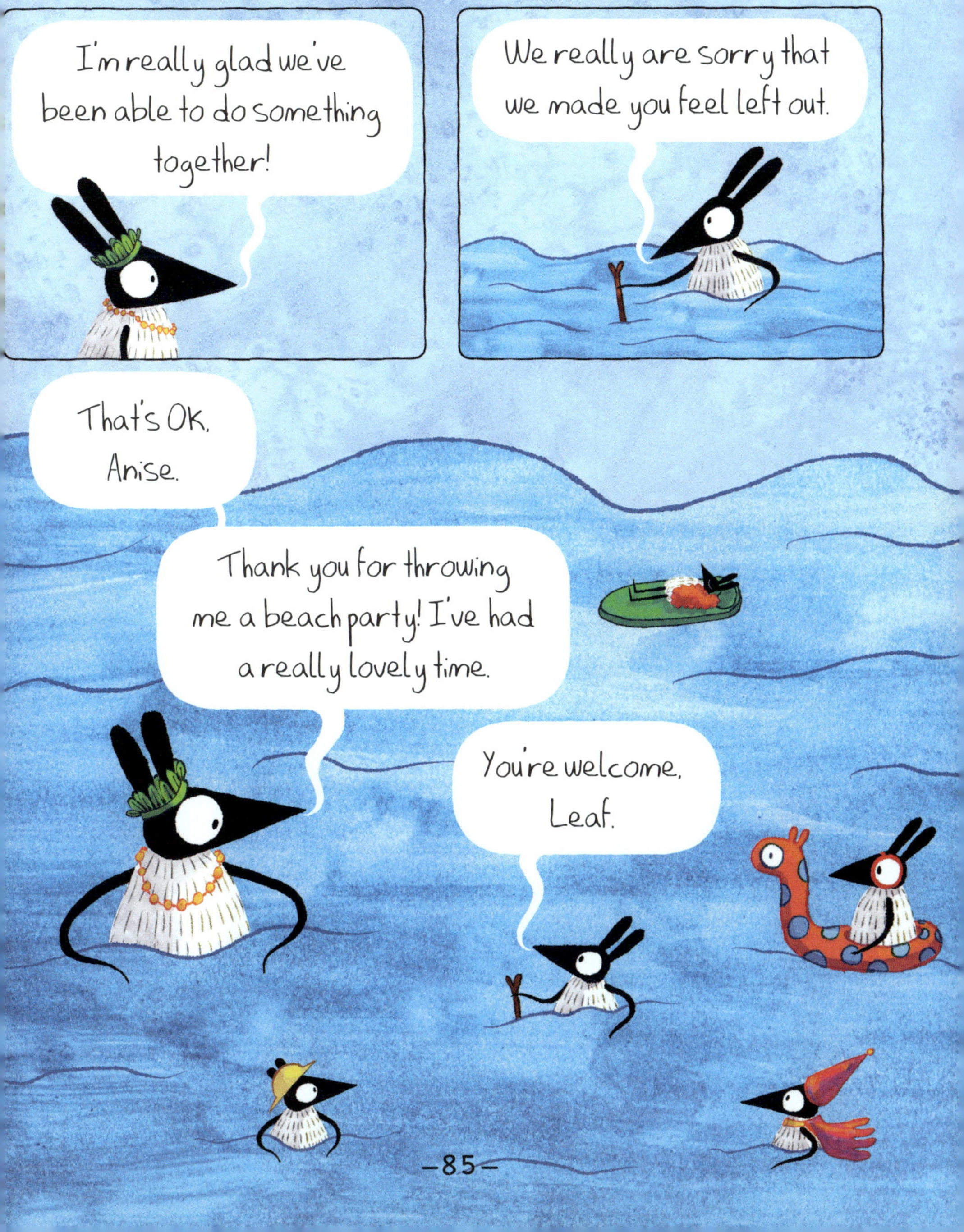
I'm really glad we've been able to do something together!
We really are sorry that we made you feel left out.
That's OK, Anise.
Thank you for throwing me a beach party! I've had a really lovely time.
You're welcome, Leaf.

The Floofs sit together on the beach, enjoying their giant cake and swimming in the sea. Leaf realizes that he doesn't need to be the same size as his friends, and the other Floofs learn that it's important to make sure Leaf feels included. Their friendship is special because of how wonderfully unique they all are.

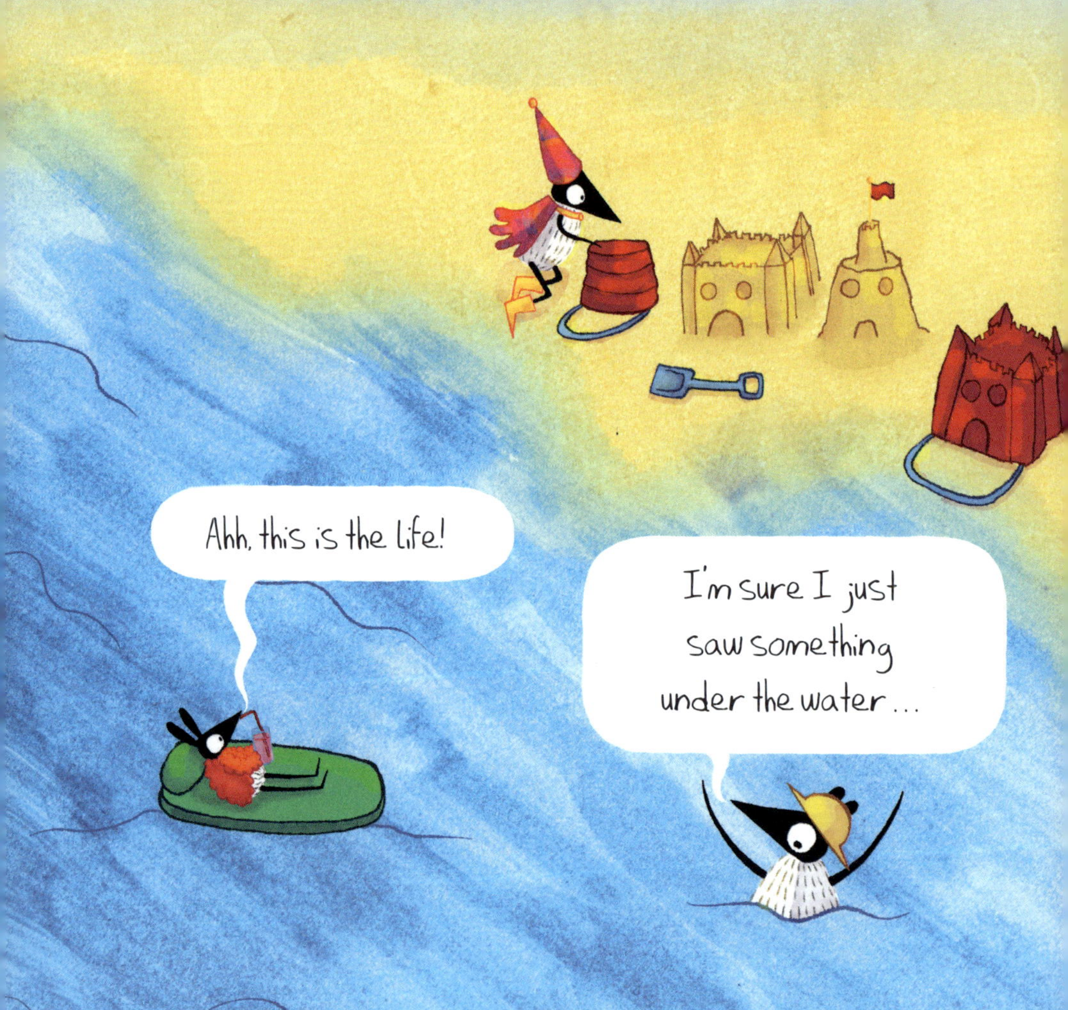
Ahh, this is the life!
I'm sure I just saw something under the water...

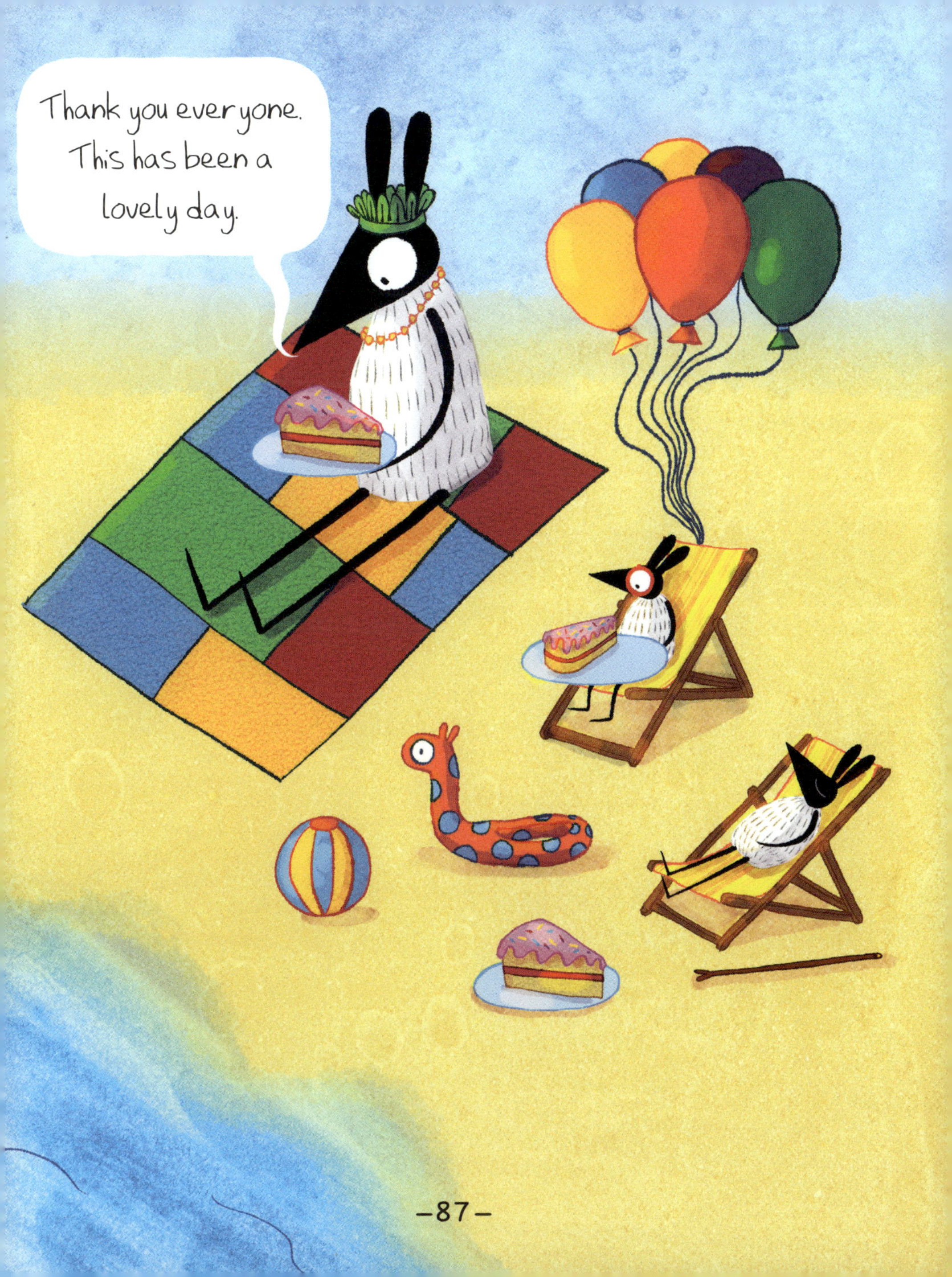
Thank you everyone. This has been a lovely day.

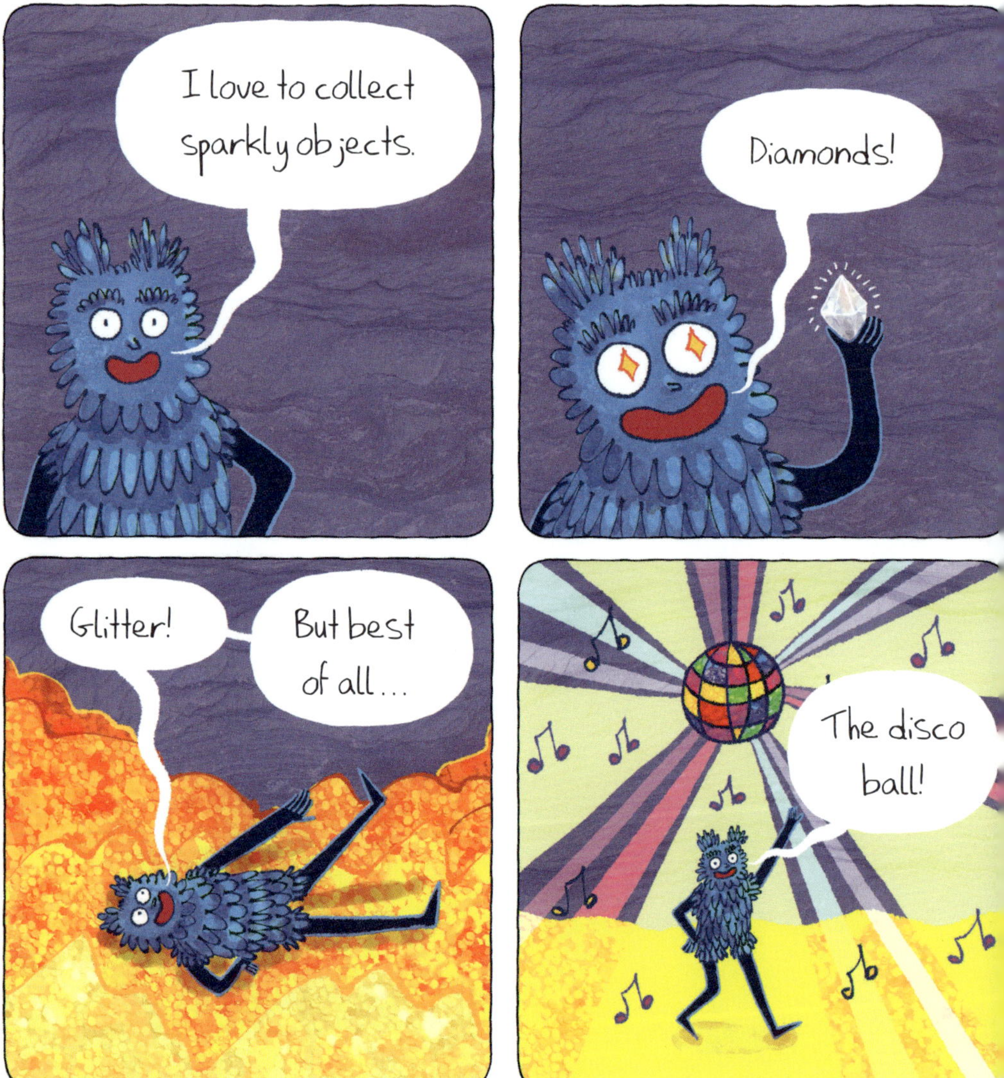
I love to collect sparkly objects.
Diamonds!
Glitter!
But best of all...
The disco ball!

FLOOF
AND THE GIANT

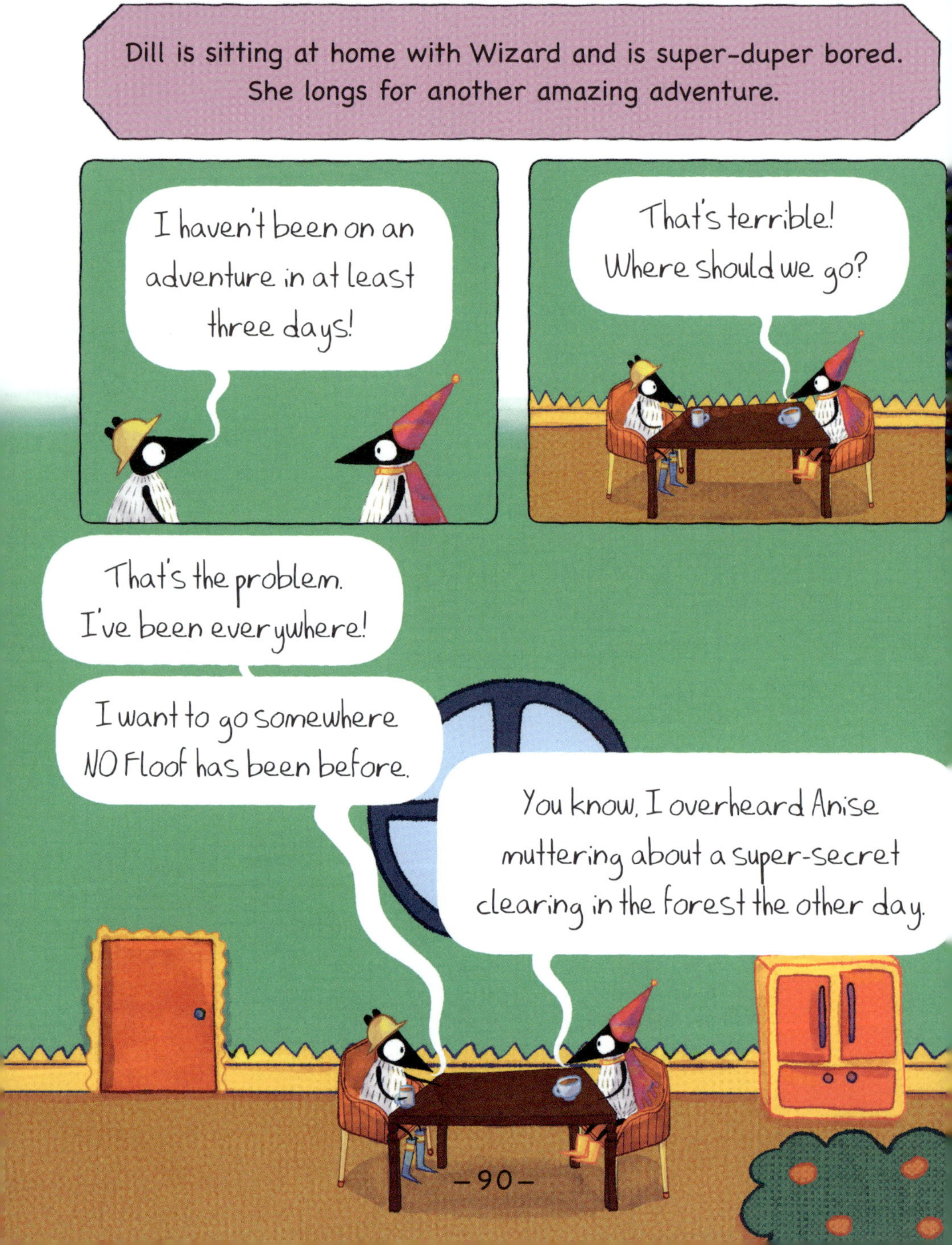
Dill is sitting at home with Wizard and is super-duper bored. She longs for another amazing adventure.
I haven't been on an adventure in at least three days!
That's terrible! Where should we go?
That's the problem. I've been everywhere!
I want to go somewhere NO Floof has been before.
You know, I overheard Anise muttering about a super-secret clearing in the forest the other day.

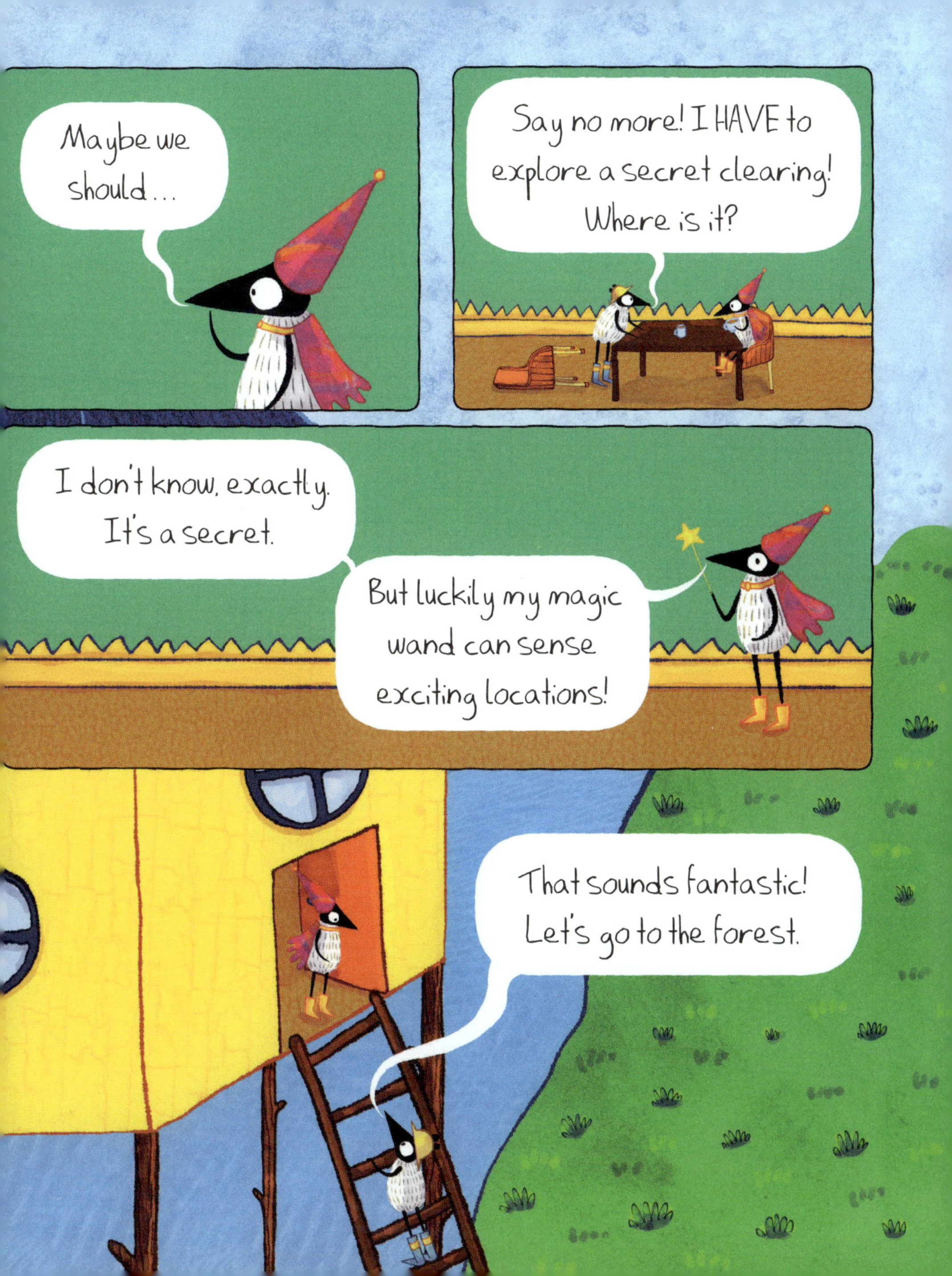
Maybe we should...
Say no more! I HAVE to explore a secret clearing! Where is it?
I don't know, exactly. It's a secret.
But luckily my magic wand can sense exciting locations!
That sounds fantastic! Let's go to the forest.

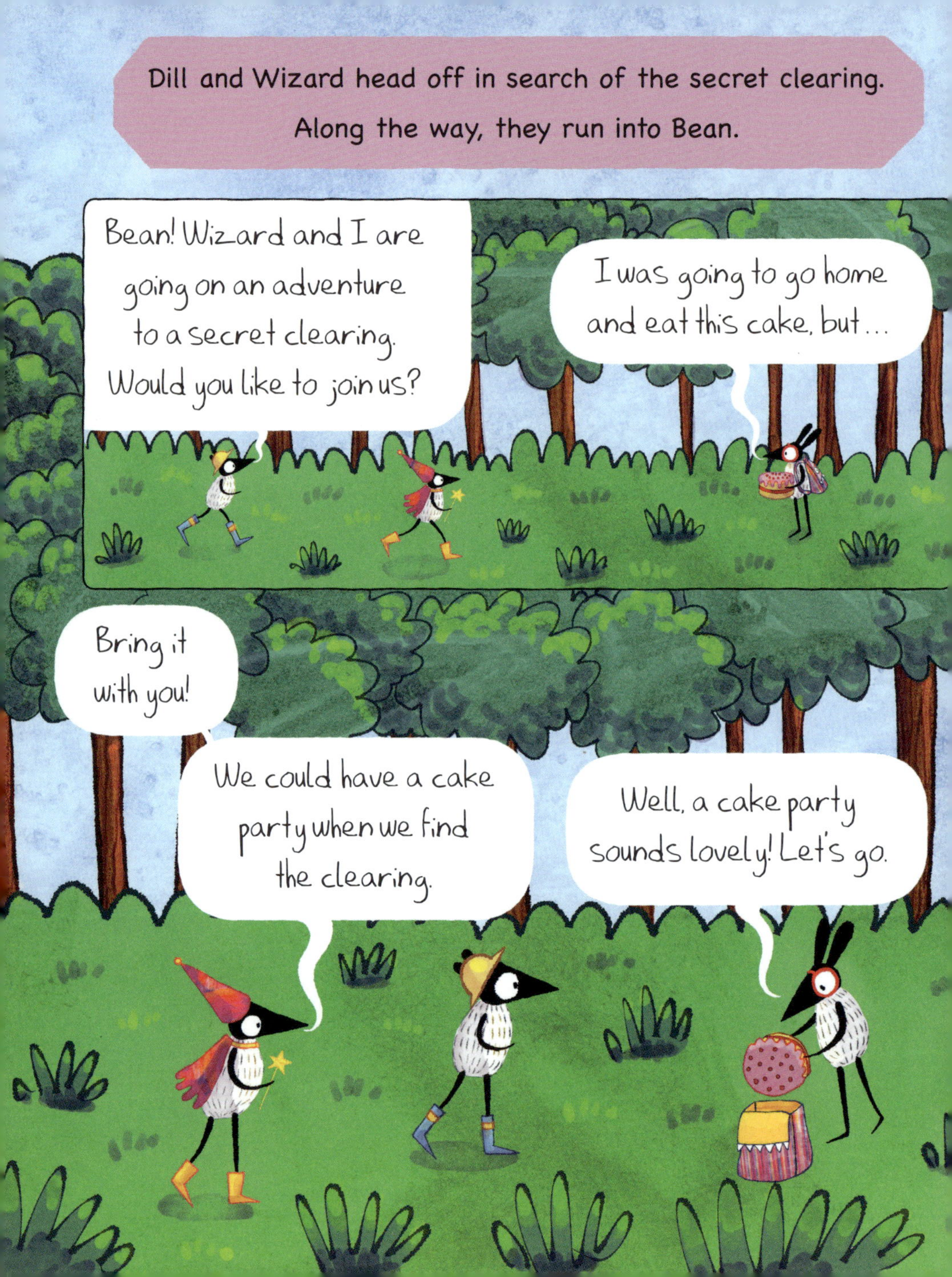
Dill and Wizard head off in search of the secret clearing. Along the way, they run into Bean.
Bean! Wizard and I are going on an adventure to a secret clearing. Would you like to join us?
I was going to go home and eat this cake, but...
Bring it with you!
We could have a cake party when we find the clearing.
Well, a cake party sounds lovely! Let's go.

Dill, Wizard, and Bean continue to the forest. Before long, with the help of Wizard's wand, they discover the secret clearing. It is surrounded by large trees and flowers of different colors, and dancing in the sunlight are all kinds of magical animals.

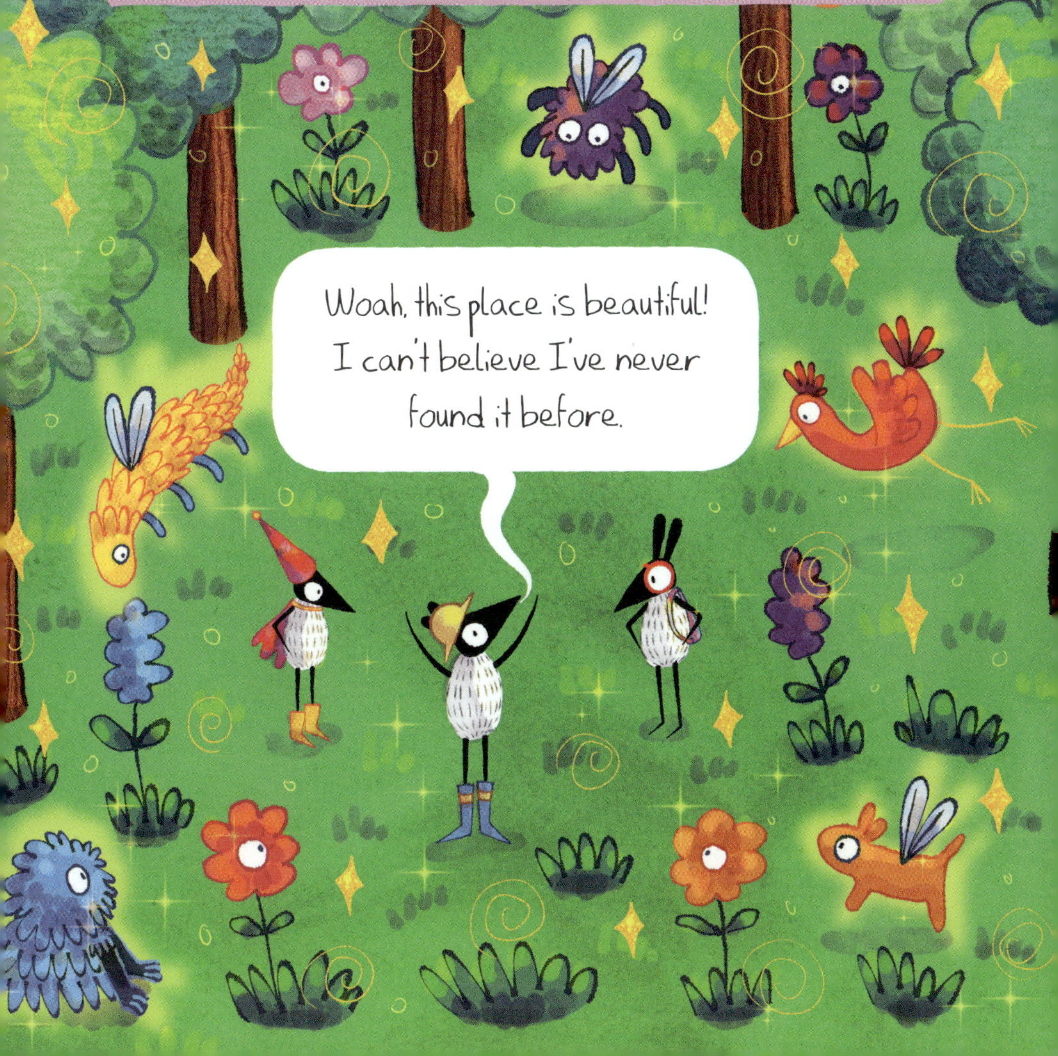
Woah, this place is beautiful! I can't believe I've never found it before.

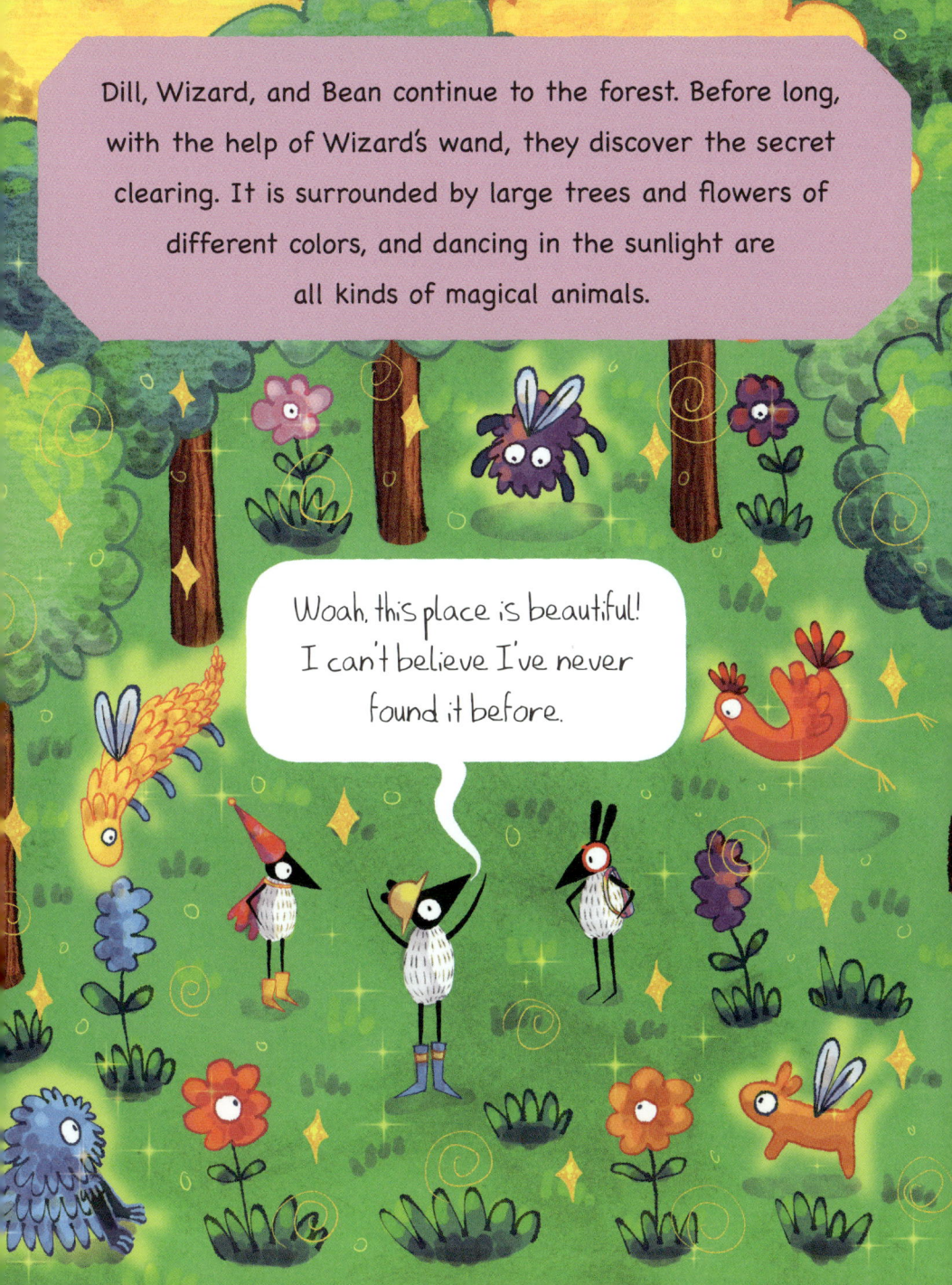

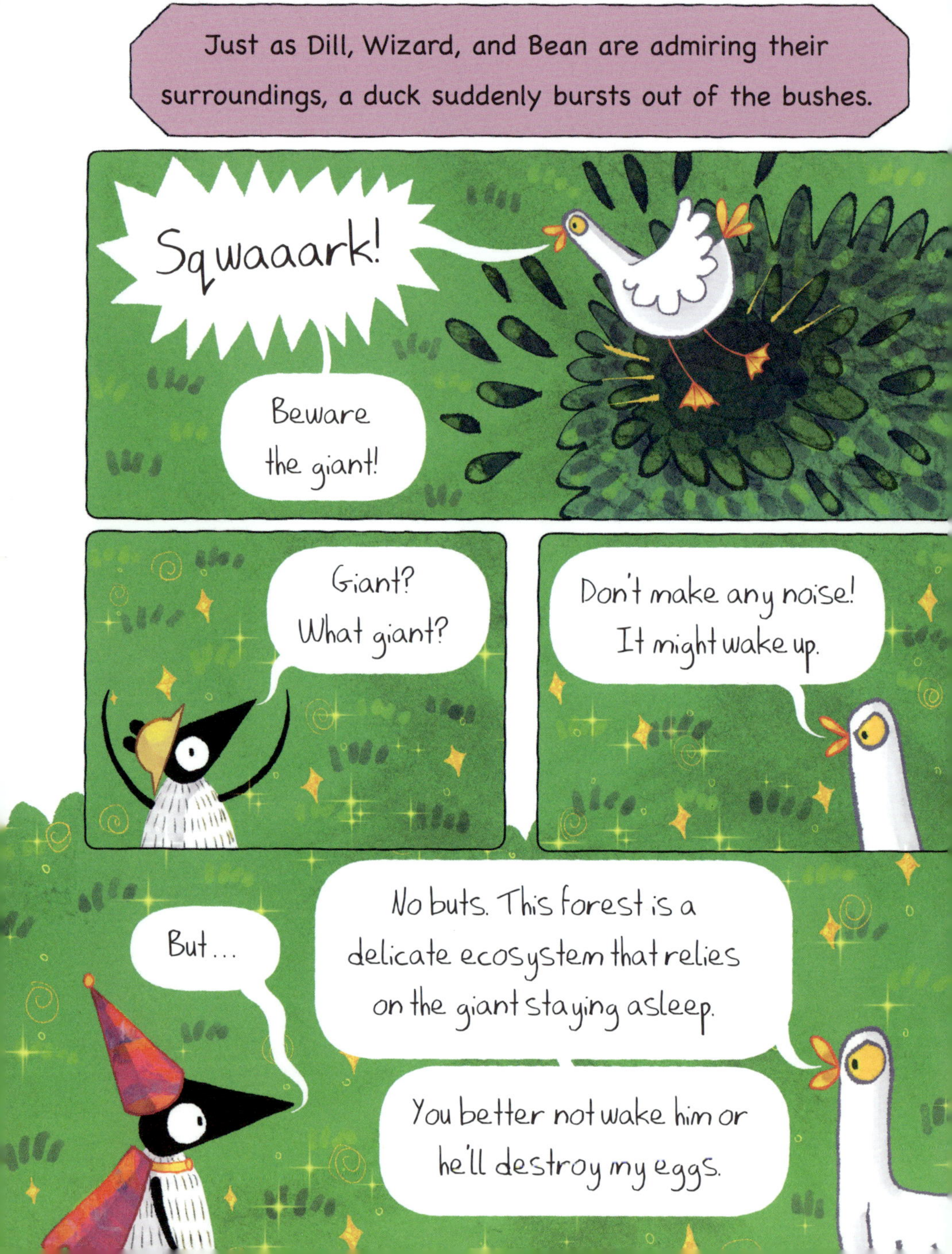
Just as Dill, Wizard, and Bean are admiring their surroundings, a duck suddenly bursts out of the bushes.
Squaaark!
Beware the giant!
Giant? What giant?
Don't make any noise! It might wake up.
But...
No buts. This forest is a delicate ecosystem that relies on the giant staying asleep.
You better not wake him or he'll destroy my eggs.

And with a flap of its wings, the duck flies away.

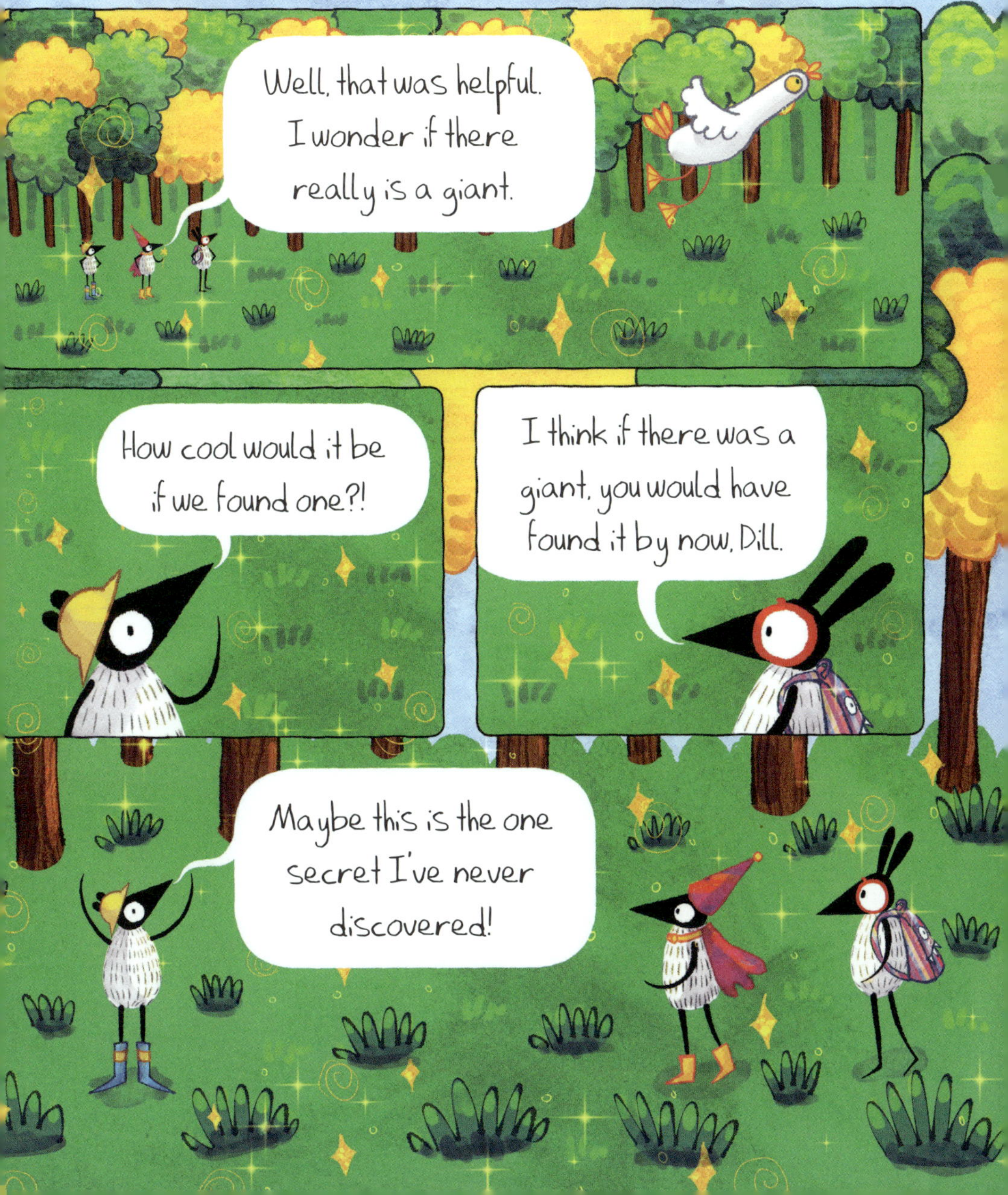
Well, that was helpful. I wonder if there really is a giant.
How cool would it be if we found one?!
I think if there was a giant, you would have found it by now, Dill.
Maybe this is the one secret I've never discovered!

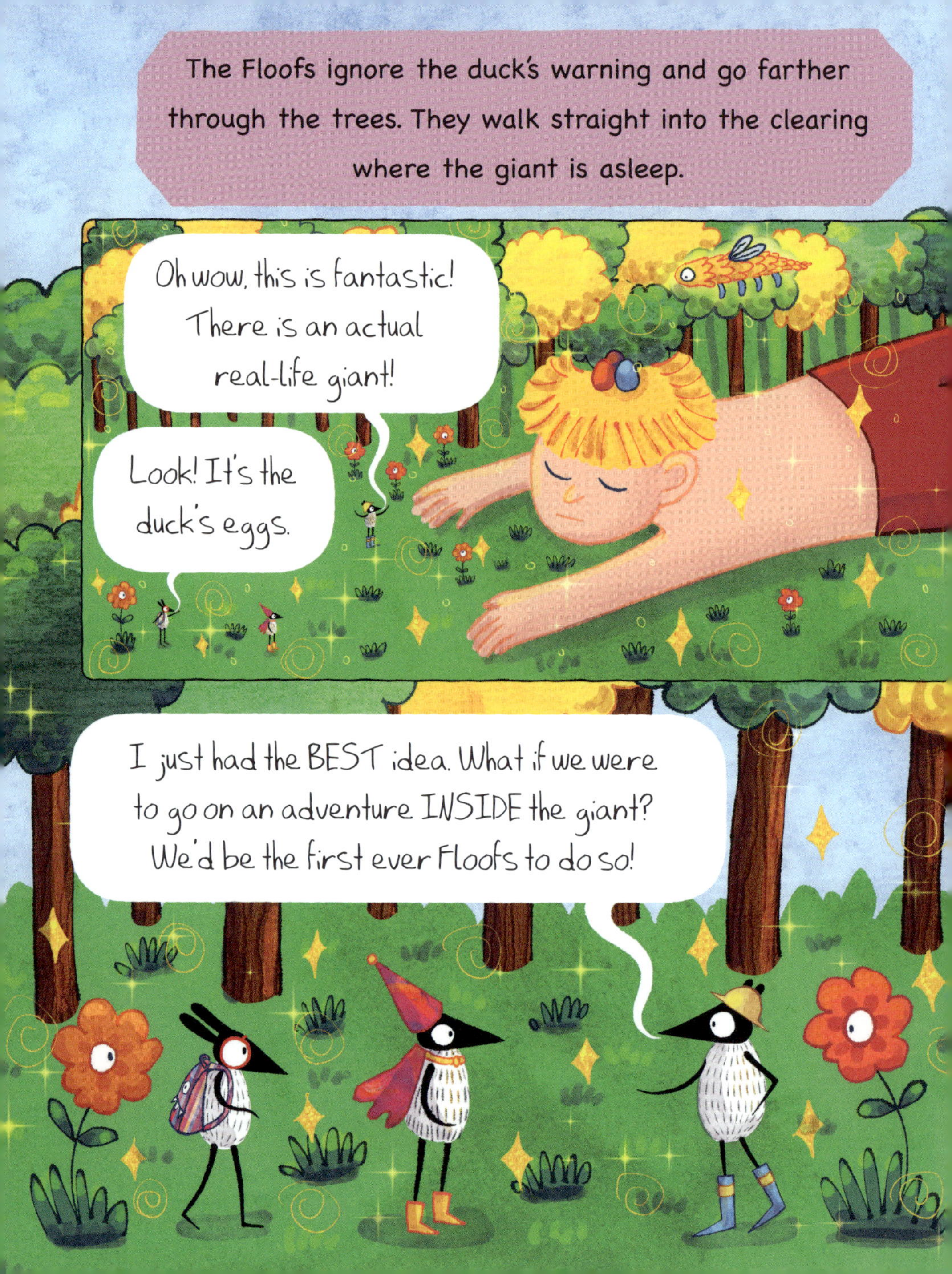
The Floofs ignore the duck's warning and go farther through the trees. They walk straight into the clearing where the giant is asleep.
Oh wow, this is fantastic! There is an actual real-life giant!
Look! It's the duck's eggs.
I just had the BEST idea. What if we were to go on an adventure INSIDE the giant? We'd be the first ever Floofs to do so!

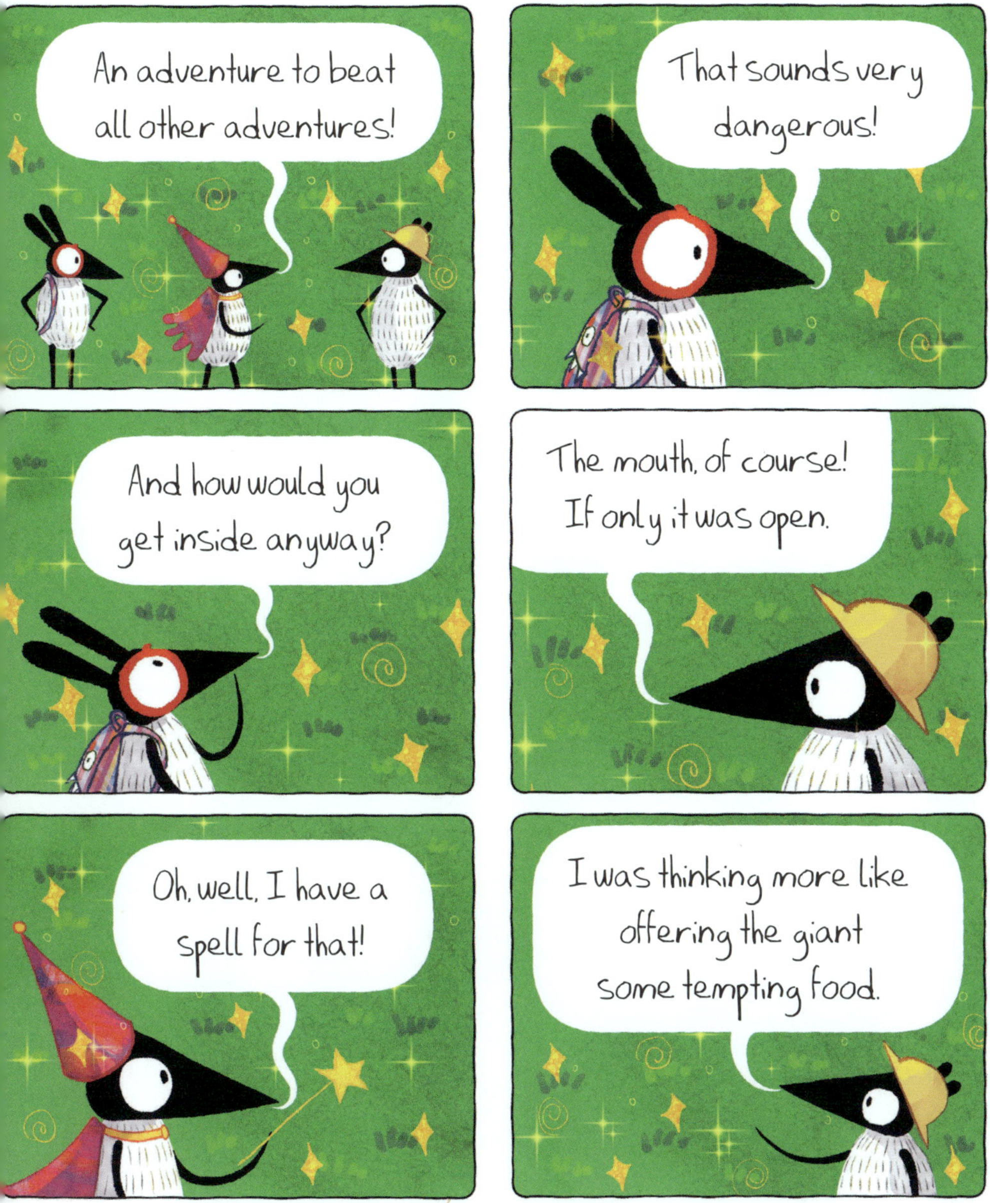
An adventure to beat all other adventures!
That sounds very dangerous!
And how would you get inside anyway?
The mouth, of course! If only it was open.
Oh, well, I have a spell for that!
I was thinking more like offering the giant some tempting food.

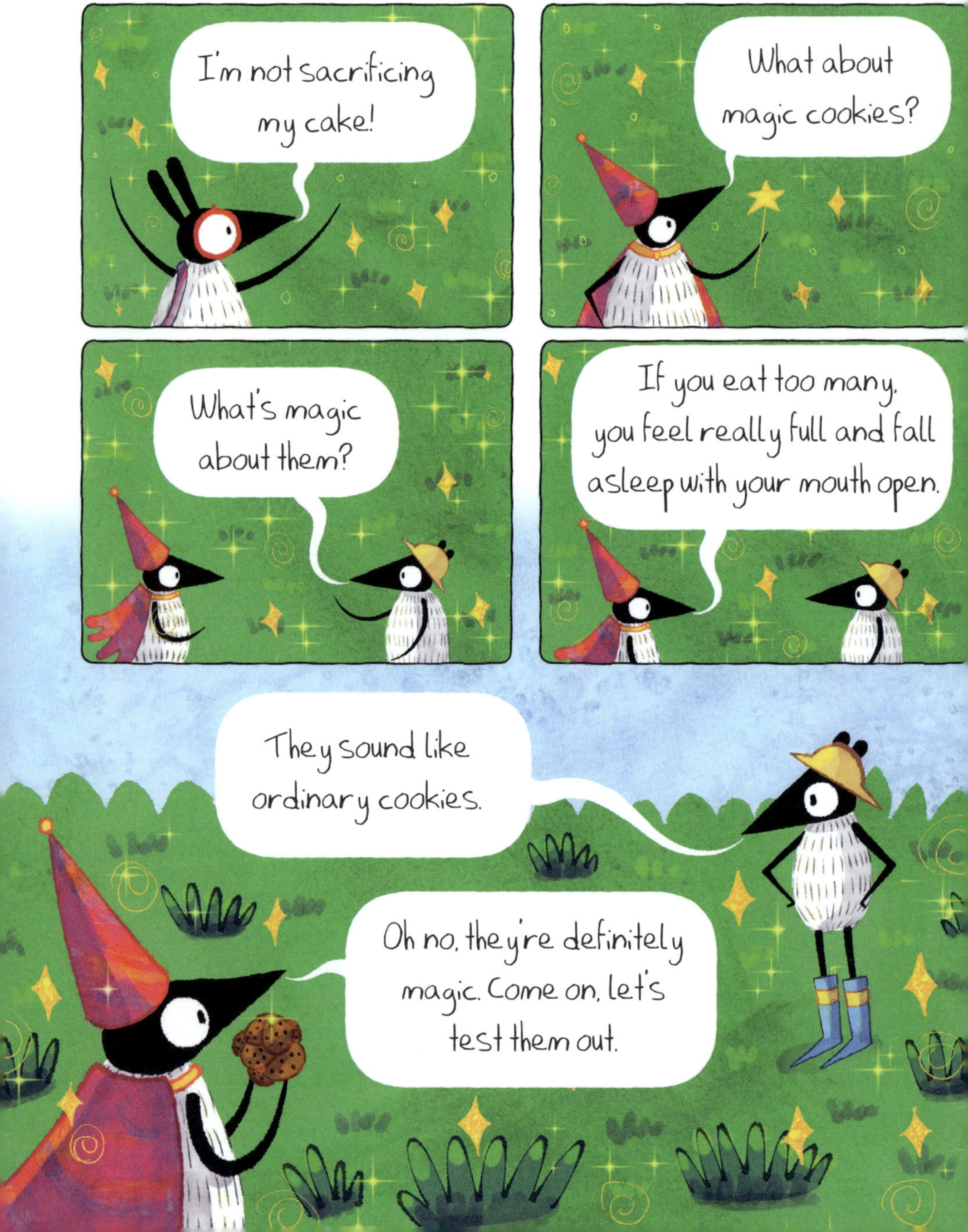
I'm not sacrificing my cake!
What about magic cookies?
What's magic about them?
If you eat too many, you feel really full and fall asleep with your mouth open.
They sound like ordinary cookies.
Oh no, they're definitely magic. Come on, let's test them out.

Wizard waves the cookies in front of the giant. His nose starts to twitch; his lip begins to quiver . . .

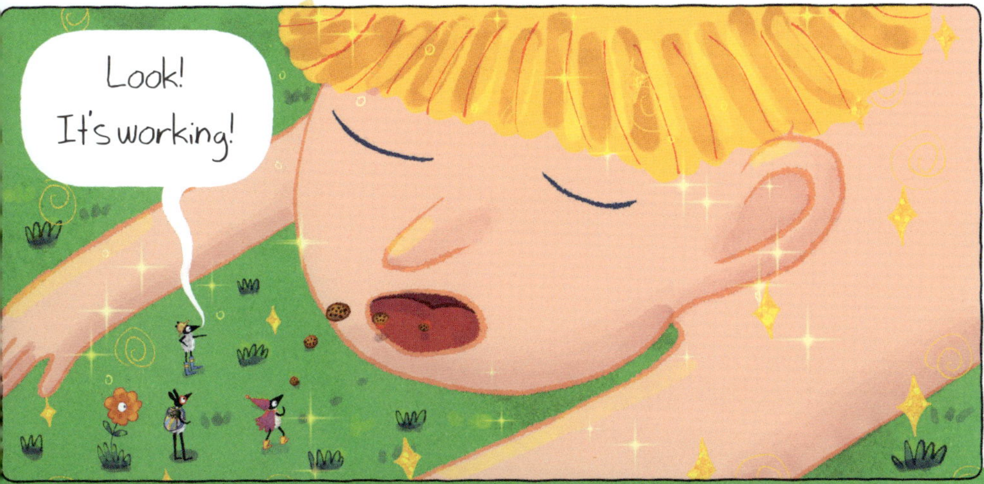
Look! It's working!

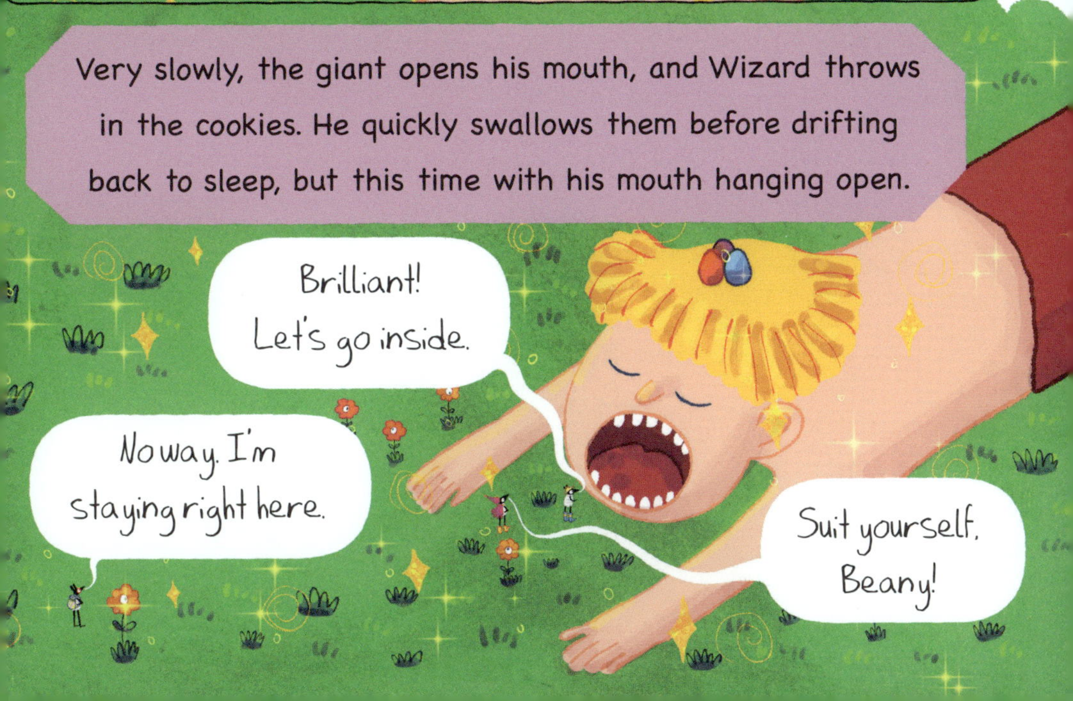
Very slowly, the giant opens his mouth, and Wizard throws in the cookies. He quickly swallows them before drifting back to sleep, but this time with his mouth hanging open.
Brilliant! Let's go inside.
No way. I'm staying right here.
Suit yourself, Beany!

Dill and Wizard climb inside the giant's mouth, excited about their new adventure. But in all the excitement, they didn't notice that when the giant was disturbed, the flowers in the clearing had began to droop. Maybe the duck was right, and they shouldn't have disturbed the giant.

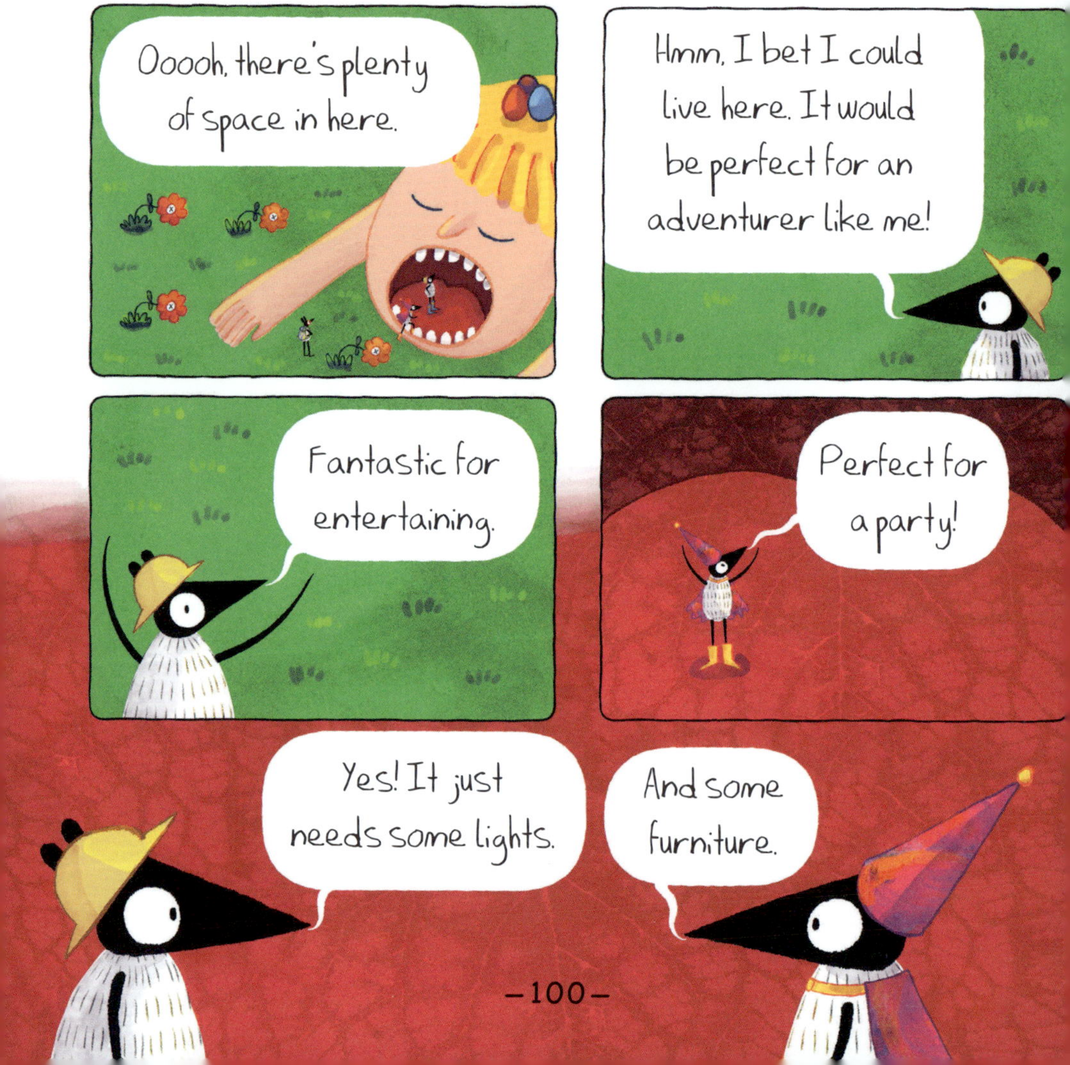

Ooooh, there's plenty of space in here.
Hmm, I bet I could live here. It would be perfect for an adventurer like me!
Fantastic for entertaining.
Perfect for a party!
Yes! It just needs some lights.
And some furniture.

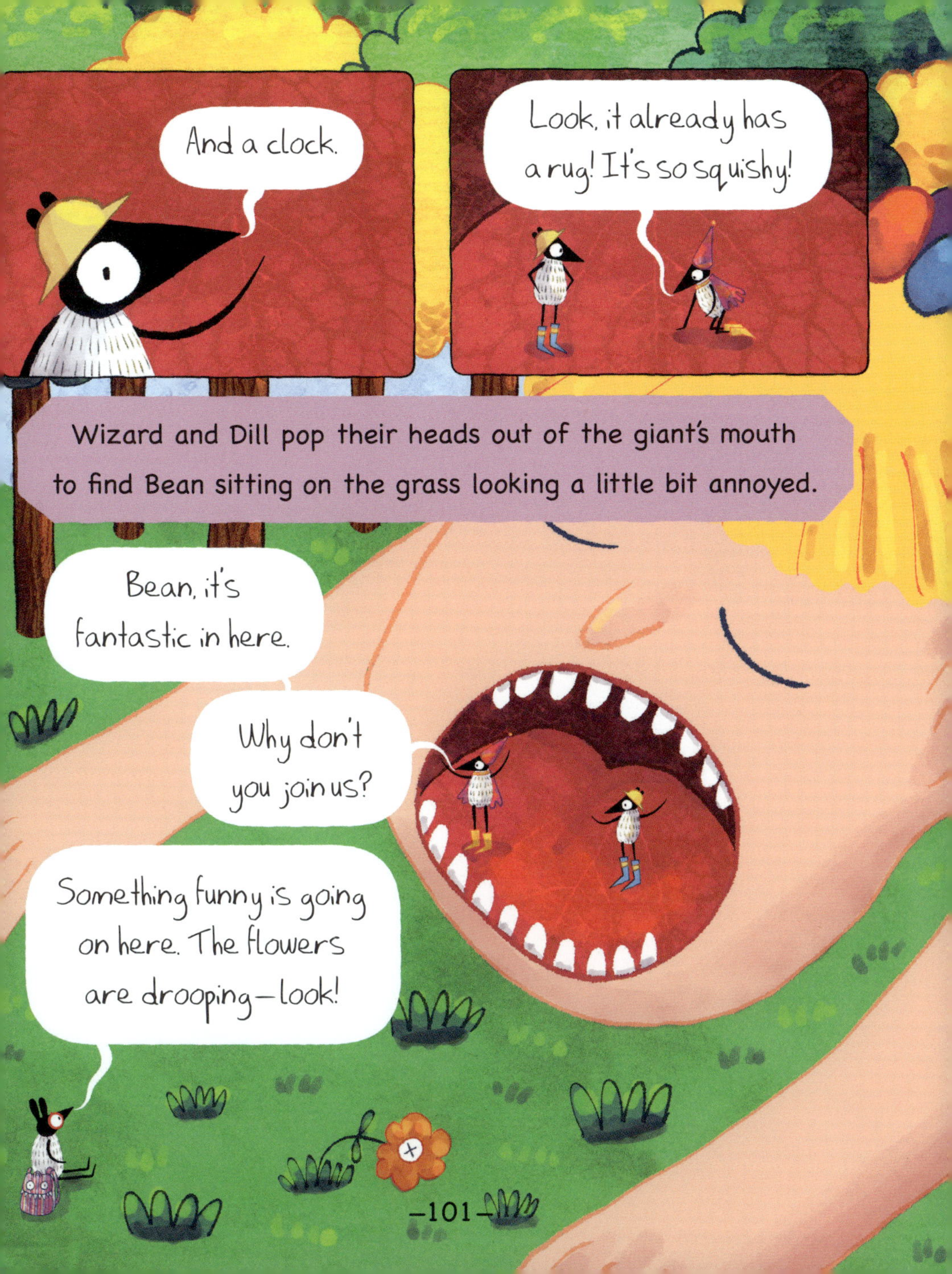
And a clock.
Look, it already has a rug! It's so squishy!
Wizard and Dill pop their heads out of the giant's mouth to find Bean sitting on the grass looking a little bit annoyed.
Bean, it's fantastic in here.
Why don't you join us?
Something funny is going on here. The flowers are drooping—look!

But Dill and Wizard don't listen to Bean.
They are too excited about their discovery.

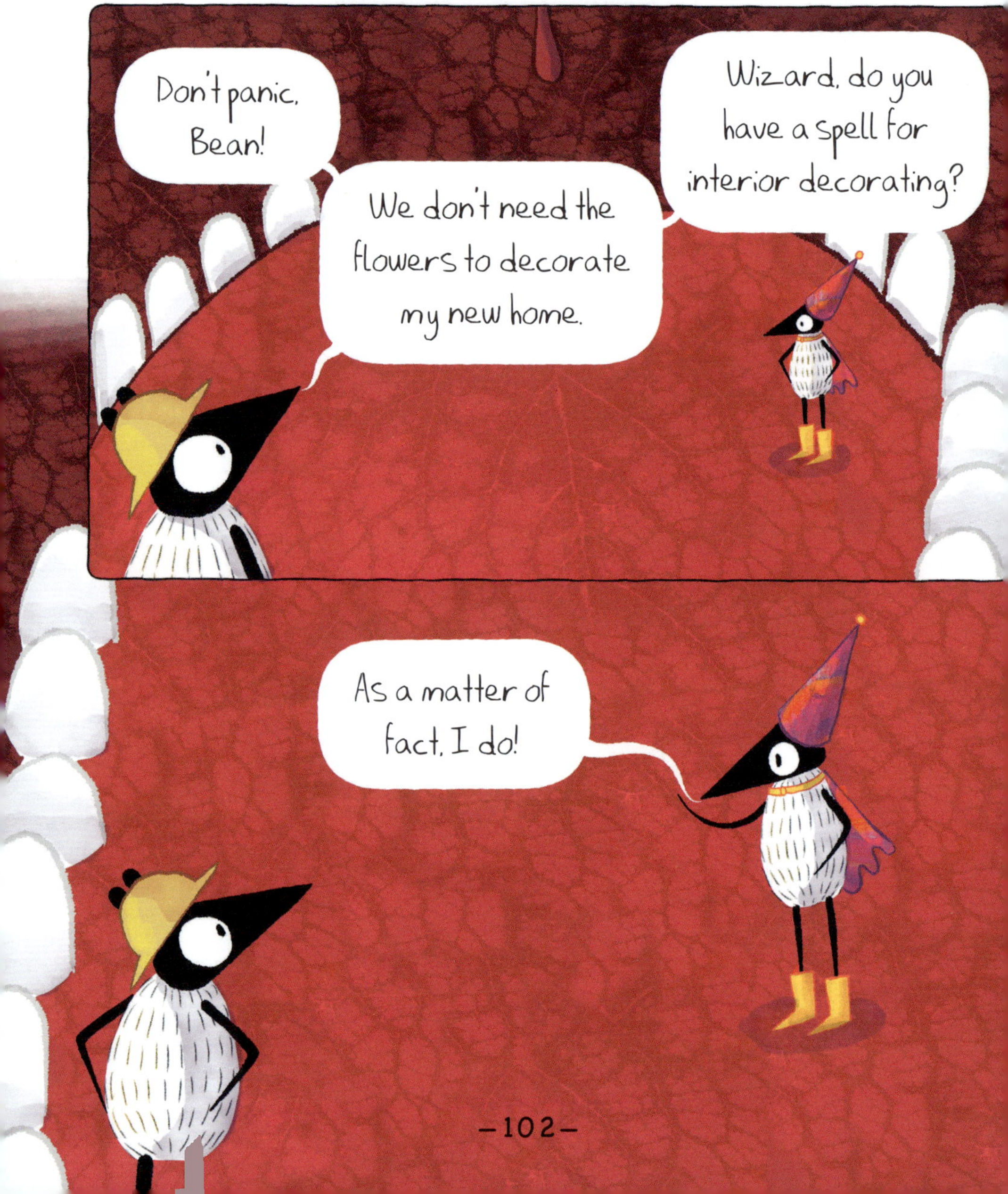
Don't panic, Bean!
We don't need the flowers to decorate my new home.
Wizard, do you have a spell for interior decorating?
As a matter of fact, I do!

Wizard pops outside and starts blasting trees with his wand and turning them into some furniture. He magics a few furry animals into chairs and a lightning bug into the perfect lamp. The clearing is left looking sad and gray. But only Bean has noticed something isn't right.

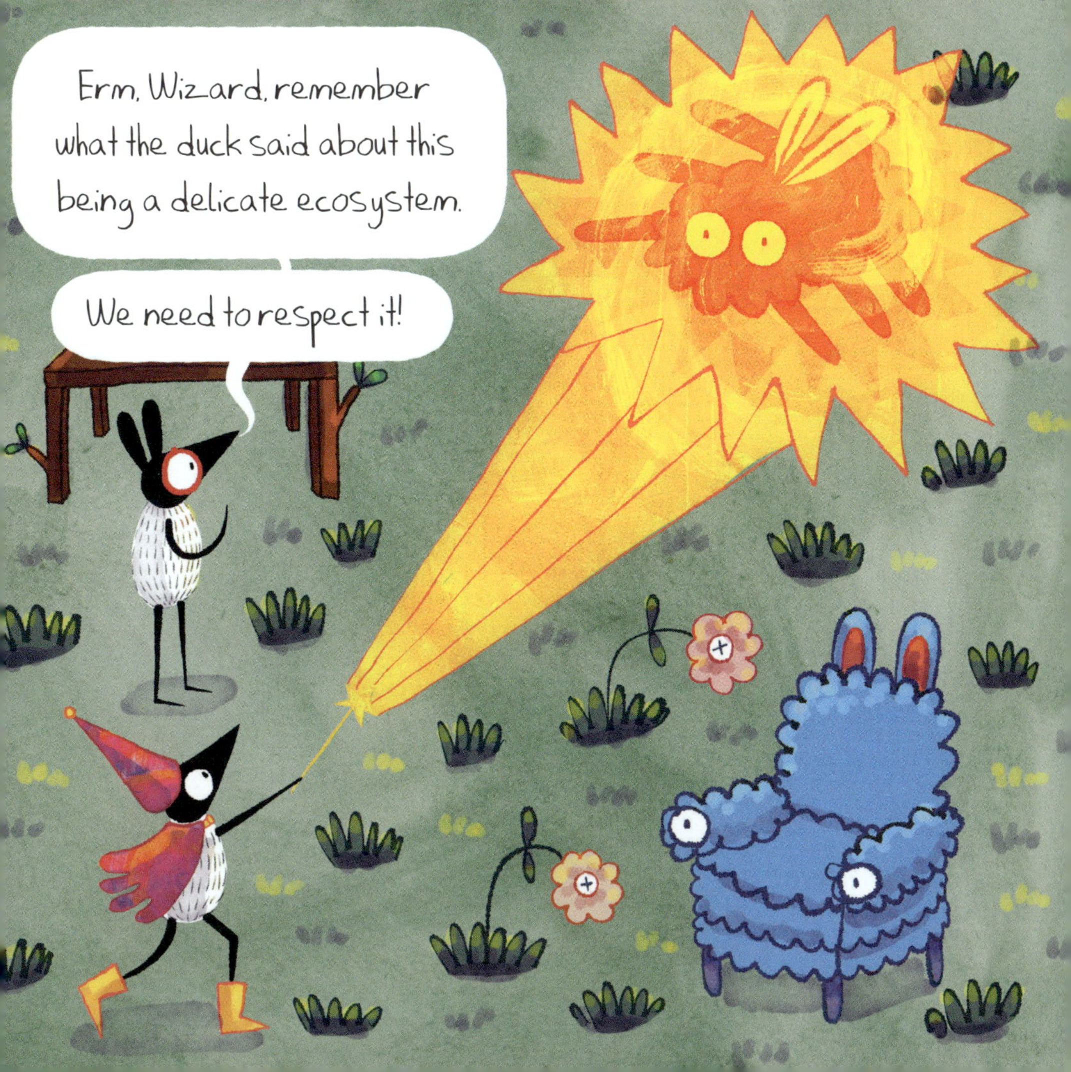
Erm, Wizard, remember what the duck said about this being a delicate ecosystem.
We need to respect it!

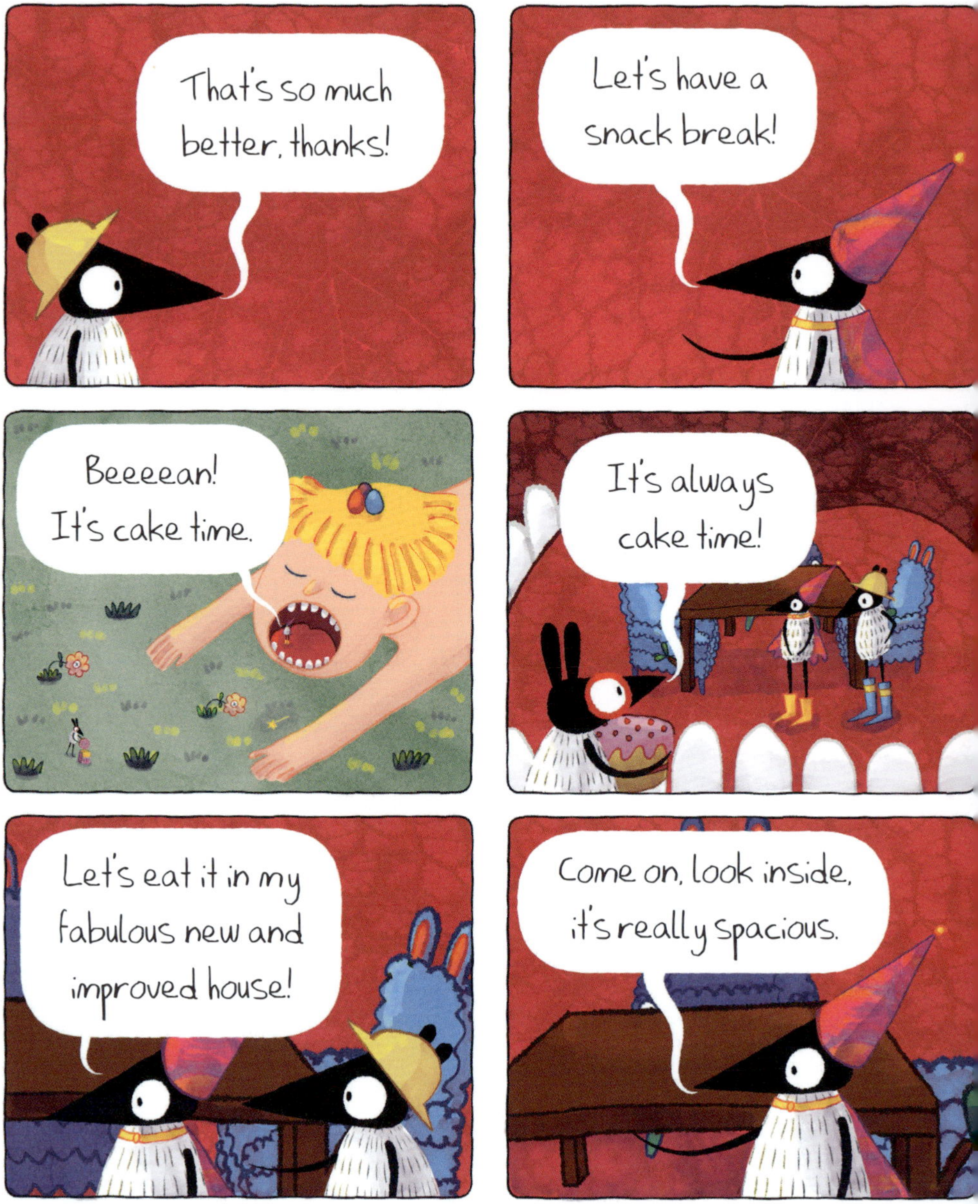
That's so much better, thanks!
Let's have a snack break!
Beeeean! It's cake time.
It's always cake time!
Let's eat it in my fabulous new and improved house!
Come on, look inside, it's really spacious.

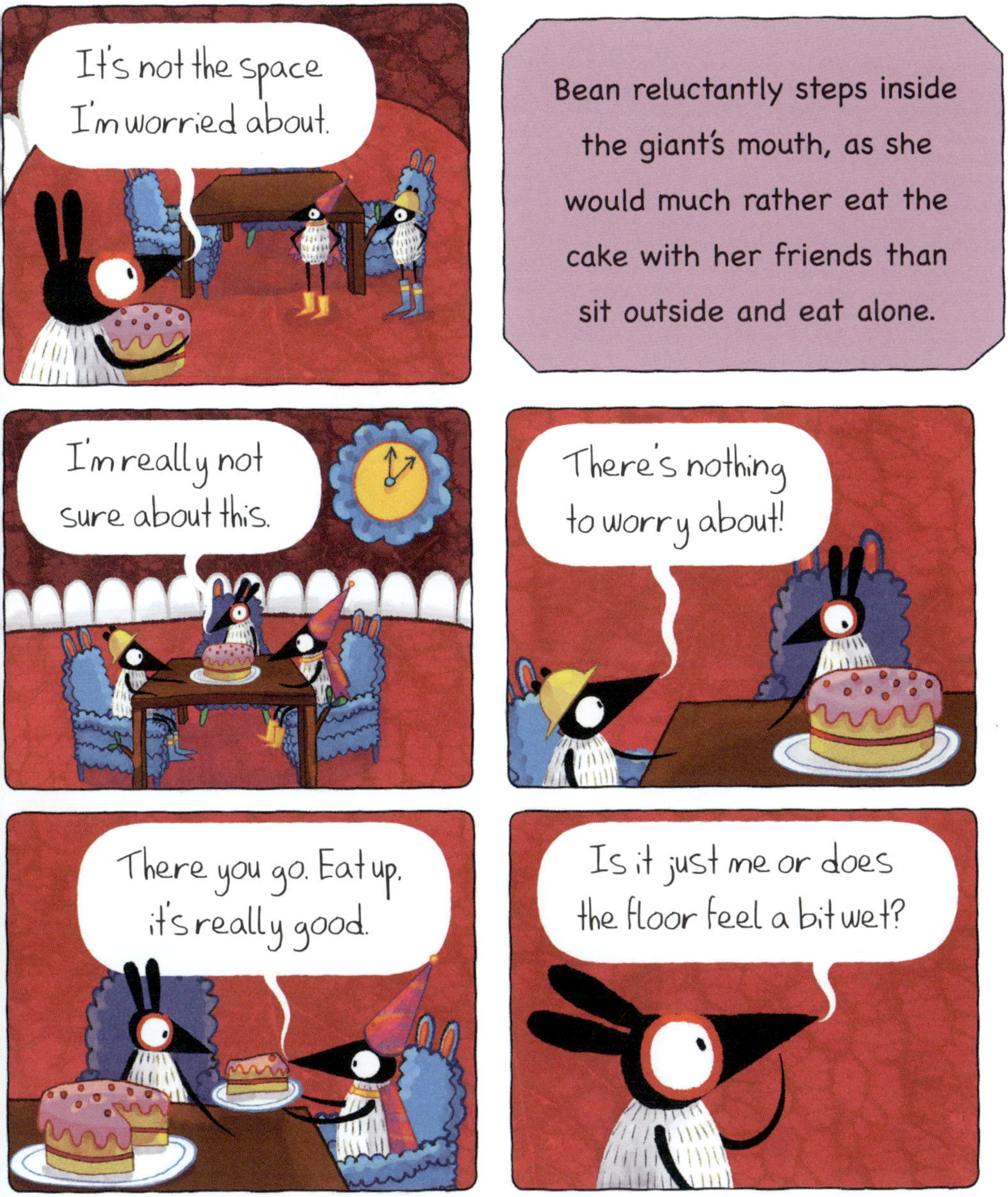
It's not the space I'm worried about.
Bean reluctantly steps inside the giant's mouth, as she would much rather eat the cake with her friends than sit outside and eat alone.
I'm really not sure about this.
There's nothing to worry about!
There you go. Eat up, it's really good.
Is it just me or does the floor feel a bit wet?

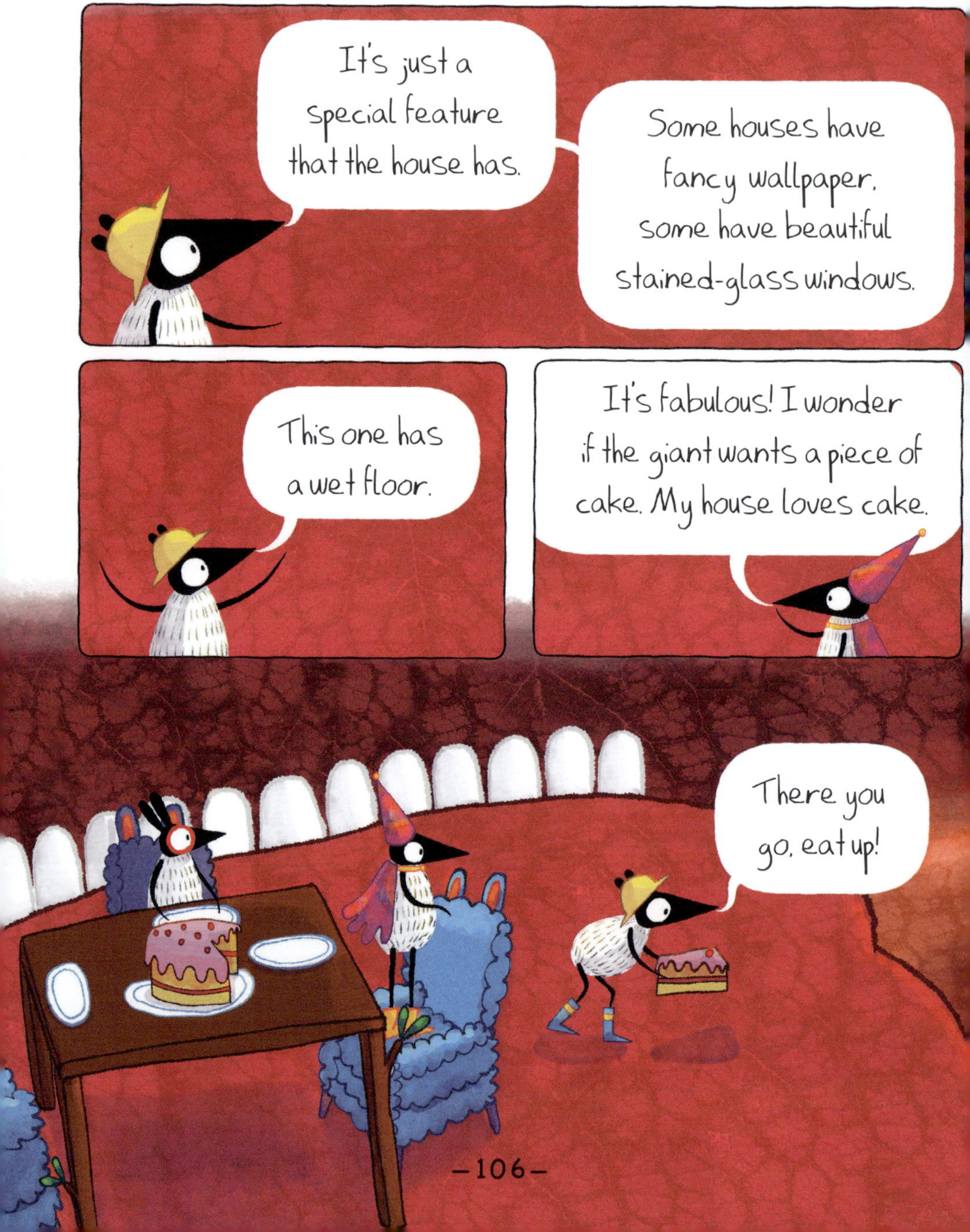
It's just a special feature that the house has.
Some houses have fancy wallpaper, some have beautiful stained-glass windows.
This one has a wet floor.
It's fabulous! I wonder if the giant wants a piece of cake. My house loves cake.
There you go, eat up!

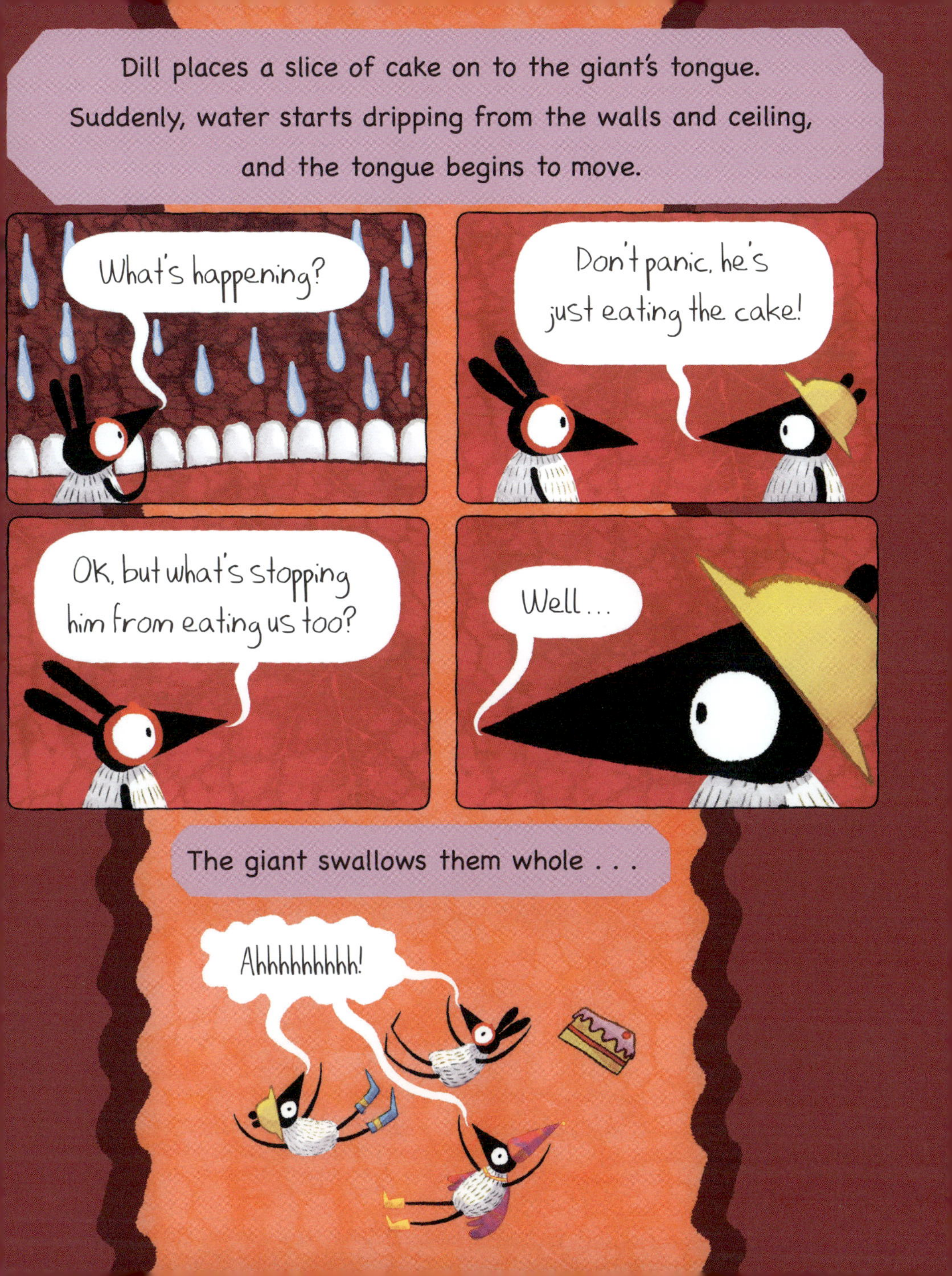
Dill places a slice of cake on to the giant's tongue. Suddenly, water starts dripping from the walls and ceiling, and the tongue begins to move.
What's happening?
Don't panic, he's just eating the cake!
OK, but what's stopping him from eating us too?
Well . . .
The giant swallows them whole . . .
Ahhhhhhhhh!

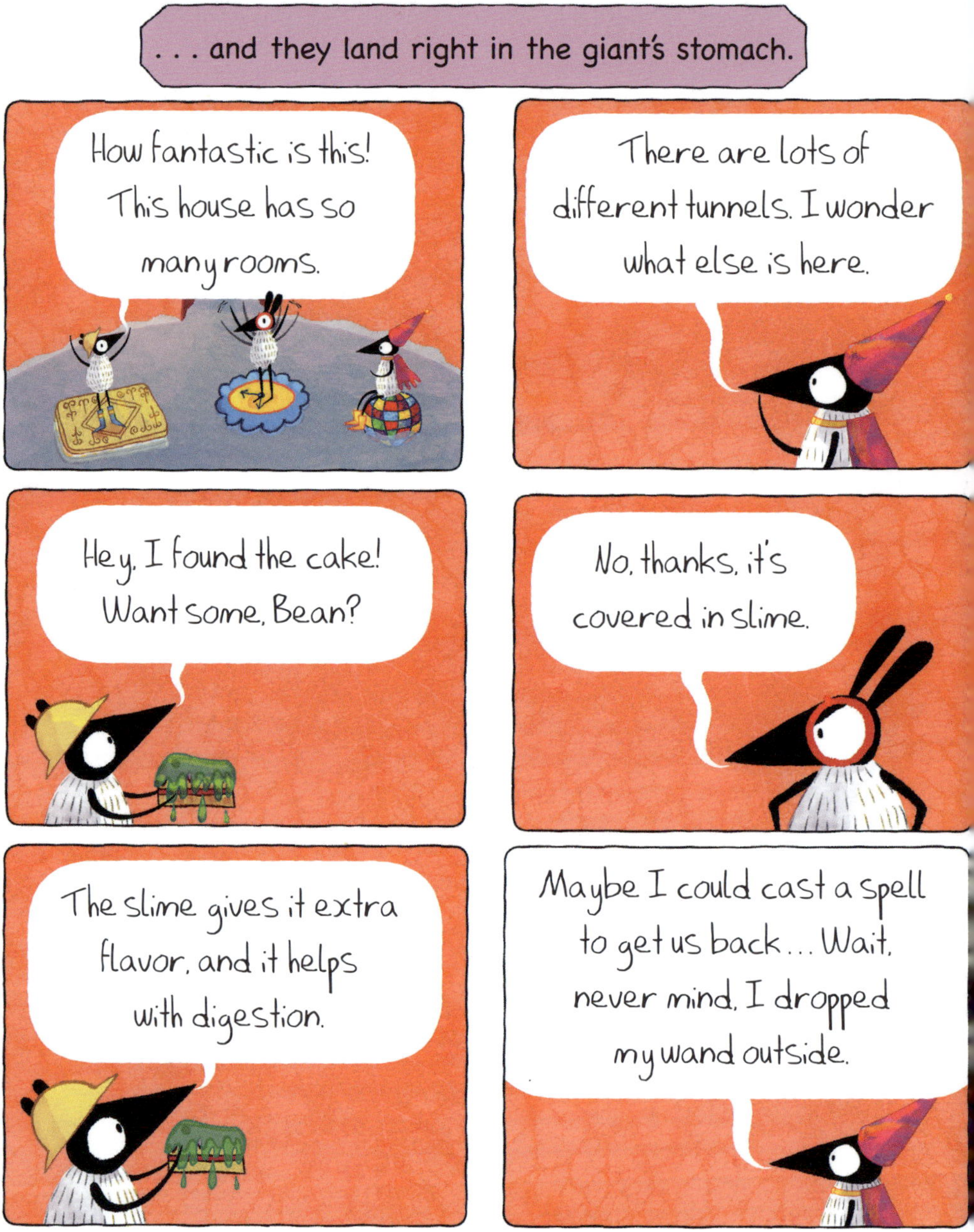
. . . and they land right in the giant's stomach.
How fantastic is this! This house has so many rooms.
There are lots of different tunnels. I wonder what else is here.
Hey, I found the cake! Want some, Bean?
No, thanks, it's covered in slime.
The slime gives it extra flavor, and it helps with digestion.
Maybe I could cast a spell to get us back... Wait, never mind, I dropped my wand outside.

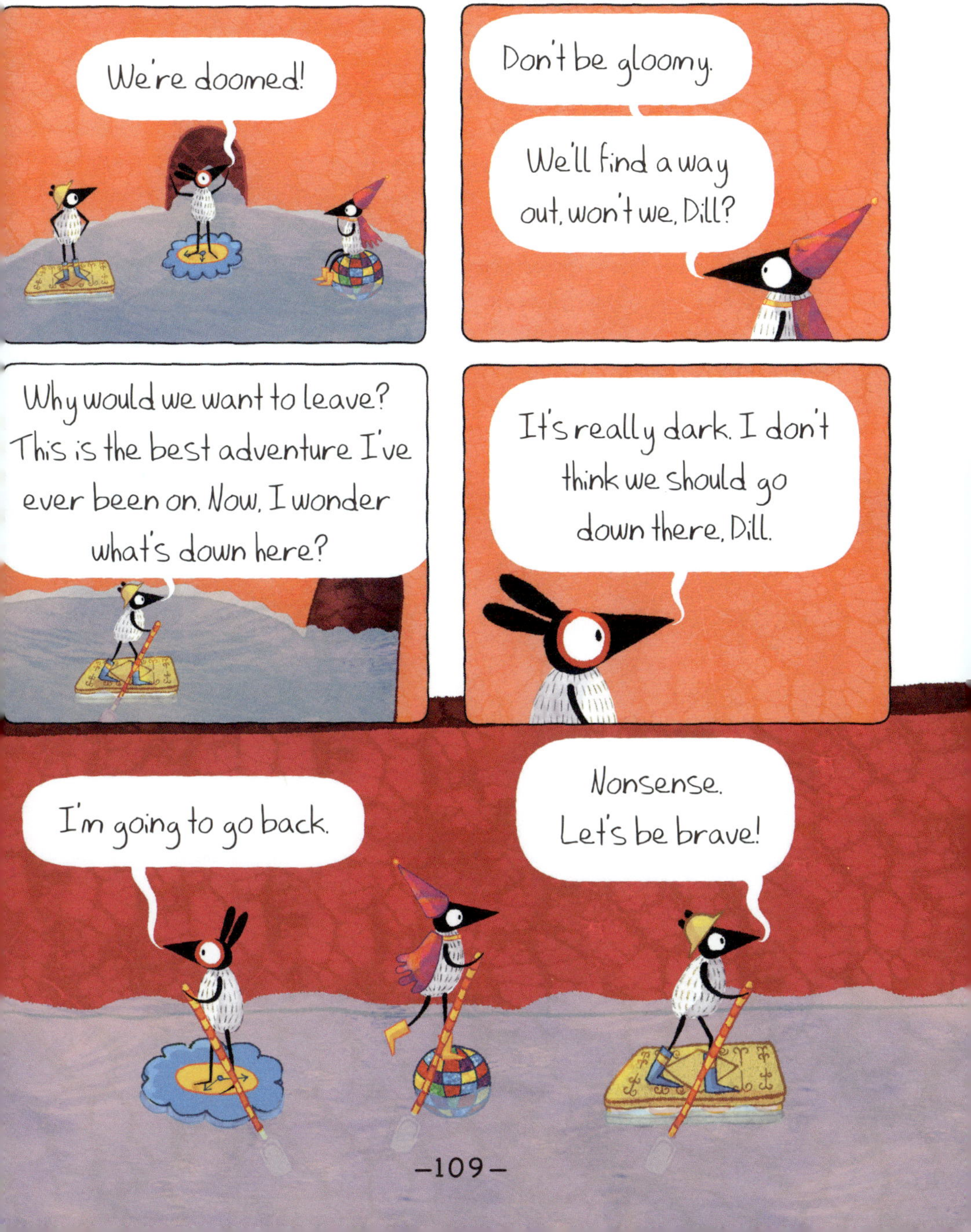
We're doomed!
Don't be gloomy.
We'll find a way out, won't we, Dill?
Why would we want to leave? This is the best adventure I've ever been on. Now, I wonder what's down here?
It's really dark. I don't think we should go down there, Dill.
I'm going to go back.
Nonsense. Let's be brave!

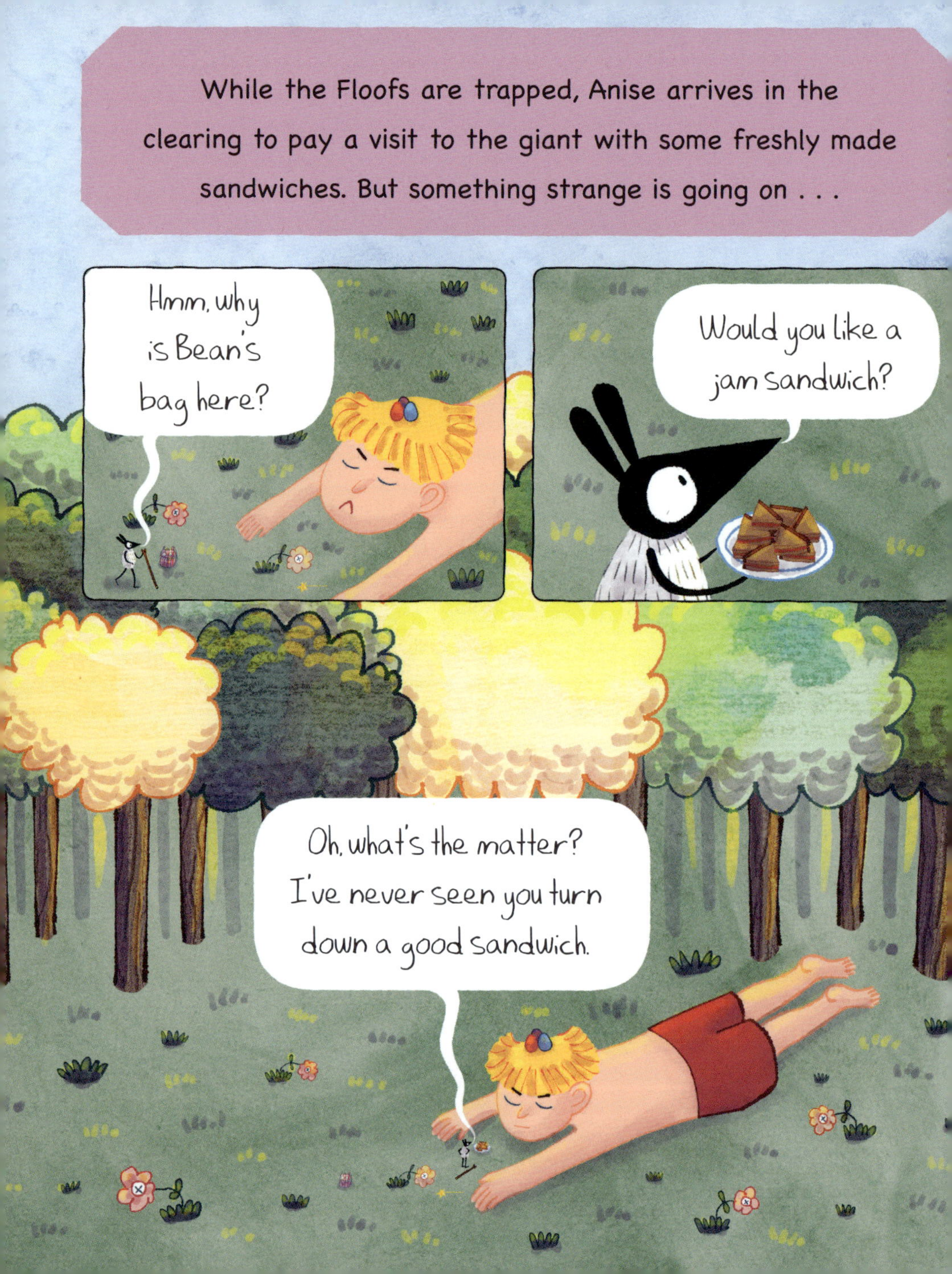
While the Floofs are trapped, Anise arrives in the clearing to pay a visit to the giant with some freshly made sandwiches. But something strange is going on . . .
Hmm, why is Bean's bag here?
Would you like a jam sandwich?
Oh, what's the matter? I've never seen you turn down a good sandwich.

Anise wanders around the giant and sees the drooping flowers. Then she hears a funny noise coming from his stomach.

"What happened to the flowers?"

"Your tummy is gurgling. Have you eaten a tree again?"

The giant can feel a tickle in his throat. He lets out a large cough and out flies Bean.

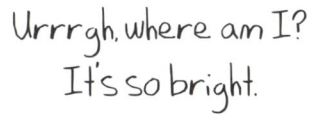

"Urrrgh, where am I? It's so bright."

"Bean! You tell me right now what you were doing inside the giant."

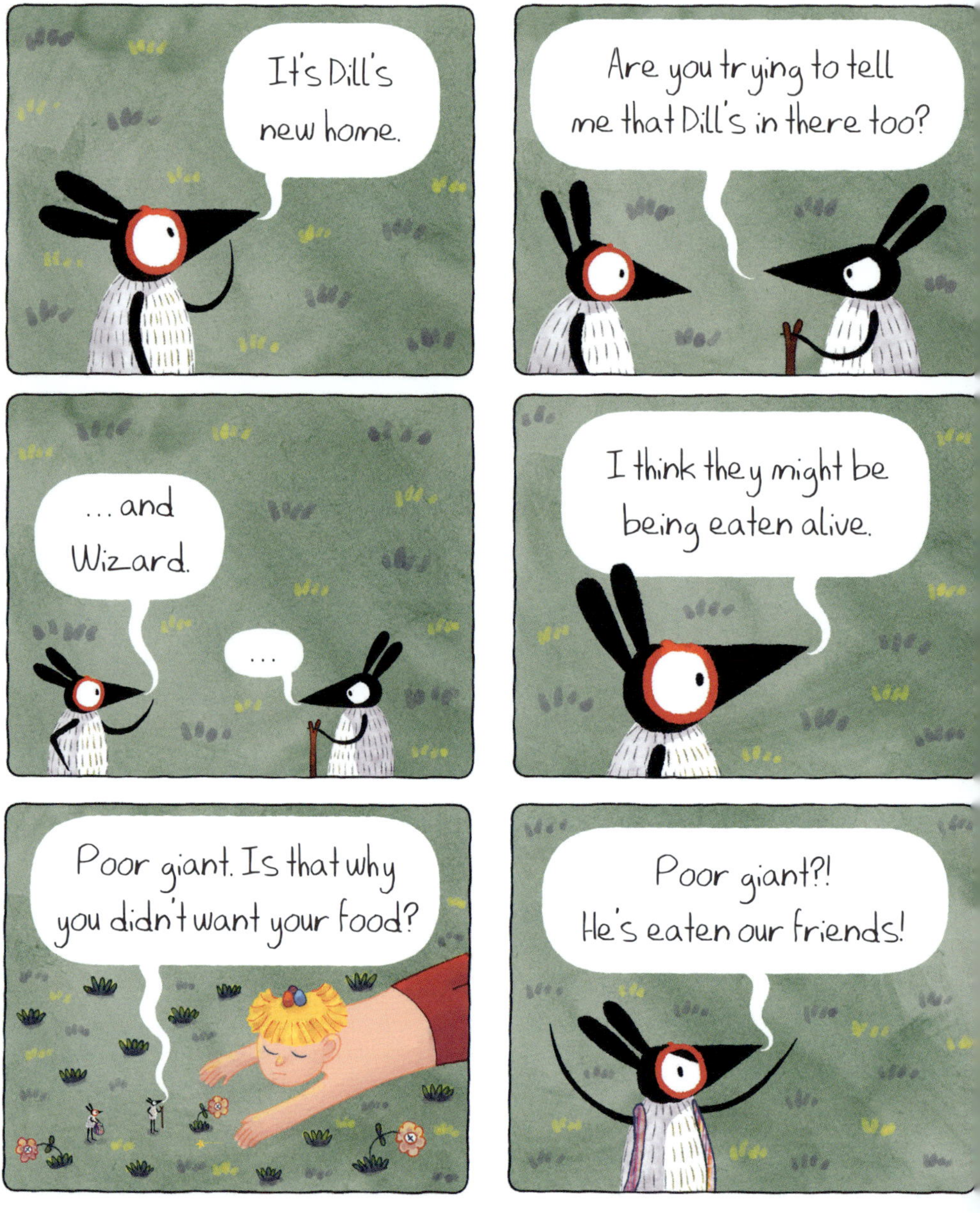
It's Dill's new home.
Are you trying to tell me that Dill's in there too?
...and Wizard.
...
I think they might be being eaten alive.
Poor giant. Is that why you didn't want your food?
Poor giant?! He's eaten our friends!

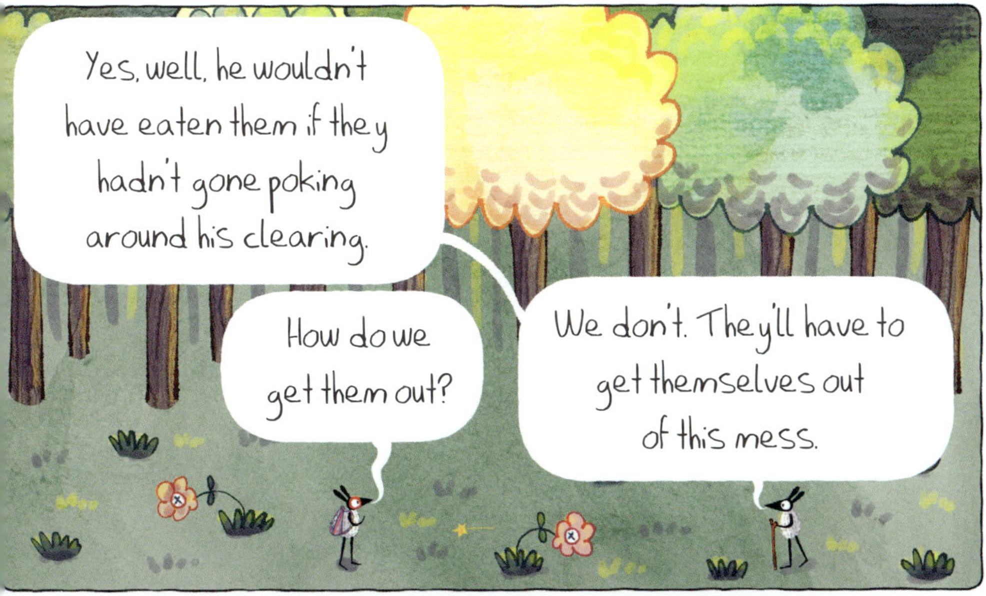
Yes, well, he wouldn't have eaten them if they hadn't gone poking around his clearing.
How do we get them out?
We don't. They'll have to get themselves out of this mess.

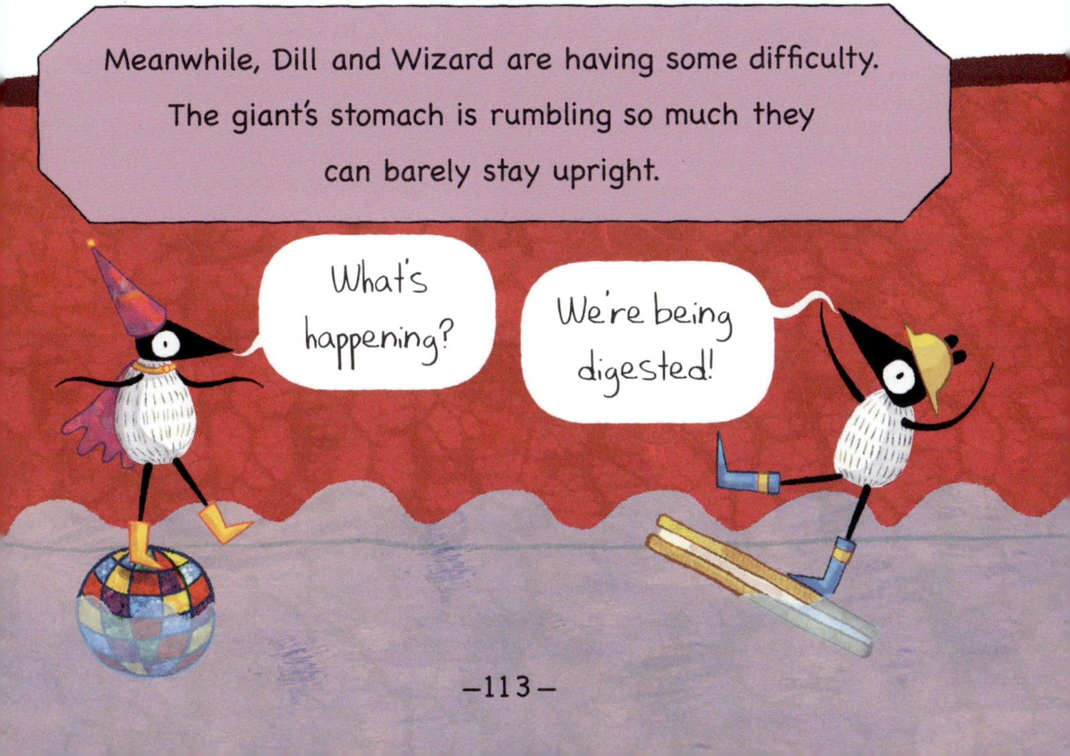
Meanwhile, Dill and Wizard are having some difficulty. The giant's stomach is rumbling so much they can barely stay upright.
What's happening?
We're being digested!

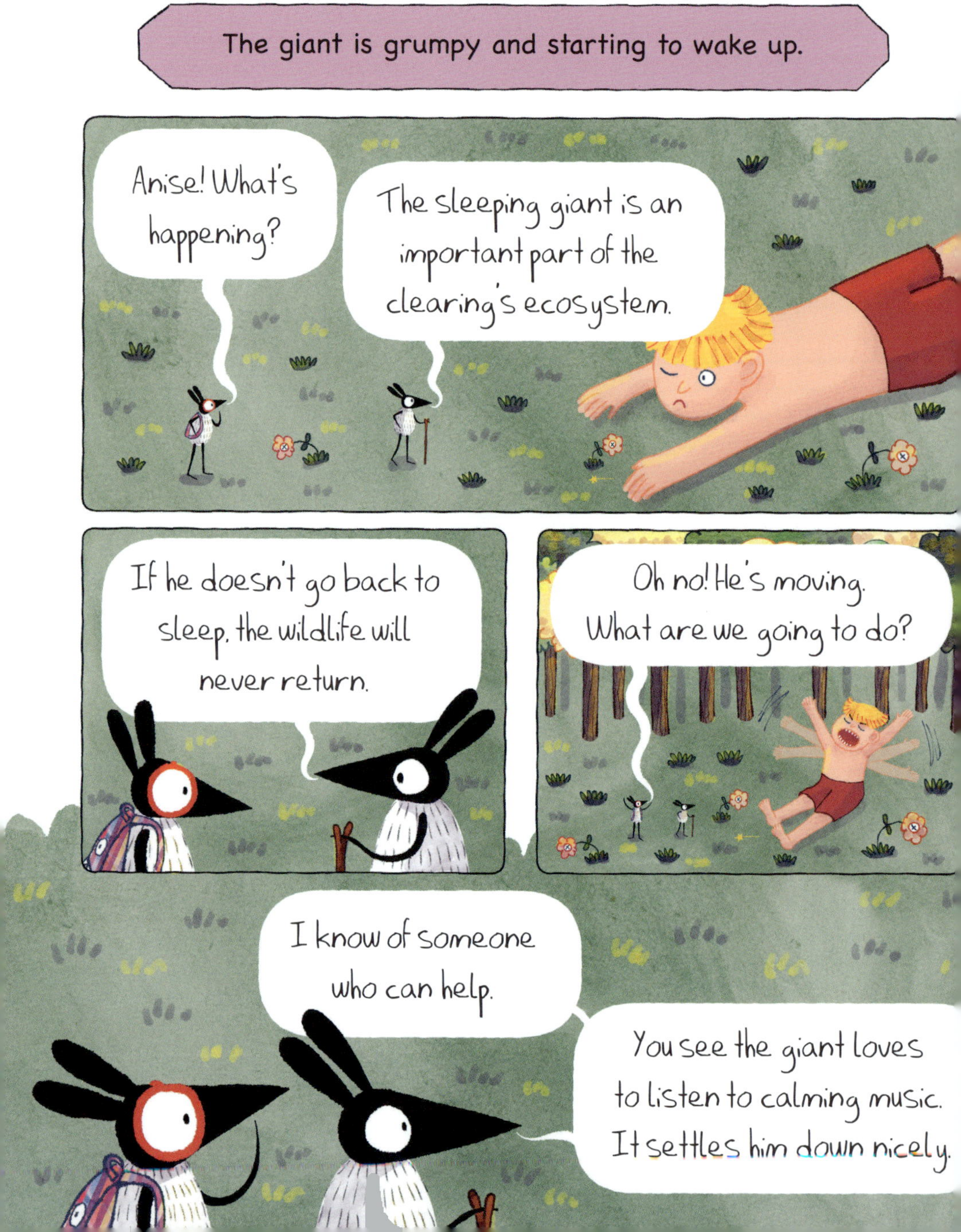
The giant is grumpy and starting to wake up.
Anise! What's happening?
The sleeping giant is an important part of the clearing's ecosystem.
If he doesn't go back to sleep, the wildlife will never return.
Oh no! He's moving. What are we going to do?
I know of someone who can help.
You see the giant loves to listen to calming music. It settles him down nicely.

Bean moves away from the giant while Anise goes to get help. She returns with Teazle who is carrying his violin.

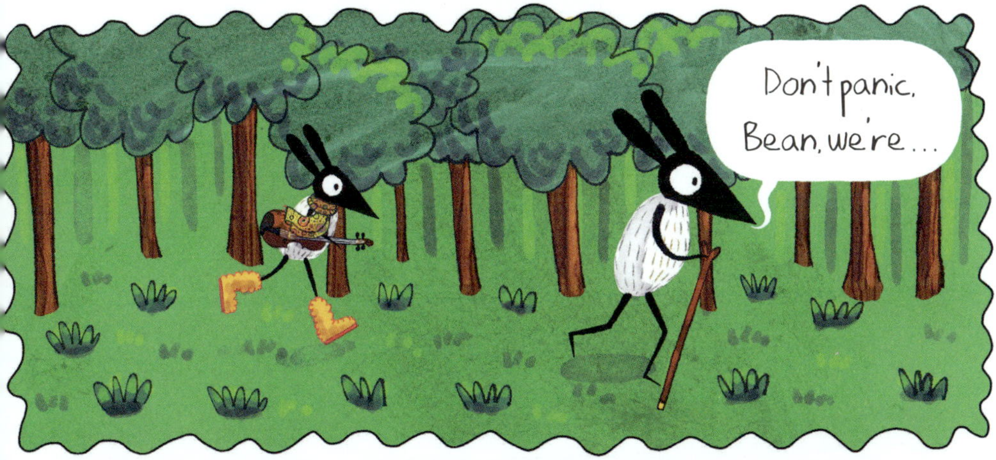
Don't panic, Bean, we're...

By now the giant has woken up and is waving his arms around and crying. The eggs that were resting in his hair fall, and Bean and Anise rush to catch them. Then, the duck arrives back and is NOT happy.

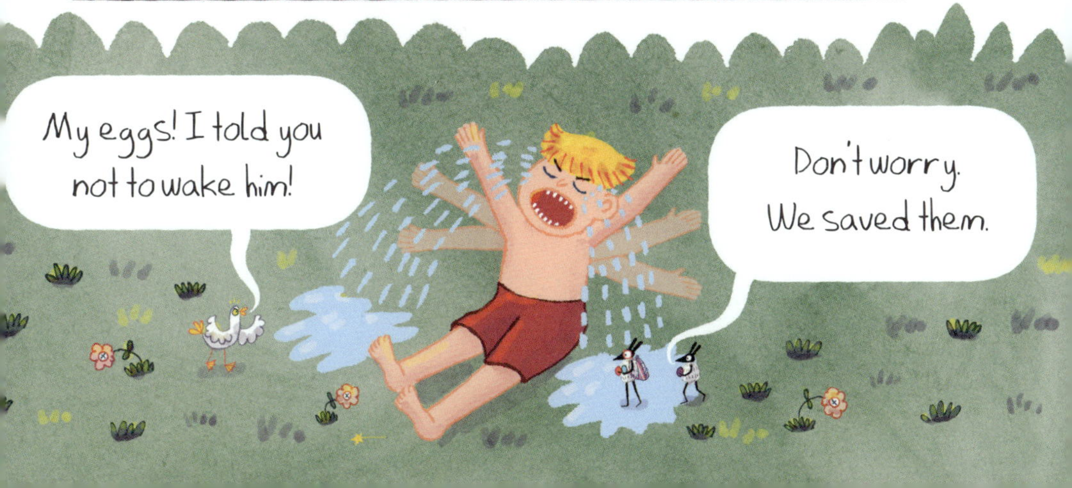
My eggs! I told you not to wake him!
Don't worry. We saved them.

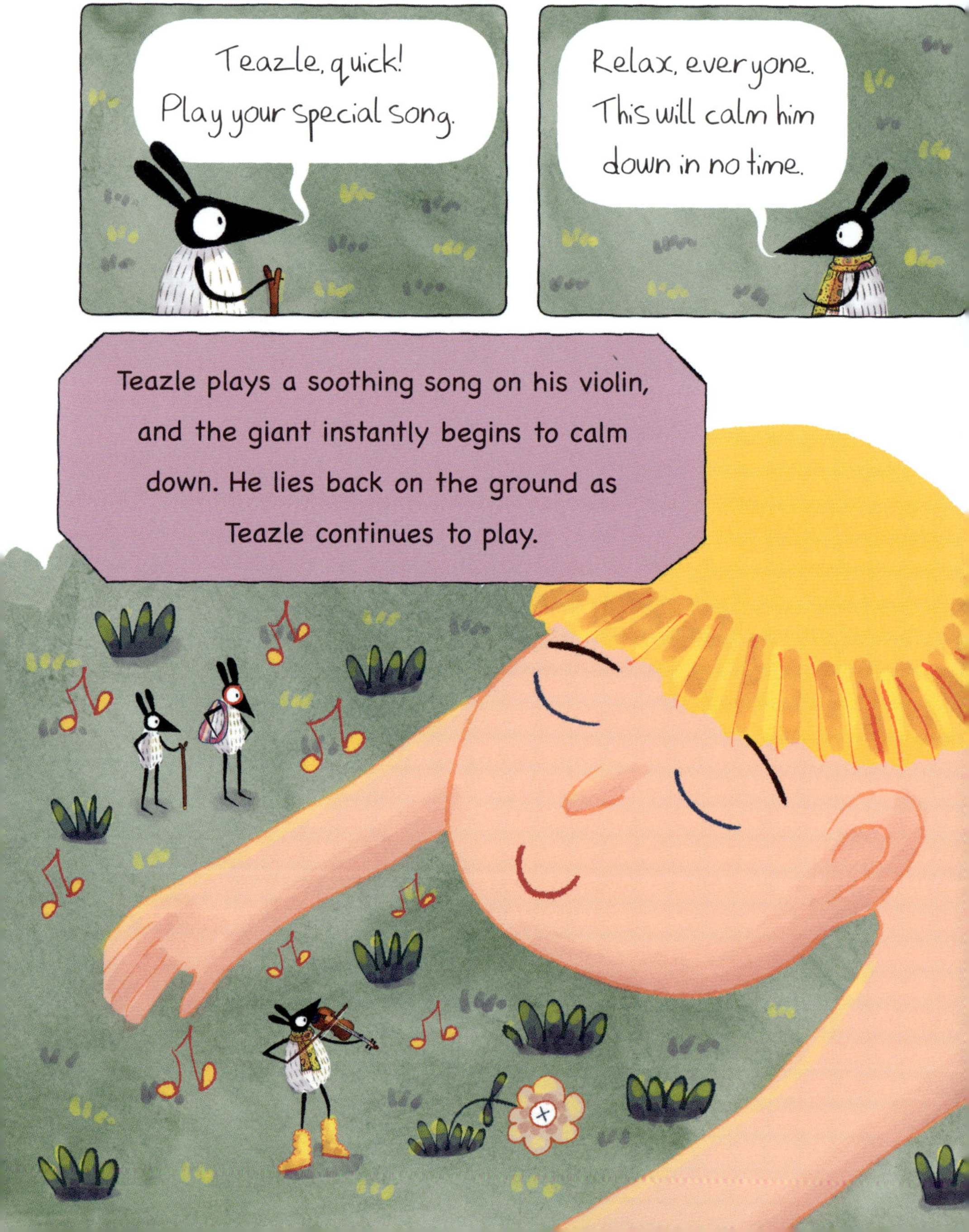
Teazle, quick! Play your special song.
Relax, everyone. This will calm him down in no time.
Teazle plays a soothing song on his violin, and the giant instantly begins to calm down. He lies back on the ground as Teazle continues to play.

The duck moves closer to the giant, hoping to put her eggs back in her nest. But she can hear a funny noise coming from the giant's mouth.

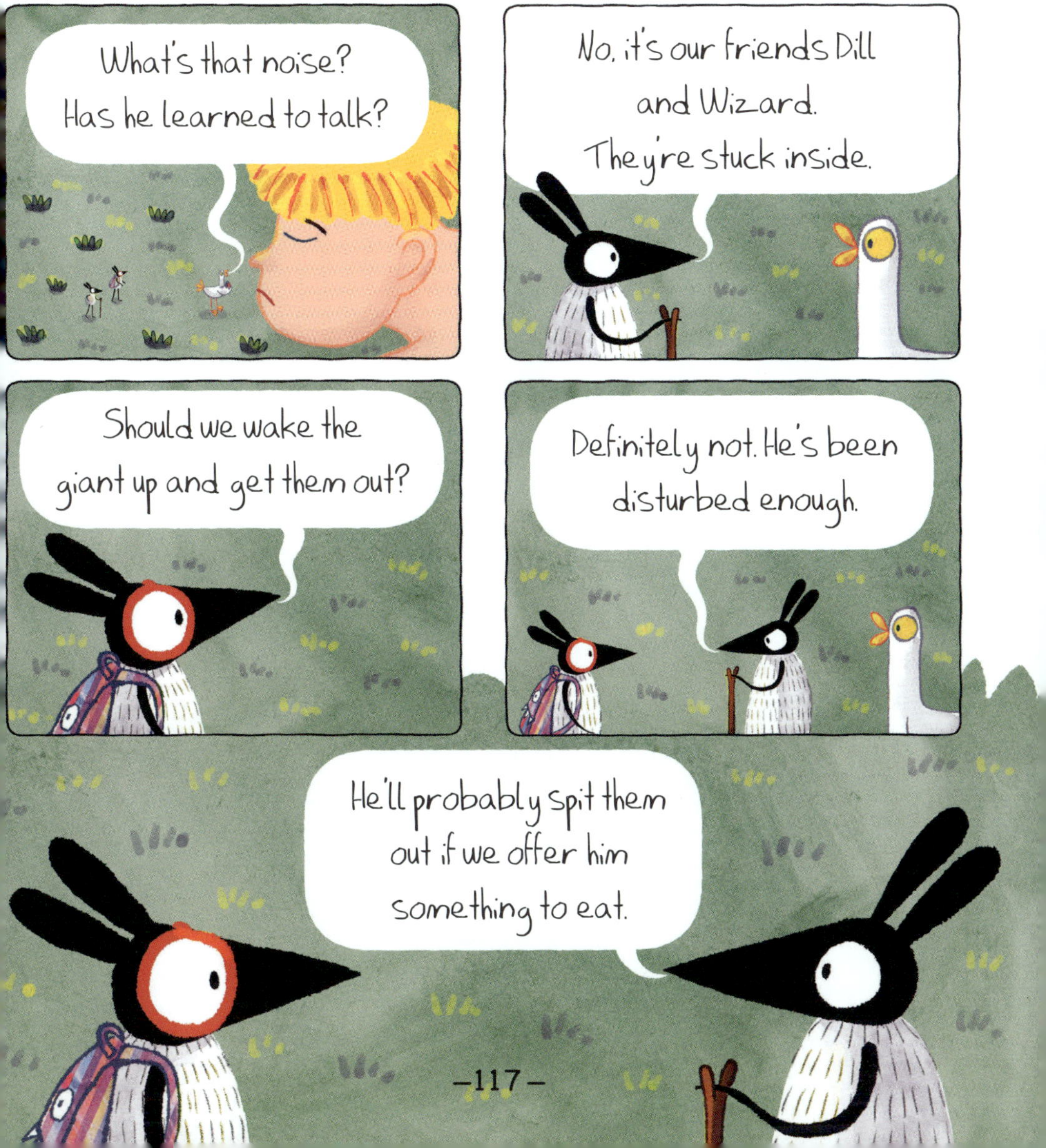

What's that noise? Has he learned to talk?
No, it's our friends Dill and Wizard. They're stuck inside.
Should we wake the giant up and get them out?
Definitely not. He's been disturbed enough.
He'll probably spit them out if we offer him something to eat.

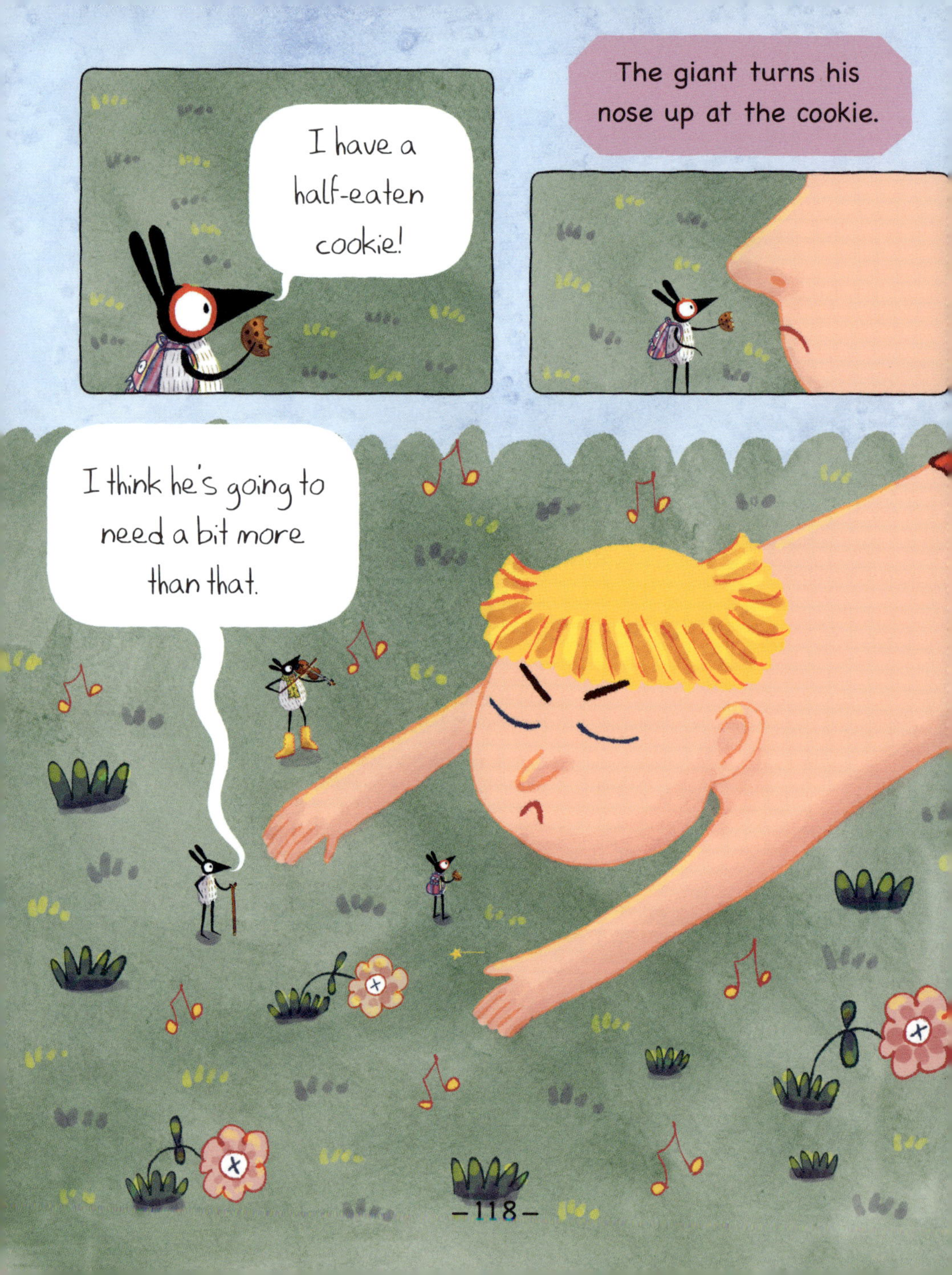
I have a half-eaten cookie!
The giant turns his nose up at the cookie.
I think he's going to need a bit more than that.

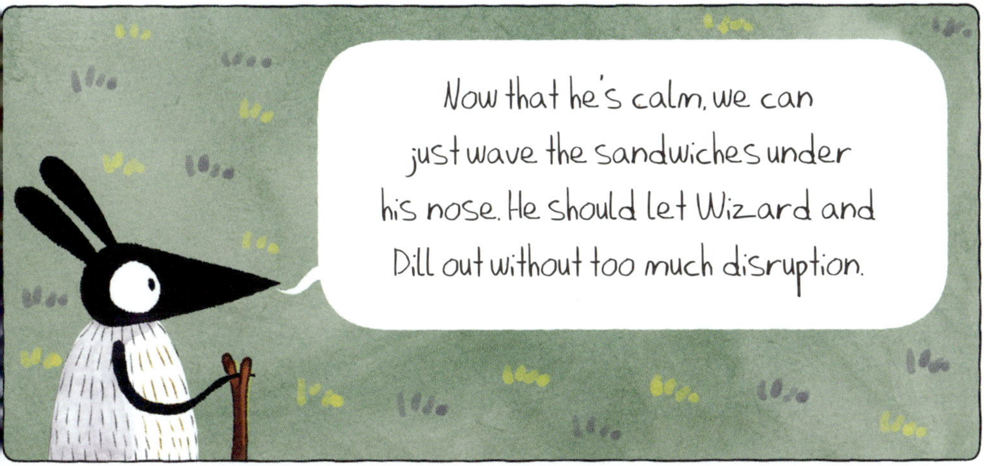
Now that he's calm, we can just wave the sandwiches under his nose. He should let Wizard and Dill out without too much disruption.

Anise offers the giant the plate of jam sandwiches.

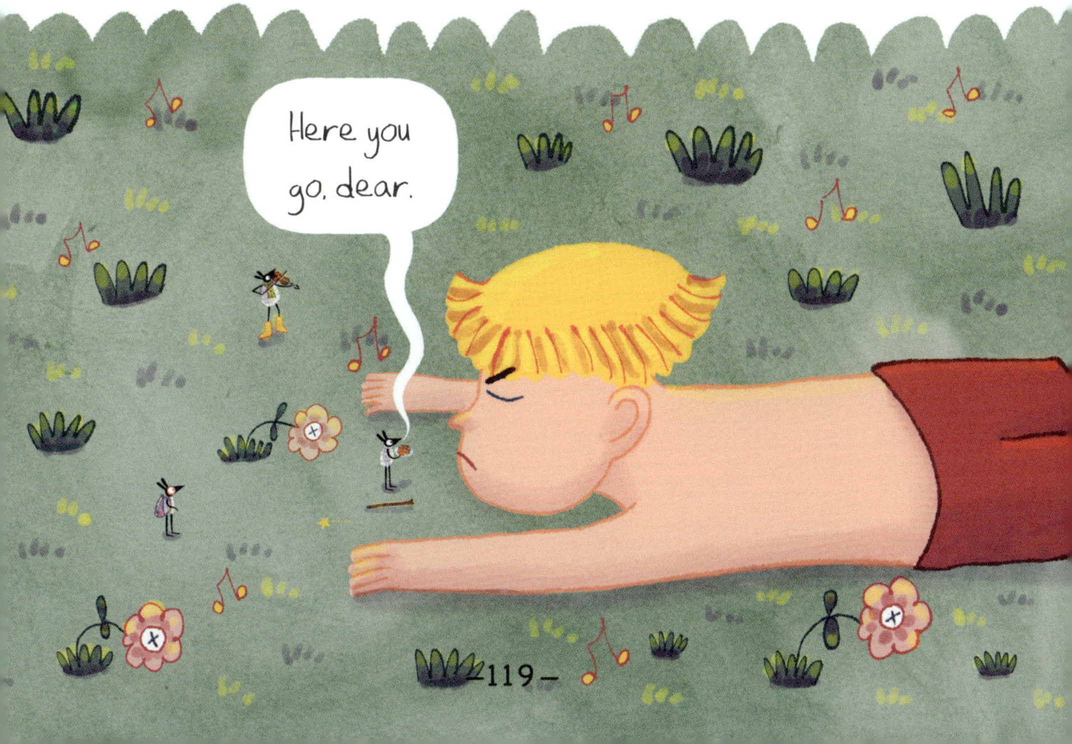
Here you go, dear.

Upon smelling the delicious sandwiches, the giant opens his mouth and burps out Dill, Wizard, and all the furniture.

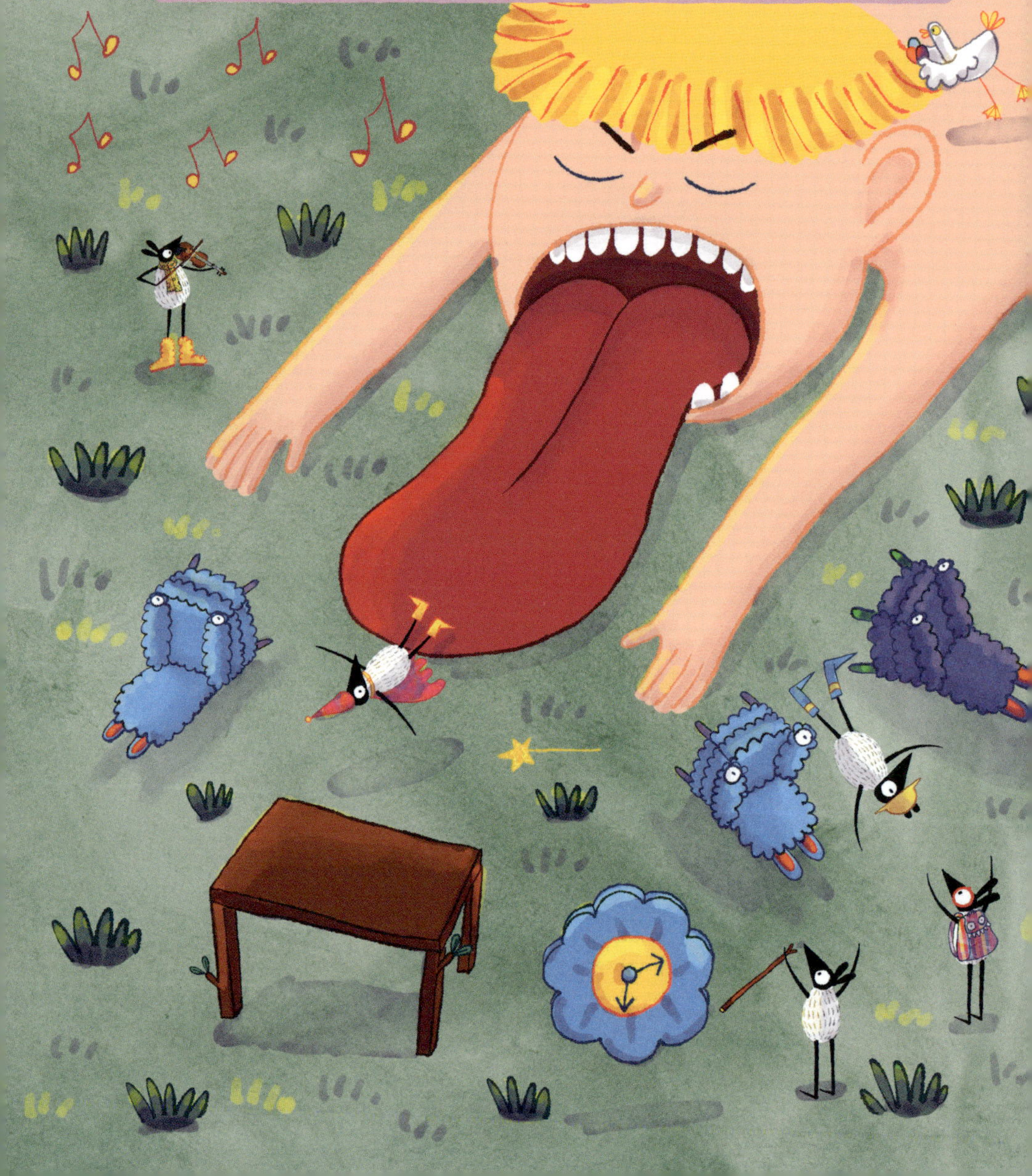

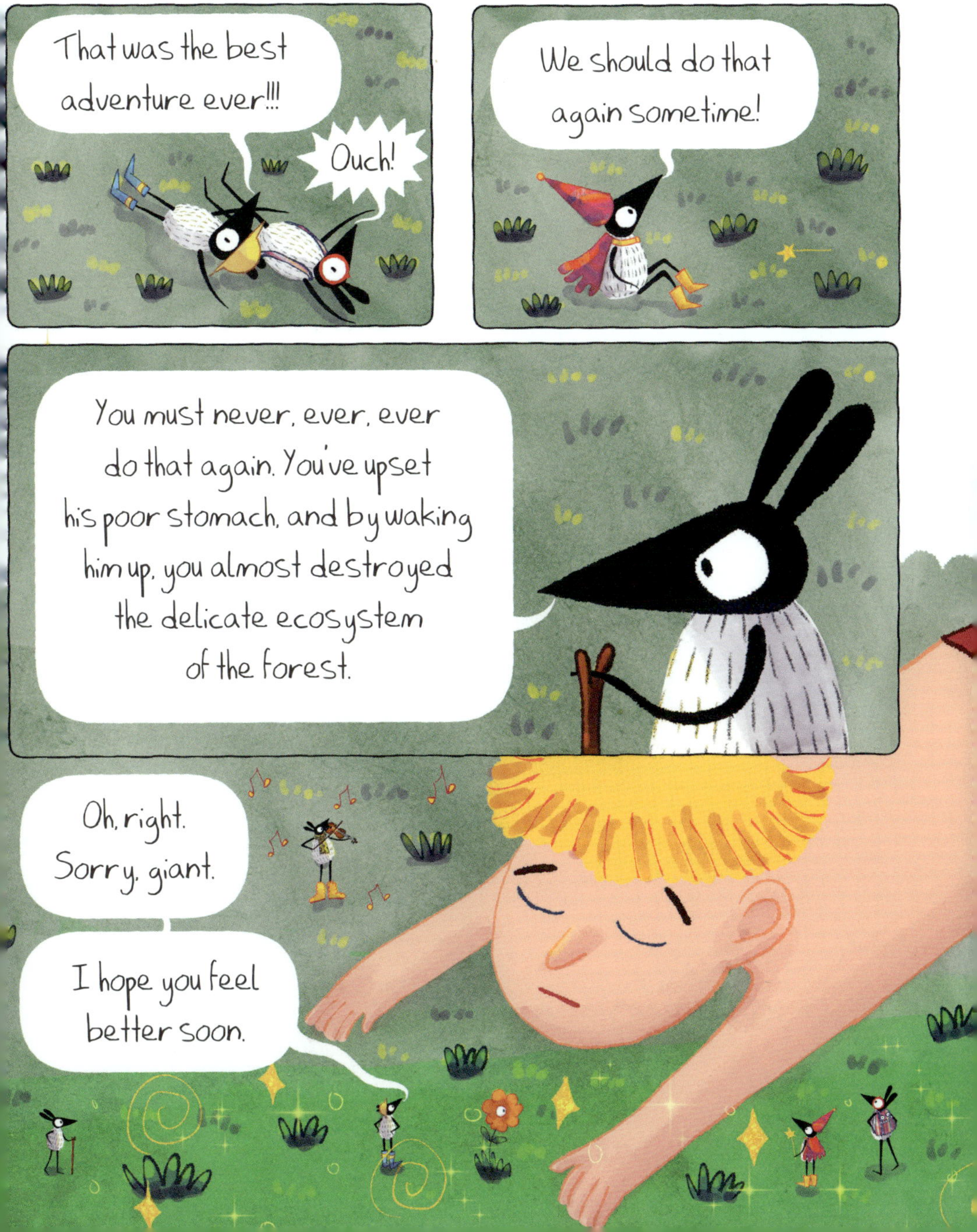
That was the best adventure ever!!!
Ouch!
We should do that again sometime!
You must never, ever, ever do that again. You've upset his poor stomach, and by waking him up, you almost destroyed the delicate ecosystem of the forest.
Oh, right. Sorry, giant.
I hope you feel better soon.

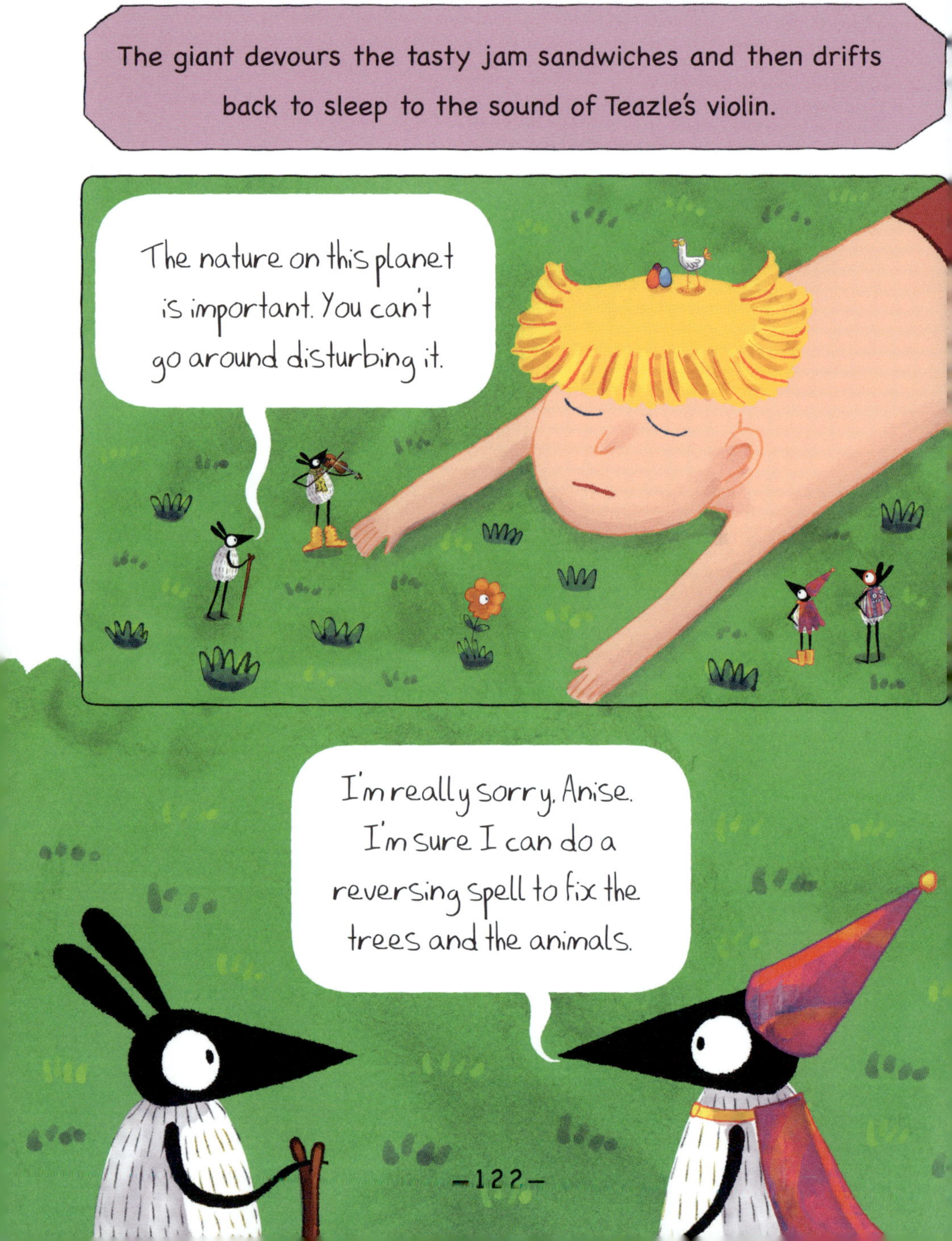
The giant devours the tasty jam sandwiches and then drifts back to sleep to the sound of Teazle's violin.
The nature on this planet is important. You can't go around disturbing it.
I'm really sorry, Anise. I'm sure I can do a reversing spell to fix the trees and the animals.

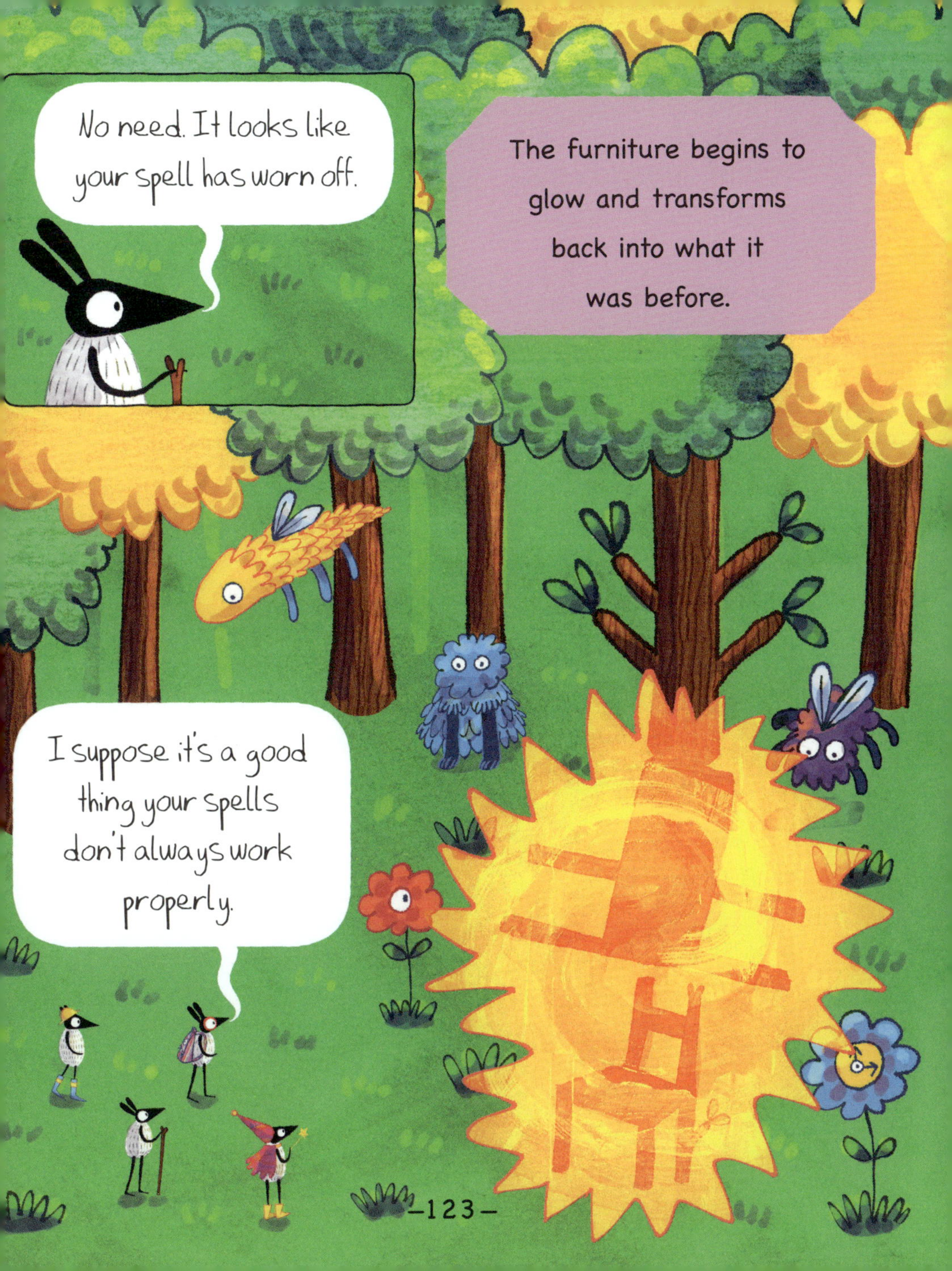
No need. It looks like your spell has worn off.
The furniture begins to glow and transforms back into what it was before.
I suppose it's a good thing your spells don't always work properly.

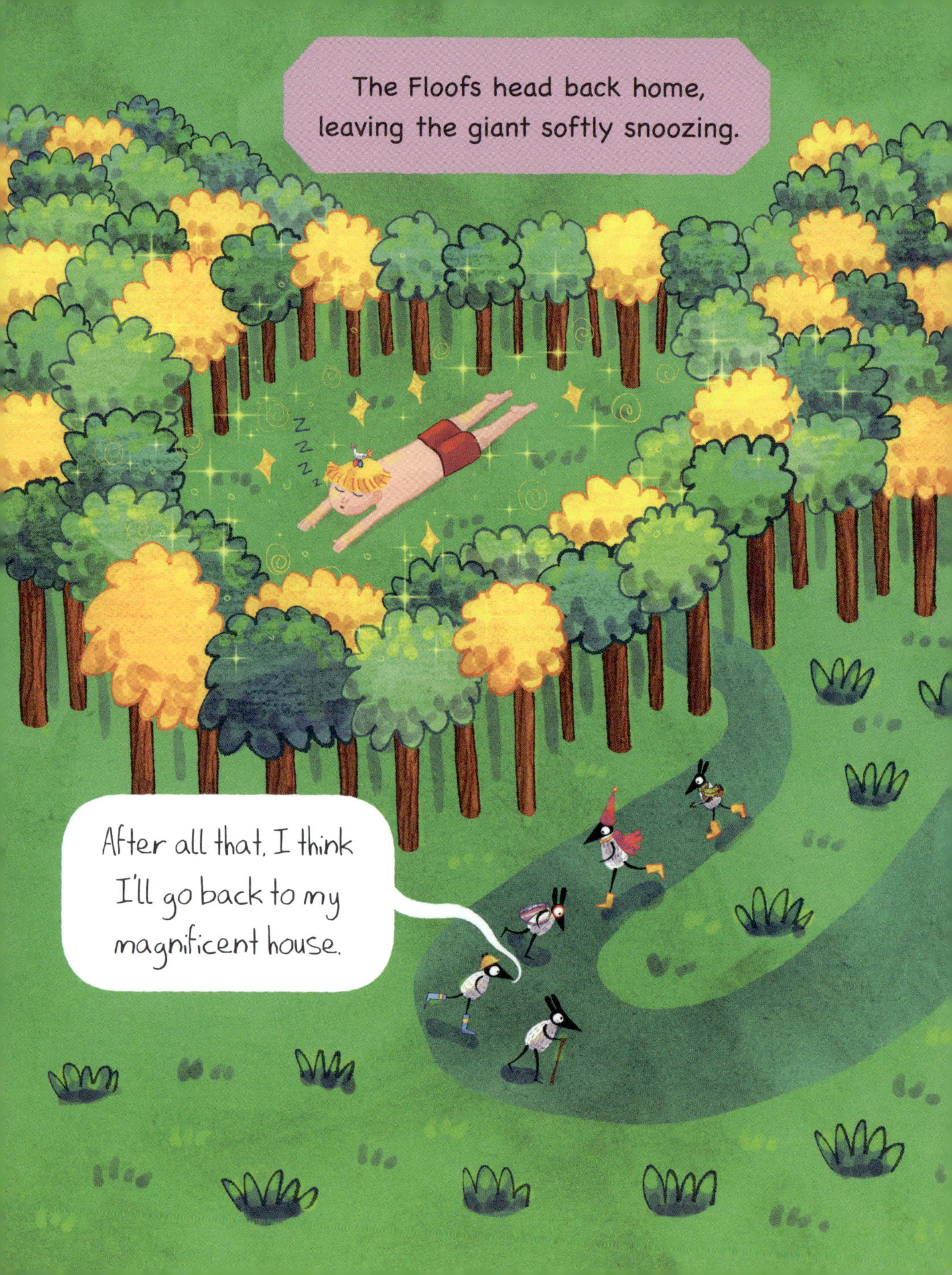
The Floofs head back home, leaving the giant softly snoozing.
After all that, I think I'll go back to my magnificent house.

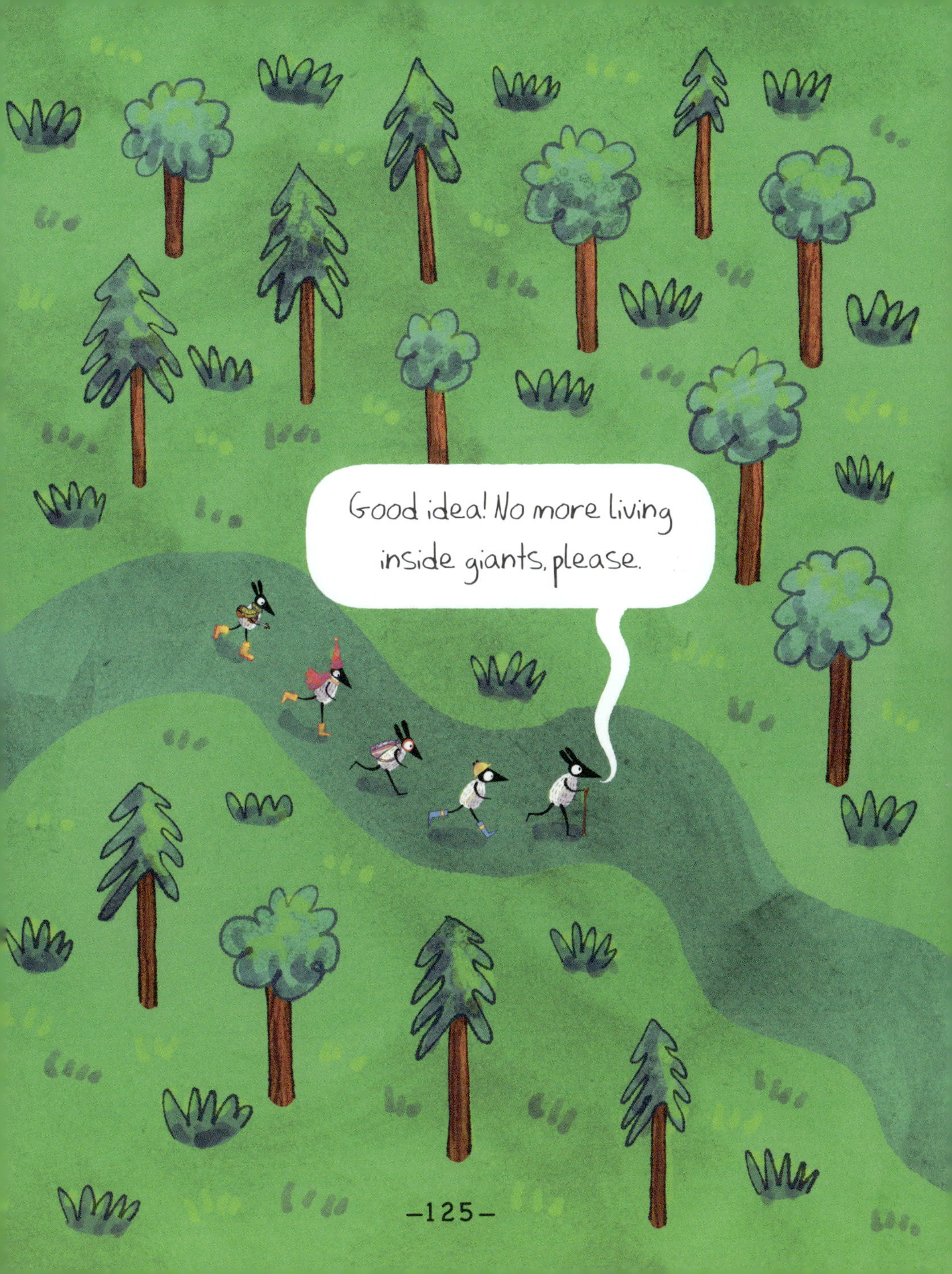
Good idea! No more living inside giants, please.

The secret clearing was happy to be returned to its natural state, free from disturbances and pesky Floofs. The flowers were blooming, the animals moved about the clearing, and the trees sparkled in the sun. All was at peace once again.

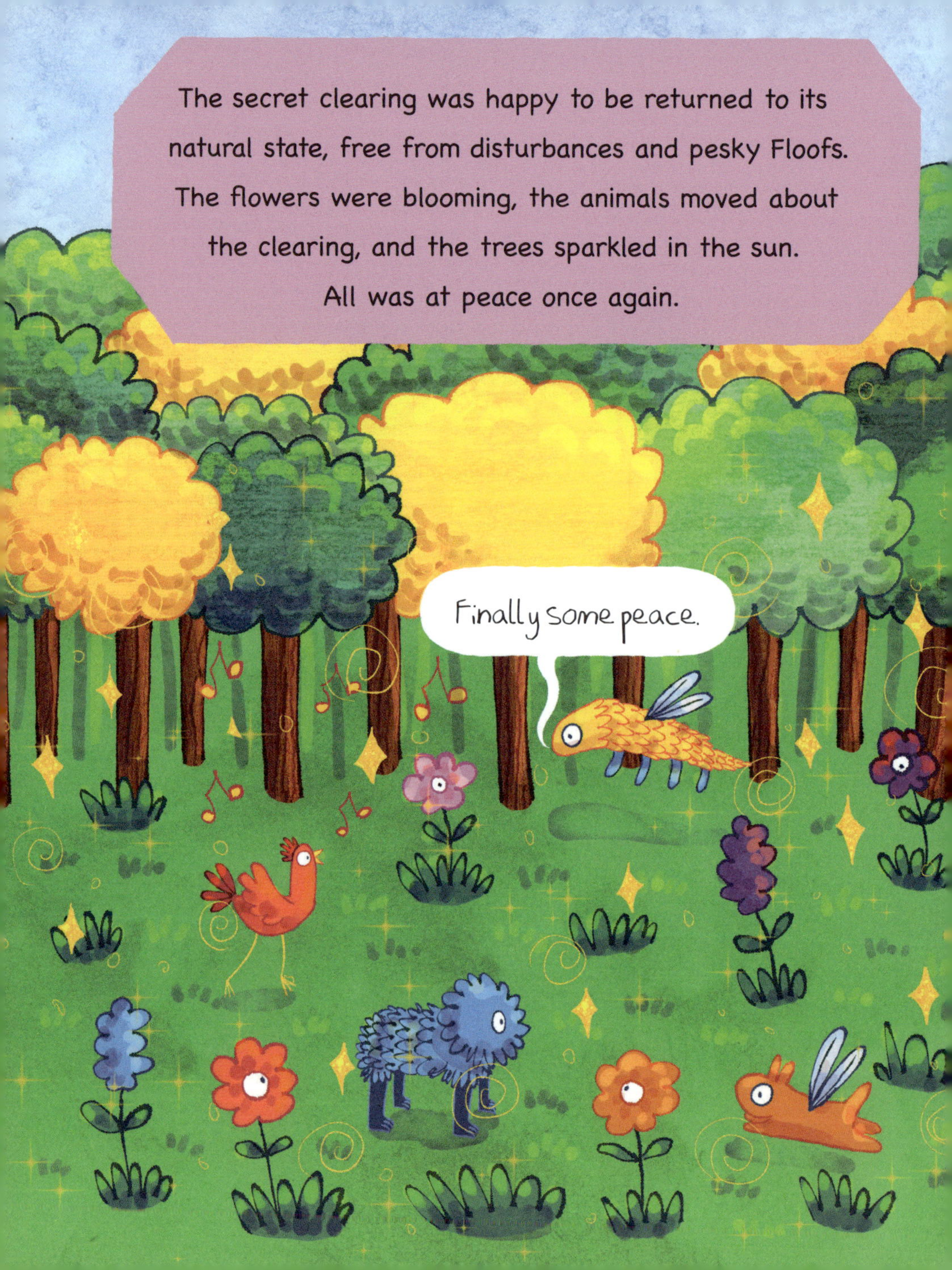
Finally some peace.

The Floofs went back to Dill's house for some tea, and to help Dill plot her next adventure . . . somewhere where they wouldn't disturb the delicate ecosystems of their beautiful world.

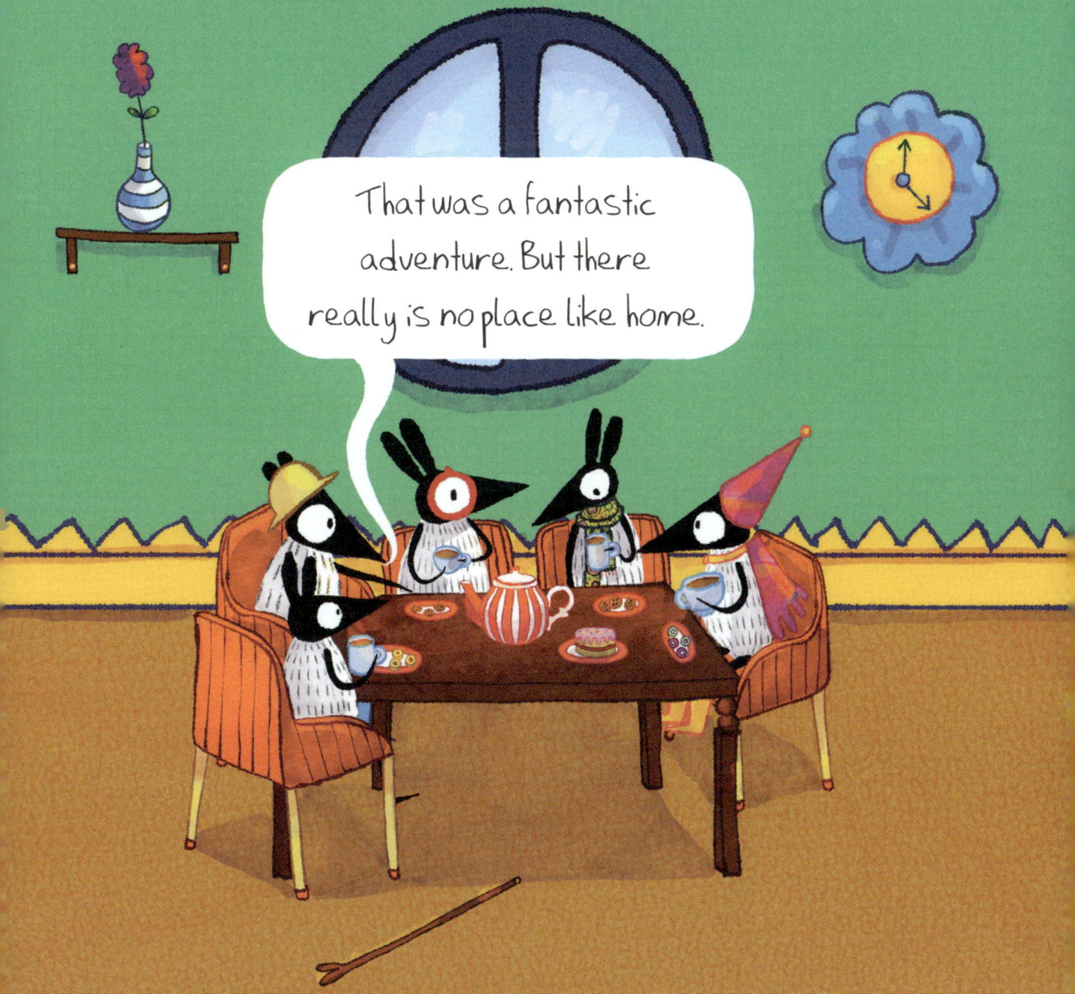
That was a fantastic adventure. But there really is no place like home.

Penelope O'Neill is an author and illustrator (and Floof expert) from South Yorkshire. She spends most of her time making Floofy comics in a studio at the bottom of the backyard. When not working, Penelope enjoys baking tasty treats, singing with friends, and swimming.